Also by Alicia Erian

The Brutal Language of Love

TOWELHEAD

A NOVEL

ALICIA ERIAN

Simon & Schuster
New York London Toronto Sydney

Simon & Schuster
Rockefeller Center
1230 Avenue of the Americas
New York, NY 10020

SIMON & SCHUSTER and colophon are registered trademarks
of Simon & Schuster, Inc.

For information about special discounts for bulk purchases,
please contact Simon & Schuster Special Sales:
1-800-456-6798 or business@simonandschuster.com

Designed by Davina Mock

Manufactured in the United States of America

10 9 8 7 6 5 4 3 2 1

Library of Congress Cataloging-in-Publication Data
Erian, Alicia, 1967–
   Towelhead : a novel / Alicia Erian.
      p. cm.
   1. Teenage girls—Fiction. 2. Suburban life—Fiction.
3. Arab Americans—Fiction. 4. Lebanese Americans—Fiction.
5. Fathers and daughters—Fiction. 6. Children of immigrants—Fiction.
7. Conflict of generations—Fiction. 8. Children of divorced
parents—Fiction. 9. Domestic fiction. 10. Bildungsromans. I. Title.

PS3555.R4265T69 2005
813'.6—dc22   2005042482

ISBN 0-7432-4494-X

For David Franklin

We all do better in the future.

—Raymond Carver,
"On an Old Photograph of My Son"

TOWELHEAD

My mother's boyfriend got a crush on me, so she sent me to live with Daddy. I didn't want to live with Daddy. He had a weird accent and came from Lebanon. My mother met him in college, then they got married and had me, then they got divorced when I was five. My mother told me it was because my father was cheap and bossy. When my parents got divorced, I wasn't upset. I had a memory of Daddy slapping my mother, and then of my mother taking off his glasses and grinding them into the floor with her shoe. I don't know what they were fighting about, but I was glad that he couldn't see anymore.

I still had to visit him for a month every summer, and I got depressed about that. Then, when it was time to go home again, I got happy. It was just too tense, being with Daddy. He wanted everything done in a certain way that only he knew about. I was afraid to move half the time. Once I spilled some juice on one of his foreign rugs, and he told me that I would never find a husband.

My mother knew how I felt about Daddy, but she sent me to live with him anyway. She was just so mad about her boyfriend liking me. I told her not to worry, that I didn't like Barry back, but she said that wasn't the point. She said I was always walking around with my boobs sticking out, and that it was hard for Barry not to notice. That really hurt my feelings, since I couldn't help what my boobs looked like. I'd never asked for Barry to notice me. I was only thirteen.

At the airport, I wondered what my mother was so worried about. I could never have stolen Barry away from her, even if I'd tried. She was 100 percent Irish. She had high cheekbones and a cute round ball at the end of her nose. When she put concealer under her eyes, they looked all bright and lit up. I could've brushed her shiny brown hair for hours, if only she had let me.

When they announced my flight, I started to cry. My mother said it wasn't that bad, then pushed me in my back a little so I would walk onto the plane. A stewardess helped me find my seat, since I was still crying, and a man beside me held my hand during takeoff. He probably thought I was scared to fly, but I wasn't. I really and truly hoped we would crash.

Daddy met me at the airport in Houston. He was tall and clean-shaven and combed his wavy, thinning hair to one side. Ever since my mother had ground up his glasses, he'd started wearing contacts. He shook my hand, which he'd never done before. I said, "Aren't you going to hug me?" and he said, "This is how we do it in my country." Then he started walking really fast through the airport, so I could barely keep up.

As I waited with Daddy at the baggage claim, I felt like I didn't have a family anymore. He didn't look at me or talk to me. We both just watched for my suitcase. When it came, Daddy lifted it off the conveyor belt, then set it down so I could pull it. It had wheels and a handle, but it fell over if you walked too fast. When I slowed down, though, Daddy ended up getting too far ahead of me. Finally he picked it up and carried it himself.

It was a long drive back to Daddy's apartment, and I tried not to notice all the billboards for gentlemen's clubs along the way. It was embarrassing, those women with their breasts hanging out. I wondered if that was how I had looked with Barry. Daddy didn't say anything about the billboards, which made them even more embarrassing. I started to feel like they were all my fault. Like anything awful and dirty was my fault. My mother hadn't told Daddy about Barry and me, but she had told him that she thought I was growing up too fast, and would probably benefit from a stricter upbringing.

That night, I slept on a foldout chair in my father's office. There was a sheet on it, but it kept slipping off, and the vinyl upholstery stuck to my skin. In the morning, my father stood in the doorway and whistled like a bird so I would wake up. I went to the breakfast table in my T-shirt and underwear, and he slapped me and told me to go put on proper clothes. It was the first time anyone had ever slapped me, and I started to cry. "Why did you do that?" I asked him, and he said things were going to be different from now on.

I got back into bed and cried some more. I wanted to go home, and it was only the second day. Soon my father came to the doorway and said, "Okay, I forgive you, now get up." I looked at him and wondered what he was forgiving me for. I thought about asking, but somehow it didn't seem smart.

That day, we went looking for a new house. Daddy said he was making a good salary at NASA, and besides, the schools were better in the suburbs. I didn't want to go back on the highway because of all the billboards, but I was afraid to say no. Then it turned out that the billboards on the way to the suburbs were for new homes and housing developments. The prices started at one hundred fifty thousand dollars—almost three times as much as my mother had paid for our town house back in Syracuse. She was a middle-school teacher, so she couldn't afford very much.

Daddy listened to NPR while I watched the road out the window. Houston seemed like the end of the world to me. The last place you would ever want to live. It was hot and humid and the water from the tap tasted like sand. The one thing I liked about Daddy was that he kept the air-conditioning at seventy-six. He said that everyone he knew thought he was crazy, but he didn't care. He loved walking into his apartment and saying, "Ahh!"

Some news about Iraq came on, and Daddy turned up the volume. They had just invaded Kuwait. "Fucking Saddam," Daddy said, and I relaxed a little that he would swear.

We went to a housing development called Charming Gates and looked at the model home. A Realtor named Mrs. Van Dyke gave us the tour, which ended in the kitchen, where she offered Daddy a cup of coffee. She talked a lot about the beauty of the home, its reasonable price, the school district, and safety. Daddy tried to bargain with her, and she said that wasn't really done. She said if he were buying an older home, that sort of thing would be fine, but that new homes had fixed prices. Back in the car, he made fun of her southern accent, which sounded even funnier with his own accent mixed in.

For dinner, we had thin-crust pizza at a place called Panjo's. Daddy said that it was his favorite and that he ate there a lot. He said the last time he'd been there, he'd come with a woman from work, on a date. He said he'd liked her quite a bit until she took out a cigarette. Then he realized she was stupid. I thought she was stupid, too, not because she smoked, but because she'd gone on a date with Daddy.

That night, on the vinyl bed, I thought about my future. I imagined it as day after day of misery. I decided nothing good would ever happen to me, and I began to fantasize about Barry. I fantasized that he would come and rescue me from my father, then we would move back to Syracuse, only without telling my mother. We would live in a house on the other side of town, and I could wear whatever I wanted to the breakfast table.

In the morning, Barry hadn't arrived yet. It was just my father, standing in the doorway and whistling like a bird. "I don't really like that," I said, and he laughed and did it again.

That day, we went to see more model homes. And more over the weekend. On Sunday night, Daddy asked me which one I liked best, and I picked the cheapest one, in Charming Gates. He said he agreed, and a few weeks later we moved in. It was a nice place with four bedrooms—one for Daddy, one for me, one for an office, and one for a guest room. Daddy and I each had our own bathroom. The name of my wallpaper was "adobe," since it looked like all these little earthen houses, and my sink and countertop were cream with gold glitter trapped underneath. It was my responsibility to keep my bathroom clean, and Daddy bought me a can of Comet for under the sink.

Daddy's bathroom was twice the size of mine. It connected to his room and had two sinks, plus a walk-in closet with one rack on top of the other, just like at the dry cleaner's. Some of his suits were even in dry-cleaner bags. His toilet was in a little room with its own separate door, and right away, after we moved in, it started to smell like pee. He didn't have a bathtub like I did, but he had a shower stall with a door that made a loud click when you shut it.

There were formal and informal living rooms, as well as a formal dining room and a breakfast nook. We started using everything for what it was named for. Breakfast in the breakfast nook, dinner in the dining room, TV in the informal living room (which also had the fireplace), and guests in the formal living room at the front of the house.

Our first guests were the next-door neighbors, Mr. and Mrs. Vuoso and their ten-year-old son, Zack. They came over with a pie Mrs. Vuoso had baked. Daddy invited them to sit down on his brown velvet couch, then brought them all hot tea, even though they hadn't asked for it. "Oh my," Mrs. Vuoso said, "tea in a glass."

"This is how we serve it in my country," Daddy said.

Mrs. Vuoso asked him what country that was, and Daddy told her. "Imagine that," she commented, and Daddy nodded.

"You must have some interesting opinions on the situation over there," Mr. Vuoso said. He was a very clean-looking man, with short, glossy brown hair and a black T-shirt. He wore jeans that looked ironed, and had very big arm muscles. The biggest I'd ever seen. They got in the way of his arms lying flat at his sides.

"I certainly do," Daddy said.

"Maybe I'd like to hear them sometime," Mr. Vuoso said, only it sounded like he didn't really want to hear them at all.

"Not today," Mrs. Vuoso warned. "No politics today." She wore a tan skirt and flat shoes. Her face was young, but her short hair was totally gray. I had to keep reminding myself that she was Mr. Vuoso's wife, and not his mother.

"Do you know how to play badminton?" Zack asked me. He sat between his parents on the couch, his legs sticking straight out in front of him. He looked a little like his father, with short brown hair and neat jeans.

"Sort of," I said.

"Do you want to play now?" he asked.

"Okay," I said, even though I didn't. I was more interested in staying with the grown-ups. I kept wondering if Mr. Vuoso was going to beat up Daddy.

The Vuosos had a badminton net in their backyard, and Zack kept hitting the birdie into my boobs and laughing. "Cut it out," I finally told him.

"I'm just hitting it," he said. "I can't help where it lands."

I let him do it a few more times, then I quit.

"Want to do something else?" he asked.

"No thanks," I said, walking to his side of the net and handing him the racquet.

We went back to my house, where the Vuosos were just getting ready to leave. "Who won?" Mr. Vuoso asked.

"I did," Zack said. "She quit."

"We don't say *she* when the person is right beside us," Mrs. Vuoso said.

"I don't remember her name," Zack said.

"Jasira," Mr. Vuoso said. "Her name is Jasira." He smiled at me then, and I didn't know what to do.

After they left, Daddy told me that Mr. Vuoso was a reservist, which meant he was in the army on the weekends. "This guy is something else," Daddy said, shaking his head. "He thinks I love Saddam. It's an insult."

"Did you tell him you don't?" I asked.

"I told him nothing," Daddy said. "Who is he to me?"

There was a pool in Charming Gates, and Daddy felt strongly that we should be using it. He said he wasn't paying all of this money just so I could sit around in the air-conditioning. I told him I didn't want to go, but when he asked me why, I was too embarrassed to say. It was my pubic hair. There was getting to be more and more of it, and some of it came out the legs of my bathing suit. I'd begged my mother to teach me how to shave, but she said no, that once you started, there was no stopping. I cried about this all the time, and my mother told me to can it. I told her that the girls in gym class called me Chewbacca, and she said she didn't know who that was. Barry said he knew who it was and that it wasn't very nice, but my mother told him that since he didn't have any kids of his own, he could go ahead and butt out.

Then one night, when my mother had parent/teacher conferences, Barry called me into the bathroom. He was standing there in his sweats and a T-shirt, holding a razor and a can of shaving cream. "Put your bathing suit on," he said. "Let's figure out how to do this." So I put my bathing suit on and stood in the tub, and he shaved my pubic hair. "How's that?" he asked when he was finished, and I said it looked good.

When it came time to shave again, Barry asked if I remembered how to do it, or if I needed him to show me one more time. I told him I needed him to show me, even though I did remember. It just felt nice to stand there and have him do such a dangerous and careful thing to me.

My mother would never have found out except that after a while, the tub got clogged. She called the plumber, and when he used his snake, all that came up were my black curly hairs. "That happens sometimes," he said. "It ain't always the hair on your head." Then he charged my mother a hundred dollars to pour some Liquid-Plumr down the drain.

"Take off your pants," she said when he left, and I did. There was no use fighting her.

"Did I tell you you could shave?" she asked. "Did I?"

"No," I said.

"Get me the razor," she said, and I told her I didn't have one, that I'd snuck and used Barry's. When he came home, she made me apologize to him for taking his property without asking. "That's okay," he said, and my mother grounded me for a month.

Then, a week later, Barry broke down and told her the truth. That he had shaved me himself. That he had been shaving me for weeks. That he couldn't seem to stop shaving me. He said the whole thing was his fault, but my mother blamed me. She said if I hadn't always been talking about my pubic hair, this would never have happened. She said that when Barry had first offered to shave me, I should've said no. She said there were right and wrong ways to act around men, and for me to learn which was which, I should probably go and live with one.

Finally Daddy forced me to go swimming. I figured he would probably like all my pubic hair, since it made me look ugly. But then, when we got to the pool and I took my shorts off, he said, "This bathing suit doesn't even cover you."

"Yes, it does," I said, looking down at the low-cut legs.

"No, it doesn't," he said. "You're falling out of it. Put your shorts back on immediately."

I put my shorts back on and sat on my towel, watching Daddy swim laps back and forth in the single lane that had been roped off for adults. Once, a little kid got confused and drifted under the lane divider, and Daddy had to stop in midstroke. I thought he would probably yell at the kid, but he just smiled and waited for him to get out of the way. I saw then that everything would be fine between me and Daddy if only we were strangers.

School started, and a lot of the janitors, who were Mexican, talked to me in Spanish. I couldn't really understand them, but I signed up for Spanish class so I could learn. Then Daddy made me change to French, since that was the only other language his family back in Lebanon spoke, and maybe one day I would get to meet them. I didn't talk very much in any of my classes, except when the teachers called on me. When the other kids heard my accent, they asked where I was from, and I said New York. They said, "New York City?," and since they were kind of excited about that, I said yes.

I got a job babysitting Zack Vuoso after school. Mrs. Vuoso worked in the billing department of a doctor's office, and Mr. Vuoso ran his own copy store at the local shopping center. He came home at a little after six, and she came home later, around seven. They called the couple of hours I spent with Zack each afternoon "keeping him company."

It made Zack pretty mad to have a babysitter. He was always pointing out that I was only three years older than he was, and also, when we played together on the weekends, his parents didn't pay me anything. "That's because they're home on the weekends," I said, but he was still insulted.

To make it seem like he wasn't being babysat, he had an idea one day to go and visit his father at work. I didn't want to, but Zack just started walking, so I followed him. I thought for sure Mr. Vuoso would fire me on the spot for not doing my job, but he seemed happy to see us. "Just in time," he said, and he put us to work in the back room, collating packets about how to knit a Christmas stocking.

After a while, Zack got bored and starting xeroxing different parts of his body. He stuck his face under the lid, then a hand, then a hand flipping the bird. "Maybe you shouldn't do that," I said, watching this, and he pulled his pants down and xeroxed his butt. Then he brought all the copies over and started collating them with the knitting packet. When Mr. Vuoso came back to check on us, he asked what was the meaning of all of this. I said I was sorry, and Mr. Vuoso said, "Did you make these pictures?" I shook my head, and he said, "Then you have nothing to be sorry about." He told Zack that he could go ahead and redo all the packets from scratch by himself, and that we would be up front waiting for him when he was done.

I didn't know what to say to Mr. Vuoso at the front of the store. Sometimes a customer came in and I didn't have to say anything; other times I just sat there on the stool he'd given me, trying not to be so quiet. I knew from Daddy that it was bad to be quiet. Except other times, when I talked, he didn't like that either. The worst thing about him was that his rules were always changing.

Finally I said to Mr. Vuoso, "I'm sorry I'm so quiet."

He laughed. He'd just taken an order for a thousand business cards, and was finishing up the paperwork. "I'll tell you what," he said. "There's nothing worse than talk for the sake of talk."

I nodded, then relaxed a little. It was nice to watch Mr. Vuoso do his job. He didn't seem to notice that I was there, and I was glad. I was tired of being noticed.

When Zack finally finished up his packets, we closed the store and rode home in the Vuosos' minivan. Mr. Vuoso told me to sit up front, even though Zack had called shotgun, and when he started kicking the back of my seat, his father told him to cut the shit. For a joke, Mr. Vuoso pulled into my driveway and dropped me off, even though we lived next door to each other. He said, "Zack and I are going to have a talk tonight about authority. I think you'll find that tomorrow will be a better day." Then he leaned over and opened my door for me.

The next day, Zack only seemed angrier. We played badminton, and he kept hitting me in the boobs. When I told him I was quitting, he called me a towelhead and stormed in the house. I went inside to find him, but he wasn't in the living room. "Zack!" I called, but he didn't answer. I went upstairs then and found him in the guest room, sitting on the edge of the bed and looking at a *Playboy*.

"What are you doing?" I asked.

"Leave me alone," he said, without looking up.

The closet door was open and I saw a whole stack of magazines in there. Some of Mr. Vuoso's army uniforms hung from the rod above. "C'mon, Zack," I said. "Put that away."

"Why?" he said. "I want to look at it."

"You're too young."

"Don't you want to look at it?" he asked.

"No."

"Then you can go downstairs," he said. "You can go watch TV."

I went downstairs and turned the TV on, but I couldn't find a show I liked, so I went back up to the guest room. "Okay," I said to Zack, "put it away."

"Look at this," he said, and he held up a picture of a woman who was riding a horse naked.

"That's stupid," I said.

He shrugged and went back to flipping through the pages. After a moment, I walked over to the closet and got my own magazine. I took it back to a wicker chair with me and opened it up to the beginning. There was already a woman without a shirt on in the Table of Contents. I closed the magazine again, then opened it back up to the middle, where the centerfold was. I didn't unfold it, but I looked at the pictures on the pages before and after it. The woman had a funny haircut between her legs. A thin strip that ran up the middle, like a Mohawk. She was wearing clothes, but they were pushed aside so you could see her private parts. There was some writing next to the pictures, different opinions that the woman had about men and dating and food that she liked. Then there was the name of the man who had taken the pictures. When I saw this, I closed the magazine again and put it back in the closet. I went downstairs and sat in the living room. Soon Zack came down, too.

"Did you put everything back the way it was?" I asked him.

He nodded, then lay down on the couch.

"You can't look at the magazines anymore," I told him.

"I can do whatever I want, towelhead."

"Stop calling me that," I said.

"Why?" he said. "You're a towelhead, aren't you?"

"No," I said, even though I didn't know what a towelhead was.

"Your dad is," he said. "If your dad is, then so are you."

I got it then, only it seemed stupid, since Daddy didn't wear a towel on his head. He was a Christian, just like everyone else in Texas. One summer, when I was seven, he'd taken me to the Arab church and had me baptized in a bathtub. I'd cried for days beforehand, scared that I would have to be naked in front of a bunch of people I didn't know, but the priest gave me a robe to wear. In the car on the way home, Daddy made fun of me for worrying about nothing, and I knew then that he'd known about the robe all along.

Zack fell asleep on the couch, and I went back upstairs to make sure there weren't any *Playboy*s lying around. I was disappointed when there weren't, so I went to the closet and took one out. I sat down on the edge of the bed and opened it up to the centerfold, this time unfolding it. I was starting to get used to the pictures a little. They didn't shock me as much as they had earlier. I especially liked the ones where the women had hardly any pubic hair. If I squeezed my legs together when I looked at them, I got a good feeling.

Mr. Vuoso came home and asked if I'd had any problems with Zack, and I told him no. "That's what I like to hear," he said, reaching for his wallet. I thought I might feel more nervous around him now that I knew what kind of magazines he read, but I didn't. Instead, I felt more comfortable. I felt like he didn't think there was anything wrong with breasts or bodies at all.

When I got home, there was blood in my underwear. At least I thought it was blood. It was kind of orange and rusty. I got on the phone and described it to my mother, and she said, "That's definitely blood."

"What do I do?" I said. It was the one thing I'd been most afraid of, getting my first period with Daddy. The night before I'd left Syracuse, my mother had given me a couple of her pads, but they weren't going to last.

"What do you mean, what do you do? Just put on a pad and tell Daddy when he gets home. He knows what a period is."

"Can't you tell him?"

"Why would I tell him?"

"I just don't want to talk to him about it."

"Why not? You're going to have to talk about it sometime."

"You don't understand," I said. "Daddy doesn't like my body."

"What's that supposed to mean?"

"I don't know."

"You're making a big deal out of nothing," she said. "Pull yourself together."

We hung up, and I went to my bathroom and put on one of the pads. As I walked around the house, I kept thinking I could hear it making little crinkling noises in my underpants. They'd shown us a movie in school saying that this was a special day, but mostly I just felt like a baby in a diaper.

When Daddy pulled into the driveway at seven o'clock, I met him at the back door. "Hi," I said.

"Hello, Jasira," he mumbled. Daddy was rarely happy at the end of the day. The people at NASA bothered him since they didn't work as hard as he did. It was best to stay out of his way and let him cook dinner by himself, only I was worried about my pad supply.

"Daddy," I said, as he set down his briefcase, "I need to talk to you about something."

"Not now," he said, untying his shoes. Then he headed for the kitchen and got a beer from the fridge.

I went in the bathroom to check my pad, which was beginning to fill up. Plus, my stomach hurt. Not my real stomach, but the part below it. It felt like someone was reaching a hand inside of me and squeezing something they shouldn't. I went back out in the kitchen and said, "Daddy?"

He was unwrapping a piece of steak and listening to a small radio on the counter. He probably heard me, even though he didn't say anything. I stood there for a while, waiting for his news report to end, then said, "Daddy?" again.

He sighed. "What is it, Jasira?"

"I have to talk to you about something."

"Just say it, would you?" he said. "I don't need all the introductions."

"Okay," I said, taking a deep breath. "I got my period."

"Your period?" he said. Finally he looked at me. "You're too young to get your period."

"I'm thirteen," I said.

He shook his head. "My God."

"I called Mom. She said to tell you."

"Well," he said, "what do you need? Do you need to go to the store?"

"Yes."

"Right now?"

"I think so."

He took off his apron and went to put his shoes back on. In the car, he said, "You can't wear tampons until you're married. Do you understand what I'm telling you?"

I nodded, even though I wasn't sure I did.

"Tampons are for married ladies," he said.

We passed the pool, which stayed lit from underwater at night. It always seemed sad to me that it was closed when it looked the prettiest.

I had hoped that he would give me money at the drugstore and let me go in by myself, but he turned the car off and got out. In the feminine hygiene aisle, he said, "Let's see," and started pulling down all different kinds of pads. Finally he turned to me and said, "Would you describe your situation as light, medium, or heavy?"

"I don't know," I said.

"What do you mean, you don't know?"

"Can't I pick them out, Daddy?"

"Why?" he said. "What's the problem?"

"Nothing."

"You're not going to wear tampons, if that's what you're thinking."

"I don't want to wear tampons."

"When you're married, you can buy all the tampons you want. Right now, you'll wear pads."

A thin, older saleslady came over to see if we needed any help. "We're fine, thank you," Daddy said.

I looked at her, and she smiled at me. "These for you?" she asked. I nodded.

"Well," she said, reaching for a green box, "this is the kind my daughter likes."

I took the box from her and started reading the side panel.

"What's wrong with these?" Daddy asked, showing the lady his box.

"They're just a little thicker. Not as comfortable."

He looked like he didn't believe her.

"Can I get these?" I asked, holding out my box.

Daddy took them from me and said, "How come they're so expensive?"

The lady put on a pair of glasses that were hanging on a chain around her neck. "Well," she said, looking at the price sticker, "that's probably the comfort issue I was referring to earlier."

"What a rip-off," Daddy said.

"You getting cramps?" the lady asked me, and I nodded again. "Here," she said, handing Daddy a box of Motrin. "Give her these."

"We have plenty of aspirin at home," Daddy said, putting the pills back on the shelf, but the woman grabbed them and gave them back.

"I'm telling you," she said, "she's going to need these. Aspirin won't work." Then she took the box of thick pads out of Daddy's arms and put that back on the shelf, too.

I could see he was mad at her, only there was nothing he could really do about it. In the car on the way home, though, he told me that from now on, I could pay for my own feminine hygiene. He said he hadn't realized how expensive this stuff was going to be, and anyway, now that I was working for the army, I could afford it. That was how he referred to my job at the Vuosos'. It still bothered him that Mr. Vuoso thought he loved Saddam. If there was anything he didn't appreciate, Daddy said, it was people making assumptions about him.

That night in bed, I fantasized again that Barry would come and save me. I figured he probably wouldn't, but still, thinking about him always made me feel better. He was someone I knew for sure liked me. Even more than he liked my mother. He liked me so much that she had to send me away, since she was jealous. This was my favorite part. The part where no matter what happened, I was better than my mother. Boys liked me better than they liked her.

In art class the next day, when I pulled my drawing tablet out of my backpack, a maxi-pad fell out with it. I tried to hide it, but it was too late. The three boys at my worktable had already seen it. They grabbed it and started tossing it around, while I tried to get it back. Then one of them opened the packet, pulled off the adhesive strip, and started wearing it on his forehead. Mrs. Ridgeway told him to take it off, and he did, but then he put red watercolor on it. A rumor started going around that it was real blood, and that I was such a dirtball that I carried around used sanitary napkins.

I didn't have any pads left then, so I went in the bathroom and put a bunch of toilet paper in my underwear. I cried a little, and one of the lady janitors heard me. "You okay in there?" she asked. I told her the problem, and she said for me to wait. A couple of minutes later, she came back and passed a tampon under my door. "I don't think I can wear that," I said.

"Sure you can," she said. "It's very small."

Then she stood outside the stall, asking a million times whether I'd gotten it in yet. "Just relax," she told me, and finally it slipped inside.

When I came out and she saw it was me, she started talking in Spanish, and I had to tell her that I couldn't understand. "Your parents don't speak Spanish at home?" she asked, and I said no, and she shook her head like it was the saddest thing in the world.

For the rest of the day, I thought a lot about what Daddy had said—that you had to be married to wear tampons. I guessed he meant that when you got married, you had sex, and when you had sex, it made more room for a tampon. Only there was already some room now. The lady janitor had said there would be, and she had been right. I started to wonder what other wrong things he had told me.

After school, Zack asked if I wanted to look at magazines, and I said okay. He sat with his back to me on the edge of the bed, and I sat in the wicker chair. I read all the interviews with the women very closely, hoping they'd talk about something important, like getting your period. But it was more of the same—descriptions of how they liked to have sex with their boyfriends, or how many times a week they liked to do it, or what color hair their boyfriends should have. I didn't realize I was pressing my legs together until Zack turned around and said, "Stop creaking the chair."

The women also talked about having orgasms, which I didn't understand. I assumed it was the feeling I got when I pressed my legs together, only that didn't seem like such a big deal. As far as I could tell, it was just a nice sensation, like when Barry had shaved me. Not some kind of actual event.

"Look!" Zack said at one point, and he came over to show me a picture of a woman with light brown skin and dark brown nipples. There was a headline above the picture that said ARABIAN QUEEN.

"So?" I said.

"She's a towelhead, just like you."

"Stop saying that," I said. "It's not nice."

He took the magazine back. "Maybe you could be in *Playboy* someday. You have big boobs."

I shook my head, remembering the names of all those men photographers.

"My dad even thinks you're pretty," he said, heading back to his spot on the bed.

"He does?"

Zack nodded. "He says you're going to have a lot of boyfriends, and your dad's going to lock you up."

"He is not," I said, feeling alarmed.

"Wait and see," Zack warned.

That afternoon, when Mr. Vuoso came home, I felt more nervous than usual. "Hi, Jasira," he said, and I said, "Fine, thank you." Zack thought this was the funniest thing he'd ever heard and wouldn't stop laughing. Even Mr. Vuoso laughed, but it wasn't mean. He just said, "Well, you're getting a little ahead of me there, but good. I'm glad you're fine." Then he went in the kitchen.

"You can go now," Zack said.

"I know when I can go," I told him.

At home, I checked my underwear. There were a few blood spots, so I put a pad on for safety. I didn't want to take the tampon out yet. Not until Daddy came home and I could walk around in front of him while I was wearing it.

"Stop walking everywhere," he told me later that night.

"Sorry," I said, and I took a seat in the breakfast nook.

"Don't you have homework?" he asked. He was standing at the kitchen counter, fixing our dinner. Tonight it was weird Middle Eastern food.

"I already did it," I said.

"Well," he said, "I'm listening to the radio right now."

"I'll be quiet."

After a moment, he said, "How's your period?"

"Fine."

"Did your cramps go away?"

"Uh-huh."

"Your mother used to have cramps," he said. "It was like she was dying or something."

"Mine weren't that bad," I said.

"I always thought she was lying about it," he said. "To get attention."

I nodded. I had actually seen her like this and thought the same thing.

"I would ignore her, and she would get mad at me and say I was heartless. I'm not heartless. I just know a liar when I see one."

I thought about my tampon then, and how he didn't really know a liar at all.

"Come and help me chop this salary," he said, which was what he called both the vegetable and his paycheck, and I said okay.

After dinner, I went and took the tampon out. It was pretty soaked, and a lot of other blood fell into the toilet with it. I had to use extra toilet paper, and when I flushed, the water wouldn't go down. I didn't know what to do, so I yelled, "Daddy! Help!" He ran in, saw what was happening, then ran out again. By the time he came back with the plunger, pink water was overflowing onto the beige carpet.

"Jesus Christ," he said, starting to plunge. This sent more water and bits of toilet paper onto the rug. Soon, though, the bowl began to drain. At the end, it made a little gurgle, then shot out a teeny bit of clear water. "Go get me a plastic bag," Daddy said, and I did, and he put the dirty plunger inside it. Then he pointed to the floor and said, "What's that?"

I looked down and saw my tampon. It wasn't as bloody as it had been when I'd taken it out, but it had still clearly been used.

"Pick it up," Daddy ordered.

I reached down and grasped its cotton body. I didn't really want to touch it with my bare hands, but Daddy was blocking the toilet paper.

"Where did you get that?" he demanded.

"At school," I said. "Some kids—"

"What did I tell you about tampons?"

"That they're for married ladies."

"Are you married?" he asked.

"No," I said.

He looked at me for a second, then said, "Follow me." In the kitchen, he opened the cupboard under the sink so I could throw the tampon away. "Now take the trash out," he said, and I did, and when I got back to the house, the door was locked. I went around to the front, but it was the same thing. I rang the doorbell, but no one answered.

It was hard to know what to do then. I checked the car doors, but they were locked, too. I thought about going over and ringing the Vuosos' doorbell, but I worried that somehow, if they knew that my father had locked me out, they would fire me.

In the end, I decided to take a walk to the pool. I remembered that there was a pay phone just outside the locker rooms, and I used it to call my mother collect. She accepted the charges, then asked what the hell was going on down there.

"I'm locked out," I said, and I started to cry.

"Well," she said, "your father just called and said you ran away."

"I didn't run away," I told her. "He locked me out, and I went to the pay phone to call you."

"Where's the pay phone?" she asked.

"At the pool."

"You shouldn't be calling me," she said. "You should be calling your father. He has no idea where you are."

"But he locked me out!"

"Listen to me, Jasira. You and I both know your father has problems. He overreacts. That means you have to adjust your behavior to take that into account. If he locks you out, you're just going to have to wait a while until he lets you back in. Do you understand me? I mean, I just can't be getting these phone calls all the time. What's the point of you even living there if I have to fix everything?"

"I don't want to live here. I want to come home."

"You haven't given it enough of a chance."

"I have," I said. "I gave it a big chance."

"What you need to ask yourself in a situation like this," she said, "is, Why did Daddy lock me out? Have you asked yourself that?"

"Yes," I lied.

"Really? Have you really?"

"No," I said.

"Because if Daddy tells you that you shouldn't be wearing tampons, and then you wear tampons, what do you think is going to happen?"

"What's wrong with wearing tampons?" I said.

"Well," she said, "that's not really the question, is it? The question is, What's wrong with wearing tampons when Daddy explicitly told you not to? Because there's definitely something wrong with that. Just like there's something wrong with shaving when your mother tells you not to."

I didn't say anything.

"Or asking someone else to shave you," she said.

"I'm sorry," I said.

"I don't want to talk about it," she said.

"All right."

"Hang up now and call Daddy. He'll come and get you."

I hung up, but I didn't call Daddy. Instead, I stood there in the passageway between the men's and women's locker rooms, pretending this was my house. The soda machine next to the pay phone hummed like a refrigerator. The smell of chlorine reminded me of the Comet I used to scrub my sink.

On the walk home, I fantasized that something terrible would happen to me. That my body would be found after a long search, and that my parents would feel awful about it for the rest of their lives. But nothing happened. I made it home safely. And though the front door was still locked, the back was now open.

TWO

I started stealing Mrs. Vuoso's tampons. She kept them in a clear glass jar on the back of the toilet, the same kind that held tongue depressors at the doctor's. I was careful to take only one or two a week, so she wouldn't notice. I slipped them in my jeans pocket, then hid them behind the Comet under my bathroom sink when I got home. The only time Daddy had ever looked there was when he'd had to clean my bathroom for me the night he locked me out. I'd come home to find the toilet smelling fresh, along with the damp carpet surrounding it. All the mushy toilet paper had been picked up, and the plunger was gone. Daddy was in his room with the door shut, but I could see that his light was still on. He didn't come out to yell at me, and he didn't come out to welcome me home. The next morning at breakfast, all he said was, "Please pass the sugar," and I did.

By the time my second period came in October, I had enough tampons to last the whole cycle. They were bigger than the ones the lady janitor had given me, and at first it was kind of hard to get one in, but I just kept pushing and it worked. I bought more pads with my babysitting money, but since I wasn't really using them, I chose the cheaper kind. "See?" Daddy said, as we stood in the feminine hygiene aisle at the drugstore. "It's a different story when it's your own money." I agreed with him about this, and it made me feel good. Anytime Daddy thought he knew something when he really didn't made me feel good.

I never flushed the tampons anymore. Not even at school, where the toilets were more powerful. Instead, I wrapped them in tissue paper and threw them in the trash, like they were maxi-pads. At school, there were little metal boxes stuck to the side of the stalls that you were supposed to use, and I loved looking inside them. Sometimes they were empty, but other times there was stuff I hadn't put in there. I began looking at all the other girls in school, trying to figure out who was getting her period besides me.

There was hardly any blood at the end of my period, but I used a tampon anyway. Then, when I went to pull the string out, it broke. It was the worst feeling in the world, standing there in the girls' lavatory and looking at both ends of it. I had no idea what to do. I couldn't reach more than one finger inside myself, I knew that. There just wasn't room. Instead, I sat on the toilet and pushed, like I was trying to poop. Nothing came out.

I felt scared for the rest of the day. I worried that without the string, the tampon would disappear inside me. Plus, I knew there was a disease you could get if you wore one too long. When I got home, I tried to take my own temperature, but I couldn't read the thermometer. At the Vuosos', I asked Zack to feel my forehead, but he said, "I'm not touching you." I tried feeling my own forehead, but it was like trying to smell your own breath. Everything seemed fine.

I thought my only hope was looking at *Playboy,* since whenever I did that, my underwear got kind of wet. It seemed like if there was enough moisture in the tampon, it would eventually slide out. That afternoon, I pressed my legs together harder than ever. I looked at all my favorite centerfolds over and over again, especially the ones where the women were smiling. I liked to think that even though they were naked and a man was taking their picture, they weren't afraid.

There was one photo I especially liked, of a woman in a golf cart with her shirt open. She was laughing and happy and didn't seem to realize that she was on a golf course where anyone could see her breasts. I tried to imagine what it would be like to be her. To be out in public and have my shirt open and a man taking my picture. To be able to smile while all of that was going on. The more I imagined it, the more I pressed my legs together. I knew I was making a lot of noise in the wicker chair, but I couldn't stop. I felt like I was chasing after something. Like if I just kept pressing, there would be a feeling that was even better than the pressing. I didn't know how I knew this, I just did. And then it happened. An orgasm.

It reminded me of breathing gas at the dentist's office, because suddenly everything felt okay. I didn't hate Daddy or my mother, I didn't care about having to live in Houston, I didn't even care about the tampon stuck inside me. For a brief moment, I was happy again. But then it wasn't like gas, because it went away. Just like that. And when it was gone, I felt even worse than before it had come, because I wanted it back again, all day long, every day.

I didn't notice that Zack had been looking at me until it was over. "What are you doing?" he asked.

"Nothing," I said.

"Why were you jumping around in the chair?"

"I wasn't," I said. "I just couldn't get comfortable."

He seemed like he didn't believe me.

"I'll be back in a minute," I said, and I got up and went in the bathroom. I sat on the toilet and pushed again, but the tampon didn't move. I went back in the bedroom to see if I could have another orgasm, but Zack was already picking up the magazines. "Hey," I said, as he took away the one with the golf cart. "I was looking at that."

"It's five o'clock," he said. This was the curfew I had placed on both of us, just to be safe.

"Really?" I said. I looked at my watch. He was right.

"What were you doing in the bathroom?" he asked.

"Nothing," I said.

"I heard you," he said. "You were pooping."

"I was not," I said.

Then he made a grunting noise, which I guessed was supposed to sound like me, even though I knew I hadn't done that.

"Shut up," I said, and I went to the closet and got my magazine.

"Hey," he said. "No looking at magazines after five."

"We can change it to five-thirty," I told him, since Mr. Vuoso never really came home before six. I just didn't think I would be able to wait another day to have an orgasm, and I didn't think it would be possible to have one without the pictures.

Zack shrugged and got his magazine, too. We took our regular seats, and I started creaking in my chair again. I could feel Zack turn around to look at me, but I didn't care. All I wanted was to feel good. To have an orgasm, then, as I was having it, to think of all the terrible things in my life and see how they didn't look so bad anymore. I thought if I did this a bunch of times in a row—if I was always pressing toward that good feeling—I would never have to feel bad again.

After the second one came, I started trying for a third. I didn't really feel like it anymore, but I just kept telling myself that I'd be happier in the end. I definitely had to work harder this time, pressing my legs together, looking at the woman in the golf cart, pretending I was the woman in the golf cart, pressing my legs together some more. Maybe if the chair hadn't been so loud, we would've heard Mr. Vuoso coming in the front door. Or climbing the stairs, or walking down the hall. But we didn't. I didn't even notice him standing in the doorway until I heard Zack say, "Dad."

"What's going on in here?" Mr. Vuoso asked. He looked different than usual. He still wore the same neat clothes and hair, but his face was tighter.

"Nothing," Zack said. He closed his magazine and got off the bed.

I closed mine, too.

"Who said you could look at my magazines?" Mr. Vuoso asked.

"No one," Zack said.

"Then why are you looking at them?"

"I don't know, sir."

"Jasira?" Mr. Vuoso said.

I stood up. "Yes?"

"Why are you looking at these magazines?"

"I don't know," I said.

"You don't know?"

I shook my head.

"You're the babysitter," he said. "You're supposed to know."

I nodded.

"So why are you doing it?"

"I don't know," I said again. It seemed like we were having the same conversation over and over, and I wished it would stop.

"Give me the magazine, Zack," Mr. Vuoso said.

Zack stepped up and handed it to his father.

"Now go and wait for me downstairs."

"Yes, sir," Zack said, and he slipped out of the room. It scared me, how fast his footsteps sounded when no one was even chasing him.

"I really would've expected more from you than this, Jasira," Mr. Vuoso said. He came over and took the magazine I was holding out, and our fingers touched for a second. I watched him put both issues back in the closet, then shut the door.

"I'm sorry," I said.

"You're sorry?" He laughed. It wasn't a nice laugh, and I wished I could go home. "'Sorry' doesn't cut it," he said.

"I guess I'm not a very good babysitter."

"I guess not." He sat down at the foot of the bed then, facing me. He looked at me for a long time. "C'mere," he said.

I didn't move. Since he'd arrived, I'd managed to inch a little closer to the door, and this seemed like the best place to be.

"Come over here," he said, a little softer this time. I looked at the door and thought about leaving. I wanted very much to leave. I took another step in that direction, then stopped when I heard his voice. "Where are you going?" he asked.

"Home," I said.

"Come here for just a second," he said.

"No."

"No?" He smiled then, like he thought I had said something funny.

"I have to go," I said.

"Where you going?" he asked.

"Home," I said again. It was like he was playing a game with me.

"All right," he said. "Fine. You go home."

I didn't move.

"Go on," he said.

"Are you going to tell my father?" I asked.

"Tell him what?"

"That I was looking at magazines."

"Your father's a fucking towelhead," he said.

I didn't say anything.

"Go on home to the towelhead."

"Please don't tell my father," I said.

"Why not?"

"Just please don't."

"What should I do, then?" he asked. "Should I just forget about it?"

"I won't do it again," I said.

"Do what?"

"Look at magazines."

"Did you like looking at them?"

I didn't answer.

"You must've liked looking at them. Why else would you look at them if you didn't like it?"

I still didn't answer.

"Tell me why you like looking at them, and I won't tell your father."

I tried to think of why, but I didn't know how to say it.

"C'mere," he said.

I took a step toward him.

"Just for a second," he said.

I got as close as his knee, then stopped.

"Tell me why you like looking at the magazines," he said.

"I can't," I said.

"Why?"

"I don't know why I like looking at them."

"But you like it?"

"Yes."

He reached a hand out then and put it around my waist. It was the strongest hand I had ever felt, and I thought about how it also touched guns. "Come and stand here," Mr. Vuoso said, and he pulled me between his knees.

I stood there for a minute, and he moved his hand down over my bottom. Then he reached up and touched my hair. He pushed it out of my face and tucked some of it behind my ear. I looked down at the floor. "Do you still want to go home?" he asked, and I nodded. "Okay," he said. "Go home."

I didn't move.

"I thought you wanted to go home," he said.

I pulled away from him then, and he let me. I turned and walked out the door, and he didn't stop me. I walked down the stairs and past

Zack in the living room and out of the house. Once I was on the front steps, I wished there was some way to go back inside, but there wasn't. Not until tomorrow.

When I got home, I sat on the toilet and pushed as hard as I could, and finally I could feel the tampon move. I could feel my muscles pushing it out. After it fell in the toilet, I reached in and got it, then wrapped it in tissue paper. I thought I had been saved. I thought Mr. Vuoso had made me feel so good that my insides had turned almost entirely to liquid. He was better than the magazines, and I couldn't wait for it to happen again.

When Daddy came home that night, he was in a good mood. A Greek woman in his office had invited him to dinner for the coming Saturday, and she was someone he actually liked. A hard worker. To celebrate, we went to Panjo's for pizza, and Daddy let me have some sips of his beer. I liked the way it made me feel dizzy for a second, right after I swallowed.

On the ride home, he told me about how he had first met my mother, even though I hadn't asked. "She had this little Fiat," he said, "and it was parked illegally, and she was standing there on the street, fighting with the guy who was going to tow it. So while they were fighting, I got in the car and locked the doors. No one can tow a car with a person sitting inside it. Did you know that?"

I shook my head.

"Well," he said, "it's true."

I guessed it was an interesting story, only I didn't want to hear any more. It bothered me to know nice things about Daddy, since that wasn't the way I usually thought of him. I was afraid of being tricked into liking him, so that the next time he turned mean—which I knew he would—it would be too surprising.

At home, Daddy said that he needed me to do him a favor.

"What is it?" I asked. I couldn't believe I had anything he wanted.

"I'd like you to write a letter to your grandma in Beirut."

"Why?" I said.

"Because," he said, "she loves you very much."

"But I don't even know her."

"That doesn't matter," he said. "She's your grandma."

He got out some paper then—onionskin, he called it. It was really thin and made crackling noises whenever you touched it. I sat down at the dining room table, and Daddy sat across from me. "Dear Grandma," he began, and I wrote it down. I hadn't known he was going to tell me what to say, and I felt pretty relieved about that. "I miss you very much," he continued, then he paused so I could write that down, too. Once I had finished, he said, "I hope you are happy and in good health. I am living with Daddy now in Houston. We have a very nice house." The next part was all about how I was sorry that I couldn't write to her in French, but that I was taking classes and would learn soon. Then, at the end, he made me put "Daddy is engaged to a very nice woman from NASA."

"Is that true?" I asked.

"No," he said.

"Then why are you saying it?"

"Your grandma won't understand dating," he said. "She'll be happier if she thinks I'm getting married."

"But what if you don't?"

"How do you know I won't?"

I didn't say anything.

"I may very well get married," he said. "This woman likes me a lot."

"Okay," I said.

He pointed to the letter. "Now write, 'I love you, Grandma,' and sign your name."

Afterward, he looked the whole thing over and told me it was very nice. "Your grandma will really like to see your penmanship," he said. Then he got a new piece of paper out of the package and started translating my English into Arabic. He said I could go, but I stayed for a while and watched him write from right to left. When he was done, he asked if I'd like to sign my name in Arabic, and I said sure. I thought he would show me how on a scrap of paper, then let me copy it onto the onionskin, but instead, he gave me the pen, then held my hand in his as he guided my movements. I knew he was just trying to help, but I really couldn't stand for him to touch me. My arm went kind of stiff, and when we'd finished, he said that Grandma was going to think I was retarded.

In bed that night, I squeezed my legs together and tried to have an orgasm just from picturing the lady in the golf cart. I didn't think it would work, but it did. When it happened, instead of thinking terrible things, I thought about Mr. Vuoso. I thought about his hand around my waist, and his nice cologne, and how he had let me go home when I wanted to. I thought about how he had called Daddy a fucking towelhead, but he still liked me.

At school the next day, I was nervous. I wondered how things would go with Mr. Vuoso that night. How we would ever be alone again so he could touch me. While I sat in Social Studies, listening to Mr. Mecoy talk about how Texas used to be its own country, I started pressing my legs together under the desk. I was very still and quiet, so no one would notice, and I had an orgasm. When it happened, I looked across the aisle at Robert Serling, the boy who had stuck my maxi-pad to his forehead. He had blond curly hair, and I realized in that moment how handsome he was.

That afternoon at the Vuosos', Zack said, "We're not allowed to look at magazines anymore. My dad put them in the garage."

"Can't we just go out in the garage?" I asked.

Zack shook his head. "My dad says he'll know if we sneak and look at them."

"All right," I said, though I was disappointed.

"He says you should've known better," Zack said.

"Yes," I said. "I should've."

"I know what you were doing in that chair."

"What?"

He laughed. "You know."

"I wasn't doing anything."

We went outside then to play badminton. For once, Zack didn't hit me in the boobs, and we actually ended up finishing a game. We had to quit in the middle of the second one, though, when we hit our last birdie into the yard next to Zack's. We thought about climbing the fence, but it was too tall. We'd have to wait until the newlyweds got back from their honeymoon. They'd moved in a week earlier, then left right away for Paris. I hadn't met them, but Zack had. He said the lady was pretty and the man was tall.

We went back inside and turned on the TV. I couldn't remember what we had done before looking at magazines, and now that they were gone, I couldn't imagine what we would ever do again. After a while, I went upstairs to steal a tampon from Mrs. Vuoso, but there were too few in the jar to make it safe.

On the way downstairs, something caught my eye in the master bedroom, and I stopped. It was a large green duffel bag at the foot of the canopy bed. I walked in and knelt down on the floor. I was quiet for a moment, listening for footsteps, and when I didn't hear anything, I unzipped it. Mostly there were just clothes: white T-shirts, camouflage pants, boots, sneakers, boxer shorts, belts. I reached a hand in to see if anything had been slipped between the neat piles, and it had. Something wrapped in plastic or cellophane. At first I thought it was candy, but then I pulled it out and saw that it wasn't. It was rubbers. A long strand of them. *Durex,* the package read. *Extra Sensitive.*

Super thin for more feeling. I ripped one off and stuck it in my pocket, then put the rest back. Downstairs in the living room, I asked Zack if his dad was going somewhere.

"Why?" he said.

"There's a duffel bag in the bedroom."

"That's in case we go to war with Iraq," Zack said.

"Oh."

"It could happen anytime. He has to be ready."

"Is it going to happen soon?"

Zack shrugged. "I don't know." Then he turned back to the TV.

I sat down on the couch then, feeling worried. I started to wonder if Mr. Vuoso really could die. Daddy had been talking a lot about the possibility of a war lately. He was really excited about it. He said, "Saddam is a bully. He can't invade another country and get away with it."

When Mr. Vuoso walked in the door that night, I stood up and smiled. "Hi," I said.

He didn't smile back. "Everything go okay?"

I nodded.

"Good to hear," he said, and he walked in the kitchen.

I didn't know what to do then, if I should follow him or sit and wait for him to come back.

"You can go now," Zack said.

"Shut up," I told him, and I pretended that I was watching something on TV. A couple of minutes later, when Mr. Vuoso still hadn't come back, I let myself out the front door.

At home, I was upset. I didn't even feel like having an orgasm. I tried to think of a reason to go back to the Vuosos', and when I couldn't, I went over there anyway. Zack opened the door. "What do you want?" he said.

"I need to talk to your father," I told him.

"About what?"

"Just get him."

He looked at me for a second, then turned and yelled, "Dad!"

"What?" Mr. Vuoso called back.

"Jasira wants to talk to you!"

He didn't answer, but a few seconds later, he came to the door. "Yes?" he said, standing behind Zack.

"Can I talk to you in private?" I asked.

He was quiet for a second, then said, "Zack, why don't you go upstairs and start your homework?"

Zack left, even though I could tell he didn't want to.

"What is it?" Mr. Vuoso asked, his hand on the doorknob.

I didn't know what to say then. I guessed I thought that he might say something—or do something—if I just set it up so that we could be alone. "Well," I said finally, "I wanted to thank you for not telling my father about yesterday."

"Yesterday," he said. "What was yesterday?"

I looked at him. He seemed so different now. "Yesterday," I said. "In the guest room."

"Nothing happened yesterday," he said. "Don't worry about it."

I was quiet for a second.

"Is that all?" he asked.

"I guess," I said.

"All right, then," he said, "we'll see you tomorrow. Have a good night."

He shut the door, and I stood there on the porch for a minute. After a while, I went home and locked myself in my bathroom. I took Mr. Vuoso's condom out of my pocket and hid it behind the Comet with his wife's tampons. Then I sat down on the edge of the tub and started to cry. I knew from health class what condoms were for, and I knew that if Mr. Vuoso got called up, Mrs. Vuoso wouldn't be going with him. That could mean only one thing, which was that he was planning to love other people. I just didn't understand why it couldn't be me.

For the rest of the week, it was the same thing. Mr. Vuoso came home and asked me how everything had gone, then went in the kitchen. I didn't know what to do. I thought about calling him or writing him a letter, but I wasn't sure what I would say. Maybe he was right. Maybe nothing really had happened.

On Saturday, Daddy wanted to get some new clothes for his date, so we went to the mall. At Foley's department store, a salesman showed him some different sport jackets, and Daddy tried them all on. He asked me what I thought of them, and I said they were nice, even though they looked exactly like the ones at home in his closet. He ended up buying a navy blue one, along with a blue striped tie. I thought we would leave then, but instead, he said I needed some new things, too. "No, I don't," I said, since shopping for clothes with Daddy sounded as bad as shopping for maxi-pads. But he said yes I did, and that I was starting to sag.

As I followed him through the store, I couldn't stop thinking about this. That I was sagging. I couldn't stop thinking that for Daddy to have known it, he would've had to be looking at my boobs.

In the ladies' underwear department, he asked the saleswoman to help us. He mentioned again that I was sagging, and she said that I probably needed to start wearing underwires. Then she got a tape measure and used it right there, in front of Daddy. I didn't have to take off my shirt or anything, but the tape got stretched across my nipples. "Thirty-four C," the saleswoman said, and Daddy whistled like he couldn't believe it.

While the two of them went off to find me some bras, I sat in a pink velvet chair next to the cash register and thought about my mother. The last time she'd taken me shopping, she'd tried to get me to wear underwires, too, but I wouldn't. They hurt too much. "You won't be happy if you end up with stretch marks," she said, but I still wouldn't do it. After a while, she gave up. We went to the food court and got hot dogs, and she told me that one day I would make some man very happy. "I will?" I asked, and she nodded. "Even with stretch marks," she said. Then she met Barry a few months later, and I guessed he wasn't the man she had been thinking of.

Soon, Daddy and the saleswoman came back with a bunch of different bras. She took me in the fitting room and told me to press a little red button if I needed help, and I said I would. I undressed and put on the prettiest one first. It was silvery gray with a tiny bow at the center. I couldn't tell if it fit or not, so I pressed the red button. When I opened the door to my dressing room, though, it was Daddy standing there. I crossed my hands over my chest, but he said to move them so he could check the fit. "Where's the lady?" I asked, and he said she was busy with another customer. When I still didn't uncross my arms, he said to stop this nonsense, that a bra was no different from a bathing suit.

I really couldn't stand the sight of Daddy in the mirror, looking at me. I couldn't stand the way he tugged at the hooks on the bra, or made adjustments to the shoulder straps. I didn't understand why he wanted to know so much about my body if he didn't even like it. I thought he should keep away from it instead. I thought only people who really and truly liked it should get to see it.

He ended up buying me seven new bras, one for each day of the week. The saleswoman told him that not many fathers would take the time to make sure that their daughters had proper foundation garments, and I could tell that made him happy. She gave him a bra club card so we could get a discount the next time we came in, and he said we'd see her next year.

As soon as we got home, Daddy told me to go put one of my new bras on and show him. I thought he meant without a shirt, like in the dressing room, but when I came out like that, he slapped me and asked what the hell I was doing. I started to cry and ran back in my room, and a little while later, he came and knocked at the door. "What's the problem in there?" he asked, and I said, "Nothing."

"Good," he said. "Because I'm still waiting to see one of those bras." When I finally came back out wearing a T-shirt, he said, "Much better."

"Thank you," I said.

He nodded. "Try to remember that we never leave our rooms unless we're properly dressed."

"Okay," I said. I went back in my room and clipped the tags off all my bras. I still didn't like the feel of the underwire, but it was true that it gave me better support. Every time I saw myself in the full-length mirror on the inside of my closet door, I couldn't believe how high up I was. And pointy. When I looked at myself from the side, I liked how my boobs made my T-shirt pull up in the front.

At seven o'clock, Daddy called me out into the living room. He was all dressed up in his new coat and tie, with a white shirt underneath. "How do I look?" he asked.

"Very nice," I said.

"Do you think Thena will like it?"

"Yes."

"Well," he said, "let's hope so."

After he pulled out of the driveway, I heated up a TV dinner in the microwave. I ate it in the breakfast nook instead of the dining room, then washed and dried my dishes. Later, when I called my mother to tell her I was finally wearing an underwire, Barry answered. "This is Jasira," I said. "I need to talk to my mother." I tried to make my voice sound like as much of a robot as possible, so nothing bad would happen.

"Jasira," he said. He didn't sound like a robot at all. He just sounded happy. "How are you doing?"

"Is my mom there?" I asked.

"No," he said. "She's not."

"Where is she?"

"She went swimming. She's on a big fitness kick lately."

"Oh," I said. I wondered why she hadn't mentioned this to me herself. "Well, can you please have her call me when she gets back?"

"Sure," he said. "Is everything okay?"

It was really making me mad, how nice he was being, when I was trying so hard not to be friendly. I thought the least he could do was be unfriendly, too.

"Jasira?" he said.

"What?"

"Are you okay?"

"No," I said.

"What's going on?" he asked.

"Nothing."

"You just said you weren't okay."

"Stop asking me questions," I said. "It's not fair."

"It's not?"

"No."

He sighed. "All right. I won't ask you questions."

"Thank you," I said.

There was silence then, and I hoped he wouldn't hang up. "Tell me what I'm allowed to say," he said finally.

"Nothing."

He laughed. "Then how are we supposed to have a conversation?"

"We're not."

He sighed again and said, "Right."

"I'll ask you questions," I said.

"Okay," he said. "Shoot."

"How are you?"

"I'm fine," he said. "Especially now."

"Don't say extra things," I said. "Just answer the question."

"Sorry," he said.

"Are you and my mom going to break up?"

"I don't know," he said.

"Why not?"

"Because we're trying not to."

I wanted to tell him that I thought he should. That my mother wasn't a very nice person, and that once she got mad at you, she stayed mad forever. Instead, I said, "I got new bras today. With underwires."

"Oh yeah?" Barry said.

"Yeah," I said. "I used to be a thirty-four B, but now I'm a thirty-four C."

"Wow."

"I went up a size."

He was quiet for a second, then he said, "I'd better go."

"No," I said, "don't," but he'd already hung up.

The phone rang a little later, and it was my mother. "Barry said you called," she said.

"Yes," I said. "Were you swimming?"

"He said you told him about your bras."

I couldn't believe it. He'd tattled again.

"Haven't you learned anything from all of this?" she asked.

"I just wanted you to know that I was wearing underwires," I said. "For better support."

"No," she said, "you wanted Barry to know."

I didn't answer her. It was true.

"No one wants to hear about your breasts, Jasira. Do you understand me? They don't want to hear about your breasts, and they don't want to hear about your pubic hair, and they don't want to hear about your period, okay? You need to keep all of that stuff to yourself. Then maybe you and I will have something to talk about."

"Okay," I said.

"Do I make myself clear?" she asked.

"Yes."

"Good."

"Are you going to hang up now?"

"Not necessarily," she said. "I mean, do you have anything else to talk about besides that famous body of yours?"

"Yes," I said.

"Great," she said. "What is it?"

"Daddy is on a date tonight."

"Oh yeah? What does she look like?"

"I don't know," I said.

"Well," she said, "you'll have to fill me in if you meet her."

"Okay."

"Anything else?" she asked.

I tried to think of something, but I couldn't. "No," I said finally.

"All right, then," she said. "I guess I'll go and wash this chlorine out of my hair."

We hung up and I went to pee. Then I went in my room and took off all my clothes. I opened the closet door and looked at myself in the mirror. When I thought about my mother or Daddy seeing me like this, I felt bad, but when I thought about Barry or Mr. Vuoso, it was better. After a while, I got down on the floor and sat with my legs apart to try to get a look at myself. It was pink and hairy and wet, and I thought it looked terrible. I started to get up, then I decided to look again. This time, it wasn't so bad. I knew from *Playboy* that there was a spot in there that made you have an orgasm, only I wasn't sure where. I started touching different parts until I found it, then I rubbed it over and over again. When the orgasm came, I looked in the mirror and thought I might be pretty, but then it ended and I changed my mind.

I went to bed before Daddy got home. The next morning, I walked out to find him standing in the kitchen with a woman I'd never seen before. They were both holding mugs of coffee and talking, and the woman had a funny look on her face, like she thought Daddy was nice or interesting.

"Good morning!" Daddy said when he saw me.

"Good morning," I said, stopping just shy of the kitchen. I couldn't tell if I should stay or go back in my room.

"Good morning," the woman said, turning around. She was tiny and had dark skin like mine and Daddy's. There were big lids on her large brown eyes, and I liked how you could see her eye shadow when she blinked. What I didn't understand was how she was standing there bare-legged in one of Daddy's shirts without getting slapped.

"Jasira," Daddy said, "this is Thena Panos."

"Hello," I said, moving forward a little.

Thena held out a hand, which was still warm from her coffee mug, and I shook it. "It's so nice to finally meet you, Jasira. Your father talks about you all the time."

"He does?" I asked, slightly confused.

Thena nodded. "You apparently have quite a zest for life."

"Oh," I said.

"That's a compliment," Daddy said.

"Thank you," I told him.

"You're welcome," he said.

There were pancakes cooking on the stove, and Daddy had Thena and me sit down in the breakfast nook so he could serve us. Pancakes were Daddy's specialty. He made them from scratch, then cooked them in a lot of oil, so that they were crispy on the outside. When Thena took her first bite, she said, "Oh, Rifat. I am your slave."

"The secret is baking powder," he said. "Lots of baking powder."

"I don't want to know the secret," she said. "I just want you to keep cooking them for me."

He laughed and said, "That shouldn't be a problem."

When the next batch was finished, Daddy brought them over on a plate and sat down to eat with us. He started telling funny stories about NASA, which I thought was fake, since he normally hated it. Then he complimented me some more, saying I was a wonderful babysitter. "You should see how much this kid next door likes her," Daddy said. "He thinks she's the greatest thing on earth."

Thena smiled. "I'll bet."

"He doesn't really like me," I said, which was the truth. Zack hated me. I had no idea what Daddy was talking about.

"Of course he likes you," Daddy said sharply. "He likes to play badminton with you."

"What's his name?" Thena asked.

"Zack," I said.

"His father is a reservist," Daddy said, raising an eyebrow at Thena.

"Uh-oh," she said.

Daddy nodded. "He found out I'm Lebanese, and now he thinks I'm in love with Saddam."

"Typical," Thena said.

"The only reason I let Jasira work for him is so she can save for college," Daddy said. "Otherwise, forget it."

"How much have you saved so far?" Thena asked me.

"I don't know," I said.

She laughed. "You don't know?"

"Daddy puts the money in the bank for me."

"I see," she said. Then she looked at Daddy and said, "How much does she have, Rifat?"

Daddy thought for a minute, then said, "Maybe two hundred dollars? Something like that."

"Wow," Thena said. "That's a good start."

"Thank you," I said.

"What do you want to be?" she asked.

"I don't know."

"You could be a model," she said.

"Forget it," Daddy said.

"What do you mean, forget it?" Thena said. "Models make a lot of money."

"She's going to college," Daddy said. "She can make a lot of money being an engineer."

"Does she want to be an engineer?" Thena asked.

Daddy shrugged. "She's good in math and science."

Thena turned to me and said, "Don't be an engineer, Jasira. It's boring. Be a model, make a lot of money, then spend the rest of your life traveling."

"Okay," I said.

"Stop putting ideas in her head," Daddy said.

"We're just having a conversation," Thena said. Then she reached over and touched her hand to his cheek, which seemed to make him forget everything.

Later, when she got up from the table to take her plate to the sink, I saw Daddy watching the backs of her bare legs. She excused herself to go to use the bathroom, and he watched her walk into his room. Then he looked at me and said, "She's nice, isn't she?"

"Yes," I said.

"Try not to look so miserable, would you?" he said, getting up to take his own plate into the kitchen. "No woman is going to marry a man with a miserable kid."

"I'm not miserable," I said, following him.

"Then why don't you smile?"

"I don't know," I said.

I tried to help him load the dishwasher, but he told me to go away. "You're depressing all of us," he said.

I went in my room and shut the door. A little while later, Daddy came and knocked. "You have to come back out again," he whispered.

"Why?" I asked.

"She wants to put makeup on you."

"Makeup?"

He nodded. "She won't stop talking about that stupid modeling."

I said all right, then followed him into the dining room. Thena was fully dressed now in a skirt and blouse, and her makeup was laid out on the table. She had me sit in the chair closest to the window, then told Daddy to go in the other room until she called him. "Can't I watch?" he asked, and she said no, that it would be better if he got the full effect.

After he left, she got busy working on me. She told me everything she was doing, right as she was doing it. "I'm starting with moisturizer," she said, lightly moving her hands across my face. "Then I'll put on foundation. Never put foundation directly on your skin. Fill your pores with lotion first."

I nodded, even though I wasn't really listening. Instead, I watched out the window as Mrs. Vuoso and Zack came out of the house dressed for church. His hair was wet and combed to one side, and she wore a blue dress with a collar. I noticed that she didn't really have any breasts, and I wondered if that was why her husband wanted to touch mine.

A couple of minutes after they drove off, Mr. Vuoso came out with a shovel and started digging in the front yard. I guessed he didn't have reserve duty that weekend.

"Close your eyes," Thena said, and I did, and she powdered me with a brush. "Always put on powder after foundation," she said. "To set it."

I nodded again, wishing I could open my eyes. But she told me to keep them shut, because now she was putting on eye shadow. "Light colors in the corners, dark colors at the edges," she said, swirling her fingertips around on my lids. It felt good, the way she was touching me. Like when Barry had shaved my pubic hair. My scalp started to tingle, and soon I didn't mind so much that I couldn't see Mr. Vuoso.

The last things she put on were mascara and lipstick. Then she handed me her compact mirror and said, "What do you think?"

At first I didn't say anything. It was strange to see myself like this. My skin was smoother, my eyes stood out more, my cheeks were pink, and my mouth looked like I had just eaten something red and wet without using a napkin. It was me, but better. "I like it," I said finally.

She nodded. "Me, too." Then she turned toward the kitchen and said, "Okay, Rifat! We're ready."

"What the hell is he doing?" Daddy said when he came in.

Thena followed Daddy's gaze out the window, then said, "Rifat, what do you think of Jasira?"

"What?" Daddy said.

"Isn't she gorgeous?"

He looked at me for a moment, then said, "Yes. She looks very nice."

"She really could be a model," Thena said.

"That's him," Daddy said to Thena, nodding toward the window. "The reservist."

Thena looked outside again. "Ah," she said.

"He's digging for oil in his front yard," Daddy said, and he and Thena both laughed.

"May I be excused?" I asked. I didn't like them making fun of Mr. Vuoso.

Daddy turned to me. "Did you say thank you to Thena?"

"Thank you," I told her.

"Oh," she said, "it was my pleasure. I just love makeup."

Back in my room, I opened the closet door and stared at myself in the mirror. Suddenly, without Thena there to say I looked nice, I couldn't see it anymore. I could only hear Daddy saying I looked very nice in that way he didn't mean. I wasn't sure why I believed him instead of her, but I did.

There was a knock at my door then, and Daddy stuck his head in. "I'm taking Thena home," he said. "Go and wash your face."

"Okay," I said.

He looked at me standing in front of the mirror and said, "You're not going to be a model."

"I know," I said.

I went in the bathroom and turned on the water, but I didn't wash my face. Then, when I was sure Daddy had left, I went next door. Mr. Vuoso was still working in the front yard, and I stood there for a while, watching him with the shovel. I liked how his arm muscles looked when they did something hard. You could see the exact shape of them for a second, then, when it was over, they'd disappear again under his skin. "What are you doing?" I asked.

"Digging," he said.

"For oil?"

He laughed a little and said, "No. For a flag post."

"Oh."

A few minutes later, he took a break. "You look different," he said.

"I'm wearing makeup."

"Your father lets you wear makeup?"

"No," I said. "His girlfriend put it on."

"Is that who that was?"

I nodded. "He went to take her home."

Mr. Vuoso didn't say anything. Just wiped some sweat off his forehead with the back of his arm and started digging again. I thought I should probably go home and wash my face, but then he said, "Jasira?"

"Yes?" I said.

"How old are you?"

"Thirteen."

"When are you going to be fourteen?"

"In June," I said. Then I said, "How old are you?"

"I'm thirty-six," he said. "I'm a lot older than you."

"Yes," I said.

"But you look older with that makeup on."

"I do?"

He nodded. "You look about sixteen."

I wasn't sure if it was a compliment, so I didn't say thank you. Instead, I said, "I miss looking at your magazines."

He was quiet for a second, then he said, "Why?"

"Because," I said. "They make me feel good."

He didn't say anything.

"They make me have orgasms," I said.

He still didn't say anything. Just kept digging. After a while, I walked home. I washed my face in the sink, then dried it, then went to change my underwear, which had gotten wet from talking to Mr. Vuoso. As I was zipping my jeans back up, the doorbell rang. I went to answer it, but there was no one there. I looked down and saw a paper bag on the welcome mat. I picked it up and opened it, and inside was a *Playboy*.

THREE

When Daddy found out that Mr. Vuoso was getting a flagpole, he got one, too. He put it in the same exact spot in the front yard as Mr. Vuoso's, and installed a floodlight that he turned on at night. You had to do this if you wanted to fly the flag at all times, he told me. Otherwise, you were supposed to take it down at sunset and put it back up at sunrise. This was what Mr. Vuoso did, and it drove Daddy crazy. "What is he trying to prove?" Daddy asked, watching him out the dining room window. "That he's more patriotic? Well, he's not. It's more patriotic to fly the flag all the time."

I knew that Daddy wasn't really being patriotic. That he just wanted to bother Mr. Vuoso and try to teach him a lesson. But I didn't care. I was glad we had a flag. For once it seemed like we were normal Americans. Like we did at least one thing just like everybody else. The next time I saw Mr. Vuoso, he asked me what Daddy was trying to pull, and I lied and said I didn't know.

It had been almost two weeks since he'd given me the *Playboy*, and we hadn't really talked about it. "Thank you for the magazine," I'd whispered the next day, slipping out the door after babysitting, and he'd looked at me and said, "What magazine?" I didn't feel hurt, though. There was something in his voice that made me think we really were playing a game, and this was just one of the rules.

He'd given me the issue with the lady in the golf cart. I wondered if he'd remembered it from that day he'd caught me and Zack in the guest room, or if it was a coincidence. Either way, I was glad to see her again. Her wonderful smile. I wanted so much to be like her. To be with a man photographer and feel good about showing him my breasts.

I used the magazine a lot. I woke up early in the morning to use it, and went to bed early at night. If I ever woke up in the middle of the night, I used it then, too. More and more, when I used it, I didn't press my legs together. Instead, I lay back on the bed, let my legs fall open, and touched myself while I looked at the pictures. I touched my nipples, too, like some of the women in *Playboy,* and it made the orgasms come faster. It was like there was some connection running from my breasts to between my legs. To test out how strong it was, I tried having an orgasm just by touching my nipples, and it worked.

I began to think that my body was the most special thing in the world. Better than other bodies, even. Not because of the way it looked, but because of all the things it could do. All the different buttons there were to push. I wanted to find out what every single one of them was. I wanted to feel as good as possible.

At the end of October, the newlyweds finally came back from Paris. "She got fat on her honeymoon," Zack said. We were sitting on his front steps, watching the lady unload her groceries from the car into the house.

"No, she didn't," I said. "She's pregnant."

"She is?"

I nodded. "Can't you tell the difference?"

He shrugged. "Not really."

We waited a little while for her to put the food away, then went over and knocked on her door. "Hi," I said, "I'm Jasira, and this is Zack. We need to get our birdies out of your yard."

"What birdies?" she said. She was eating almonds from a plastic container. Her T-shirt was snug and showed the shape of her stomach. She had partly blonde hair and partly brown hair. The brown part was at the roots. A whole crown of it. Up by her left eye were a couple of tiny moles that made it look like she was crying black tears.

"We shot some birdies into your yard while you were on your honeymoon," Zack said. "We just want to get them back."

"Oh," she said. "You mean shuttlecocks."

"What?" Zack said.

"Shuttlecocks," she said. "That's the real word for birdies."

"It is not," Zack said.

"You want to bet?" she said.

Zack thought for a minute, then said, "No."

"Smart move," she said. Then she stepped back from the door a little. "C'mon in. Sorry about the mess."

There were boxes everywhere, and a lot of rolled-up rugs. Instead of carpeting, the lady and her husband had wooden floors. NPR was playing somewhere, though I couldn't see a radio.

The lady offered us some of her almonds, but we said no. "What grades are y'all in?" she asked, and we told her. She wanted to know if we liked the schools here, and Zack said yes. I said I liked the ones back home better, and she said, "Oh yeah? Where's home?"

"New York," I said.

"Where in New York?" she said, and for the first time since I'd moved to Texas, I told someone that I was from Syracuse.

"You're kidding," she said.

"No."

"My husband went to SU."

"C'mon, Jasira," Zack said. "Let's go get the birdies."

We went outside then and picked them all up. When we came back in, the lady said, "Jasira. What kind of name is that?"

I hesitated for a second, and Zack said, "She's a towelhead."

"Excuse me?" the lady said.

"It's a towelhead name," Zack said, and he laughed a little.

"Who taught you that word?" she asked.

Zack didn't answer.

"Don't ever use that word in this house again," she said, and she walked off and left us standing alone in the kitchen. After a second, we turned and let ourselves out the front door.

"What a bitch," Zack said once we'd reached the sidewalk.

"I thought she was nice," I said.

"You would."

"She's right," I said. "You shouldn't be using that word."

"I'll say whatever I want, towelhead."

We played a little badminton then, and I purposely hit a few of the birdies into the lady's yard so we could go back and see her to-morrow.

Later, when we went inside, Zack got the dictionary and looked up *shuttlecock.*

"Does it mean birdie?" I asked, and he nodded. "See?" I said. "She wasn't trying to trick you."

Next he looked up *towelhead.* "It's not in here," he said.

"That's because it's a bad word," I told him.

"Oh yeah?" he said, and he flipped the pages around to show me *spic* and *nigger.* "It's just a new word," he said. "They'll put it in all the new dictionaries."

He went to watch TV, and I went upstairs. I was getting worried about my tampon supply for November. I had only three left in my bathroom cabinet, and Mrs. Vuoso had stopped refilling the jar on the back of her toilet. It seemed like it had been the same five tampons in there for weeks. And today was no different. I was going to go back downstairs without taking one, but then I changed my mind and slipped one in my pocket. I really couldn't stand the idea of having to use pads again. They were dirty and smelly, and sometimes I thought this was the real reason Daddy wanted me to wear them. To make me think my body was terrible.

When Mr. Vuoso came home, Zack told him that the lady next door had yelled at him. "What for?" Mr. Vuoso asked.

Zack looked at me, then got up on his tiptoes and whispered something in his father's ear. After he'd finished, Mr. Vuoso said, "All right. We'll talk about it later." Then he turned to me and said, "Everything else okay, Jasira?"

I nodded.

"Good," he said, and he walked past me into the kitchen.

I left then, and as I headed down the Vuosos' front walk, the lady's husband pulled into the driveway next door. He drove an old blue truck, which made me think he'd be wearing jeans when he got out, but he wasn't. He had on a gray suit and carried a briefcase. "Hi there," he said, and I said hi back. I thought about asking him about Syracuse, but he was already almost to his front door.

When Daddy got home that night, he gave me a letter with my name on it. It had foreign stamps, and the person who'd sent it didn't know how to write the address. The city and state and zip code were all on separate lines. I turned the letter over and saw that it was from someone I'd never heard of. "Who's Nathalie Maroun?" I asked, and Daddy said, "She's your grandma." He told me to open the envelope, and I did, and the whole letter was written in French. I asked Daddy if he would read it to me, but he said no. He said that I could take it to school and ask my teacher for help, and that he expected a full translation tomorrow night.

We ate dinner, then I went and sat on the couch with my grandmother's letter. She used the same blue onionskin paper as Daddy, and her handwriting was long and slim. *Ma chère Jasira,* it began, which I knew meant *My dear Jasira*. I read that part over and over again, wondering how I could be dear to someone who'd never even met me. I guessed if I tried, I could probably have figured out the rest of the letter, but I didn't want to try. I didn't want to hear a bunch of nice things from someone I didn't even know. It didn't mean anything.

The next day, at the beginning of French class, I showed Madame Madigan my letter and asked if she would help me. She got very excited, then stood up from her desk and said she'd be right back. A few minutes later, she returned with Xerox copies of the letter. She had the whole class break into five groups, and we were each assigned a paragraph to translate. My group got the one that said: *I hope that one day we will meet and I will be able to kiss your cheeks and tell you how much I love you. It is important for you to know your Lebanese family. Please come to Beirut as soon as possible. Grandma.*

By the end of class, everyone was calling me a towelhead. They also called me a sand nigger and a camel jockey, which I'd never heard of before. Even Thomas Bradley, who was black, called me a sand nigger.

I felt really terrible all the way home. On the bus, I sat by myself at the back and thought about the lady in the golf cart, squeezing my legs together. That helped a little, but then, when I got to the Vuosos', there was a note for me on the kitchen table. It was from Mrs. Vuoso, and the envelope was sealed. "What's this?" I asked Zack, and he said how should he know. I opened it, and it said: *Dear Jasira, I've noticed that my tampons seem to be disappearing from the back of the toilet. I wondered if maybe you had borrowed some? If so, I would appreciate it if you would stop. They're kind of expensive, and I'm sure if you asked your father, he would get you whatever supplies you need. Thanks, Mrs. V.*

"What does it say?" Zack asked.

"Nothing," I said, putting the note in my pocket.

"Are you in trouble?"

"No."

"Then what is it?"

"We need to go next door to get the birdies I lost yesterday."

"Why?" he said. "We still have a bunch left."

"I'm going next door," I told him.

"I don't want to go," he said.

"So stay here."

"You're supposed to be babysitting me," he said.

"I thought you didn't need a babysitter."

He ignored this and said, "If you go next door, you can't get paid for when you're gone."

"Fine," I said.

He checked his watch. "You can't get paid from starting now."

"Fine," I said again, and I left.

I went over to the lady's and knocked. At first no one answered, then she came to the door wearing a pair of pajama pants and a T-shirt. "Hi," I said, "I need to get our birdies again."

"Sure," she said. "C'mon in."

I followed her through the living room and into the kitchen. She was setting up a large spice rack on the counter, and I noticed that she had a lot of the same ones as Daddy: cumin, coriander, turmeric, cardamom, fenugreek.

"Where's your friend?" she asked.

"Zack?"

She nodded.

"He's at home."

"What a mouth on that kid," she said, shaking her head.

"He didn't mean it," I said. "He's only ten."

"I don't care how old he is."

She started alphabetizing the spices. She seemed very organized, like Daddy, even though she dressed kind of messy. After a while, I went outside and got the birdies. When I came back in, I tried to think of something else to talk about so I wouldn't have to go back to the Vuosos'. "What's your name?" I asked.

"Melina," she said.

I nodded. "Do you have any tampons?"

She laughed. "Tampons? What would I be doing with tampons?"

I didn't know what she meant by this. She stopped working then and looked at me. "You don't get your period when you're pregnant," she said. "All that blood stays in your uterus to keep the baby cushioned."

"Oh."

"Why?" she said. "Do you need a tampon?"

"Not right now," I said. "But I will soon."

"Can't your parents buy you some?"

"It's just Daddy," I said. "That's who I live with."

"Well," she said, "can't you ask him?"

I shook my head. "No."

"No?"

"I'm not allowed to wear them," I said. "Not until I'm married."

"Huh," she said. "I guess I never really heard of that."

"That's Daddy's rule," I told her.

"Where's he from?" Melina asked.

"Lebanon," I said, and for the first time, I didn't feel so embarrassed about it.

"Huh," she said again. Then she said, "What's with the flag?"

"Excuse me?" I said.

"You guys live on the other side of the Vuosos, right?"

I nodded.

"So why does your father fly the flag?"

"Daddy hates Saddam," I said.

She looked at me like she didn't really understand.

"Mr. Vuoso thinks Daddy loves Saddam," I tried to explain, "but Daddy doesn't. That's why he put the flag up. To prove it."

"Why does your father care what that guy thinks?"

I thought for a second, then said, "I don't know."

"Because that guy is a pig," Melina said.

"Who?" I said.

"Vuoso," she said. "He reads *Playboy*."

"He does?" I said. Suddenly it seemed like something I should keep a secret.

Melina nodded. "We got some of his mail on accident yesterday."

"Did you give it back?"

"Hell no," she said. "I threw it out."

"You threw out his *Playboy*?"

"Why shouldn't I?" she said.

I didn't answer.

"I'll throw out whatever I want."

I felt really upset then. Not just because Melina had thrown out a *Playboy*, but because she seemed to think it was such a bad thing to like. I didn't want her to think that way. I wanted her to like it as much as I did. I wanted us to think the same way about everything. "Well," I said, "I guess I better go."

"All right."

"Sorry about the birdies," I said.

"Don't worry about it."

It was a short walk back to the Vuosos', but I slowed it down by not cutting across their front lawn. When I walked in the door, Zack said, "What took you so long?"

"I was only gone ten minutes," I said.

"You were gone fifteen minutes," he said. "That means you lose fifty cents."

"Whatever," I said. I didn't really care. Mostly, I just wanted to think about Melina. How you could see the nub of her belly button poking through her T-shirt.

When Mr. Vuoso got home, Zack tried to tattle on me for having left him alone. "You can't stay by yourself for fifteen minutes?" his father asked, and Zack said he could, and Mr. Vuoso said that he didn't see what the problem was then. After his dad went in the kitchen, Zack gave me the finger and whispered that I was a dirty towelhead, and I whispered back never to call me that again.

Later that night, Daddy made me translate Grandma's letter for him. When I finished, he told me I'd done a very good job, then asked how much Madame Madigan had had to help me. I thought about telling him that the kids at school had called me names, but then I didn't. I just couldn't bring myself to say those words out loud. Somehow, I thought Daddy would think I was talking about him.

The next afternoon at the Vuosos', I hit four birdies in a row into Melina's backyard. "You suck!" Zack screamed.

"Sorry," I said. "I'll go get them."

"No!" he yelled, but I ignored him.

"Birdies?" Melina said when she answered the front door, and I nodded. There were pencils sticking out of the messy bun at the back of her head.

After she let me in, she asked if a picture she'd just hung on the living room wall looked straight, and I said it did. It showed a sandy-colored building set into a rocky cliff. "What is that?" I asked.

"Gil's old house," she said.

"In Syracuse?" It didn't really look like Syracuse.

She laughed. "No. Yemen."

I tried to think of where that was.

"He used to be in the Peace Corps," she said.

"What did he do?"

She shrugged. "A lot of stuff. Mostly, he dug sewage systems."

"Oh," I said.

"Toilets," she added.

I nodded.

"Squat down," she said.

"What?"

"Bend your legs and squat."

I did this, and she said, "No, more."

I squatted more.

"Even more," she said. "As far as you can go without letting your butt touch the floor."

When I'd gotten as low as possible, she said, "That's how they go to the bathroom over there. There's no real toilets. They just dig a hole in the floor and crouch over it."

"They do?" I said, standing back up. My thighs were kind of sore.

She nodded. "Can you imagine doing that when you're pregnant?"

"No."

"Me, neither," she said, laying a hand on her stomach.

"I guess I'll go get the birdies."

"Oh," she said. "Okay."

I went through the kitchen and let myself out the back door. I didn't really like when Melina touched her stomach, and I didn't want to talk about her being pregnant. I wasn't sure why, and I felt kind of bad about it, but that was just the way it was.

Zack had already gone inside by the time I got back. He was sitting in the living room, trying to watch HBO. His parents didn't subscribe to it, but sometimes it seemed like you could see naked people through all the scramble lines. "Don't you want to play badminton anymore?" I asked.

He shook his head, keeping his eyes on the TV.

"Why not?"

"Because," he said, "you're hitting the birdies over there on purpose. So you can go and talk to that lady."

"I am not," I said.

"I'm never playing badminton with you again," he said, and he got up and went to his room. I turned the TV off, then went to the bookshelf and took down the dictionary. There was an atlas at the back and I found Yemen, right under Saudi Arabia.

That night at dinner, I said to Daddy, "You know the people that moved in next to the Vuosos?"

"Do I know them?" he said. "No, I don't know them."

He liked to do this sometimes. Answer my exact question instead of the real one I was asking. I sighed and said, "Do you know that some new people moved in next door to the Vuosos?"

"Yes," he said this time. "I do know. The woman needs to cover her stomach more when she comes outside. No one wants to look at that."

"Well," I said, "her husband used to live in Yemen."

Daddy crunched on the cartilage from his chicken drumstick for a moment, then swallowed and said, "How do you know?"

"Melina told me," I said. "That's his wife."

"We don't call adults by their first name," he said.

"But she said I could."

"I don't care what she said. Find out her last name and call her that."

After dinner, Daddy packed up his clothes and went over to Thena's for the night. They had been seeing each other regularly since their first date, but Daddy wouldn't let her come to our house anymore. He said he didn't want to have to deal with her fussing over me with her makeup. "You hog all the attention," he said. "I don't know how you do it, but you do." Then he said that he needed attention, too, and that I was a big enough girl to spend a couple of nights alone each week.

I didn't mind being by myself. Actually, I preferred it. I could walk around the house without worrying so much that I was about to do something wrong. I could have orgasms with my bedroom door open. I could read my *Playboy* on the couch. That was what I was doing when the doorbell rang at around nine o'clock. It was Mr.

Vuoso. He was wearing a white T-shirt and jeans, and his breath had a nice beer smell. "Hey," he said. "Is your father home?"

"No," I said.

"Well," Mr. Vuoso said, "his floodlight is out. You might want to tell him."

"He'll be back tomorrow," I said.

"Tomorrow?"

I nodded. "He's over at his girlfriend's."

"You're a little young to be staying alone, don't you think?"

"I can do it," I said.

He looked at me. "You're not afraid?"

I shook my head.

We didn't say anything for a few seconds, then he said, "What're you reading?"

"What?" I said.

He nodded toward the couch behind me, and I turned around. "Oh," I said, wanting to play our game right. "Nothing."

He smiled a little. "Nothing, eh?"

I didn't know what to say then, so I smiled a little, too.

"I couldn't decide which one to give you," he said. "I just grabbed one off the top."

"It's my favorite," I said.

"Really?" he said. "Why?"

"I like the lady in the golf cart."

"The lady in the golf cart," he said, like he was trying to remember her.

"Her shirt is open, but she doesn't notice it," I said.

"Oh yeah?" he said.

I nodded.

"That's what you like?" he said. "That she doesn't notice?"

"Yes," I said. It made me so happy to finally be talking about this. To say things I knew only he would understand.

"Well," he said. "Don't forget to tell your father about that light."

"Do you want to come in?" I asked.

"No," he said. "I need to be getting back."

"Oh."

"You call us if you need anything," he said.

"All right," I said, wishing I could think of something to make him stay.

"Good night," he said, but he didn't leave.

"Good night," I said.

He reached out then and squeezed my shoulder a little bit. Then he moved his hand down the front of me, over one of my breasts. Then he turned and walked away.

After he left, I sat on the couch and had an orgasm just from touching my breast and thinking about him. When it was over, I remembered what Melina had said, that he was a pig. I didn't think that was true. It just didn't seem possible, that someone who could make me feel so nice could also be so terrible. I liked Melina a lot, and I thought she seemed very smart, but I also thought there might be some things she didn't understand. Mostly, I believed that anything that could give me an orgasm was good. I believed that my body knew best.

In the cafeteria the next day, Thomas Bradley brought his tray over to my table. "Mind if I eat with you?" he asked.

I shook my head, and he sat down. He had only a thin sheen of hair, and his eyes were a much lighter shade of brown than his skin. We didn't say anything for a while, then he said, "I'm sorry I called you that name the other day. I don't know why I did that."

"It's okay," I said.

"No," he said, "it's not."

I didn't know what to do then, so I kept eating my ravioli. When the bell rang, Thomas offered to clear my tray, and I said okay. He piled my plate and silverware and milk carton onto his tray, then stacked my empty tray beneath it. "I'll be right back," he said, which I guessed meant I was supposed to wait for him, so I did. When he returned, he said, "Okay, ready," and we walked to his locker together. He asked me if I needed to go to mine, and I lied and said I did. It was just nice, having someone to do things with.

Later, when I was bored in Social Studies, I tried to have an orgasm by thinking about Thomas, but it wouldn't work. Not like when I thought about Mr. Vuoso touching my breast, or when I imagined a man photographer taking my picture. So I gave up and started thinking about those things instead. I thought I was very lucky to have a system like this. To be able to test out different people and decide if I really loved them.

At the Vuosos' that afternoon, I checked the tampons on the back of the toilet seat, just in case Mrs. Vuoso had given up on trying to catch me. She hadn't. It was still just the four. I went downstairs then and told Zack I needed to go next door for a second. "No way!" he said, muting the TV. "There aren't any birdies over there."

"It's not that," I said. "I need to find out Melina's last name."

"Why?" he said.

"Because," I said, "I'm not allowed to call her Melina anymore. My father won't let me."

Zack didn't say anything.

"I'll be right back," I said. "Okay?"

He turned away and unmuted the TV.

When Melina opened the door, I said, "I can't stay very long. I just need to ask you something."

"Shoot," she said, walking back inside the house.

I followed her into the living room, where she was unpacking a box of books onto a tall wooden shelf. I noticed that some of them had Arabic writing on the spine. "I need to know your last name," I said.

"Sure. It's Hines. Why?"

"Because," I said, "I'm not allowed to call you Melina anymore."

"Oh yeah?"

I nodded. "It's Daddy's rule."

"Wow," she said. "He sure has a lot of rules."

"Uh-huh."

"Well, maybe you could just call me Melina when he's not around."

"Okay," I said.

"Great," she said.

"Melina?" I asked.

"Yes?"

"If I gave you some of my babysitting money, would you be able to buy me some tampons?"

She was quiet for a second. "Well, I don't know about that, Jasira."

"Why not?" I asked.

"I guess I don't feel comfortable going against your father."

"But you just said I could call you Melina when he wasn't around."

She sighed. "Oh boy."

"I don't see why I can't wear tampons," I said. "They fit me fine."

"Can't you talk to your mother about this?" Melina asked.

I shook my head. "No."

"Why not?"

"Because," I said, "she just tells me to listen to Daddy."

"Is she Lebanese, too?"

"No," I said. "Irish."

"Wow," Melina said. "What a mix you are."

It bothered me, how she was trying to talk about my nationalities now, instead of tampons. "I better go," I said finally.

"Are you sure?" she said.

"Yes," I said. "I'm not supposed to leave Zack alone."

"I'm really sorry, Jasira. I wish I could help you. I really do. I'm sure you'll figure something out."

"Thanks," I said, and I left.

I felt really angry with her on the way back to Zack's. It was like she had tricked me or something. Like she had said all that stuff about Daddy's rules being weird, but then it wasn't true. She thought I should listen to him just like everybody else did.

When I walked into the Vuosos' living room, Zack said, "Long time no see, towelhead."

"Don't call me that," I said.

"Okay," he said. "Camel jockey."

"Shut up," I said.

"Okay," he said. "Sand nigger."

I took a step forward then and hit him in the arm. It wasn't hard, but he acted like it was, and he made himself cry. "You're in big trouble!" he screamed, and he ran up to his room and slammed the door.

I sat at the kitchen table then, waiting for Mr. Vuoso to come home. I guessed it was probably true, that I would be in trouble. If only I had hit Zack on the weekend, when we were just playing, nothing would've happened. We would've just been two kids.

At around six, I heard Mr. Vuoso's key in the lock, and I went in the living room to meet him. "Where's Zack?" he asked.

"Upstairs," I said.

"Everything okay?"

"Yes," I said, and I walked quickly out the door.

Back at home, I wasn't sure what to do. I got myself some water, then washed and dried my glass. As I was putting it back in the cupboard, the doorbell rang. I went to answer it, and Mr. Vuoso was standing on the front steps. He was still wearing his light blue oxford from work. "Did you hit my son?" he asked.

I was quiet for a second, then I said, "Yes."

He stepped inside the house and closed the door behind him.

"What kind of babysitter are you?" he asked, standing on the square tiles of the entryway.

"I don't know," I said.

"Every day there's some new problem."

"I'm sorry."

"Don't you know enough not to hit small children?"

"Yes."

"Well," he said, "apparently you don't."

I didn't answer him.

"Do you?"

"No."

"I want my magazine back," he said.

"What?"

"Go and get my magazine. I want it back."

I didn't move. I didn't want to give the magazine back.

"Where is it?" he asked.

"In my room," I said.

"Go and get it," he said. "Now."

When I still didn't move, he took a step toward me. He reached his hands out and put them on my shoulders, then turned me around so I was facing the back of the house. "Go and get that fucking magazine," he said, and I tried to, but he wasn't letting go. Instead, he moved his hands off my shoulders and slid them down over the front of me, over my breasts. He started squeezing them. I tried to move again, but the more I pulled away, the tighter he held me.

Now his hands moved farther down the front of me, into my jeans. "I'll go and get the magazine," I told him, but he wasn't listening. He was putting his fingers inside my underwear, then moving them down between my legs. "No," I said, "don't," terrified that he would feel all my pubic hair and think I was ugly just from touching me. But he didn't say anything about this. He just kept going, farther down. He started to rub me then, and at first it was kind of rough, but then he would pass over the certain spot and there would be a good feeling. I got a little bit wet, and soon his fingers started to move more easily.

I thought it wouldn't be so bad if he just wanted to touch me like that for a while, but then he stopped. Instead, he started poking me with his fingers, like he was looking for something. Soon, I could feel him pushing up inside of me. It didn't hurt too much at first, but then it seemed like he was using more than one finger. "Don't," I said, and I tried to get free of him, but my arms were pinned under his. "You're hurting me," I said, but he just kept doing it. It was terrible, to have a pain like that in the place that always felt so good. All I could think was that he was breaking something. That nothing down there would ever work again. I started to cry, and that was when he finally stopped. He pulled his hand out of my pants and there was blood all over it. For a second I thought it was my period, but then I knew that it wasn't.

"Oh Jesus," Mr. Vuoso said, looking at his hand. "Oh my God." He went in the kitchen and I heard the water running. When he came back, he said, "I didn't mean to do that. I didn't."

I had almost stopped crying, but now that he sounded so sorry, I started all over again.

"Oh Jesus," he said.

I took a step forward for him to hug me, but he took a step back. "I have to go," he said. "I have to get home to Zack."

"No," I said, "I don't want you to go."

But he already had his hand on the doorknob. "I didn't mean to do that," he said again, and he left.

I stood there crying for a few minutes. Then I went in the bathroom and undid my pants. There was blood all over my underwear and some had leaked through to my jeans. There was blood on my stomach from when Mr. Vuoso had pulled his hand out. I took off all my clothes and got in the shower. When I came out, I got a clean pair of underwear and stuck one of the big maxi-pads inside. Then I started washing my clothes in the bathroom sink. I tried to hurry, since I knew Daddy would be home soon. The jeans came pretty clean, but no matter how hard I scrubbed the underwear, there was still a brown stain. Finally, I just wrapped them up in some toilet paper and threw them in the trash.

I went in the living room then and waited for Daddy. I actually looked forward to seeing him, in a strange way. It was just that I wanted company, and I knew Daddy didn't like Mr. Vuoso, and that seemed like the best company to have.

I tried not to like Mr. Vuoso myself, but it was hard. Especially when I thought about how sorry he had seemed. No one had ever acted sorry to me before, and it gave me such a nice feeling. It was almost worth having someone do something mean to you if they were going to be like that afterward.

The first thing Daddy did when he got home was yell at me for not turning the floodlight on. I told him about Mr. Vuoso's visit the night before then, and he said, "You must be kidding me."

"No," I said.

"Well, that's just great," Daddy said, reaching up to loosen his tie. "I bet he thought he was really hot stuff, coming over here like that."

I nodded.

"You didn't tell him that I'd be out all night, did you?" he asked.

"No," I lied.

"Good," he said. "Because that's none of his business."

I sighed a little then, and Daddy looked at me.

"What's the matter with you?" he asked.

"Nothing," I said.

"You seem depressed."

"I'm not."

"Did you have a bad day at school?"

"No."

"Do you think that every time you feel depressed, someone is going to ask you all kinds of questions to find out why?"

"No," I said.

"Because they're not."

"I know."

"I give up," he said, and he went to cook dinner.

I went in the bathroom then to check on my pad. The blood wasn't so bad anymore. I just felt sore. I was afraid to wipe myself after I peed, so I sat there and dripped dry. After a while, there was a knock. "Everything okay?" Daddy asked.

"Yes," I said, getting up and zipping my jeans. The door was locked, but I still worried that he would find a way to come in.

"Have you got your period?" he said. "Is that what it is?"

"Yes," I said after a second.

"Did you take any medicine?"

"No."

"Well, take some," he said. "There's no reason to sit around feeling miserable."

"Okay," I said.

I started to feel a little bit better during dinner. It was the medicine, but also, Daddy was in a good mood from his night with Thena. He described the food she had made him, a delicious casserole called moussaka, and also her terrible baklava. "Of course I told her it was very good," he said. "But she uses sugar syrup instead of honey. That's her mistake." Then he said that she might try to call me to see if I wanted to go shopping with her, and that I was to tell her no. "Just say you have homework or something," he said.

"All right," I said, even though I wished I could go.

"She needs to find friends her own age," Daddy said.

Later, he told me I could lie on the couch while he did the dinner dishes. When he had finished, he came in and read the newspaper in his chair. At around eight, the doorbell rang. I was about to get up and answer it, but Daddy said to stay put. He set his paper down on the floor and got up. When he opened the door, it was Mrs. Vuoso and Zack. "Oh," he said. "Hello."

I sat up on the couch then, wondering if Mr. Vuoso was somewhere behind them.

"Hello, Rifat," Mrs. Vuoso said. She pronounced his name with the word *fat* in it, instead of the way Daddy pronounced it, with the *fat* rhyming with *hot*. "May we have a moment of your time?"

"Certainly," Daddy said, and he stepped back so they could come in. I saw then that it was just the two of them. Zack wouldn't look at me, but Mrs. Vuoso was looking at me a lot. Her eyes were gray, just like her hair.

"Well," Mrs. Vuoso said, once they were standing in the middle of our living room. "We've come to give Jasira her last paycheck. I'm afraid it won't be possible for her to babysit Zack any longer."

"Zack is going to babysit himself now?" Daddy asked.

"No," Mrs. Vuoso said. "I mean, we're going to have to find another babysitter."

"She hit me," Zack said to Daddy.

Daddy looked at him. "Who hit you?"

"Jasira," Zack said.

Daddy turned to me on the couch. "You want to tell me what's going on here?" he said.

I stood up, but before I could answer him, Zack said, "She hit me really hard in the arm."

"Is this true?" Daddy asked me.

I nodded.

He was quiet for a second. "Why did you hit him?"

"Well," Mrs. Vuoso said, "I just don't think there are any circumstances under which hitting would be appropriate."

Daddy kept looking at me. "Was it because of a game?"

I shook my head.

"It wasn't because of anything!" Zack said.

"I just think Jasira seems like a very unhappy little girl," Mrs. Vuoso said. "I mean, I hate to say it, but this isn't the first problem we've had with her."

"What are you talking about?" Daddy said.

"He called me a towelhead," I said then, terrified that Mrs. Vuoso would start talking about her missing tampons.

Daddy looked at me. "A what?"

"A towelhead," I said.

"A towelhead?" Daddy repeated. Then he turned to Mrs. Vuoso and said, "Did you know your son called my daughter a towelhead?"

Mrs. Vuoso looked at Zack then, like she hadn't known at all.

"And a camel jockey," I said.

Daddy looked at me again.

"And a sand nigger," I said.

He laughed. "Jesus Christ."

"I don't think this is something to joke about," Mrs. Vuoso said. "I mean, if Zack used inappropriate language, I apologize. But violence is violence. I just think Jasira must be a very unhappy little girl."

"Where's the check?" Daddy said.

"Pardon me?" Mrs. Vuoso said.

"You said you had Jasira's last check," he said. "Where is it?"

"Oh," Mrs. Vuoso said. She hesitated for a second, then reached inside her jacket pocket. "Here you go."

After Daddy took it, he showed it to me. "Is this the right amount?"

I looked at it, even though I was too nervous to read it. "Yes," I said.

"All right, then," Daddy said. "I think we must be finished here."

"Well," Mrs. Vuoso said, "I don't think we are finished."

"Thank you very much for coming," Daddy said, and he went and opened the door for them.

After a moment, Mrs. Vuoso said, "Well, all right," and she and Zack left.

I thought Daddy would hit me once they'd gone. I thought maybe he was just pretending to be nice to me in front of Zack and his mom. But he didn't hit me. He said, "What was she talking about when she said she'd had other problems with you?"

"I don't know," I said.

"What did you do?" he demanded.

"Nothing," I said.

"You must've done something."

"Once I left Zack alone to go and get birdies from Melina next door," I said finally.

Daddy looked at me.

"I mean, Mrs. Hines."

He nodded. "Is that all?"

"Yes."

"Big deal," he said.

He went outside then to take our flag down so we wouldn't be un-patriotic. When he came back in, he said, "Guess whose flag is still up?"

"Whose?" I said.

"Who do you think?" he said.

I went to the dining room window and pulled the curtain aside. It was hard to see at first, but after a moment, I noticed Mr. Vuoso's flag, drooping in the still air. I thought then about how he had been with me at sunset. How he had been unpatriotic because of me.

"I should go over there and say something," Daddy said. But he didn't. He folded our flag and put it in the closet. Then he sat in his chair and picked up his newspaper. I lay back down on the couch. I must've fallen asleep, because the next thing I knew, Daddy was stand-ing over me, whistling his awful wake-up song. When I opened my eyes, though, it wasn't so terrible to see his face.

FOUR

stopped bleeding the next day. Then, a few days after that, I stopped feeling sore. I tested myself out to see if I could still have an orgasm, and I could. I was glad everything still worked down there, but I didn't really want to have orgasms anymore. They didn't make me feel that much better.

My period came, and the tampons went in more easily than ever. There were only a few of them, though, and soon they ran out. I had an idea that I could ask Mr. Vuoso to buy me more—that he would want to get them for me, since he had hurt me. But then, when I watched him from the dining room window taking his flag down, I changed my mind. He didn't look so sorry anymore.

Zack's new babysitter was Melina. She played badminton with him in the backyard, just like I used to do. She didn't really run that much, maybe because of the baby. She just stood still while Zack hit the birdies to her. Sometimes he hit her in the stomach, and she would yell at him to cut it out. I thought about telling her what Mr. Vuoso had done to me so that she would feel terrible about working for him, but I didn't. I was too ashamed.

Mostly, I looked forward to when Daddy came home at night and he would call the Vuosos names. He said they were ignorant and sons of bitches and hicks. He said that Mr. Vuoso was going to get called up soon enough, and that Saddam would gas him and that that would serve them all right. I asked Daddy what happened when you got gassed, and he said, "You fall to the ground, and you don't see, and you can't feel. And you're so thirsty. Except any water you can find to drink is filled with the gas, and it makes you even sicker."

"I thought you hated Saddam," I said.

"Of course I do," he said. "These are just the facts."

I nodded. It was nice, feeling closer to Daddy. Ever since Mrs. Vuoso had fired me, it seemed like he was trying to make me feel better. He even called my mother to tell her what had happened. "She just went ahead and hit him," I heard him say. "Right in the arm." Later, when it was my turn to talk, my mother said, "If you have a problem with someone, see if you can talk it out first before resorting to violence."

"Okay," I said.

"What's she telling you?" Daddy demanded, since he was standing right there.

"That I should try to talk things out first," I said.

"Give me that," he said, and he took the phone away from me. Then he started fighting with her about how she was Irish and didn't know anything. Eventually, he hung up on her and we went to have pizza at Panjo's. We sat on a picnic bench outside the restaurant, even though it was the end of November, and Daddy said, "Your mother is coming to Houston for Christmas."

"She is?" I hadn't heard that part of their conversation.

He nodded. "She wants to stay with us so she won't have to pay for a hotel."

"Okay," I said, thinking he wanted my approval.

"What do you mean, 'Okay?'" he said. "Is it your house?"

"No."

"That's right," he said, gnawing on his crust. "It's my house. I decide who stays."

I didn't say anything.

"I told her she could have my study, even though it's against my better judgment."

I nodded.

"Your mother can be very hard to live with," he said. "She thinks she knows everything."

"How long is she staying?" I asked.

"Too long," he said. "A week."

"Wow," I said.

"If she starts to get difficult, I told her I was kicking her out."

I wasn't sure how I felt about my mother coming to visit. I hadn't seen her since July, and I didn't really miss her that much anymore. I worried that if she noticed this, she would get mad. She already seemed mad that I'd stopped calling her so often. "What's going on down there?" she'd say, calling me herself. "I hardly ever hear from you." I'd tell her nothing was going on, and she'd say that couldn't possibly be true. She was right—except that I couldn't tell her what was going on. I just didn't do regular things.

Once I tried to tell her about Melina, but she got bored. "Why would I want to hear about a pregnant woman who can't be bothered to go out and buy herself some decent maternity clothes?" she asked.

"Her husband used to work in Yemen," I said.

"So?"

"I just thought it was interesting."

"Well," my mother said, "I want to hear about you. That's what's interesting to me. Tell me about school."

"What about it?"

"Do you have any friends?"

"Yes."

"Who?"

"Thomas Bradley."

"Fine," she said, "tell me about him."

"We eat lunch together," I said. "Then he clears my tray for me."

"You can't clear your own tray?" she asked.

"I can," I said. "He just does it first."

"You're too young to have a boyfriend," she said. "Remember that."

"He's not my boyfriend," I said.

"Right," she said.

"He's not," I insisted.

In a way, though, he was. The kids at school teased us about it, and when they did it in front of Thomas, he never told them it wasn't true. Sometimes I wanted to tell them myself, but I was afraid that if I did, they would start calling me names again. They had stopped when they thought I was Thomas's girlfriend. I wasn't sure why, since Thomas didn't seem all that popular. He was a lot bigger than most of the other kids, though, and he did help the YMCA swim team win most of their meets.

At the beginning of December, he asked me over to dinner at his house. "My parents want to meet you," he said.

"Why?" I said.

"Why do you think?"

I shrugged. "I don't know."

"Well," he said, "do you want to come or not?"

"I have to ask Daddy," I said.

"All right," he said. "Just let me know by tomorrow. My mother has to buy the food."

That night at dinner, when I told Daddy about my invitation, he said, "No. You're too young."

"But his parents are going to be there," I said.

"I don't care," he said. "If you want to go over to a friend's house, you should try to make friends with a girl."

The next day, when I told Thomas that I couldn't come, he said, "What if my mom called your dad? Would that help?"

I shook my head. "I don't think so."

"Why not?" he said.

"Daddy doesn't like that," I said, even though I didn't know for sure that this was true.

That night, Thomas's mom called Daddy anyway. I didn't know it had happened until I heard him yell, "Jasira!" I was in my bathroom, hand-washing my bras with the Woolite Daddy had bought me. When I got out to the kitchen, he slapped me. It was the first time he had been mean to me since I'd gotten fired, and I started crying immediately. After I'd calmed down a little, he said, "That was Mrs. Bradley on the phone. Do you know Mrs. Bradley?"

I nodded, even though I didn't know her personally.

"She was calling to convince me to let you go to dinner at her house this weekend. Do you know how embarrassing that was for me?"

I nodded again.

"When I say no, it means no. It doesn't mean tell your friend to have his mom call and try to change my mind."

"But I told Thomas not to do it," I said. "I told him you wouldn't like that."

He looked at me. "How come when you tell people no, they think you mean yes?"

"I don't know," I said.

"Well, I do," he said. "It's because you say yes and no in the exact same way. No one can tell what you're really thinking. You need to learn to speak with more emphasis. Do you understand me?"

"Yes," I said, trying to sound forceful.

He nodded. "That's better."

"I'm sorry that Mrs. Bradley called you," I said.

"Don't let it happen again."

"I won't."

"And you're not allowed to go in that boy's room with him. I already told his mother."

I didn't know what to say to this. I'd assumed I wasn't going.

"You are restricted to the common areas of their home."

"Okay," I said.

That Saturday, Daddy took me to the mall so we could buy a box of Godiva chocolates for Mrs. Bradley. I felt embarrassed to give someone I didn't even know a present, but Daddy said that was what you did when you were a dinner guest. Then we went to the liquor store to buy her a bottle of wine.

When I came out of my room that night, Daddy looked at me and said, "Don't you have anything besides jeans?"

I shook my head.

"You can't go to someone's house for dinner in jeans."

"Thomas wears jeans."

"I don't care what Thomas wears," Daddy said, and he walked past me toward my bedroom. I followed him, and when I got there, he was holding one of my cotton skirts. "I thought you said you didn't have anything besides jeans."

I looked at him.

"What's this?" he asked, shaking the hanger a little.

"A skirt."

"Put it on," he said, handing it to me.

"I can't."

"Why not?"

"Because," I said.

"Because why?"

"Can't I just wear jeans?"

"Why can't you wear a skirt?" he demanded.

"Daddy," I said, "my legs are too hairy."

He looked at my legs then, even though they were covered. "All right," he said, "hold on a second." He handed me the skirt and walked out. A few moments later, he came back with some shaving cream and his fancy razor. "Go in the bathroom and use these," he said. "Then put the skirt on and let's go."

"Okay," I said.

"Hurry up," he said.

I couldn't believe I was finally going to get to shave. I did my calves as quickly as possible, then my bikini line. The pool was closed for the winter, so Daddy would never find out. "What's taking so long?" he yelled, and I yelled back that I was trying not to cut myself. Luckily, the tub had one of those crisscross drains, so I was able to scoop all the hairs out afterward.

"Now you're going to be late!" Daddy said when I finally came out. "What's the point of going to all this trouble if you're not even going to be on time?"

"Sorry," I said.

"It's rude to be late," he said, and he grabbed his keys and walked out the back door.

On the drive over to the Bradleys', he told me to make sure not to talk with my mouth open, and to say that the food was good even if it wasn't. "Okay," I said.

"And don't sit there looking miserable," he said. "Try to smile a little."

I nodded.

"I don't want to hear any more of this shit about how people think you're an unhappy little girl. Is that clear?"

"Yes."

"Practice smiling now," he said, and I smiled a little, and he said, "Good. Just keep doing that."

The Bradleys lived two developments over from us. We'd looked at the model homes there, and even though they were a little bit nicer than ours, Daddy had decided that they weren't worth the money. As we turned onto the Bradleys' street, he said, "They probably paid twenty thousand more than I did, and for what? An extra bedroom? Idiots." He pulled into their driveway, which was wide enough for two cars, even though there was only one in it now. I remembered then that the color of the pale bricks on the outside of their house was called "champagne."

"All right," Daddy said, putting the car in park, "get out." It was the way he talked to me when he wanted to be nice without using nice words, and suddenly I felt happy. I even thought about leaning over and kissing him good-bye, but I knew that would ruin every-thing, so I didn't. "Thank you for the ride," I said.

He nodded. "Call me when you're ready to come home."

"Okay," I said, gathering up the wine and chocolate.

"No later than ten," he said.

"Okay," I said again, and I got out of the car. Just then, Thomas opened the front door and walked out onto the steps. "Hi," he said. He was dressed up a little bit, too, in khaki pants and a gray turtleneck sweater.

"Hi," I said.

He looked over my shoulder. "Is that your dad?"

I turned around then to see what Daddy was still doing in the driveway. I waved good-bye to him, but he didn't wave back. He wasn't looking at me. He was looking at Thomas.

"Does he want to come in?" Thomas asked.

"I don't think so," I said.

After a second, Daddy put the car in reverse and backed out. I waved again, but he ignored me and drove off.

"You look nice," Thomas said when I'd turned back around.

"Thanks."

"Your leg is bleeding a little," he said.

I looked down to see what he was talking about. It was true. There was a cut on my right ankle, just above the back of my loafer.

"C'mon," he said. "I'll get you a Band-Aid."

I followed him inside, and he left me standing in his living room while he went upstairs. There was a long tan couch with high seat backs, like in an airplane, and their Christmas tree was already up. I liked how it stood next to the stairs. It seemed like you could probably climb them when you wanted to decorate the higher branches.

When Thomas came back, he got down on the floor and swabbed my ankle with a gauze pad, then put the Band-Aid on for me. "How'd you cut yourself?" he asked.

"From shaving," I said. "I was in a hurry."

"Try to go slower next time," he said, and he stood up. We went in the kitchen then to meet his mom. She didn't hear us at first because she was running the blender, but then Thomas yelled, "Mom!" and she turned around. Her hair was a short Afro just like Thomas's, and she was tall and pretty. I liked how she had two gold studs in her left ear. "This is Jasira," Thomas said, and Mrs. Bradley stepped forward to shake my hand.

"It's so nice to meet you," she said. "Welcome to our home."

"Thank you," I said. Then I held out the wine and chocolates and said, "These are for you."

"Aren't you sweet?" she said, taking them from me.

"Daddy picked them out," I said.

"Really?" she said, and she laughed a little. "He didn't even want you to come."

I nodded. "He thinks I should have more friends that are girls."

"Don't you have any?" she asked.

"No."

"Huh," she said.

"The girls at school are jerks," Thomas said. He turned to me then and asked if I wanted to see his room. I looked at Mrs. Bradley, waiting for her to say no, but she didn't. She said, "Thomas, while you're upstairs, tell your father that I need him to come down and open the wine."

Mr. Bradley was in his office, working on a computer. "Dad," Thomas said from the doorway, "this is Jasira."

"Jasira!" Mr. Bradley said, and he came over to shake my hand. "So nice to meet you." He wore khaki pants like Thomas's, except he was a little bit fat, so he had to fit the waistband under his stomach. "I hear your father works at NASA," he said.

I nodded.

"How interesting," he said. "I might like to talk to him sometime. I'm sort of an amateur astronomer."

"Okay," I said.

"C'mon, Jasira," Thomas said. "My room is down here."

"Leave the door open, please, Thomas," Mr. Bradley called after us.

"I will," Thomas said.

He had a double bed instead of a single, like mine, with a dark blue quilt on it. There were swimming ribbons stuck to the cork-board above his desk, and a small TV in one corner. His walls were covered with music posters, only I didn't really know any of the bands. My parents listened mostly to classical.

"Want to sit down?" Thomas asked.

"Sure," I said, and I settled myself on the edge of his bed.

"Check this out," he said, and he picked up a guitar on a stand near his desk. He put the strap over his shoulder and started playing, but it was hard to hear since there was no amplifier. When he was fin-ished, he asked me if I recognized the song, and I said no. "It's 'Hey Joe,'" he said. "Jimi Hendrix."

"Oh," I said.

He asked if I wanted to play something then, and I said okay. I got up off the bed, and he slipped the guitar strap over my head. I was a little embarrassed about how it squashed my left boob, but Thomas didn't say anything. "Put your fingers like this," he said, and he started positioning them for me on the strings. When he finally had them in place, he told me to strum a little with my right hand. "Recognize that?" he said, and I shook my head. "It's Neil Young," he said. Then he said, "Here," and he took the guitar back and played the song better than I had. "Recognize it now?" he said, and I nodded, pretending that I did.

When the song was finished, he took the guitar off, and we sat down on the edge of his bed. After a minute, he lay all the way back, with his feet still touching the floor. I wasn't sure if I was supposed to stay sitting or lie back with him. Finally, I lay back. "How far up do you shave?" Thomas asked me.

"What do you mean?" I said.

"I mean, like, do you shave your pubes?"

"Yes," I said.

"All of them?"

"No. Just the sides."

"I like how it looks when girls shave all of them," he said.

I didn't say anything.

"Maybe sometime you could do that."

"Maybe," I said.

We lay there for a few minutes, until Mrs. Bradley called us down to eat. In the dining room, she had laid out hummus, baba ghanoush, lamb kebobs, salad, pita bread, rice, and tabouleh. I said it was good, and it was, even though it wasn't my favorite kind of food. While we ate, Mr. Bradley asked me different questions about my family in Lebanon, and I felt kind of embarrassed that I didn't know the answers. I couldn't tell him when my grandfather had died, or what he had done for a living, or even the name of my father's older brother. I tried to switch the conversation to my mother being Irish, but Mr. Bradley didn't seem as interested in that country.

For dessert, there were ice-cream sundaes that we got to make ourselves using cherries, nuts, bananas, hot sauce, M&M's, whipped cream, and sprinkles. Once we'd started eating, Mrs. Bradley asked me what my mother did, and I said she was a teacher. Mrs. Bradley nodded. "So you just prefer to live with your dad?"

"No," I said. "I prefer to live with my mom."

"Oh," Mrs. Bradley said, and I noticed that she looked across the table at Mr. Bradley.

After dessert, Thomas and I went in the family room to listen to music, while his parents stayed in the kitchen to clean up. I kept thinking they would come and join us, but they didn't. Mr. Bradley only poked his head in later and said that he and Mrs. Bradley were going upstairs and to please keep the volume down.

We listened to Jimi Hendrix, and Thomas stood in front of the fireplace, playing air guitar. Any time there was a solo, he scrunched up his face, like he was in pain. After a while, he came and sat next to me on the couch. He played drums on his thighs, and whenever there was a cymbal part, he hit one of my thighs.

A slow song came on, and Thomas reached over and started touching my breasts through the outside of my shirt. Then he reached a hand under my shirt and touched them through my bra. Somehow he knew to keep touching the nipples, and I had an orgasm. I started to cry then, and he seemed really worried. "Did I hurt you?" he said. "I didn't mean to hurt you."

"No," I said.

"What happened?" he asked.

"Nothing," I told him, and I crossed my arms in front of me.

Thomas got up for a second, and when he came back, he had a tissue. "Here."

I took it and wiped my face.

"Are you sure I didn't hurt you?"

"I'm sure."

"Then why are you crying?"

"I had an orgasm," I said.

"You did?"

I nodded.

"Was that the first time?"

"No."

"Oh," he said. He seemed disappointed. "Well, when did you have one before?"

"With myself," I said.

"Oh," he said again.

"But I don't want to have them anymore."

"Why not?"

"I just don't."

"You don't like them?"

"No."

"I thought everyone liked them."

"I don't," I said.

"That's too bad," he said.

I shrugged.

"I like them," he said.

I didn't say anything.

"I wish I could have one now."

"You can if you want," I said.

"Will you watch?"

"I don't know."

"You don't have to do anything," he said. "Just sit there."

"What about your parents?" I asked.

"They won't come down."

"How do you know?"

"They don't like Jimi Hendrix."

I thought about this for a second.

"Just watch," he said, and he unzipped his pants and pulled out his penis. He wrapped his fingers around it and started moving his hand up and down. After a while he said, "Okay, I'm going to come," and he reached over and took my hand and used it to catch what came out. He was breathing kind of heavily, so I waited a minute before I asked him what to do with it. "You can go wash it off," he said.

I got up then, being careful not to spill, and went in the bathroom. I sniffed it a little before turning on the faucet, then stuck the tip of my tongue in it. I knew from *Playboy* that men liked for women to drink it. I thought maybe it would taste like pee or glue, but it didn't. It was just thick.

After I washed my hands, I looked under the sink and found a box of tampons. I didn't really have any place to put them, so I just carried a bunch of them out in my hand. "Can I have these?" I asked Thomas. He was still sitting on the couch, but he'd zipped up his pants.

He shrugged. "Sure."

"Could you bring them to school for me on Monday?"

"Can't you just take them home with you tonight?"

"No," I said. "Daddy won't let me wear them."

"Why not?" he asked.

"I don't know."

"Because you're a virgin?"

I looked at him.

"You're not a virgin?"

"I don't know," I said.

"How can you not know?"

I didn't say anything.

"I could tell if you are."

"No," I said. "I don't want to."

"All right," he said. "We don't have to."

"Don't tell your mother about the tampons," I said.

"She probably wouldn't care."

"Just please don't tell her," I said, and he said okay.

When I hadn't called Daddy by nine o'clock, he called Thomas's mom to say that he was on his way, and to please make sure I was waiting outside for him. Mrs. Bradley gave me a bag of leftovers and said, "Tell your father that I'm sure it's not as good as what he's used to, but I hope he enjoys it." Then she hugged me good-bye, even though we had only just met.

While we waited for Daddy on the front steps, Thomas leaned down and kissed me. His lips were a little bit open, and they caught one of mine in between. While he was kissing me, he started squeezing one of my breasts again, and touching my nipple. I tried to push his hand away, but he kept it there. It was the first time all night that I really liked him.

A few minutes later, Daddy pulled into the driveway. "See you Monday," Thomas said, and he leaned down and kissed me again, this time on the cheek.

"See you," I said, and I went and got in the car. "These are leftovers from Mrs. Bradley," I told Daddy, showing him the bag.

He nodded, then put the car in reverse. As we pulled out, I waved to Thomas, and he waved back. When we were finally driving away, Daddy said, "I have to talk to you about something."

"Okay," I said.

"You're not allowed to see that boy again."

"Thomas?" I said.

He nodded. "When you told me about this dinner, you didn't give me the full information. So I could make a proper decision."

I didn't know what to say to this.

"Do you understand what information I'm referring to?" he asked me.

"I think so," I said, even though it didn't make any sense.

"Good," he said. "Because if you continue to visit this boy's house, no one will respect you. I know what I'm talking about."

The smell of Mrs. Bradley's food had begun to fill the car then, and I took a deep breath of it.

"Are you listening to me?" Daddy asked.

"Yes," I said.

"Then say so."

"I'm listening," I told him.

"Good," he said.

When we got home, he told me not to go to bed yet, because my mother wanted to talk to me. Then he dialed her number and handed me the phone. "Jasira?" she said.

"Yes?"

"Your father told me about your friend Thomas. It's very important that you listen to your father's rules about him. Do you understand?"

"No," I said.

"What don't you understand?"

"I like Thomas," I said.

"That's fine," my mother said. "I'm glad you do. But you can't visit his house anymore, because it will be very difficult for you later on."

"What's she saying?" Daddy asked.

"That it will be very difficult for me to visit Thomas's house," I said.

He nodded. "That's correct."

"Tell him to shut up," my mother said. "Tell him I'm talking."

"It's okay," I said. "I'm listening to you."

She was quiet for a second, and I knew she was mad that I wouldn't tell Daddy to shut up for her. I was mad at her, too, since if I had done what she wanted, Daddy would've hit me. Finally, she said, "Your father isn't even black, and people used to call me all kinds of names."

"Like what?" I said.

"Like nigger lover."

I didn't understand how this would work, since the kids at school already called me a sand nigger. It seemed like that would make Thomas a nigger lover, too. Plus, I didn't even know if we loved each other.

"Do you want people to call you that?" my mother asked me.

"I don't know," I said.

"Well," she said, "trust me, you don't."

"What do I tell Thomas?"

"About what?" she said.

"About going to his house."

"Has he already invited you back?"

"No."

"Well, maybe he won't. Then you won't have to worry about it."

"He will," I said.

"Oh really?" she said, and she laughed a little. "We're very sure of ourselves, aren't we?"

I didn't say anything.

"If he invites you back, just tell him you can't come. Tell him your parents think you're too young to be going to boys' houses."

"He'll know I'm lying," I said.

"Well," she said, "maybe the next time something like this comes up, you'll be sure to give us all the details. Consider it a learning experience."

"Is she finished?" Daddy asked me then.

"Daddy wants to know if you're finished," I said.

"Oh," she said, "so you can pass along his messages to me but not the other way around?"

"Here's Daddy," I said, and I handed him the phone, and they started arguing about how bad it was to interrupt each other.

I went in the bathroom then and sat on the edge of the tub. I looked down at the Band-Aid Thomas had put on my ankle, and I decided I'd had a nice time with him. I decided that what my parents were saying didn't really make any sense. Being Thomas's girlfriend in school hadn't hurt me—it had helped me. And even if it did start to hurt me sometime later on, I didn't care. I'd still never tell him what my parents wanted me to tell him. Not in a million years.

On Monday at lunch, Thomas gave me a bag with the tampons in them. "Thanks," I said.

"No problem."

"Thomas?" I said.

"Yeah?"

"Does your mom have any razors?"

"Why?" he said.

"Because I need razors, too."

"Your dad won't get them for you?"

I shook my head.

"But you shaved the other day."

"That was a special occasion," I said.

He took a sip of his milk. When he was done, he said, "Sure. I could get you some razors."

"Thanks," I said.

"How far up are you going to shave?"

"I don't know."

"You should shave everything," he said.

"I'll think about it."

After Thomas cleared my tray, I walked with him to his locker, then he walked with me to mine. On the way there, he held my hand, and I noticed that some of the kids around us were looking. There were a few other couples in school who held hands, too, but no one cared about them because they were all white.

There was nothing to do when I got home except homework

and TV. While I was doing some of my English reading, I heard Melina and Zack playing badminton in his backyard. I got up and put my shoes on and went outside. I crossed the driveway and stood on the spot where our concrete met the Vuosos' grass. Melina noticed me immediately. "Jasira!" she yelled. "C'mon over!"

Zack, who had his back to me, turned around and said, "No way! I'm not supposed to play with her anymore!"

By now, though, Melina had already set her racquet down and walked over to where I was standing. "Hey, stranger," she said, and she reached out to ruffle my hair.

"Melina!" Zack yelled, not moving from his side of the net. "Come back! Let's finish the game."

She ignored him. "So what's up?" she asked me.

I shrugged. "Nothing."

"How's school?"

"Fine," I said. "I have a boyfriend."

She smiled. "Really? That's great."

"Thanks."

"Melina!" Zack yelled.

Finally she turned around and said, "Zack? I'm talking to Jasira right now. So you're going to need to shut up for a second. You got it?"

He didn't say anything, and she turned back around and rolled her eyes.

"Mrs. Vuoso fired me," I said.

"I heard," Melina said. "She came to see me."

"You took my job."

"No, I didn't."

"Yes, you did."

"Are you kidding?" she said, lowering her voice. "I don't want to babysit this kid. I'm doing it as a favor to his mother. Till she finds someone else."

"Why are you doing her a favor?"

"I don't know. I felt sorry for her. She was all freaked out that Zack was going to be alone."

I wanted to say that I was alone all the time and no one freaked out about it, but I didn't.

"I'm going inside!" Zack yelled. He pointed at me with his racquet and said, "I'm not supposed to be anywhere near her!"

"Good!" Melina yelled back. "Beat it!"

"You can't talk to me like that!" he said.

"Oh, don't be such a baby," she said.

He stormed onto the patio and through the sliding-glass door. He tried to make a loud noise closing it, but it didn't really work.

"I have to go inside, too," I said.

"Why?" she said.

"I have to do my homework."

She sighed. "Are you still mad at me about the tampons?"

"No," I lied.

"If you were mad at me," she said, "I would understand."

"Thomas gets me tampons now," I said.

"Who's Thomas?" she asked.

"My boyfriend."

"Oh."

"He gave me a whole bunch today at school."

"Well," she said, "he sounds like a pretty cool guy."

"He is," I said. I thought about giving her the full information, but I didn't. I was too mad. I just didn't understand why she wouldn't get me tampons, then, when someone else did, she said they were cool. It didn't make sense.

We said good-bye, and I went back inside to finish my homework. When Daddy came home, he asked me if I'd told Thomas that I couldn't see him anymore, and I lied and said that I had. "Good," he said. "It's for the best."

After dinner, we worked on his study, preparing it for my mother's visit. As Daddy filed away the papers on his desk, he got into a bad mood. He said he didn't understand why my mother had to stay with us. He said she had a perfectly good job, and she could afford a hotel just fine. He decided to call her to tell her this, and they ended up having a fight. I heard him say something like, "Don't think you're going to come crawling into my bed, because you're not." I didn't know what she said back to him, but whatever it was, it made him hang up on her.

At lunch the next day, Thomas gave me a bag of plastic razors. "Thanks," I told him.

"Are you going to shave today?" he asked.

"I just shaved on Saturday."

"You know what I mean," he said.

"Oh," I said. "Right."

"I could do it for you," he said.

I looked at him.

"I'd be really careful. I promise."

I said no, but then later, in French class, I couldn't stop thinking about it. I remembered all those times with Barry in our bathroom in Syracuse, and I started to get a good feeling between my legs. I tried to ignore it at first, but then it got too strong and I had to press my legs together.

After class, I headed for my locker. Thomas came along and asked me what I had been doing under my desk. "What do you mean?" I said.

"You were squeezing your legs together."

"No, I wasn't."

"Did you have to pee or something?"

"No," I said.

"I read where girls can have an orgasm that way," he said.

"What way?"

"Squeezing their legs together."

I didn't say anything.

"Is that what you were doing?" he asked.

We had reached my locker by then, and I started working on the combination.

"Jasira," Thomas said, leaning his head against the locker next to mine.

"What?"

"Let me shave you."

"No," I said, but it wasn't forceful, and when I got on my bus after school that day, he was already there, saving me a seat.

At home, Melina and Zack were out in the street, kicking a soccer ball back and forth. "Hey!" Melina called as we walked up. She kicked the ball to Zack and came over to meet me and Thomas in my driveway. I introduced the two of them, and they shook hands. Then Melina turned to me and made kind of an excited face.

"Is that your son?" Thomas asked her, nodding toward Zack. He hadn't moved an inch since we'd shown up. He was just standing there in the street with his foot on top of the soccer ball.

"God no," Melina said.

"That's Zack," I said. "He lives next door to me."

"Hey Zack!" Thomas called, but Zack didn't say anything.

"What are you guys up to?" Melina asked.

"Nothing," I said.

"Just hanging out," Thomas said.

"Want to play soccer?" Melina asked.

"I'm not allowed to play with them!" Zack yelled then.

Thomas looked at him. "What's that kid's problem?"

"Just ignore him," I said.

"I was just trying to be nice," Thomas said.

"He's a brat," I said. "It doesn't matter."

Thomas didn't seem to be listening to me. "I mean, what kid doesn't want to kick a ball around?"

"A weird kid," Melina said.

Thomas looked at her. "But he was just kicking it around with you."

"He's used to me," Melina said. "If he knew you better, he'd kick it around with you, too."

Thomas didn't say anything. Neither did I. I was pretty sure that even if Zack did know Thomas, he wouldn't want to kick a ball with him.

"Is it hot out?" Melina asked, fanning her face with her hands. "I feel hot."

"Not really," I said.

"Maybe it's just me," she said, laying a hand on her stomach.

I hated how she always figured out some way to start talking about her baby.

"Is it a boy or a girl?" Thomas asked.

"A girl," Melina said. "Dorrie."

"Dorrie?" he said.

She nodded.

"What kind of name is that?"

"It was my grandmother's."

"Oh."

"It's also the name of a witch," I said.

"Yes," Melina said, "that's true."

"What witch?" Thomas asked.

"Dorrie the Witch," I said. "She's a character in these books."

"She's a good witch, though, right?" Melina asked.

"I don't know," I said, even though I did.

"I think she is," Melina said.

"We have to go," I said, and I took Thomas's hand and led him down my driveway.

Inside, I asked him to take off his shoes. "I didn't know you could play sports when you're pregnant," he said, bending down to untie his laces.

"She wasn't really playing," I said. "She was just standing there kicking the ball."

"When is she going to have the baby?" he asked.

I shrugged. I didn't really like to think about Melina's baby.

Thomas asked if he could have something to drink then, and I went to the fridge and got him a Coke. When I came back, I said, "You can't stay very long."

"Why not?"

"Because," I said, "I didn't ask Daddy."

"So?" he said. "We're friends."

"It doesn't matter," I said. "I still have to ask Daddy."

He finished his Coke, then asked me to give him a tour of our house. I wasn't going to show him Daddy's room, but then he said, "What's in there?" and I opened the door a little so he could take a peek. I was about to shut it again, but he said he wanted to go inside. "We'd better not," I said.

"Why not?"

"Because," I said, trying to think of a reason.

"Just for a second," Thomas said, and he went in.

There wasn't really much to see. Daddy was very clean. He always made his bed in the morning, his clothes were always draped neatly over his valet, his shoes were always lined up against the wall. He had shoe trees for every pair, and their cedar smell filled the room.

In the bathroom, Thomas opened and closed the shower stall door, then stuck his head in the toilet room. I wondered if he would notice that it smelled like pee, but he didn't say anything. After flipping through some of Daddy's suits in his closet, he picked up a can of shaving cream on the sink counter. "Hey," he said. "We need this."

Finally we left and went to my part of the house. I showed

Thomas my bathroom and the study where my mother would be sleeping, then finished the tour in the doorway of my own bedroom. "This is it?" he asked.

I shrugged. It was true, I didn't have any posters or pictures on the walls. There was just a twin bed on a metal frame, a large wooden chair with cushions, a dresser, and a nightstand.

"Show me your closet," Thomas said, and I did, and he said, "You don't have very many clothes."

"No," I said.

He reached out and touched the skirt I'd worn to his house. "I like this."

"Thank you."

"What else do you have?" he asked.

I looked around the room. Finally I went to my mattress and pulled out the *Playboy*.

"Where'd you get that?" Thomas said.

"I found it."

He came over and took it from me. "Where?"

I thought for a second, then said, "In the garbage."

"Huh." He sat down on the bed and started flipping through it, and I sat next to him. After a while, he stopped. "See?" he said, pointing to a woman with a thin strip of pubic hair. "This is how I think you should shave."

I'd seen that particular picture a million times before, but I still looked at it like I didn't know what it was.

"I promise I'll be careful," Thomas said.

"Okay," I said.

"Where are the razors?" he asked, and I went and got them from my backpack in the living room. When I came back, he was waiting in the bathroom. "Ready?" he said, and I nodded, and he told me to take my pants off.

"Should I put on my bathing suit?" I asked.

"How am I going to shave you if you're wearing your bathing suit?"

I shrugged. That was just how I had done it with Barry.

"C'mon," he said, and he reached out and started undoing my jeans himself. He pulled them down around my ankles, then waited for me to step out of each leg. Then he pulled my underwear down. We stood there for a second doing nothing. He just stared at me naked. "You look nice," he said finally.

"Thanks."

"Do you want to stand up or sit down?"

"Usually I stand," I said, thinking about Barry.

"Okay," he said. "We can try that."

I got in the tub then, and he reached for Daddy's shaving cream. He shook the can and squirted some into his hand. When he put it on me, he didn't put it all over, just at the edges. Then he turned the tub faucet on low and started shaving me. After every stroke, he rinsed the razor under the water, and a lot of hair came off. Then he'd put on more shaving cream. Soon, he got a new razor, even though he hadn't used the first one for very long. "It's getting dull," he said.

He was very careful, just as he had promised. Just as Barry had always been. And I started getting the old feeling that I used to have with Barry, about someone doing a dangerous thing to me. It was nothing like that time with Mr. Vuoso. He had done a dangerous thing, but he hadn't been careful at all. It had hurt and there had been blood and it had made me stop wanting to press my legs together forever. Now, though, with Thomas, I was starting to feel a little bit better. I was starting to remember some of the things I used to like.

It took him a long time, but eventually, I had a thin strip, just like the lady in the magazine. And no cuts. Thomas made a cup with his hands and collected water to wash off any remaining hair or shaving cream. Then he reached for my bath towel and patted me dry. "Do you like it?" he said.

I nodded. It seemed very grown-up, even though it also made me look like a little girl. "Do you like it?" I asked him.

"Yeah," he said. "I like it a lot."

"Thanks for doing it," I said.

"You're welcome."

I was about to step out of the tub, but he said, "Wait. You can't get dressed yet."

I stopped and looked at him. "Why not?"

"Because," he said, and he started undoing his jeans. "I want to have an orgasm."

"What time is it?" I asked.

"It won't take long," he said. "I promise." He pulled out his penis then and started touching it like he had the night before. While he touched it, he stared at where he had just shaved me. "You look so good that way," he said, and soon the white stuff came out and spilled onto his hand.

I waited a minute until he'd caught his breath, then got out of the tub and put my clothes on. I was beginning to panic. Every sound I heard seemed like it could be Daddy coming home.

By the time we'd cleaned everything up, it was after six. "You really have to go now," I said, and I walked him to the living room.

While he was putting his sneakers on, he said, "Let me know when it grows back. I can shave it for you again."

"Okay," I said.

He kissed me and I opened the front door for him. After he left, I went around the house making sure everything looked normal. I returned Daddy's shaving cream to his bathroom. I checked my bathtub drain for hairs. I put the *Playboy* back under my mattress. I tried to look at the place the way Daddy always did: searching for problems. When I didn't think I could find any, I went and started my homework at the dining room table. Right after I sat down, though, the doorbell rang. I went to answer it, and it was Mr. Vuoso. "What the hell do you think you're doing?" he said.

His hair was messed up in the front, and the shoulders of his jacket were a little crooked, as if he'd put it on too quickly. I tried to shut the door on him, but he stuck his foot in it. "What do you think you're doing with that nigger?" he said.

"Don't call him that," I said.

"Call him what?" Mr. Vuoso said.

I didn't want to say the word back to him.

"You're going to ruin your reputation," Mr. Vuoso said. "Do you understand me? If you hang around with that kid, no one will ever want you."

"You ruined my reputation," I said.

He looked at me.

"It's already ruined." I tried to shut the door again, but he wouldn't move his foot.

"Jasira," he said.

I kept pushing the door on his foot.

"Jasira," he said again, and he put his arm up to hold the door still. "What?"

"Do you need a doctor?"

"Why?" I said.

He didn't answer me.

"Why?" I said again.

"You know," he said, lowering his voice.

I acted like I didn't.

Finally he said, "For the other day. When I visited you."

"No," I said.

"Are you sure?"

"Leave me alone," I said.

"Hey," he said, "I'm trying to help you here."

"Leave me alone or I'll tell my father what you did!"

He didn't say anything then. He just stood there, breathing. I worried that he didn't believe me. That he knew I could never, ever say the words I would need to say to tell Daddy what had happened. Soon, though, he moved his foot. He took his hand off the door and let me shut it in his face. After I'd locked it, I went to the dining room window to watch him take his flag down. Only he didn't. He walked straight past the pole and into his house.

FIVE

The Saturday after Mr. Vuoso called Thomas a nigger, I helped Daddy plant some Persian cyclamen in the front yard. They were these tall red and white flowers, and the lady at the nursery told Daddy that they could survive the cooler weather. First we dug up the grass lining either side of our front walkway, then we pulled the plants out of their pots and stuck them in the ground, careful not to damage the roots. Daddy said he wanted the place to look nice for when my mother arrived. He said if she thought she was the only one who could plant a decent garden, she was about to experience a rude awakening.

While we were planting, Mr. Vuoso and Zack came over. We were kneeling on the ground with our backs to their house, so we didn't see them until they were right in front of us. "Good morning," Mr. Vuoso said.

Daddy looked up. He was wearing dirty green garden gloves and holding a trowel. "Yes?" he said.

Mr. Vuoso cleared his throat. "Zack and I were wondering if we could talk to you and Jasira."

Daddy looked over at me, then back at Mr. Vuoso. "Aren't you talking to us now?" he said, and he laughed a little.

I could see Mr. Vuoso was getting irritated. "There's no need for that," he said. "We're just here as friends. That's all."

"What friends?" Daddy asked then, looking around. "Where are the friends?"

"We're here to apologize," Mr. Vuoso said. "Right, Zack?"

Zack looked up at his father.

"Go ahead," Mr. Vuoso told him.

After a second, Zack took a deep breath and said, "I'm sorry I called you a towelhead."

"Not to me," Mr. Vuoso said, because Zack was still looking at him. "To Jasira."

He turned away from his father and toward me, then repeated what he had said.

"Good," Mr. Vuoso told him. "What else?"

Zack hesitated. Then he said, "Will you be my babysitter again?"

I didn't know how to answer this. I turned to Daddy for help, but he just shrugged. "Do whatever you want," he said. "But since they want you so much, I'd ask for a raise."

"Sure," Mr. Vuoso said. "We can give you a raise."

"How much?" Daddy asked.

"A dollar more an hour," Mr. Vuoso said.

Daddy didn't say anything.

"A dollar fifty," Mr. Vuoso said.

"What about Melina?" I asked.

"That was only temporary," Mr. Vuoso said.

"What do you think?" Daddy said. "A dollar fifty and an apology. Is that enough?"

"I don't know," I said.

Mr. Vuoso looked at me. "I want to apologize, too."

"For what?" Daddy said.

"For saying things I shouldn't have. I mean, maybe Zack heard me, and maybe that's why he said those things to you."

Daddy laughed. "*Maybe*?"

"All right, fine," Mr. Vuoso said, snapping his head toward Daddy. "Probably, okay? Probably he heard me, and probably that's where he picked it up."

"I would say so," Daddy said.

"Did anyone ever teach you how to accept an apology?" Mr. Vuoso said. "Because you're not very good at it."

"Why should I be good at it?" Daddy barked, and he stood up and peeled off his green gloves. "Why!"

"I don't want to be Zack's babysitter," I said.

No one seemed to hear me, so I said it again, more forcefully. Mr. Vuoso turned to me. "What?"

"I have other things to do after school," I told him.

"Like what?" he said. "What do you do after school?"

"What do you mean, 'What do you do after school?'" Daddy said. "She does her homework. That's what she does. She's a smart girl."

Mr. Vuoso looked at me long and hard, and I looked back at him. "All right," he said. "Fine."

"Can we go now?" Zack said to his father.

"Sure," Mr. Vuoso said, and the two of them turned and walked off.

Daddy said he was very proud of me then. He said that it was clear that the Vuosos knew how wrong they were to fire me, and that now they were just trying to cover their asses. I didn't tell Daddy that he didn't know what he was talking about. That Mr. Vuoso had put his fingers inside me, and that I had bled, and that that was why he wanted me back. To try to make it up to me.

We finished planting the rest of the flowers, and when we were done, Daddy said that now our yard looked like the Lebanese flag:

red, white, and green. He said that all Arab flags had the colors of either red, white, green, or black. He said it was one of the few things
the Arabs had ever managed to agree on, then he sighed and said how
pathetic.

That afternoon, I started to worry about Mr. Vuoso. I worried that I
had hurt his feelings. It was the same way I sometimes felt after Daddy
hit me. I hated him, but I didn't want him to feel bad. I wasn't sure
why this happened. It just seemed like it would be worse to be him in
those moments than it was to be me.

I went in Daddy's room while he was getting ready to go and
meet Thena. He had on slacks and an undershirt. "Blue or beige?" he
asked me, standing in his bathroom doorway, a dress shirt in each
hand. "Beige," I said, and he nodded. He put the blue one in his
closet, then came back and took the beige one off its hanger.

"Maybe I should've said yes to Mr. Vuoso," I said.

Daddy put his arm through one of his sleeves. "I already complimented you for saying no. If you change your mind, I take my compliment back."

I thought about this. I guessed I didn't really want to lose Daddy's
compliment.

"We don't go back on our decisions," he said, buttoning his shirt.
"Once we make a decision, we stand firm."

"But he apologized."

"He owed you that apology. You owe him nothing."

"Okay," I said.

"Try to have a little more resolve," he said, turning around so I
wouldn't see him unbutton his pants and tuck his shirt in.

After Daddy left, I went in the kitchen and put my frozen macaroni and cheese in the microwave. Daddy always bought me lettuce
I was supposed to wash and make into a salad for myself, but I never

did. I just ripped some of the leaves off, wrapped them in paper towels, and took them out to the garbage can.

Later, while I was watching TV, the doorbell rang. It was Mr. Vuoso. "Hi," he said. His cheeks were clean-shaven, his hair was neatly combed to one side. He looked like he was on his way somewhere.

"Hi," I said.

"Don't worry," he said. "I don't want to come in."

I didn't say anything.

"Zack and his mom went to visit his grandma."

"Oh."

"Her cat just had kittens. I guess they're pretty cute."

I nodded.

"Is your dad at his girlfriend's?" Mr. Vuoso asked.

"Yes."

"What's she like?"

"Daddy doesn't like her to come here anymore because she pays too much attention to me."

"Figures," Mr. Vuoso said.

"She thinks I should be a model."

He laughed a little. "I bet your father loves that."

"No," I said, "he doesn't."

"I'm just kidding," he said. "I know he doesn't."

"Oh."

"Anyway," he said, "I'm pretty bored."

I looked at his shirt cuffs. They poked out from under his jacket the same exact amount on both sides.

"Are you bored?" he said.

"No," I said, even though I was.

"You must be. There's nothing to do."

I shrugged.

"Maybe we could do something together."

"No, thank you."

"Maybe I could take you somewhere."

"I have to stay here."

"Why?"

"In case Daddy comes home."

"I thought you said he was staying at his girlfriend's."

"He is."

"So?" Mr. Vuoso said.

"He could change his mind and come home," I said. "I have to be here in case he does."

Mr. Vuoso shrugged. "Zack and his mother could come home, too. But they probably won't."

I looked at him. His voice had softened a little, and he'd put his hands in his pockets. I had been trying to have resolve, like Daddy said, but it was hard when Mr. Vuoso was being so nice. "Where would we go?" I asked.

"There's always a movie. You like movies?"

"No," I said, even though I did.

"Or we could go out to eat. Are you hungry?"

I shook my head.

"We could go and get some Mexican," he said. "I know a great place."

It was a weird thing, but I had never eaten Mexican food since I'd moved to Texas. Only pizza, and Daddy's Middle Eastern cooking. And Thomas's mother's Middle Eastern cooking.

"C'mon," Mr. Vuoso said. "Let's get something to eat."

When I didn't respond, he said, "How about this," and he reached into his pocket and pulled out something I couldn't recognize.

"What is it?" I asked.

He flipped out part of it, and I saw it was a knife. "See?" he said, showing me the blade. Then he quickly folded it back in. "It's for you."

"From the army?" I said. It was green.

He nodded. "You can borrow it for the night. To protect your-self."

I let him set it in my palm. Then I picked it up with my other hand and turned it over a couple of times.

"Put it in your pocket," he said.

I put it in my pocket.

"Now go get your coat. I'm hungry."

We didn't talk much in the car. I'd moved the knife from my pants pocket to my coat pocket, where I could reach it more easily, and now I took it out and opened the blade.

"Be careful," Mr. Vuoso said. "It's sharp."

I guessed he could've taken me anywhere that night and done what he wanted with me. The knife didn't really matter. I could never imagine using it against anyone. Plunging it into their body. My mother had once dated a man who was diabetic, and every day he had to give himself a shot, and I couldn't imagine that, either.

"Want to hear some music?" Mr. Vuoso asked.

"I don't care."

He turned the radio on to a country station. He started to hum along a little with the song, but then it ended and a bunch of com-mercials came on. They were loud and blaring, and Mr. Vuoso had to reach over and turn down the volume. "That's illegal," he said.

"What?" I asked.

"Making the commercials louder than the songs. But they all do it."

I thought it was stupid of him to be talking about things that were illegal, but I didn't say so.

It took a long time to get to the restaurant. For the last half hour of the trip, I was pretty sure it was all a big lie. Especially since just be-fore we got there, we had to go through a really bad part of down-town. But then suddenly, there it was. A place with flashing neon lights and a full parking lot, and music seeping out the back door, where a couple of Mexican men in white aprons were smoking cigarettes.

"This is it," Mr. Vuoso said, turning off the car.

"Wow," I said.

"You like it?" he asked.

I nodded. It seemed like a tiny carnival.

We went inside, and a man at the door told us we would have to wait a few minutes for a table. He said, "You and your daughter can sit at the bar," and Mr. Vuoso didn't correct him.

"I'm not your daughter," I said once we'd taken our stools. There were piñatas hanging from the ceiling above us, and everything had so much color. It seemed like Mexicans must be very happy people.

"Obviously," Mr. Vuoso said. "He just had to call you something."

The bartender came and set two margaritas in front of us—one for adults, one for kids. I took a sip of mine. It was like a lime Sno-Kone. There was salt around the rim of the glass, and I couldn't see why I would want to lick it, as Mr. Vuoso was doing. "What am I?" I asked him.

"What do you mean?" he said.

"If I'm not your daughter."

He thought for a second, then said, "You're my neighbor."

"What else?" I felt drunk, or like I wanted to be.

"That's all."

"I'm Zack's babysitter."

"Not anymore," he snapped.

I didn't say anything.

He sighed. "Sorry. I know that's my fault."

"I'm your girlfriend," I said. I wished I could say I was his wife, but that was already taken.

"You're too young to be my girlfriend."

"You did that thing to me," I insisted. "I'm your girlfriend."

He took a long sip of his drink. "That thing," he muttered.

I stared at him.

"Jesus," he said, and he rubbed his eyes a little.

By the time we'd finished our drinks and Mr. Vuoso had ordered us new ones, the man from the front of the restaurant came to tell us that our table was ready. It was near a tiny fake waterfall surrounded by plastic plants, and Mr. Vuoso said the whole setup was going to have him pissing all night. He got up to go to the bathroom, and while he was gone, I switched our drinks. His made me feel dizzy after a few sips, and I liked it. By the time he returned, I still hadn't switched them back.

"Did you look at the menu yet?" he asked.

"Yes," I lied.

"See anything you like?"

"I don't know what this food means," I said.

"What it means?" he said. "What are you talking about? There's enchiladas, burritos, tamales. Don't you know Mexican food?"

I shook my head.

"Well," he said, "then you should get chicken enchiladas. Everyone likes chicken enchiladas."

The waiter came, and Mr. Vuoso ordered for us. Afterward, he took a couple of sips of his drink, then looked at his glass funny. He looked at my glass and reached over and took a sip from it. "Jesus, Jasira," he said, switching them back.

"I'm drunk," I said.

"How do you know?"

"I feel happy."

"Oh yeah?" he said. He smiled a little. "You think being drunk makes you happy?"

I nodded.

"Well," he said, "I guess it does. Sometimes."

"Can I have another sip of your drink?"

"No," he said. "That's enough." Under the table, his leg touched mine for a moment, then he pulled it away.

"Why do you like me?" I asked.

"Why?" He sighed. "Oh, I don't know."

"I know," I said.

"Why?"

"My boobs."

He took a sip of his drink. "Maybe," he said. "But that's not all."

"My hair."

He nodded. "You have nice hair."

"When I grow up, I want to be in *Playboy*," I said.

"No, you don't."

"Why not?"

"Because," he said. "It's for sluts. Are you a slut?"

"I don't know," I said. I didn't think so, but I wasn't sure.

"Well, you're not," he said. "That's why you're not going to be in *Playboy*."

The food came, and we put our napkins in our laps and started to eat. After a few minutes, Mr. Vuoso said, "If you keep going around with that black kid, you'll be a slut."

"That's not true."

"Yes, it is," he said.

"He's better than you," I said. "He only touches me when I say he can."

Mr. Vuoso didn't say anything to that. He didn't even eat. He just sat there. I knew he wanted me to look at him or feel sorry for him that he felt so terrible or ashamed, but I didn't care. I was drunk and my enchilada was good, and I could feel my knife in my pocket, and Mr. Vuoso's drink made me think I could maybe use it if I had to.

For dessert I ordered fried ice cream, which was melted ice cream with a crust on top. Mr. Vuoso said he didn't want anything, but when my dessert came, he asked for a bite.

"No," I said. It was really delicious, and I didn't feel like sharing. I thought he would take a bite anyway, since he was paying for everything and technically it was his, but he didn't. He just looked disappointed and put his spoon back on his coffee cup saucer.

On the ride home, I took his knife out of my pocket again. "You like that?" Mr. Vuoso asked.

"Yes."

"Good," he said. "I'm glad."

"I guess you can have it back," I said.

"You trust me?"

I shrugged. "We're almost home."

"Keep it till we get there," he said.

Suddenly I worried that this was it. That he'd bought me dinner and lent me his knife and not eaten my ice cream in exchange for having done a mean thing to me. In exchange for me not telling on him. I'd had a good time that night, and now I was afraid that it would never happen again. "I still might tell on you," I said quickly. "I haven't decided."

Mr. Vuoso nodded. "I understand."

When we got home, he pulled into his driveway and turned off the car. We sat there for a while, our seat belts still on. "We're going to war with Iraq," Mr. Vuoso said finally.

"I know," I said. Daddy was always talking about it these days. How stupid it was to wait until after the holidays. How Kuwait was burning, but the president wanted to make sure that people spent money on Christmas presents. In protest, Daddy said he wasn't going to buy any presents this year, for anyone. He said my present would have to be knowing that my father was not a pawn of the regime.

"I'll probably get called up," Mr. Vuoso said.

"That's too bad," I said.

"Will you write me letters?"

"Sure."

He nodded. "That would be nice."

I reached in my pocket. "Here's your knife."

"See?" he said, taking it from me. "You can trust me."

"I have to go," I said, and I got out of the car. It was dark outside except for the streetlights. A lot of the new houses on our block remained unsold, and I hated how there were never any lights in the windows.

As I headed home on the sidewalk, I heard someone call my name. I turned to see Gil at the foot of his driveway, taking out his garbage. "Oh," I said. "Hi."

"Hi," he said, looking over at the Vuosos' minivan. Mr. Vuoso still hadn't gotten out. "Were you in that car?" Gil asked me.

"No."

"You weren't?"

"I'm just taking a walk," I said.

"I thought you were in that car."

"I was on the sidewalk," I told him.

He didn't say anything.

"Well," I said, "good night."

"Good night," he said.

I felt a little nervous that he had seen me, but I was more nervous about whether or not Daddy had tried to call. When I got inside and checked the answering machine, though, there was only a message from my mother. I called her back and she said, "Where have you been?"

"In the shower," I said.

"An hour-long shower?"

"I just forgot to check the machine when I got out."

"Where's your father?" she demanded.

"At Thena's."

"Does he stay over there? He doesn't stay over there, does he?"

"No," I said. "Of course not."

"You're too young to spend the night alone."

"He never stays over," I said.

"He'd better not."

"Don't worry."

"Don't tell me not to worry. I don't like it."

"Sorry," I said.

"Are you excited about Christmas?"

"Yes."

"You don't sound it."

"I am."

"I hope you like your presents," she said. "I spent a fortune."

"I'm sure I will."

"Don't get me anything," she said. "I don't want anything."

"Okay," I said. I didn't tell her that even if I had thought about getting her something, which I hadn't, Daddy wouldn't have allowed it. He wouldn't even let us buy a tree, in protest of the timing of the war. Instead, he'd put some tiny white lights on a large ficus plant by the front window.

"Listen," my mother said. "Do you like living there? With your father?"

"It's okay," I said. I tried to sound like it didn't matter either way, since I wasn't sure what the right answer was.

"Barry and I broke up," she said.

"What?"

"He moved out."

"Oh." I tried not to sound sad, but for a second it really hit me, that I'd probably never see him again.

"I guess it's just a little lonely here without you," she said.

"Well," I said, "that's too bad. About Barry, I mean."

"You know what?" she said. "It's not. Because he was an asshole. I have to say, Jasira, I feel terrible about what went on here last summer. When I took his side over yours."

"That's okay."

"No," she said. "It's not. Not at all."

"Well," I said, "I guess I really should finish out the school year here. I like my school."

"Oh," she said. "I hadn't realized that."

"I learn a lot there."

"I thought you didn't like it."

"No," I said. "I do."

"I thought you didn't like Daddy."

I didn't know what to say to that. She was right, in a way. I didn't like Daddy. But I was used to him. And I didn't want to have to leave and get used to her all over again. It was too much work.

"Well," my mother said curtly. "I guess I must've misunderstood. Okay then. See you next week. Sleep tight. 'Bye." And she hung up on me.

I knew she was mad. I knew she was trying to make sure that I knew this, and to scare me, too. Normally it would've worked. Now, though, I just felt lucky. Lucky that Daddy hadn't called or come home while I was out. Lucky that my mother was mad and would stop bothering me about coming home. Lucky to find a little bit of caramelized sugar between my teeth, and to pick it out with my tongue, and to remember how sweet the night had been.

When Daddy came home from Thena's the next morning, I told him about my mother and how she wanted me back. "What?" he said. "Who the hell does she think she is?"

"I don't know," I said.

"You have to finish the school year."

"That's what I told her."

"You like it here."

"I know."

"You're not going anywhere," he said. "I can't believe she's pulling these kinds of tricks. Calling you behind my back and trying to steal you."

"I don't want to go," I said.

"Of course not!" he said. "Why should you?"

We had one of our nicest days ever then. Daddy told me a little about his evening with Thena, how they were making plans to go to Cape Canaveral. There was a launch coming up in March, and since they had both designed parts for the shuttle, they would be invited to attend. I worried for a second that I would have to go, too, but then Daddy said, "You can stay by yourself for a couple of days, can't you?" and I said sure.

Later he asked me what kind of meal I thought he should cook for Christmas. I said I liked turkey, and he said, "Fine. That's what we'll have." He left to run his errands, while I went for a walk. Mostly I was hoping to see Mr. Vuoso. He wasn't outside, though, and my waiting on the sidewalk in front of his house wasn't making him come out. It made Melina come out instead. "Jasira!" she called, standing on her front steps.

I looked at her. "Yeah?"

"C'mere," she said, like I should've already known to do that. I walked over to her front yard.

"Were you in Mr. Vuoso's car last night?" she asked me.

"What?" I said, trying to act confused.

"Gil said he saw you last night in Mr. Vuoso's car."

"I wasn't in his car." I looked her right in the eye, since I had seen a TV show that said liars always looked to one side.

"Uh-huh," she said. I could tell she didn't believe me.

"I wasn't," I said.

"Come with me," she said, heading inside.

I followed her into the house, then upstairs, where I'd never been before, and down the hall. There were more pictures on the walls of Yemen and all the toilet holes Gil had dug.

Melina's bathroom didn't look anything like the Vuosos'. It was simple and modern, and the words CHAUD and FROID were written on the hot and cold sink taps. "Here," Melina said, reaching inside the cabinet beneath, and she offered me a box of tampons. "I was wrong not to give you these before. I'm sorry."

"But I already have some."

"You'll run out," she said. "Then you can use these. And when you run out of these? Just come and tell me and I'll get you some more."

I looked at the box.

"Take them," she said. "Please."

"Okay," I said. "Thanks."

After a second, she said, "Are you sure you weren't in that car?"

"Yes," I said. I might not have looked her in the eye that time.

"Mr. Vuoso is a pig," she said. "Just so you know. Any man who wants a girl your age to be his friend is a pig. Do you understand?"

"I wasn't in his car."

She ignored me. "If he asks you to be his friend, I want you to come and tell me. Okay?"

"Okay," I said.

"I mean it, Jasira."

"I will."

Back at home, I put the tampons under my sink with all the other ones Thomas had given me. Then I went and lay on my bed. I thought about the night before, when Gil had seen me on the sidewalk. I tried to imagine his going inside and telling Melina. I thought about her getting all mad and bossy, like she'd been today. I thought about the two of them making decisions about me, worrying. It was the strangest feeling I had ever known. It made me smile a lot, even though I was alone.

★ ★ ★

At lunch the next day, Thomas asked if I needed him to shave me again yet. "Maybe," I said.

"How long is the hair?" he asked.

"Not too long. We could wait a few days."

"Oh," he said, "okay." Then he said, "Could I come over and look at it?"

"I didn't ask Daddy," I said.

"I'll leave before he comes home again."

I thought about this for a second, then said, "Okay." I liked Thomas. I didn't think hanging around with him made me a slut or ruined my reputation or any of that stuff. Mostly, he just reminded me of Barry, the way he always wanted to shave me.

The bus let us off at the end of my block. Since there was never any traffic, we walked down the middle of the street to my house. We'd been holding hands on the bus, and Thomas didn't let go now, even as we saw that Zack was outside, kicking his soccer ball around.

"Hi, Zack!" Thomas yelled in a fake way.

Zack stopped kicking for a second and looked up. I wasn't sure if he saw our hands or not, but I figured he probably did. Then he went back to kicking his ball.

"What the fuck is the matter with that kid?" Thomas said, letting go of my hand.

"I don't know," I said.

"Yes, you do," Thomas said. "You know exactly what's wrong with him." We had reached my house by then, and Thomas yelled, "Hey, Zack! Kick that ball over here!"

Zack ignored this and kept playing by himself. He was moving away from us, toward Melina's house.

After a second, Thomas went after him. He didn't chase him, exactly, but he moved in really close. The next thing I knew, Thomas had taken the ball away from Zack and was kicking it back toward me. "Hey!" Zack yelled. "Give that back!"

"You say hi to me and I'll give it back," Thomas said.

I noticed that he was very good at kicking the ball, even though his main sport was swimming.

"Fine!" Zack yelled. "Hi!"

"Now say hi to Jasira."

Zack looked at me.

"Say hi to Jasira, and I'll give you the ball back," Thomas said.

"Hi," Zack said to me.

"Hi," I said.

He turned to Thomas and said, "Now give it back."

Thomas ignored him. He kicked the ball a little closer to Zack, but his feet were moving so quickly that Zack would never have been able to steal it. "Where's your babysitter?" Thomas asked.

"Give me my ball," Zack said.

"Tell me where your babysitter is, and I will."

"I don't have a babysitter anymore," Zack said.

"She quit?" I said.

Zack glared at me. "I'm old enough not to have a babysitter."

"Oh yeah?" Thomas said. "How old are you?"

"Eleven," Zack said.

"I thought you were ten," I said.

"I was," he said, "but then I had my birthday."

"Oh yeah?" Thomas said. "What'd you get?"

"Give me my ball!" Zack yelled.

"Tell me what you got first," Thomas said. He'd hopped the curb with the ball and was now on the sidewalk in front of Zack's house.

"I don't have to tell you anything," Zack said.

"Of course you don't," Thomas said. "And I don't have to give you this ball."

"Yes, you do," Zack said.

"What'd you get for your birthday?" Thomas said. "It's a straight-forward question. Answer it, and you can have your ball."

"I've already answered your questions," Zack said. "You said five questions ago that you would give me my ball, but you didn't keep your word. That just proves it!"

Thomas stopped kicking then. "Proves what?"

Zack didn't say anything.

"Proves what?" Thomas said again, and he picked the ball up and walked over to Zack.

"Nothing," Zack said.

"What'd you get for your birthday?" Thomas said. He was standing right in front of Zack now, hovering. It was strange to see him like this. So mean.

Zack turned to me then for help. I felt sorry for him, only I wanted to see what Thomas was going to do. "Just tell him what you got for your birthday and he'll give you the ball," I said.

Zack looked like he was going to cry. He looked like he thought I was as bad as Thomas. Finally he turned back to Thomas and said, "I got a kitten."

"What kind of kitten?" Thomas asked, and though it didn't seem possible, he moved in even closer to Zack.

"Get away from me," Zack said.

"We want to see the kitten," Thomas said.

"You can't," Zack said. "No one's allowed in the house."

"So bring it outside."

"No," Zack said. "She's an indoor cat."

"It won't hurt her to come outside for a second," Thomas said.

Just then, Zack reached out and punched the soccer ball out from under Thomas's arm. It fell and started to roll a little, and Zack quickly chased it down. Thomas stood calmly and watched. He acted like Zack could've had his ball all along, if only he'd asked for it.

Once he'd scooped up the ball, Zack ran in his house and slammed the door. "What a brat," Thomas mumbled.

I nodded.

"I want to see that cat," he said. "I like cats."

"We'll see it another time," I said. "Let's go inside now."

He didn't move.

"C'mon," I said.

Thomas eyed Zack's house. "Let's go over there and ring his doorbell."

"No," I said. "I don't want to."

"Did you see how scared he looked when I was talking to him? Why was he so fucking scared?"

"I don't know," I said.

"Yes, you do."

We went inside eventually and I gave Thomas a Coke. Then we went in my room. He lay back on my bed and I took my pants off. I went and stood next to the bed, and he reached out and touched me a little. After a minute he said, "I'm too mad to shave you. I might slip and cut you. I'd better not."

"Okay," I said, and I went to get my pants.

"No," he said, "wait." He pulled out his penis then and started to touch it, but nothing really happened. He stared at me and touched it for a long time, but it didn't get as big as usual. Finally he gave up and let go of it.

"Can I get dressed now?" I asked.

"Yes."

I went and got my clothes.

"I guess I'm too mad," he said, zipping up his fly.

"It's okay," I said. I was about to go and sit with him on the bed, but then I remembered something and went to my dresser. I opened the top drawer and pulled out a silver key. "Look," I said, bringing it to Thomas.

"What is it?" he asked.

"The Vuosos forgot to take it back from me when I got fired."

He hiked up on his elbows. "Really?"

I nodded. "We can go and see the kitten."

He took the key and looked at it.

"We'll just see the kitten, though, okay? I don't want to be mean to Zack anymore."

"That's all I want to do," Thomas said. "See the kitten."

"Okay," I said, and we went to put our shoes on.

Zack wasn't in the living room when we let ourselves in. I thought he might be in the kitchen getting himself a snack, but when we tiptoed in there, it was empty. There were small bowls of food and water beside the refrigerator, with a few pieces of the food spilled onto the floor. There was something else, too. A different smell. I went and looked in the half bath beside the kitchen and found it. A litter box. It was lumpy and mounded from use, and I could see a piece of poop poking up. A can of air freshener sat on the back of the toilet.

Thomas came in and found me. He was eating an apple from the fruit bowl on the kitchen table. "Pee-yew," he said, chewing and looking over my shoulder.

"Zack must be in his room," I whispered.

Thomas nodded. "You go first," he said, and he stepped aside to let me out of the bathroom.

We were quiet as we went up the stairs. At the top, I peeked in the Vuosos' bedroom and saw that Mr. Vuoso's duffel bag was still at the foot of the bed. "Look," I whispered to Thomas, pointing at it. "That's for when Mr. Vuoso gets called up."

"Called up for what?" Thomas said.

"The war. He's a reservist."

"Oh."

"There are condoms in there," I told him.

"How do you know?"

"I looked."

Thomas was quiet for a second. Then he said, "What about his wife?"

I shrugged.

"Shit," Thomas said.

We moved down the hall toward Zack's room. I thought he'd be in there doing his homework or something, but he wasn't. He was in the guest room, looking at *Playboys*. He was sitting on the bed with his back to the doorway, so he didn't notice us at first.

The kitten did, though. She was sitting on the bed with him. A little white puffball with blue eyes. She looked at me and made a tiny cry. For the first half of it, no sound came out.

"Hi, Zack," Thomas said.

Zack jumped. This made the kitten jump, too. Then she ran to the edge of the bed, hopped off, and crawled underneath it.

"Oh no," I said, dropping to the floor to see if I could find her.

Zack set his magazine down and got off the bed, too. His face turned bright red, and he started to cry. "What do you want?" he said, looking at Thomas. "Are you trying to kill me? Get out of here! Just get out of here!"

"Shut up!" I said, still on the floor. "You're scaring the kitten."

"Don't touch her!" Zack yelled. "You leave her alone!"

"Zack," Thomas said. "Calm down. Would you just calm down?"

Zack wouldn't calm down. He started crying even harder as he backed himself against the bedroom wall. "How did you even get in here?" he wailed. "Did you break in?"

I got up from the floor then. The kitten was out of my reach. "Zack," I said, "just shut up, okay? Stop saying that stuff."

"We just wanted to see the kitten, man," Thomas said. "That's all."

"Well, you can't," Zack choked. "She's afraid of you."

"No, she's not," Thomas said. "She's afraid of you. You're the one who jumped."

"Because you scared me," Zack said.

"There's nothing to be scared of," Thomas told him.

"You broke into my house," Zack said.

"We did not," Thomas said.

"Then how did you get in?"

"The door was open," I said.

"No, it wasn't," Zack said. "No way."

"Yes, it was," Thomas said.

Zack looked at me. He was quiet for a second, then he said, "You still have your key."

"No, I don't," I said.

"Give it back!"

"I don't have your key," I said.

"I'm telling my dad," he said.

"You're not going to tell your dad anything," Thomas said. "We just came over to see your kitten. That's all. You got upset about nothing."

Zack sniffled a little.

"We're just waiting for the cat to come out," Thomas said.

"She's not going to come out as long as you're here," Zack said. "She doesn't like you."

Thomas ignored this. He looked at the *Playboy* on the bed and said, "Is that yours?"

"It's my dad's," Zack said.

"There's more in the closet," I said, and Thomas went over to look.

"Shit," he said, looking at the stack. "You gotta let me borrow a couple of these."

"No!" Zack said.

Thomas borrowed a couple anyway. "I'll bring them back tomorrow," he said. "Maybe the cat will be out by then."

"You can't come back here!" Zack yelled.

"Fine," Thomas said. "I'll keep the magazines."

Zack looked at him.

"C'mon, Jasira," Thomas said, and he walked out of the room.

"You better give that key back," Zack said to me.

"The door was open," I said, and I turned and followed Thomas out.

Back at my house, Thomas wanted me to take my pants off again so he could try to have an orgasm, but I said no. "But I'm not mad anymore," he said, sitting down on the edge of my bed. "It'll probably work."

"It's too late," I said. "Daddy could come home."

"So what? I mean, what's the big deal? He knows we're friends."

"That's just the way he is," I said.

"We're not even doing anything."

"It doesn't matter."

"What if your dad came home right now and we were just talking?"

I thought for a second, then said, "He would yell."

"Is that all?"

"Yes."

"Would he hit you?"

"No."

Thomas was quiet. I couldn't tell if he believed me or not. I might've answered the question too fast. Finally, he said, "Okay, I'll go."

"You will?" I said, relieved.

"Yes," he said, standing up. "I don't want you to get in trouble."

"Thank you."

I walked him to the front door then, and he kissed me. He put his tongue in my mouth for a long time, and I put mine in his. We moved them all around each other, along the sides and over the tops and bottoms. We pressed our mouths even tighter together to try to make our tongues reach farther. It seemed hard and rough in a way, but also kind of soft, since we were really just trying to get closer.

★ ★ ★

That night, Mr. Vuoso and Zack came over and knocked on our door. "What do you want to apologize for this time?" Daddy said, and he laughed a little.

"We don't want to apologize," Mr. Vuoso said. "We just want our key back."

"What key?" Daddy said.

"The key Jasira had when she used to sit for Zack."

"She already gave that back," Daddy said. "To your wife."

"No, she didn't," Mr. Vuoso said.

"Did you give the key back?" Daddy asked me.

I nodded. I didn't know what else to do.

"She's lying," Zack said. "She broke into my house today with her friend. They scared my cat."

"What friend?" Daddy said.

"Her black friend," Zack said.

Daddy turned to me. "Were you with a black friend?"

I didn't say anything.

"Girl or boy?" he demanded.

"Boy," I said.

I thought he was going to hit me then, so I flinched. Only he was just touching his hand to his forehead. Mr. Vuoso saw it, though. "We're not here to get anybody in trouble," he said. "I don't think there's any reason for that. We just want our key back."

Daddy kept looking at me. He moved his hand again, and I couldn't help it, I flinched again. "Why are you doing that?" he yelled. "Why do you keep doing that?"

"I don't know," I said.

"Well, stop it!"

I looked at Mr. Vuoso. I wanted to tell him not to leave. That as soon as he left, things would be worse for me than ever.

Mr. Vuoso took a deep breath. "I don't think anyone meant any harm here," he said calmly. "These are just the kinds of things kids do."

"What do you mean?" Zack wailed. "That was breaking and entering!"

"Zack," Mr. Vuoso said, "you can go home now."

"But—" Zack said.

"I'll see you at home," Mr. Vuoso told him.

Zack looked at his father, then slowly turned and let himself out the front door. When he was gone, Daddy turned to me and said, "Go and get that key."

I did as he told me. On the way back to the living room, though, I heard him and Mr. Vuoso talking, so I stopped in the kitchen and listened.

"You hit her," Mr. Vuoso said, "and I'll call Protective Services."

"The discipline of my child is none of your business," Daddy said. "You discipline your child; I'll discipline mine."

"You hit her," Mr. Vuoso said, "and I'll know it, and I'll call Protective Services. You got it?"

I came back in then and gave Mr. Vuoso the key.

"Thanks," he said.

"Get out now," Daddy told him.

"Remember what I said," Mr. Vuoso warned, and he looked at me and left.

Daddy shut the door. Then he turned to me and raised his hand like he was going to hit me. He didn't, though. He just swung his hand close enough to my face so that I thought he would. He did this two more times and each time I flinched. Then he stopped. He said, "You're grounded. You're to come straight home after school and stay indoors. I will be calling to make sure that you do this. If you don't, I will find a way to beat you so that no one will ever know. Do you understand?"

I nodded.

He turned and went to bed then. So did I. As I lay there, I thought over and over again about what Mr. Vuoso had said. *Protective Services.* What were Protective Services? Were they part of the army? I had no idea. But I thought I could tell what kind of place it was from the name, and I was pretty sure it was a place that wouldn't like Daddy.

SIX

We picked up my mother from the airport three days before Christmas. Daddy didn't talk in the car. He hadn't really talked to me much at all since the night Mr. Vuoso came and got his key back. It was hard for me to tell what he was thinking. In a way, that was worse than usual. At least when he yelled at me or hit me, it was all over with.

I hadn't been to the airport since I'd arrived in Houston the previous summer. I noticed as we got closer that a lot of the billboards were different now, but that they were all still sexy. I tried not to feel like they were my fault this time, but it was hard. I just wished Daddy would say something about them, even if it was mean. I wished we didn't have to ignore them.

Daddy parked in the airport garage, then turned off the car and looked at me. He said, "If you want to go back to Syracuse with your mother, that's fine with me." He didn't seem particularly mad or anything, just tired.

"I don't want to go back," I told him.

"You may change your mind when you see her."

"No, I won't."

"Well," he said, unbuckling his seat belt. "You do whatever you want. I can't seem to control you."

The video monitor in the airport said that my mother's flight was on time. We found her gate, then waited outside it with a bunch of other people. Soon, the plane landed and the passengers started coming off. My mother was somewhere in the middle. When I saw her, I was sort of surprised. It wasn't that she looked different or anything—she didn't; she looked exactly the same. It was just that it hit me how long it had been since I'd seen her. And that I did kind of miss her.

I waved to her and she smiled and waved back. When she reached us, she bent down to hug me. As she pulled away, I noticed she was crying a little, and that made me cry, too.

"Try to calm down," Daddy told us.

"Shut up, Rifat," my mother said, dabbing at herself; then she gave him a hug and a kiss. He put his hands lightly on her waist and acted as if he didn't like it, but I was pretty sure he did. His face relaxed a little, like it did when he spoke Arabic to his mother on the telephone.

"Where's the baggage claim?" my mother asked, and Daddy led the way. My mother walked beside me, carrying her handbag and a small briefcase. She wore a pale blue sweaterdress and a long black wool coat. I felt sorry for her that she would be too hot as soon as we stepped outside.

"My God," Daddy said, pulling off the three big bags my mother pointed to on the conveyor belt. "You're only staying a week."

"They're Christmas presents," my mother told him. "Don't be such a complainer."

"Just so you know," Daddy said, "Jasira and I have decided not to exchange gifts this year."

"Why not?" my mother asked.

"Because," he said. "We're protesting the fact that Bush is waiting until after the holiday to wage war. It's disgusting."

"Do whatever you want," my mother said.

Outside, she took off her coat and gave it to me to carry. "So this is Houston," she said, even though it was dark and you couldn't really see anything.

"Yes," Daddy said.

"Well," she said, smiling down at me, "I look forward to getting a tour."

"Look," Daddy told her, "just because you're on vacation doesn't mean I am." He was pushing her luggage on a cart that had cost him a dollar to rent.

"You can lend Jasira and me your car, can't you?"

He didn't answer.

"We'll take our own tour," she said.

"Houston is a big city," Daddy said. "I think you'll find it can be somewhat difficult to navigate."

"We'll figure it out," my mother said.

On the way home, I felt like I could finally relax when we passed all the billboards for the gentlemen's clubs. And that was before my mother said, "My God. How many strip joints can one city have?"

"A lot," Daddy said.

She laughed. "I guess so."

At home, when we pulled into the driveway, she said, "What's with the flag?"

"I'm an American citizen," Daddy said. "I can fly the flag if I want to."

"Why do you want to?" she asked.

"To show support for the war."

She laughed. "You just said you were protesting the war!"

"I'm protesting one aspect of the war and supporting another aspect," he said. He added, "You know, the mark of intelligence is the capacity to hold two conflicting ideas in your head at one time."

"Uh-huh," my mother said, like she didn't believe him.

"I don't need your permission to fly the flag."

"I didn't say you did," she said, then she turned to me and made a face like Daddy was crazy.

I was very careful then to act like I didn't think Daddy was crazy. To not make a face back. Part of me had begun to worry that he might send me home with my mother, even if I didn't want to go. That all his silence meant he was sick of me.

Inside, my mother said our house was beautiful. We showed her the whole place. The only thing she didn't like was the ficus plant with Christmas lights on it. "We're getting a real tree tomorrow," she said. "That's it."

"No," Daddy said. "We're not. That's part of the protest."

"Look," my mother said. "I've got all these presents, and I've spent a fortune, and I'm putting them under a real tree. No one says you have to pay for it, so don't worry."

"I suppose you want to borrow my car for this tree?"

"Who else's car am I going to use?" she demanded, and he didn't answer.

My mother and I shared my bathroom. I had taken all the secret things out from under my sink and put them in my room, which was a good thing, since the first place my mother looked was under the sink. "Good storage space," she said, and I nodded.

That night, after we brushed our teeth and washed our faces, she came in my room to tuck me in. "Have you thought any more about coming home with me?" she asked.

"Yes," I lied.

"And?"

"I have to finish the school year," I said.

She sighed.

"I'm sorry."

"I don't have anyone," she said. "It's very lonely for me."

"I'll come back next summer," I told her, even though I didn't want to. She had just been so nice to me all night. I felt like I had to say something.

"Next summer?" she said. "That's a long way away." Then she got up and went back in her room without kissing or hugging me, or even turning out the light. I got up after a few minutes and went and knocked on her door. "Yes?" she said.

I pushed it open. She was propped up in bed, reading. "Are you mad?" I asked.

She looked up from her book. "Why would I be?"

"Because I won't come home."

"I'll live," she said.

I wasn't sure what that meant. I wasn't sure if it was really true that she would live, or if I was supposed to feel guilty and then eventually change my mind.

"Good night, Jasira," she said.

"Can I kiss you?" I asked.

"Sure."

I walked over to the bed and leaned down. I waited to feel her arms around me, but it didn't happen. It was just a plain old kiss that I gave her, while she held on to her book.

The next morning, Mom asked Daddy to make us his special pancakes, but he said no, that there wasn't enough time. I hadn't had them myself since the day I'd met Thena. "Then you can make them Christmas morning," my mother said.

"We'll see," Daddy told her.

We all got in the car to take Daddy to work. With Mom there, it was kind of like Daddy and I were on vacation from each other. He couldn't get mad at me and hit me in front of my mother, which meant that I didn't have to worry so much about what I did or said. I could just sit in the backseat and read the black painted house numbers off the curbs as we made our way out of our development.

At one point Daddy turned down the volume on NPR and said, "If I find any scratches on this car, I'm going to be very angry."

"If there hadn't been a war, and you weren't boycotting Christmas," my mother told him, "you would've gotten a tree and scratched the car yourself. So shut up."

Daddy didn't say anything. It was kind of exciting to hear her talk to him like that and have him not be able to answer back.

"I don't want any sticky resin on the car, either," he said. "It's impossible to get off."

"Can't you stop threatening people for even one second?" my mother asked. Then she turned around to look at me in the backseat. "I mean, how do you live with this?"

I wished she wouldn't keep doing that. Trying to get me to say bad things about Daddy in front of him. It always made me tense, especially with Daddy glaring at me in his rearview mirror, waiting for me to mess up.

Finally I said, "I don't know."

Daddy rolled his eyes and shifted his gaze back to the road. "Her stock answer," he muttered.

"How can you not know?" my mother said.

I shrugged.

"Well," she said, turning back around. "If you can stand him, you can have him."

I didn't say anything. Just stared at the road in between their two seat backs.

"You'd be surprised at who can stand me," Daddy said.

"Oh yeah?" my mother said. "Who's that? Your girlfriend?"

"Yes," he said. "My girlfriend."

"Goody for her," my mother said.

"That's right," Daddy said.

They didn't talk for the rest of the way. To show that she was mad, when we dropped Daddy off at his office, my mother drove off while he was still trying to tell her something through the driver's-side window. "Asshole," she mumbled. I was in the front seat now, and I forced myself not to look back at Daddy. I worried that I might feel sorry for him.

We had a map that he had drawn for us the night before. It showed where he thought we could get a good tree, and also where the grocery store was, since we needed a few things. There were three twenty-dollar bills attached to the map with a paper clip, and my mother told me to take the money off and put it in her purse. When I opened her wallet, I found a picture of Barry. "What's this?" I said.

She looked over at me. "What do you mean, what's this?"

"I thought you didn't like him anymore."

"He doesn't like me," she said. "They're two different things."

"Oh." I hadn't seen Barry in so long. His messy light brown hair and the dimple in his chin. It seemed like I should be the one to have the picture, since I was pretty sure he still liked me.

"Did you put the money away?" my mother asked.

"Yes."

"Then close up the wallet," she said, and I did.

At the tree place, she picked the expensive kind, a Douglas fir. The man said the needles would stay on longer. He tied the tree to the top of the car for us, then we went to the grocery store. Mom got everything on Daddy's list, then asked if I needed anything. "No," I said.

"What about period stuff? Sanitary napkins?"

"No," I said, "I don't need any."

We went and stood in the checkout line. My mother took a *Peo-*

ple magazine off the rack and read a little. I already felt tired from the whole visit.

On the way out of the store, my mother parked our grocery cart beside the self-service Xerox machine. She reached in her purse and pulled out a few strips of paper, then lifted the lid of the copier and laid the papers out on the glass.

"What are you copying?" I asked.

She put a few coins in the slot and said, "Your father's pay stubs."

I didn't say anything, just watched the copies slide out on the paper tray. There were three total, and when the machine stopped, my mother picked them up and folded them in half. She stuck them in her purse, then lifted the copier lid and took out the originals. "Okay," she said. "All done."

In the parking lot, we loaded the grocery bags into Daddy's back-seat. I pushed the empty cart off to one side, while my mother got in the car. A moment later, as I was buckling my seat belt, she said, "I don't need you blabbing to your father about this. I mean, apparently, the two of you are pretty tight, but I'd really appreciate it if you'd keep your mouth shut."

I knew she wanted me to say that I wasn't tight with Daddy, so I didn't. Instead, I said, "Where did you get his pay stubs?"

"His desk," she said.

"But his drawers are all locked."

"Well," she said, "those aren't very good locks." When I didn't an-swer, she said, "Look, Jasira, I have to protect myself. In case you hadn't noticed, your father is a stingy man. If you ever do decide to come back home, I need proof that he makes plenty of money. Teenagers are expensive."

I nodded.

"So you'll keep your mouth shut?"

"Yes."

We got home and untied the tree, then carried it inside. We'd bought a stand, too, and I held the trunk at the bottom while my mother tried to make sure the tree was straight. Once we had it screwed in, we took the lights off the ficus and put them on the Douglas fir. We spent the rest of the afternoon popping popcorn and stringing it for decoration. My mother said she was tired then, and she went to take a nap. I sat on the couch, looking at the tree and eating the leftover popcorn. I remembered the tree at Thomas's house, which had been so much bigger and prettier. I started to think that if our tree had any feelings, they would be hurt to have to spend Christmas with us.

The doorbell rang at around four, and I set my bowl of popcorn on the floor to answer it. It was Melina, and she was holding a present. "Hey," she said. "I just wanted to bring you over a little something for Christmas."

"Oh," I said. "Thank you." I felt bad that I didn't have anything for her. "I'll put it under the tree," I said, taking the package.

"No," she said. "Don't do that. Just open it."

"Now?" I asked.

"Why not?"

"Okay." I started to take the paper off.

"Just rip it!" she said, smiling, so I did. Inside was a large paperback called *Changing Bodies, Changing Lives*. There was a picture of a whole bunch of smiling teenagers on the cover.

"It's so you can learn how your body works," Melina said.

"Thank you," I said, flipping through a couple of pages. It seemed interesting.

"Jasira?" my mother called from behind me.

I turned around.

She came into the living room looking sleepy. "Who are you talking to?"

"This is Melina. Our other neighbor."

"Oh," Melina said. "I'm sorry. I thought Jasira was alone."

"My mother is visiting for Christmas," I told her.

"Oh," Melina said again. She looked a little nervous.

"I'm Gail," my mother said, holding out her hand.

"Melina," Melina said.

"What's that?" my mother asked, looking under my arm, where I had tucked the book.

"It's a present. From Melina."

"I hope it's all right," Melina said quickly. "I just thought it might be helpful."

"May I see it, please?" my mother asked me.

I didn't move.

My mother reached for the book and took it herself. "Huh," she said, when she saw the cover.

"I didn't mean to intrude," Melina said. "I really didn't. It's just that I know Jasira has questions sometimes."

"Does she?" my mother asked. Then she turned to me and said, "Do you?"

"Sometimes," I said.

"Why don't you call me?" she said.

"I don't know."

"I think I messed up," Melina said. "Please forgive me."

"No," my mother said, but I could tell she was lying. "This is a very thoughtful gift. Don't you think, Jasira?"

"Yes," I said.

"Very thoughtful," my mother repeated.

"Well," Melina said. "I'd better go."

"When are you due?" my mother asked cheerfully.

"April," Melina said.

"Well," my mother said. "Good for you. Seems like you'll be a terrific mom. Anyway. Nice meeting you." Then she turned and went back to her room.

"Give me the book," Melina said.

"No," I said. I wanted to keep it.

"Give it to me," Melina said, this time taking it out of my hands.

"But it's my book."

"Yes," Melina said. "It is. We're just going to keep it at my house. You can come over and read it whenever you want. Okay?"

I knew she was probably right. I just felt disappointed, since her book seemed better than my *Playboy*. Not the pictures, but the writing. "Okay," I said finally.

"Merry Christmas," she said. She leaned down and kissed me on the forehead, adding, "Sorry."

After Melina left, I went to see if my mother was still awake. "Yes?" she said when I knocked on her door. I opened it, and she said, "Where's your book?"

"Melina took it."

"Why?"

"She said it would be better if I read it at her house."

"What's the difference where you read it?" my mother asked.

"I don't know."

"There's no difference," she muttered.

"It's almost time to get Daddy," I said.

She looked at her watch. "We have a little while yet."

I could tell by the way she went back to her book then that she would rather be alone, so I left.

I went in my room and lay down on my bed. It was almost Christmas, and I didn't care. Christmas, to me, was as bad as any weekend, and weekends were bad because I couldn't see Thomas or Mr. Vuoso on any kind of regular schedule. Weekends were the time when I was trapped inside with Daddy all day, or else trapped outside with him.

And now, being with my mother wasn't much better. All she wanted to do was lie around and read books. She was so boring. I wasn't sure why I'd ever liked her so much. Maybe it was just that I had liked Barry, and she had introduced me to him. At least Barry had wanted to do things, even if they weren't the right things.

I wished I had Melina's book back. I couldn't imagine what it would be like to get to read about my body. Everything I wanted to do—everything I liked—was always so far away. I thought about Dorrie and how much I hated her and how lucky she was going to be to get born to Melina and Gil. Everything she liked would be right there, in her own house. When she got older, she could even read my stupid book.

After a while, I heard my mother get up and use the bathroom. Then she came to my door and said, "Ready?"

"Uh-huh," I said, sitting up on my bed.

"What kind of room did he give you?" my mother asked, looking around at my blank walls, my bed on its metal frame, my off-white venetian blinds. She shook her head. "This isn't a girl's room."

"I don't mind," I said.

My mother made a face. "You know, Jasira, it's getting a little old—the 'I love Daddy' routine. Just cut it, would you?" She turned and left.

We met in the living room and went out the back door to get to the car. At the same time, Mr. Vuoso came outside to take his flag down. "Who's that?" my mother asked, pausing at the driver's-side door.

"Mr. Vuoso," I said. "Remember? I used to babysit his son."

"Oh right," my mother said. She was still watching him. He wasn't wearing a jacket, and every time he reached up to yank on the rope pulley, his arm muscles flexed.

"Daddy doesn't like him," I said.

"Your father is very easily intimidated."

Just then, Mr. Vuoso noticed us staring at him.

"Hi there!" my mother called.

He nodded and smiled a little.

"C'mon," my mother said, moving away from the car. "You can introduce me."

I waited a second, then followed her down our driveway and into the Vuosos' front yard. "Hi," I said. "This is my mom."

Mr. Vuoso looked at me. We hadn't been together since the Mexican restaurant. We said hi sometimes when we saw each other on the sidewalk, but that was about it. I'd been missing him ever since the night he'd threatened to call Protective Services on Daddy. I kept hoping he would come and take me for dinner again.

"Gail Monahan," my mother said now, holding out her hand.

"Travis Vuoso," Mr. Vuoso said, shaking with her.

"Nice to meet you, Travis," she said, and I felt jealous that she was old enough to call him by his first name.

"Same here," he said. Then he turned to me and said, "Hi, Jasira."

"Hi."

"How are you?"

"Fine, thank you."

"Yeah?" he said. "Everything going okay?"

I nodded.

He paused for a second, then said, "Good. Glad to hear it."

"I'm here for Christmas," my mother said, even though no one had asked.

"Oh yeah?" Mr. Vuoso said, turning to her.

She nodded. "Jasira and I haven't seen each other since last summer."

"You must miss her."

My mother nodded. "I'm trying to get her to move back home with me."

Mr. Vuoso looked at me. "You're moving back?"

I shook my head. "I have to finish the school year."

"Oh," he said.

"It's not like we don't have schools in Syracuse," my mother said.

"Well," Mr. Vuoso said, "I guess it can be hard to change in the middle of the year."

My mother shrugged. "People do it all the time." She seemed like she was changing back into her regular self now, and I felt relieved. She was much harder to like that way.

"We're going to be late to get Daddy," I said.

My mother looked at her watch. "Okay, let's go."

"Nice meeting you," Mr. Vuoso said.

"You, too," my mother said, and she turned and walked back to the car.

On the way to NASA, she wanted to know what Mr. Vuoso had been talking about.

"When?" I said.

"When he was asking you if everything was okay a million times. What's not to be okay?"

"Nothing," I said. "He was just trying to be friendly. People in Texas act friendly."

"I didn't think he was that friendly," she said, then she turned on the radio. After a minute, she moved the dial from the news on NPR to a classical-music station, and I stopped myself from saying that Daddy didn't like anyone touching his dial.

When we got to Daddy's office, he was waiting outside with Thena. As soon as he saw us, he grabbed her and kissed her on the lips. After a couple of seconds he let her go, and she waved to me. I wanted to wave back, but without even looking, I could feel how angry my mother was from the front seat, so I just made a small smile. Finally, Thena turned and walk back toward the office building. "That's just lovely," my mother said when Daddy got in the passenger side of the car.

"What?" he said, though I could tell he knew.

"Fuck you, Rifat."

He laughed a little, then said, "Don't be like that, Gail. I'm sure you have plenty of boyfriends. You're a very attractive woman."

She ignored him. To try to make her feel better, Daddy said he would take us out for pizza. "I don't want pizza," my mother said. "I want Mexican food. Why would I come to Texas and eat pizza when I could eat Mexican food?"

"I don't know any Mexican places," Daddy said.

"What do you mean? They're everywhere."

"Yeah, but they might not be good."

"I know a place," I said.

"What?" Daddy said.

"Where?" my mother said.

"It's called Ninfa's," I said. "It's kind of far."

"Ninfa?" Daddy said, dropping the *s*. "How do you know about this place?"

"I read about it. In the newspaper."

"What newspaper?"

I thought for a second, trying to remember the name of Daddy's paper. "The *Chronicle*."

"In the food section?" he asked.

"Yes."

"I never saw you reading the food section."

"Who cares?" my mother said. "Let's just go."

"Pull over," Daddy said, pointing at a gas station. "I need to call and get the address."

Daddy used a pay phone and got the address, then came back and found the restaurant on his Houston city map. He said it was definitely far, but that we could still go. He and my mother switched places so he could drive.

On the way there, my mother's mood got better. She said finally she felt like she was about to have an authentic Texas experience. Then she and Daddy asked each other a little about their work. Mom described a problem she was having with another teacher. This man wasn't doing a good job with his students, and so when Mom got them, she had to reteach all the stuff he'd messed up, plus her own stuff. Daddy told her this guy sounded like a stupid idiot, and that Mom should tell the principal on him. Mom said it wasn't that simple, and Daddy asked her if she wanted to keep busting her ass or not. She sighed and said no, not really.

Then Daddy told Mom that he was going to get to go and watch a shuttle launch in March, since he had designed a part for the mission. "Rifat!" my mother said. "That's incredible!" She really seemed to mean it, too. Then my mother asked if Thena would be going, and Daddy didn't answer. "She *is* going?" my mother said. When he still didn't answer, she yelled, "I put you through graduate school, and she gets to see the fucking shuttle launch with you?"

"Calm down," Daddy told her, and she said *fuck you* to him again.

When we got to the restaurant, it was happy hour, and Daddy ordered regular margaritas for him and Mom, plus a nonalcoholic one for me. I wished they would go and pee together so I could sip from their glasses, but they only went one at a time. "Your mother is a pain in the ass," Daddy said while she was in the restroom. "I can't imagine why I ever married her." Then, when Daddy was in the restroom, my mother said, "I swear to God, if he tries to split the bill with me, I'm going to break out those fucking pay stubs."

"You didn't put them back in his desk yet?" I asked.

She shook her head, sipping her margarita. "Don't worry. I'll do it tonight."

I got really nervous then about when the bill would come. I didn't see why Daddy would try to split it if he'd already said he was taking us out, but maybe he'd only meant the offer for pizza.

Our food came, and I couldn't really concentrate on it. "What's the matter?" Daddy asked. "You don't like your dinner?"

"No," I said. "I do." I'd ordered the same chicken enchiladas I'd had with Mr. Vuoso.

"Then eat," he said, and I nodded.

A few minutes later, I got a really hot pepper. My eyes started watering, and they wouldn't stop. "Drink this," my mother said, handing me my water, and I did, but it didn't help. She signaled the waiter for more water, but it didn't seem to matter. No matter how much I drank, my mouth wouldn't stop burning.

My parents looked at me. "Pull yourself together, would you?" Daddy said.

"I'm trying," I said. My voice came out hoarse.

"It's just a pepper, for godssakes," my mother said.

"I know," I said. "I can't help it."

They looked at each other and made faces. The faces said that they both thought I was being a baby, that I was making things up, even though the waiter had gone to get the manager, and she'd come to apologize. She was an older lady with gray and black hair, and I wondered if she was the real Ninfa. "This happens sometimes," she explained to my parents. "The cooks are very careful, but it does happen." Then she put her hand on my back, like since she had hurt me, I was hers.

When the bill came, it said that our dinner was free. "Look at that," Daddy said, and he smiled.

"How nice of them," my mother said, and Daddy's pay stubs stayed in her purse.

In the car on the way home, I held my unfinished enchiladas in a bag on my lap. Slowly, my mouth began to burn less, which I guess should've made me happy, but it didn't. I found that I didn't want the burning to go away. As long as it was there, I could feel Ninfa's hand on my back, trying to make me feel better.

On Christmas morning, we got up and Daddy made us pancakes. Then I opened the presents my mother had brought me. Mostly, they were clothes—pretty ones that fit me perfectly. When my mother saw that we really didn't have any presents for her, she got upset. She told Daddy she thought he'd been kidding about that, and he said why would he have been kidding? Then she told me that at least I could've made her something in art class. I wanted to remind her that she'd told me not to give her anything, but I didn't think she would like that.

I wasn't sure what to do then. I liked my new clothes and wanted to wear one of the outfits, but I had a feeling they weren't mine anymore since I hadn't gotten my mother a present. I would've liked to have gone to Melina's to read my book, but ever since the night before there had been a lot of cars in her driveway that I didn't recognize, and I didn't feel comfortable going over and knocking on the door.

My mother got up and went in her room. I figured she was going to get in bed and read her book, but then she came back with some papers in her hand. "You're a cheap bastard!" she said, waving them in my father's face. "I put you through fucking graduate school so you could make this kind of money, and you can't even buy me a fucking bottle of perfume!" She threw the papers on the floor, and I saw then that they were the pay stubs.

Immediately Daddy bent down and picked them up. "Where did you get these?" he demanded.

"What do you mean where did I get them? I got them where you keep them. Don't you remember where you keep them?"

"My salary is none of your business," he said.

"Of course it's my business! We have a child! She costs money!"

"Where did you get the key to my drawers?"

"I didn't need a key."

He looked at me then. "Did you give it to her? Did you find the key and give it to her?"

"No," I said. "I don't even know where the key is."

"I don't believe you!" he said. "I don't believe you in the least!"

"Oh, she didn't give me the key!" my mother said. "For godssakes, I used a nail file."

"No!" Daddy said. "Those are good locks! You couldn't have used a nail file."

"Well, I did. So lay off her."

"It's not the first time she's broken into something, you know."

"What?" my mother said.

"She broke into the neighbor's house with that black boy."

My mother looked at me. "What is he talking about?"

"Daddy," I said, turning to him, "I didn't give her the key."

"'Her'?" my mother said. "We don't say 'her.'"

"I didn't give my mother the key," I told Daddy.

"What house did you break into?" my mother asked.

"The Vuosos'," Daddy said; then he told her the whole story, except for the part about how Mr. Vuoso had threatened to call Protective Services.

"But you're not supposed to see that boy," my mother said.

I didn't say anything.

"She does what she wants," Daddy said. "I can't control her."

"What do you mean you can't control her? That's why I sent her down here."

"I can't control her," Daddy repeated. "Period. That's it. She's uncontrollable."

"You're a grown man!" my mother said.

My father didn't say anything. He just shrugged.

"Well, then she can come back and live with me," my mother said.

"No," I said. "I have to finish the school year."

"What is this school year bullshit?" she said.

Daddy sighed. "Let her live where she wants."

"I want to live here," I said.

"But you hate your father!" my mother yelled. "That's what you told me on the phone."

"I did not!" I said.

She turned to Daddy and said, "You might as well know that all she did was complain about you when she first moved down here."

"I don't hate you," I told Daddy. "I never said that."

He looked at me.

"Selective memory," my mother said.

I thought Daddy would kick me out for sure then. I knew my mother thought so, too. But he didn't. He turned to her and said, "You have invaded our privacy." Then he said he was going to Thena's and walked out. My mother went in her room.

I didn't want to talk to my mother. I was mad at her for bringing out the pay stubs, but mostly for lying to Daddy. It was true, I had hated him when I'd first moved to Houston. But I'd only thought it. I'd never said it. And then I'd changed my mind. It wasn't that I loved Daddy now; I could never imagine loving him, or even liking him very much. It was something different from all of that. What I had learned about Daddy was that it was very hard for him to be nice, so when he was, it would've been wrong not to try to appreciate it.

I just wished my mother would stop acting so jealous. I could understand how she didn't want me and Barry to like each other, but me and Daddy, too? He was my own father. He was supposed to like me. Most of the time he didn't, but then today, when it seemed like he did just the teeniest bit, when he said I could live wherever I wanted, she had to go and wreck it.

I wished I could be at Thena's with Daddy. Instead I went and knocked on my mother's door. "Do you want to do something?" I asked.

"Come in here," she said.

I opened the door and saw that she was packing her suitcase. "Where are you going?" I asked.

"Home," she said. "Where else?"

"But your plane isn't for two days."

"I'm changing it."

I didn't say anything, just watched her fold her clothes.

"I need you to call me a cab. Do you think you could do that?"

"Sure."

"It's going to cost me a fortune," she said, laying her pale blue sweaterdress in the suitcase.

"Sorry," I said.

"This is your last chance," she said. "If you want to come home with me."

I tried to think of something else to say besides that I needed to finish the school year, but I couldn't.

"You know what?" she said. "Never mind. I don't want to live with someone who doesn't want to live with me. Just call me a fucking cab."

I went to the kitchen and took out the phone book. I looked in the yellow pages under *cab,* but it said to look under *taxi.* There were a lot of different companies, so I picked the one that said it specialized in taking people to the airport. When I called, a man put me on hold for a minute, then came back and said, "What's your address?" I told him, then he said, "Where you going?" and I told him that, too. "Twenty minutes," he said, and he hung up on me. I wished I could go and tell my mother what I had just done, since I'd never really called a cab for anyone before, but I knew she wouldn't care. Instead I just told her it would be twenty minutes.

She stayed in her room until the cab came, then carried her bag out by herself. The extra bags that had held my presents had been nylon duffels, and I assumed she had folded them into her one hard case. I tried to help by reaching for her purse or briefcase, but she said, "I've got it." Then, when she got to the curb, she let the cabdriver help her a lot.

I stood on the sidewalk, even though I knew she wasn't going to hug or kiss me. She just got in the car and slammed the door. The window was open a crack, and she didn't shut it or make it bigger. She didn't look at me, either. Just stared straight ahead. I knew all of this was important to her, to try to make me feel bad. I understood this, and stayed out on the sidewalk as her cab pulled away and she didn't turn around and wave.

When she was finally out of sight, I went back inside and tried on some of my new clothes. There were khakis and a skirt and some pretty shirts. I thought about calling Daddy to tell him that my mother had gone, but he had once warned me to use Thena's number only in case of emergency. I thought it might've been him when the phone rang around dinnertime, but it wasn't.

"Jasira?" a woman's voice said. It was strange to hear my name pronounced like this, with the *s* like a real *s*, instead of a *z*.

"*Oui?*" I said, almost without thinking.

"*Bonne Noël, Jasira!*" my grandmother said.

"*Merci,*" I said.

"*C'est votre grand-mère!*" she said.

"*Oui,*" I said. "*Je sais.*"

She laughed. "*Comment ça va?*"

"*Je vais très bien.*" It seemed funny to say lines from the character dialogues of my *French in Action* textbooks. It was the kind of talk I'd learned, but never thought I'd actually use.

"*Bon, bon,*" she said.

"Um," I said, "*mon père n'est pas ici maintenant.*"

"*Ah non?*" she said.

"*Non.*"

"*Et ta mère?*"

"*Non,*" I said again. I got confused then, unsure if my grandmother knew my mother had been visiting, or if she thought my parents were still married. I began to panic a little, worried that I would say the wrong thing.

"*Mais, tu es seule à Noël?*"

"They'll be back soon," I said, feeling too nervous to think in French.

"*Eh?*" my grandmother said.

I thought for a second, then said, "*Vous pouvez téléphoner Daddy à—*" and I read her Thena's number off the list beside the telephone. She wrote it down, then said she didn't understand why Daddy wasn't home on Christmas. I lied and acted like I couldn't understand her. She repeated herself a couple of times, but I kept saying, "*Je ne comprends pas.*" Finally she gave up and said she would call Daddy. She said she loved me and I said it back to her. I wasn't sure if I really meant it, but I was happy to have someone to talk to.

After we hung up, I got nervous. Grandma calling wasn't an emergency. I should never have given her Thena's number. I barely slept that night, worrying about what Daddy was going to do to me. When he came home the next afternoon, though, he didn't seem mad. Especially when he saw that my mother had left. "Good riddance," he said.

"She tried to make me go with her one more time, but I said no."

He nodded, then bent down to untie his shoes.

"Did Grandma call you?" I asked.

"Yes," he said.

"I'm sorry I gave her Thena's number."

"Don't worry about it," he said, straightening up. "I know she's a pain in the ass."

"I just didn't know what to do."

"Don't worry about it," he told me again.

I went to hug him then. I couldn't help it. Not just from that moment, but from the day before, when it had seemed like he'd been defending me a little to my mother. As soon as I reached my arms toward him, though, he hit me in the face. I fell backward onto the breakfast nook floor. "We don't hug people we hate," he said, then he went in his room and shut the door.

When I woke up the next day, I had a black eye. I couldn't stop looking at myself in the mirror. I felt very, very excited. I had seen boys in school with black eyes, boys who had been in fights. Everyone knew from the way they looked that this was what had happened to them. Now, I thought, people would know about something that had happened to me.

When I went out for breakfast, Daddy looked at me but didn't say anything. Then, in the middle of eating his cereal, he said, "Just so you know, if anyone sees you like that, you won't be able to live with me anymore."

I looked at him.

"You'll have to go and live with your mother," he said.

I didn't say anything.

"So show it to whomever you want," he said. "As long as you're ready to go and live with your mother."

I stayed inside for the rest of that week. When school started up the following week, Daddy told them I was sick and picked up my assignments on his way home from work. Thomas called to see why I wasn't in school, and I said I had the flu. "I'll come and visit you," he said.

"No," I said. "You can't. You'll get sick."

"No, I won't. I never get sick."

"You can't come over," I said.

"Why not?"

"Because," I said. "You're black."

"Ha-ha."

"I'm serious," I said. "My parents don't want me to be friends with a black boy."

He was quiet for a second. "I really hope you're kidding."

"I'm not," I said. "I already told you."

"Why would you listen to them if they said something like that?"

"Because. They're my parents."

He hung up after a moment, without saying good-bye.

I felt terrible about having to tell him the truth, but I couldn't help it. I was too afraid of making Daddy mad. I didn't want him to send me back to my mother.

There wasn't much to do, being stuck in the house. Mostly I just watched CNN while they prepared for the war to start. Sometimes I checked my bruise in the mirror and felt sad that it was healing. It was the best proof I'd ever had of what Daddy was really like.

At the beginning of the third week, he bought me some concealer makeup to cover the little bit of bruise that was left. I went back to school and tried to sit with Thomas in the cafeteria, but when I set my tray down at his table, he picked his tray up and left.

After school, I went to Melina's to see if I could read my book. "Where've you been?" she said. "I must've rung your bell a million times."

It was true, she had, but I'd ignored her. "I was sick," I said.

"With what?"

"The flu."

"Huh."

"Can I read my book?" I asked.

"Sure," she said, and she stepped aside to let me in.

We sat in her living room together, Melina on the couch, me on the floor. She read a book about babies, while I read about my body. When I came to the part about how I had a hymen and how it might hurt when someone broke it, I couldn't help it, I started to cry. Especially the part that said if I wanted it to hurt less, my partner could put a finger inside me and try to gently stretch it out a little first. "What's the matter?" Melina asked, looking up.

"Nothing," I said. I shut the book so she couldn't see what page I was on.

"Something's the matter."

"I was just thinking about my mother," I said. "I miss her."

"Uh-huh," Melina said, like she didn't believe me. She reached for a tissue on the table beside her and handed it to me. I dried my eyes a little and blew my nose.

"What's that?" she asked.

"What?"

She squinted at the right side of my face. "It looks like a bruise."

"Where?" I said, like I didn't know.

"That's a black eye," she said.

"No, it's not."

"Jesus Christ."

"It's not a black eye," I told her. "I was trying on makeup at school. It got smudged."

She didn't say anything then. She just kept staring at me.

"Thank you for getting me this book," I said finally. "I really like it a lot."

"You're welcome," she said.

"Sorry I didn't get you anything."

"It's okay."

I didn't know what else to do, so I went back to my reading. I knew Melina hadn't gone back to hers because I couldn't hear the pages turning. I just heard her strange short breaths, which she had once explained to me were because of Dorrie, who was beginning to squash her lungs.

SEVEN

The day the war started, Daddy was in a good mood. "Finally!" he said at breakfast that morning. He had NPR on in the kitchen, and CNN on in the living room, and he kept getting up from his seat in the breakfast nook when he thought there might be something interesting on TV. "This won't take long at all," he said. "Saddam will be dead in a couple of days."

At school, all the kids were kind of excited. They said we were going to blast the ragheads out of Kuwait. I tried to sit next to Thomas again at lunch, and this time he let me. "Did you hear about the war?" I asked him.

"Duh," he said.

I picked up my fork and cut one of my raviolis in half. "Daddy says it'll be over in a couple of days."

"I really don't give a shit what your dad says."

"Sorry," I said.

We didn't talk for the rest of lunch, but I was glad that we were at least sitting together.

A couple of days later, when Saddam started shooting Scud missiles at Israel, Daddy got depressed. On CNN they showed all these Palestinian people acting really happy about it, and Daddy said it was bullshit. "Those are a bunch of idiots!" he yelled. "All they want to show is a bunch of idiots!" He got even angrier when they showed a video of Yasser Arafat hugging Saddam. "What a traitor," Daddy said. "He makes me want to change your name."

"Why?" I said.

"Why?" he said. "Because you're named after him."

"Oh," I said. I hadn't known this.

"It was your mother's stupid idea. I wanted to name you Estelle."

"That's a nice name," I said.

Daddy nodded. "It's French."

"Can we change my name now?" I asked.

Daddy shook his head. He was talking to me and watching TV at the same time. "Too late."

"Why?" I said.

He shrugged. "It just is. No one would remember to say it."

I went in my room and took out a piece of paper. I wrote the name Estelle over and over, and felt cheated. It was fun to write. It was French. French was more normal than Arab.

Daddy wouldn't stop watching TV and listening to the radio at the same time. On the Saturday after the war started, we drove to Kmart so he could buy TV tables for the living room. You could see the TV from the dining room table, but Daddy wanted to get closer to make sure he didn't miss any of the writing on the screen.

I ate my dinner in the living room with Daddy and watched the news, too. It got kind of boring sometimes, especially when they talked about different models of airplanes or different types of ammunition. I liked when Christiane Amanpour came on, though, because Daddy said she was sexy. Whenever he said that, it made me want to jump up from the couch and do a dance. I just felt so happy to hear him talk about adult things in front of me.

I started to think that I might want to be a reporter. There was a meeting for the school newspaper that week, and I told Daddy I was going to go. "Good idea," he said. "The Arab voice is underrepresented in the press."

Since it was a junior-high newspaper, the *Lone Star Times* came out only every other month. My English teacher, Mr. Joffrey, was the faculty adviser. He didn't do much, just sat at his desk eating a sandwich and grading papers. The editor in chief was a kid named Charles; he had coarse brown hair and blue eyes. He stood in front of the chalkboard when the meeting began, asking different people if their articles or reviews were done. Then he asked the new people at the meeting to say their names and what kind of writing they were interested in doing. It was me and one other girl whom I knew from English class. Her name was Denise, and she was pretty and blonde and a little bit fat. She had a high voice and said weird things that I could tell made the other kids in class think she was stupid, but when I looked at all her tests and essays that got handed back, they always said A+.

I raised my hand and Charles pointed to me. "My name is Jasira," I said. "I'm interested in war reporting."

A couple of kids laughed, but Charles didn't. He said, "What kind of war reporting?"

"Well," I said, trying to think, since I didn't really have an answer. "I guess I'm interested in reservists and what it's like to get called up."

Charles was quiet for a second, then said, "Okay, good angle. Talk to me after the meeting."

Denise raised her hand next and said she was interested in writing book reviews.

"We already have enough book reviewers," Charles told her.

"Oh," she said. "Well, what don't you have enough of?"

"We've been thinking of starting a horoscope section. Could you do that?"

"Sure," she said.

Denise and I both hung around after the meeting to talk to Charles. "When do you think you can have that reservist piece done by?" he asked me.

"I don't know," I said. "Two weeks?"

"If you make it a week and a half," he said, "we can get it into the March issue."

"Okay."

"Same for your horoscopes," he said, turning to Denise.

She nodded. "Should I just make them up?"

"Sure," Charles said. "Just make sure you do a little research about the signs first. You know, like, Virgos are uptight, so write something about how they might feel tense, but around the fourteenth, something will happen to make them feel more relaxed. See what I mean?"

"I guess," Denise said, and she giggled.

When we finished talking to Charles, Denise and I walked out of the school together. I had never really thought of being her friend because she had such a weird voice and people were always laughing at her. I figured I was unpopular enough. Now, though, I found her kind of easy to be with. "Why did you join the paper?" she asked me.

I shrugged. "I might want to be a journalist when I get older."

"Oh," she said. After a second, she said, "Know why I joined?"

"Why?" I said.

"You can't tell anyone," she said.

"I won't."

"It's because I'm in love with Mr. Joffrey. I want to have sex with him."

"Really?" I said. Mr. Joffrey was short and had small eyes and small round glasses. He hadn't said one word during the meeting.

"I think he's sexy," Denise said.

"I guess I hadn't really noticed," I admitted.

"Good," she said. "I don't want any competition."

We walked outside to wait for the late buses. As we were about to cross a small drive, I didn't notice a car coming, and Denise grabbed my arm. "Wait!" she yelled.

"Oops," I said, stopping.

"Okay, you can go now," she said, once the car had passed. I noticed that she kept her hand on my arm for a couple of extra seconds, and it made me feel like I had known her for a long time already.

When I got home, Zack was outside with his kitten. He had her on a small harness and leash, and was walking her up and down the sidewalk. Except she wouldn't really walk. When he pulled the leash, she just stopped, or lay down.

"Can't you just let her walk around without a leash?" I asked him.

"I don't want her to run away," he said.

"She won't," I said. "She's too small."

"You don't know anything," he said.

"Let go of the leash and let her walk, then if she gets too far away, just grab it."

He thought about this, then surprised me by taking my suggestion. Finally the kitten started moving around a little and sniffing things. I kind of wanted to say, "See?" but I forced myself not to. Instead I said, "Did your dad get called up yet?"

"No," Zack said.

"Well," I said, "I'm writing an article for the school paper about reservists. I need to interview him."

Zack didn't say anything. He was watching the kitten jerk her head around to the movements of a small bird.

"Do you think he'll let me?" I asked.

"Maybe. If he's not too busy."

"Cool."

The kitten tried to chase the bird then and Zack stepped on her leash, snapping her neck a little.

"Be careful," I said. "You'll hurt her."

"This is a dumb idea," Zack said, and he picked the leash back up, and the kitten fell into the grass in protest, making him pull her wherever he wanted her to go.

Inside, I sat at the dining room table, watching the war on TV and making up a list of questions for Mr. Vuoso:

1. Are you scared to get killed?

2. Do you think you'll kill an Iraqi?

3. What kinds of things will you take with you from home?

4. Will your wife come and visit you?

5. Can you receive packages?

6. Do you think this is a war for oil?

Christiane Amanpour came on CNN while I was working, and I thought it would be nice to have a tan jacket like hers, with all those pockets.

When Daddy came home and I told him about the school paper meeting, he said it sounded good. Then I told him about my reservist article, and he got mad. "How is that representing the Arab view?" he asked me. "Here you are, living with an Arab, and you want to interview the scumbag next door? What kind of stupid idea is this?"

"But what if Mr. Vuoso gets called up?" I said. "Then I won't be able to interview him. That's why I want to do it now, while he's still here."

"Do whatever you want," Daddy muttered, and he went to the fridge and got a beer.

"I can interview you next," I said.

"The Arab perspective," he said, opening his Heineken. "That's what's missing in the news. You could've made a difference, but instead you chose the easy way out."

While I was washing the dinner dishes that night, the phone rang. Daddy set down his drying towel and went to answer it. "It's for you," he said, and I pulled off my rubber gloves and went to take the phone. I figured it was my mother from the angry look on Daddy's face, but it wasn't. "Jasira?" a man's voice said.

"Yes?"

"This is Mr. Vuoso." When I didn't say anything, he added, "From next door."

"Yes," I said. "I know." I was afraid to talk since Daddy was standing right there, staring at me.

"How are you?" he asked.

"Fine, thank you."

"Good," he said. "I was a little worried. I haven't seen you in a long time."

"I was sick," I said.

"With what?"

"The flu."

"Oh."

"I'm better now," I told him.

"Well," he said, "Zack mentioned something about you wanting to interview me for your school paper?"

"Yes," I said. "I wanted to write an article about reservists."

"Okay, sure. When did you want to do this?"

"I don't know," I said.

"How about Saturday?" he said. "Zack and his mom are taking the kitten to the vet. You could come over then."

"Okay," I said.

"Say, around noon?"

"Sure."

"Hopefully I won't get called up before then," he said, and he laughed a little.

"I hope not, either."

"What do you hope?" Daddy asked, once I had hung up the phone. He was still standing there with his dish towel, staring at me.

"That Mr. Vuoso won't get called up before the interview," I said. I walked around him so I could get back to the sink and finish the dishes.

"You'd better watch what you say to him," Daddy said.

"I'm just going to ask him questions about being a reservist. That's all."

"This guy thinks he's a real vigilante," Daddy said.

I didn't know what a vigilante was, but I didn't feel like asking.

The next day at school, Denise asked me if I wanted to come over to her house that weekend to work on our articles. "I can't," I said, and I explained to her about how I was going to be interviewing Mr. Vuoso on Saturday afternoon.

"Well, then I'll come over to your house," she said. "After the interview. We can have a sleepover. Want to?"

"Um," I said. "Well, I need to ask."

"Okay," she said, then she wrote down her phone number and told me to call her that night.

I had lunch with Thomas again in the cafeteria. "What do you want?" he said, looking at me as I pulled my chair out.

"Nothing," I said.

"Why are you sitting here if you're not supposed to?"

"My parents don't know what I do in school."

"Wow," Thomas said. "That's really brave of you. I mean, going against your parents when they can't even catch you. I really admire that." He stabbed his pointed straw into his milk container and took a big sip.

"I can go sit somewhere else," I said.

Thomas put his milk down. He didn't answer me.

"Should I go?" I asked.

"Fuck you," he said.

"Don't swear at me."

"Shut up," he said.

I decided to stay. I knew that sometimes when people got mad at you, you were supposed to sit there and take it. Like when my mother called the cab to the airport. At the end of lunch, I hoped that Thomas felt a little bit better from having given me the silent treatment.

At dinner that night, I asked Daddy if I could have a friend sleep over on Saturday.

"What friend?" Daddy said. He was sitting in his chair with his TV tray in front of him. He had cooked a couple of steaks for us in the broiler and made a salad. My plate was covered with little clumps of gray gristle I couldn't chew into small enough pieces, but there was no gristle on Daddy's plate. I couldn't tell if he was a better chewer than I was, or if he'd had a better piece of steak.

"A girl from the newspaper," I said. I added, "A white girl."

"Don't be so stupid," Daddy said. "It doesn't matter what color she is if she's a girl. Don't you dare try to make me out to be a racist when I have your best interests at heart."

The nice thing about the TV trays was that with me on the couch and Daddy in his chair, we were too far apart for him to reach over and slap me, which he might've done if we had been sitting at the table.

"You can have as many girlfriends over as you want," he said. "I am not a racist."

"Okay," I said. "Sorry."

We watched the news for the rest of the night. Daddy was getting madder and madder about the Scuds. Saddam kept shooting them at

the Israelis, and that made the Palestinians happy, and they kept showing the happy Palestinians on TV. "This is not the Arab perspective!"
Daddy yelled.

Every day he hoped the Americans would kill Saddam. He said
that then the Scuds would stop flying and the Palestinians would have
nothing to cheer about. More and more, this was all he seemed to
want from the war. He threw his pistachio shells at the TV when the
dancing Palestinians came on. He yelled, "This is not the real news!
Everyone knows they hate the Jews! Tell me the real news!"

I didn't really understand much about the Palestinians and the
Jews. I knew that the Jews had had the Holocaust, and that it had
been terrible, but I didn't really know what the Palestinians had had.
When I asked Daddy, he said, "Well, if you were interviewing me, I
would tell you. Too bad you're not interviewing me."

On Saturday morning, Daddy said we could go shopping so I could
pick out some junk food for Denise and me. He listened to the war
on the way to the store, and every time they said something that
made him mad—like that the Israelis wanted to enter the war—he
would turn the radio off. Then, a minute later, he would turn it
back on again. The other thing he didn't like was when anyone
talked about the Powell Doctrine, which said that we shouldn't kill
Saddam—just get the Iraqis out of Kuwait and go home. "Colin
Powell," Daddy said, turning off the radio for the second time, "is
the biggest stupid idiot that ever walked the face of the earth. He's
going to ruin everything. He's doing everything wrong."

"Maybe you could write to the president and tell him," I said.

"Well," Daddy said, "I already have written to the president."

"You have?"

He nodded.

"What did you say?"

"Are you interviewing me?" he said. "I thought you were going to interview the reservist."

"I am," I said.

"Well," Daddy said, "maybe if you ever decide to interview me, I'll tell you what I said to the president."

I didn't say anything. I wished he would stop doing this.

"Don't pout," he said.

"I'm not."

For Denise and me, I picked out Coke, Doritos, apple turnovers, ice cream, Hershey bars, Bugles, and macaroni and cheese. Daddy said we were going to be sick, but he let me have all of it. While we unpacked the groceries at home, my mother called.

"Hello, Gail," Daddy said. "What is it?" He was quiet for a moment while she talked, then he said, "Do you want to talk to Jasira? She's right here if you want to talk to her. I'm not really interested in talking to you myself."

He handed me the phone, and when I put it to my ear, I could still hear her talking to Daddy. "It's me now," I said.

She went quiet for second, then said, "That son of a bitch."

"Hi, Mom," I said, trying to sound friendly.

"Hi."

"Did you have a good trip home?"

"It was fine."

She didn't ask me anything about myself, so I said, "I'm on the school paper now."

"Oh yeah?"

"I'm going to interview Mr. Vuoso today about being a reservist."

"The guy your father hates?"

"Uh-huh."

She laughed a little. "Good."

"I might be a journalist someday," I told her.

"Well," she said, "it can be a very noble profession."

"I'll send you a copy of my article when it comes out."

"Thanks," she said.

"You're welcome."

"I have a new boyfriend," she said.

"You do?"

"His name is Richard. He's the guidance counselor at school."

"Oh," I said.

"He's very good with kids. Very appropriate."

We hung up a few minutes later, and I went in the living room to tell Daddy that I was going next door to Mr. Vuoso's now. "Do whatever you want," he said.

Charles had let me borrow a tape recorder from school, and I took that with me, along with my list of questions. He'd also gotten me a camera from the Audiovisual Department. He told me to try to take a picture of Mr. Vuoso in his army uniform, preferably in front of a flag.

As I walked toward the Vuosos', Melina came out of her house to get the mail. She was wearing green doctor pants, flip-flops, and a red hooded sweatshirt stretched tight across her stomach. "Hey," she said. Melina always said *hey* instead of *hi*.

"Hey," I said back, wishing I could be a Texan like her. I was about to turn up the Vuosos' front walk when she said, "Oh, I don't think they're home. I just saw their van pull out a few minutes ago."

"That was probably just Mrs. Vuoso and Zack," I said. "They're taking his kitten to the vet."

She raised her eyebrows. "Oh yeah?"

I nodded. "Mr. Vuoso is still home. I'm going to interview him for my school paper. About being a reservist."

"You're interviewing him all by yourself?"

"Uh-huh," I said. I shook my shoulder bag a little and said, "I have a tape recorder."

"Does your dad know about this?" Melina asked.

"Yes."

"He knows that you're going over to the Vuosos' when Zack and his mother aren't home?"

"That's the best time for Mr. Vuoso to do the interview," I said. "When it's quiet."

"Is that what he told you?" Melina said.

I nodded, even though I couldn't exactly remember how the conversation had gone. Even if he hadn't said it, I was pretty sure it was what he'd meant.

"So your dad doesn't know," Melina said.

"He knows I'm going to interview Mr. Vuoso," I said. "What's the big deal?"

"Jasira," Melina said. "Mr. Vuoso is a grown man. It's not appropriate for a grown man to spend time alone in his house with a thirteen-year-old girl. Do you understand me?"

"It's just an interview," I said. "God."

"A grown man who is a pervert and reads *Playboy*."

I didn't say anything.

"Can't you just interview him over the phone?" she asked.

"No," I said. I was about to tell her that I needed to take his picture, too, but then I stopped. Somehow I thought that if Melina knew I also had a camera in my bag, she really wouldn't let me go any farther. Instead I just said, "The tape recorder wouldn't work over the phone."

Melina sighed. "You're really stressing me out here."

"Why?" I said.

"Because I think you're lying to me, that's why."

"I'm not lying."

"If anything ever happened to you, I'd never forgive myself."

"Nothing will happen to me," I said, even though it already had.

I could feel Melina's eyes on me as I turned and walked up to the Vuosos' front steps. I knocked, and Mr. Vuoso looked happy to see me when he opened the door. Then he spotted Melina back on the sidewalk and he didn't look so happy anymore. "What does she want?" he asked.

"I don't know," I said, turning around to look at her.

"Hey, Travis," Melina called. "Have a good interview."

"Thanks," he called back. Then he looked at me and said, "Get in here, would you? She's making me nervous."

He shut the door behind me, and we stood facing each other. I always had a feeling that I wanted to put my hands on Mr. Vuoso's biceps and have him me lift me into the air simply by raising his arms. I'd seen him do this with Zack a couple of times, as if his son were a kind of barbell. I didn't touch his arms, though. I didn't touch any part of him, and he didn't touch me. He just took a long time looking up and down my body.

Finally, he said, "Can I get you something to drink? Or to eat? Are you hungry?"

"No, thank you," I said.

"What's your father doing?" he asked.

"Watching the war."

"Does he know you're over here?"

I nodded. "He's jealous. He thinks I should be interviewing him instead of you."

Mr. Vuoso laughed a little. "Oh yeah? Why's that?"

"To get the Arab perspective."

"The Arab perspective?" Mr. Vuoso said. He shook his head. "That's the whole fucking problem."

"Why?" I said.

"Don't get me started," he said.

"Why not?"

"I thought you wanted me to talk about being a reservist."

"I do."

"Then let's talk about that."

"Okay," I said, and I went and sat down at one end of the couch.

"What's in there?" Mr. Vuoso asked, pointing to my bag.

I took out the tape recorder, microphone, and camera, setting them all on the long rectangular coffee table.

"Ah," he said, "tools of the trade."

"I need to take a picture of you later in your uniform."

"Sure," he said.

"Do you have a plug for the tape recorder?"

"Uh-huh." He came over and took the adaptor from me, then got down on his hands and knees, ducking his head beneath the small end table beside me. As he did this, the side of his body brushed against my leg. Before I could decide whether to move or not, he was already pulling his head back out. "See if that works," he said, sitting up on his knees.

I hit Play and Record at the same time, then said, "Test one-two-three," copying what Charles had done at school. Then I rewound the tape and played back my own voice.

"Sounds good," Mr. Vuoso said, standing up.

I nodded.

"Where should I sit?" he asked.

"The microphone cord isn't very long."

He nodded, then sat close to me on the couch.

"It's longer than that."

He moved over a little.

I took out my list of questions and studied them one last time. Mr. Vuoso tried to read them over my shoulder, and I said, "Don't look, please."

"Sorry," he said, backing away.

"Are you ready?" I asked him.

"Ready."

I leaned forward and started the tape recorder. "Are you scared to go to war?" I asked, speaking clearly into the microphone. Then I held it in front of Mr. Vuoso's face, waiting for an answer.

After a moment, he said, "No, I'm not scared."

I brought the microphone back, asked, "Why not?" then replaced it in front of him.

"Well," he said, "I'm not in a fighting unit."

"Then what do you do?"

"You know," he said, "more humanitarian-type stuff. Passing out food or whatever."

"What about the gas?" I asked.

"What about it?"

"Saddam says he's going to gas all of the troops."

Mr. Vuoso shrugged. "I'll use my gas mask."

"What if it doesn't work?"

"It'll work."

"Daddy says it won't," I told him. "He says the gas is too powerful."

"Well," Mr. Vuoso said, "I guess I would expect that from someone who loves Saddam."

"Daddy doesn't love Saddam."

"Whatever you say."

"If you say he does," I said, "you're making an assumption about him based on his nationality. That's racist. Like when you used to call us towelheads."

Mr. Vuoso leaned forward and pressed the Stop button on the tape recorder. "Look," he said. "I didn't know you were going to ask me this stuff. It makes me look bad."

"You can't do that," I said, and I leaned forward and pushed Play and Record again.

Mr. Vuoso just sat there.

"Daddy doesn't like Saddam," I said into the microphone.

I put it in front of Mr. Vuoso's face and he said, "Fine. He doesn't like Saddam."

"He probably wants Saddam dead even more than you do."

"Fine," Mr. Vuoso said again.

I wasn't sure why I was defending Daddy so much. Mostly I just liked bossing Mr. Vuoso around, since he couldn't do anything back to me. "Are you ready for my next question?" I asked.

Mr. Vuoso nodded. "Yes. Please."

"Okay," I said. "Why did you pack rubbers in your duffel bag if you're married?"

Mr. Vuoso grabbed the microphone from me. He leaned forward and pushed Stop on the tape recorder. "How the hell did you know about that?"

"I looked in your duffel bag."

"Who said you could do that? Go through my personal things?"

I didn't answer him.

"Jesus," he said. He leaned back on the couch and rubbed his face with his hands.

"Why did you pack them?" I asked, even though the tape recorder was still off.

"Why do you think I packed them?"

I looked at him. He was still holding the microphone.

"Look," he said, "you can either ask me decent questions, or we can forget the whole thing."

"Okay," I said. I took the microphone back and started the tape recorder again. I asked him only decent questions from then on, about what it was like to live each day wondering if you were going to get called up, about who would run his copy shop if he did get called up, about who would raise and lower his flag. When I didn't have any more questions, I turned the tape recorder off. "Should I go change into my uniform now?" Mr. Vuoso asked.

"Sure," I said.

He paused for a second, then said, "Do you want to come?"

"Why?"

"I don't know," he said. "Never mind." He got up off the couch and went upstairs.

While he was gone, I thought about how he was in his room at that very second, taking his clothes off. I wondered what we would've done if I'd gone up there with him; if we would've used his rubbers before he even got to Iraq. I knew from movies that before men went away to war, the women they liked were supposed to have sex with them. You were supposed to do this because the men might never come back, and it would be a nice thing for them to think about before they got killed. On the other hand, Mr. Vuoso had said himself that he wasn't in a fighting unit.

I unplugged the tape recorder and packed it up, then picked up the camera. It was a 35 millimeter, which I had never used before. There was a light meter inside, and if you saw a red blinking dot, you were supposed to use a flash.

Mr. Vuoso came down while I was loading the film, all dressed up in his green uniform. The same one that had hung in the closet in the guest room above the *Playboy* magazines. "How do I look?" he asked.

"Fine," I said, snapping the back of the camera shut.

"Fine," he said. "Wow." He laughed a little.

"Ready to go outside?"

He nodded. "Let's go."

When we walked out onto the front steps, Melina was sitting on Mr. Vuoso's front lawn, her legs stretched out and crossed at the ankles. She had moved up a little from where we'd last seen her on the sidewalk. "Hey," she said. "How'd the interview go?"

"Oh," I said, because she had surprised me a little, being there. "Good."

Mr. Vuoso didn't say anything, just looked at her for a second, then made his way over to the flag. It was on the opposite part of the lawn from where Melina sat.

"Now I have to take Mr. Vuoso's picture," I said.

"Oh right," Melina said.

"Here, Jasira?" Mr. Vuoso asked. He had positioned himself directly in front of the flagpole.

"Sure," I said. "That looks good."

"Nice camera," Melina said.

"The school loaned it to me."

She nodded. "Cool."

I moved out into the street then, just off the curb, so I would be back far enough to get both the flag and Mr. Vuoso. "On the count of three," I said, then I counted, and Mr. Vuoso looked exactly the same on *one* as he did on *three*: arms straight at his side, mouth set, legs together. I took a few more shots, then walked back onto the lawn and said, "Okay, I'm done."

Mr. Vuoso relaxed a little then, and I wished I had a picture of that. "Thanks," he said, and he turned to go inside.

"See you, Travis," Melina said. She was still sitting on his front lawn.

Mr. Vuoso stopped and looked down at her. "Is there something I can do for you?"

"I'm waiting for Jasira," Melina said.

"I'll be right out," I told her. "I just need to get my tape recorder."

"Take your time," she said. "I can't get up without help anyway."

Mr. Vuoso headed for the front door and I followed him. When we got inside, he turned to me, angry. "What's her fucking problem?" he said. "Did you tell her something?"

"No."

"Then why is she fucking harassing me?"

"I don't know."

"You better not have told her anything."

"Stop yelling at me."

He went quiet.

"I didn't tell her anything," I said. "I didn't tell anyone. I could've, but I didn't. You can't yell at me."

He sighed and rubbed his forehead. "Okay," he said. "Sorry."

"I'm going home," I said, putting the camera back in my bag.
"That bitch ruined everything."

"She's not a bitch," I said.

"Yes, she is."

"I like her. She's my friend."

"I hardly get to spend any time alone with you," he said. "Then I get this one chance, and she has to ruin it."

I looked at him. "Why do you want to be alone with me?"

"Oh Jesus," he said. "I don't know."

"So you can hurt me again?"

"No. Of course not."

I got the good feeling then. The feeling of how wrong he knew he had been. It made me want to be nice to him, and I said, "Daddy is going to Cape Canaveral in March."

"Oh yeah?"

I nodded.

"You going to babysit yourself?" he asked.

"I guess so."

"Well," he said, "you'll be all grown up then."

"I'm already all grown up."

He didn't say anything.

"Remember?" I asked.

"Yes," he said quietly. "A thousand times, yes."

"I have to go," I said, picking up my bag. "Thank you for the interview."

We looked at each other for a long time. It was like a staring contest. Finally he took his hat off and held it in his hand. "I hope I don't get called up before March," he said.

"I hope you don't either," I said, and I turned and walked out.

Melina was waiting for me on the front lawn, just like I knew she would be. "See?" I said. "I told you I'd just be a minute."

"Help me up," she said, and I set my bag on the lawn so I could take both of her hands. As I pulled her, there was a moment when it felt like she was going to pull me back down, but instead we just kind of hung there, like a teeter-totter in balance. I put in some extra strength then, or maybe she did, and she came up all the way. "Thanks," she said, dusting off her butt.

"You're welcome."

"I was sitting there for a long time," she said.

"It wasn't that long."

"Felt like it was."

"Well," I said, "I have to go. I have a friend coming over."

"Thomas?" she asked.

"No," I said. "Denise."

"Nice," she said. "A girl."

"Well," I said, "bye," and I turned and headed home.

"What garbage did he tell you?" Daddy demanded when I first came in. He was sitting in his chair with his TV table and nuts.

"I don't know," I said. "I just asked him the questions and he answered."

"Give me the tape," Daddy said. "I want to listen to it."

"What?"

"I want to hear what kind of crap he told you."

"No," I said, "you can't."

"What do you mean I can't?"

"You can't," I said. "It's private."

"Private?" he said. "Nothing you have is private."

"It's confidential," I said. "That's what I meant. Because I'm a journalist."

Daddy laughed. "You're not a journalist. You're a kid. Now give it to me."

I looked down at my bag. I couldn't imagine playing him the tape. It wasn't just the words I was afraid of his hearing. It was the way I talked to Mr. Vuoso. Like I was the boss.

"Bring it," Daddy said, pushing his nuts aside on the tray table. "There's a plug right here."

When I didn't move, he pushed the tray table to one side and started to get up. I took a step back, and just then the doorbell rang.

"I'll get it," I said, taking my bag with me to the door.

It was Denise. "Hi," she said. "I hope you don't mind that I'm early. My mother had some errands to run, so she just dropped me off."

"No," I said, "that's fine." She was standing there on the front steps with a small duffel bag. I liked how she always wore makeup: blush, lipstick, and cream-colored eye shadow. When she put on her eyeliner, she always left a tiny sliver of space between the blue pencil and the very edge of her eyelid. It seemed like it was something she did on purpose, though I had no idea why. "C'mon in," I said, stepping aside.

"Thanks," she said.

"Daddy," I said, closing the front door, "this is Denise."

"Hi!" she said, and she made a small wave.

He was still standing there in the middle of the living room, waiting to take my bag. "Very nice to meet you," he said. Then he smiled in a way that I had never really seen before. Like he was trying to seem as cheerful as Denise.

"May I have a glass of water?" she asked, turning to me. "I went jogging before I got here, and I'm still really thirsty."

I was about to say sure, but then Daddy said, "Of course," and he went into the kitchen. When he came back with the water, Denise drank it down in one gulp. She had cream-colored fingernail polish on her hands.

"Thank you," she said, handing Daddy back the glass.

"Are you on the track team?" he asked her.

"No!" she said, like it was the craziest question she had ever heard. I worried that Daddy would get mad since he didn't like people acting like he was crazy, but instead he just looked a little embarrassed and said, "Oh, sorry."

"I'm just trying to lose weight," Denise said. "You know."

"Ah," Daddy said, nodding. "Well, you look very nice to me."

She giggled. "Thanks." Then she looked around the house and said, "This is a nice place."

"Give Denise a tour, Jasira," Daddy said.

I held on to my bag while we walked around the house, Denise sticking her head in different places. We finished up in my room, which Denise said was really boring. "You need to decorate this place," she said. "Hang some posters."

"Okay," I said, even though I was pretty sure I wouldn't do that.

"Your dad seems nice," she said, dropping her duffel bag on the floor and sitting down on the edge of my bed.

I set my bag next to hers, then sat down on the floor beside it. "He's not that nice."

"Why not?"

I shrugged. "I don't know. He gets mad sometimes."

"So?" Denise said. "My dad does, too."

I wasn't sure what to say. I couldn't tell if Denise's dad got mad in the same way mine did.

"They get over it, though," she said.

"I guess," I said, even though I was pretty sure Daddy had never gotten over anything.

"My dad does this thing where he introduces himself to the waitress every time we go to a restaurant. He's like, 'Hi, my name is Porter and this is my daughter, Denise. What's your name?' I hate it. It's so embarrassing."

I nodded. I tried to think of something embarrassing that Daddy did, but I couldn't. It actually seemed like it would be kind of fun, if he were to do something embarrassing.

"Plus, he talks really loud," Denise said. "He's like, 'HI, MY NAME IS PORTER AND THIS IS MY DAUGHTER, DENISE. WHAT'S YOUR NAME?' He has a hearing aid in his right ear."

"Oh," I said.

"At least your dad isn't deaf."

"Yeah," I said. Suddenly, though, I felt disappointed. Like I wished Denise wasn't there. She just didn't seem to be understanding what I was trying to tell her about Daddy. I wasn't even sure what I was trying to tell her. Mostly I just didn't want her to like him so much when she didn't even know him. "Is your dad a racist?" I asked.

"What?"

"A racist," I said again.

"No," she said. "Why?"

"My dad is."

She frowned a little. "Really?"

I nodded. "He said I couldn't go out with Thomas anymore because it would ruin my reputation."

"You're kidding."

"Nope."

"But your dad is an Arab."

"I know."

"He comes from the African continent."

"It ruined my mother's reputation for her to go out with Daddy, and now he doesn't want mine to get ruined by going out with Thomas."

"Geez," Denise said.

"I miss Thomas a lot," I told her.

"I guess I noticed you two haven't been hanging out as much."

"He's mad at me because I'm following my father's rules."

"I'd be mad at you, too."

"You would?"

"Definitely," she said. "Your father is wrong. So if you do what he says, then you're wrong, too. You're a racist, too."

"No, I'm not."

"Yes, you are."

"You don't understand," I said. "If I don't do what he says, he'll send me back to live with my mother."

"So?"

"I don't want to live with my mother."

"Wouldn't you rather live with her than be a racist?"

"No," I said.

"I would," Denise said.

"I can't leave Houston," I said. "Ever."

"Why not?"

I thought for a second, then told her the truth. "I'm in love with someone."

"Thomas?" she asked.

"No. Mr. Vuoso."

"Who's that?"

"The reservist. Who I interviewed."

"Oh."

"How would you feel if you had to move away from Mr. Joffrey?" I said.

"I guess I wouldn't like it," she said.

"See?"

"Does he like you, too?" Denise asked. "Mr. Vuoso?"

"Yes."

"How do you know?"

I wasn't sure how to answer that question. Finally I said, "Because he took me out for dinner."

"Really?" Denise said. "Like on a date?"

I nodded.

"Wow," she said. "Where was your dad?"

"At his girlfriend's."

Denise sighed. "You're so lucky. I wish Mr. Joffrey would take me on a date."

"You can't tell anyone what I just told you," I said.

"Of course not," she said.

"Mr. Vuoso could get in trouble."

Denise nodded. "He could get in big trouble."

"I'd definitely have to go live with my mother then," I said.

"Don't worry," Denise said. "I don't want you to go and live with your mom. Then I wouldn't have any friends!"

She smiled at me, and I wondered if that was really true, that I was her only friend.

Daddy knocked on the door then and asked if we wanted to go see a movie. It was called *Vincent & Theo,* and we sat across the aisle from Daddy so it would seem like we were there on our own. The movie was about the painter Vincent van Gogh and his brother, Theo, who took care of him. I think Daddy thought it would be educational, but it turned out that there were a lot of scenes where naked ladies posed for Vincent. Whenever this happened, Denise started to laugh. "Shh!" I told her, worried that Daddy would hear her and think it was me.

In the car on the way home, he said, "I had no idea there would be nudity in that film. I apologize, Denise."

"Oh, I don't care," she said.

"Your parents might care."

"No, they won't. They only care about violence. Not sex."

"Well," Daddy said, "maybe I should call and tell them anyway."

"I'm telling you, don't worry about it!" Denise said, and she laughed.

I thought Daddy would get mad to have a girl my age talking to him like that, but he didn't. He said, "Okay. Whatever you say."

It kind of bugged me, how Denise was allowed to act like that and I wasn't. Even if I started to act like her right now, I knew Daddy would get mad at me and tell me to cut it out. I knew it was too late for me to try something new with him.

Back at home, Mr. Vuoso was out in his yard, taking his flag down. "Is that him?" Denise asked me.

"Who?" Daddy said.

I didn't know what to say. I couldn't believe she was telling my secret already. Then she realized what she had done and caught herself.

"The reservist guy," Denise said, "who Jasira interviewed."

Daddy nodded. Then he looked at me through the rearview mirror and said, "Jasira, I want to hear that tape when we get inside."

"What tape?" Denise asked.

"The interview tape," he said.

"You can't listen to Jasira's tape!" she said.

"No?" Daddy said. He looked at her like he thought she had said something cute. "Why not?"

"Because," Denise said. "She's a journalist. Her sources are confidential. If you listen to that tape, you're breaking her confidentiality."

"Oh," Daddy said. "I see."

I couldn't believe it, that he believed Denise about confidentiality, but not me.

"You'll have to wait for the article to come out," Denise told him.

"But that's too long," Daddy said.

"Well," Denise said, "that's just too bad."

"This is a tough friend," Daddy said, looking at me in the rearview mirror again, and I nodded.

That night, after eating some of our junk food, Denise and I worked on her horoscopes. For Daddy's sign, Capricorn, she wrote: *Something very bad is going to happen to you if you don't shape up! Be nicer to other people and don't be a racist. Life will improve for you if you change your ways.* For Mr. Joffrey's horoscope, Cancer, she put: *You will fall in love with a beautiful woman who is just as smart as you but much younger. Try to give her a chance. You might be surprised!*

"What if it's a woman reading the horoscope?" I asked Denise.

"What?" she said.

"Then it's a woman falling in love with a woman."

"Oh," she said, "right," and she changed *woman* to *person*. She worried that it sounded too vague in terms of the message she wanted to send to Mr. Joffrey, but then she agreed that the other way was just too weird.

That night, I slept in a sleeping bag on the floor, while Denise slept in my bed. I thought about showing her my *Playboy* before we turned the light off, but then I changed my mind. I worried that she might think it was gross, like Melina did.

In the morning, Daddy made us pancakes. It was taking a long time for Denise to compliment him on how good they were, so finally I asked her, "Do you like the pancakes?"

"Oh yeah," she said. "They're great."

"They're the best ones I've ever had," I said.

She nodded, then took another bite. I looked over at Daddy, who was standing at the stove with his apron on, but I couldn't tell if he'd heard us.

Denise's mom came to get her at eleven. She rang the doorbell and introduced herself to Daddy and me, then complimented us on the Persian cyclamen we'd planted out front. Daddy got his scissors then and cut her a small bouquet. After Denise and her mom had pulled away in their car, we went back inside the house. As soon as he'd closed the door, Daddy said, "Okay, give me the tape."

"What?" I said.

"I want to hear that tape."

"But you told Denise you would wait for the article to come out."

"I did not. She told me I would have to wait, and I said that was too long."

I looked at him.

"Give it to me," he said.

I went in my bedroom and got it. There was nothing else I could do. When I came back, Daddy was standing in the informal living room, where the stereo system was. I gave him the cassette, and he put it in the tape deck. He stood next to the stereo while it played, like he was guarding it or something.

When the first part came on, about the gas masks, he laughed a lot. "Good for you!" he said. "You really gave it to him." When the part about the condoms came on, he didn't say anything. Then there was the sound of Mr. Vuoso turning the tape recorder off, then the sound of the tape recorder coming back on again, and me asking only decent questions. That was when Daddy hit Stop. "What did I just miss?" he asked.

"Nothing," I said.

"Why did the tape turn off?"

"Mr. Vuoso got mad that I asked him that question. He hit Stop."

"Then what happened?"

"He asked how I knew about his condoms."

"How did you know?"

"I found them in his duffel bag."

"You must be kidding me."

I shook my head.

"What kind of person goes through another person's things?"

I didn't answer.

"Do you go through my things, too? When I'm not here?"

"No," I said.

"Condoms," Daddy said, shaking his head. "You have a foul mouth and a foul mind." He came over and slapped me across my mouth then, like he was trying to fix that one part of me. When I pulled away, he grabbed my arm and squeezed hard. That hurt worse than the slap. With my arm, it was like the blood pressure cuff at the doctor's, when you think your arm will burst, but then the nurse releases the little valve, and you wonder how she knew to do it at the exact right moment. Except Daddy didn't let go.

In the morning, there were purple marks on my arm that were the same size as Daddy's fingertips. I put on a long-sleeve shirt and went and sat down at the breakfast table. Daddy had already started his Cheerios. "May I please have my tape?" I asked. "I need to transcribe it for my article."

"No," he said. "It's my tape now."

"But what about my interview?"

He shrugged. "You can interview me."

"I don't want to interview you."

He stopped eating and looked at me. "Fine. Don't."

We finished our cereal and I watched Daddy drink the milk from the bottom of his bowl. When he was finished, he got up and took his dishes to the sink. He rinsed them out with only water, then put them in the drainer. He didn't know that when I came home after school every day, I always rewashed them with soap.

EIGHT

I wrote the interview with Mr. Vuoso anyway. I still had all my questions on a piece of paper, and rereading them helped me to remember his answers. Sometimes, when I couldn't remember, I made up something that I thought he might've said. Like for the question "Can you receive packages in Iraq?" I made him say, "Yes, I can. When family, friends, and neighbors send packages, it helps me to know that people are thinking about me back home." At the end, when the interview was a little too short, I added a question: "What would you say to people who love Saddam?" "Well," I made Mr. Vuoso say, "I would tell them to look out, because I have my eye on them."

"Good ending," Charles said, when I showed him the interview on Monday, and I said thank you.

At lunch that day, I told Thomas what I had done. "Are you trying to impress me or something?" he asked. It was spaghetti day, and he had red sauce at the corners of his mouth.

"Yes," I said.

"Well," he said, "I'm not impressed."

"What would impress you?"

"Nothing," he said. "It's too late. You can never impress me again."
He stuck a forkful of twirled spaghetti in his mouth.

Later, between classes, I stopped at Denise's locker to tell her
about my conversation with Thomas. "He won't even give me a second chance," I said.

"Can you blame him?" she asked.

"I guess not."

Denise had a small round mirror on the inside of her locker door,
and after checking herself in it, she reached in her purse and pulled
out a small square of waxy-looking paper. She pressed it to her forehead, and when she pulled it away, it was clear with makeup grease.
"Eww," she said, showing it to me.

"I'm not a racist," I said. "I don't care what you and Thomas say.
I have to do what my father tells me."

"Why?" Denise asked.

"I just do."

"What if you don't?"

"He'll get mad."

"So?"

"He's really mean when he gets mad."

"I already told you," she said, "he'll get over it."

"No he won't," I said. "You don't know him."

"Just don't act so afraid of him."

"I can't help it."

"Pretend he's a dog," she said. "You know how you're not supposed to act afraid of dogs because they can smell fear?"

I nodded.

"Well," she said, "it's the same with your father. If you just ignore
him, he'll leave you alone."

I felt really bad for the rest of the day, like it was my own fault
that Daddy got mad at me. Like it would never happen if I would just

act in some certain way. Maybe Denise was right, but the problem was, I didn't know how to act the way she was describing.

Even so, I tried to practice being a little braver that night while we sat with our TV trays, watching the war. Colin Powell was giving a press conference on CNN, and it was making Daddy madder and madder. He talked a lot about Colin Powell's unsuitability for the job of Chairman of the Joint Chiefs. "Why is he unsuitable?" I asked. It had begun to occur to me that Daddy didn't like him because he was black.

"What do you mean, 'Why is he unsuitable?' Look at him! He wants to take Saddam home with him and tuck him into bed all safe and sound!"

"But why is he unsuitable for the job?"

"I just told you," Daddy said.

"But he's very smart."

"How do you know? Did you meet him?"

"No."

"Then shut it."

I tried to think of something else to say so it wouldn't seem like I was afraid to talk when Daddy told me not to, but I couldn't. Anyway, I didn't really care about being brave anymore. When Daddy told you to shut up, it was a kind of gift. A promise that he wouldn't hit you if you stopped talking right now. It just didn't make sense to ignore it.

At lunch the next day, Thomas said, "I thought of something you could do to impress me."

"What?" I asked. It was hamburger day and I was tearing open a plastic packet of mustard.

"Have sex with me."

"Okay," I said.

"Really?" he said. For the first time in a long while, he sounded kind of friendly.

"Yes."

"Great," he said. "When?"

"Whenever you want."

"Well," he said, "I guess we need to figure out a place first."

"We can't do it at my house," I said. I couldn't risk Mr. Vuoso and Zack telling on me again.

Thomas nodded. "We can do it at my house."

"What about your parents?" I asked.

"They'll be at work."

"What if they come home?"

"They won't. They never come home early."

"I'll have to walk home," I said.

"You can take a taxi," Thomas said. "I'll pay for it."

I thought about this, then said, "All right."

"Can we do it today?" he asked.

"Do you have a condom?"

"No."

"Then we'll have to wait until tomorrow. I have one at home I can bring."

"Where'd you get it?"

"From Mr. Vuoso's duffel bag."

"I don't want to use that racist's condom."

"You have to," I said. "It's the only one we have."

He said okay, even though he seemed kind of bothered.

When I met Denise at her locker later and told her about my deal with Thomas, she said, "No way! He's using you!"

"No, he's not," I said.

"He's totally using you. You can't have sex with him in exchange for not being a racist. That's ridiculous."

"But I want to have sex with him."

She looked at me. "You never told me that. You told me you were in love with that guy next door."

"I am," I said, "but I want to have sex with Thomas, too."

"Then you won't be a virgin anymore."

"So?" I said.

"So?" she said. "It's important that the first person you have sex with is someone special. Not someone who's using you."

"Well," I said, "I'm probably going to do it."

"I can't believe you," she said, and she closed her locker and walked away. I thought about chasing after her and telling her not to worry, that I already wasn't a virgin, that the person I had done it with was special, even if he had only become that way later on. But I didn't, of course. Besides the fact that I didn't want to get Mr. Vuoso in trouble, I didn't think Denise would understand. If I couldn't explain to her why Daddy was bad, then I probably couldn't explain why Mr. Vuoso was good.

All the way home, I thought about having sex with Thomas. I disagreed with Denise. I didn't think he was using me. I thought he was making a fair trade. Plus, I missed him. I wanted to be his girl-friend again.

After getting off the bus, I went to Melina's house. "Can I read my book for a while?" I asked.

"Sure," she said.

I followed her inside, noticing how skinny she always looked from behind. It was nice because for a couple of seconds, I could pretend she wasn't pregnant.

In the living room, Melina sat down on the couch beside a ball of yellow yarn and a tiny sweater, stuck on knitting needles. "That looks like doll clothes," I said.

"Yup," she said.

"Maybe when your baby gets older, you could give her those clothes for her dolls."

Melina shrugged. "If she plays with them."

My book was on the coffee table, where I'd left it last time. I wondered if Melina and Gil ever had company over, and if they ever wondered what it was doing there. "Shouldn't you keep this some- place else?" I asked, reaching for it.

Melina looked up from her knitting. "Why?"

"I don't know."

"There's nothing wrong with that book," she said. "I'm happy for anyone who comes into my house to see it."

She went back to her knitting and I looked around for a place to sit. There was a chair, but I decided to take the floor. I wanted to be far enough away from Melina that she couldn't see what I was read- ing. Plus, I liked being lower than her. It made me feel young.

The book said that if I decided to have sex, I could get a lot of diseases, and that I needed to use a condom. It said that the part of me where the orgasms came from would feel a vibration when Thomas's penis was inside me. There was a section, too, where it said that vir- ginity was seen as something that made a girl pure, but that really, a girl could do whatever she wanted and that she wasn't anyone's prop- erty. In a way I liked that, but in a way I thought it seemed very sad. Most of the time, I really wanted to belong to somebody.

"Jasira," Melina said.

I looked up. "Yes?"

"I have something for you."

"What?"

"Hold on a sec." She set her knitting down on the couch and went into the kitchen. When she came back, she handed me a key. "Here."

"What's it for?" I asked.

"My house. This way, if you ever needed to come over here, at any time, for any reason, you can just let yourself in."

"Really?" I said.

"Yes. And you don't even have to tell me why. You can just come over, watch TV, read your book—whatever."

"What if you're not home and it's just Gil?" I asked.

"It doesn't matter," she said. "He knows I'm giving you a key and that you might use it."

I thought about walking into Melina's house with only Gil there and how I wouldn't know what to say. It would be embarrassing. "Well," I said, "thank you."

"You're welcome," she said, sitting back down on the couch.

"I probably won't need it," I said.

She picked up her knitting. "You never know."

I tried to start reading again, but I couldn't pay attention. I kept thinking about coming into Melina's house and never leaving.

That night before bed, I told Daddy I was taking a shower, but really I shaved my pubic hair. I used one of the razors Thomas had given me, and I did it just like he liked, with the thin strip down the middle. When I was finished, I collected all the black hairs from the drain, wrapped them in a piece of toilet paper, and threw them away.

In the morning when I woke up, I dressed in my nicest bra and underwear. For the first time, I noticed that they didn't match. The bra was one of the gray ones Daddy had bought me, and the underwear was white cotton. I put my jeans and sweater on, then took my backpack in the bathroom and slipped Mr. Vuoso's condom in the small zip pocket.

When I got to school, Denise was waiting for me at my locker. "You're not going to do it, are you?" she said.

"Yes," I said. "I am."

"But why?"

"Virginity doesn't make me pure," I said.

"What?"

"I'm not anyone's property."

"I never said you were," she said. "I just don't think it's fair for Thomas to make you trade your virginity for his forgiveness."

"It's not like that," I said.

"Then what's it like?"

"I already told you," I said. "I want to have sex with Thomas. If it also helps him to forgive me, then that's good, not bad."

"This is stupid," Denise said. "I hate that I know anything about this." She walked away, and I watched the back of her hair bounce from how heavy she was stepping.

At lunch, Thomas wanted to know if I had remembered the condom, and I said I had. "Just one?" he asked, and I nodded.

After school, I walked past my bus and met Thomas in front of his. We got on together and took a seat toward the back. He held my hand all the way, like he used to in the halls at school. Every once in a while he would lean over and whisper in my ear, "I'm going to have sex with you." I wasn't sure what to say back to him, so I just nodded.

When we got to Thomas's house, he reached inside his shirt for a key he wore on a chain around his neck. He didn't take the chain off, just lowered his neck to the level of the doorknob and leaned forward a little until the key reached the lock.

The first thing I noticed when we got inside was how much bigger the living room looked without the Christmas tree. There was still a pine smell in the air, though. Thomas set the mail he'd collected from outside on a table beside the door. "Do you want something to eat first?" he asked.

"Okay," I said. I was a little nervous.

I followed him into the kitchen, with its clean counters and dirty breakfast dishes in the sink. Daddy always said we could never, ever leave dishes in the sink or the roaches would come, but I didn't see any bugs at Thomas's.

"What do you want?" he asked, opening the fridge and leaning slightly into it.

I pulled out a chair at the table and sat down. "What are you going to have?" I asked.

He shrugged. "I'm not really hungry." Then he knelt down and opened the crisper. "How about an apple?"

"Sure."

He got two of them and bit into his without washing it. I did the same, even though Daddy had always warned me about pesticides on fruits and vegetables.

"I'm getting really turned on," Thomas said after a few bites.

"You are?"

He got up from his chair and came and stood in front of me. He took my hand and put it on his pants. "See?"

I nodded, feeling his erection.

"Are you ready?" he asked.

"Can't I finish my apple?"

"Sure," he said, and he went back to his seat.

Thomas finished his apple first and ate the core and the seeds, too. It was like Daddy with his chicken bones. "Why do you eat the core?" I asked.

"It's just roughage."

"You want mine?" I said, offering it to him. Daddy liked me to pass him my chicken bones when I was done so he could crunch on the cartilage.

"No thanks," Thomas said, but he did take my core and toss it in the trash under the sink. Then he came back and said, "Let's go to my room."

We walked up the stairs. I went first, and Thomas squeezed my butt while I climbed. On the way to his room, he stopped at a hall closet, opened it, and took out a towel. "We'll probably need this," he told me. "There's going to be blood."

When we got to his room, he said, "I'm taking my clothes off," and in a few seconds he was naked. He had nice broad shoulders, from swimming I guessed, and his stomach had a couple of ripples in it. His penis stuck straight up, nearly hugging his stomach. He unfolded the towel and laid it out on the bed. Then he lay down on top of it. "Now you take your clothes off," he said.

It took me longer than it had taken Thomas. I had never played strip poker before, but I undressed as if that was what we were doing now. Where you only took off your bra and underwear at the very, very end.

"You shaved," Thomas said when I was finally naked.

I nodded.

"That looks good," he said. "C'mere."

I walked over to the side of the bed where he lay. He reached out and put a hand on the little bit of hair I had left. "Lie down," he said, scooting over to make room for me.

I lay down on the towel on my back. I was worried about how there wasn't going to be any blood at all, and what Thomas would think about it.

He rolled onto his side, then reached out and ran a hand over my stomach. "Your skin is soft," he said.

"Thank you."

He moved his hand up to my breasts and pinched one of my nipples. "Ow," I said.

"Really?" he said. "That doesn't feel good?"

"No."

He looked confused. "It's supposed to feel good."

"It doesn't," I told him.

He touched my nipple in a softer way and said, "How's that?"

"Better."

I wasn't sure what to do with my legs—whether I should open them or keep them closed. Soon, though, Thomas was moving in front of me, opening them himself. I thought we were going to do it then, but instead, he bent my legs at the knees then pushed them apart as wide as they would go. After he did that, he just stared. He stared and stared and stared. He wouldn't stop. Even though he wasn't touching me, it was exciting. It was like the girls in *Playboy*, having their picture taken by men photographers who wouldn't hurt them.

Soon, he put his head between my legs. He started to lick me there, or kiss me—I couldn't tell. It felt good, though. Warm. He did it for a long time before he finally pulled his head up and said, "I think you're ready."

"Okay," I said.

"Where's the rubber?"

"In my pocket."

He reached for my jeans, which I had hung over his desk chair, and took the foil packet out. I watched him tear it open and roll the condom on. It looked a little tight. "These are for guys with little dicks," Thomas said.

I wondered about Mr. Vuoso then, if he had a little dick. "Does it hurt?" I asked Thomas.

"It's okay," he said. "Don't worry about it."

I had closed my legs while he put the condom on, and now he opened them again. He lay down between them, this time with his face up by mine. I could smell myself around his mouth. The smell that was on my hands every time I had an orgasm alone.

"Listen," Thomas said, "I promise to be careful. I won't hurt you."

"I know," I said.

"Just tell me if you want me to stop and I will."

"But then you'll think I'm still a racist."

"What?" he said.

"You said if I had sex with you I would impress you and you wouldn't think I was a racist anymore."

This seemed to bother him. "Forget about that, would you?"

"All right," I said.

He reached for his penis then and started to put it inside me. "Just try to relax," he said.

"Okay."

He pushed a little harder now. "It'll only hurt for a few seconds."

I nodded. It was true. It did hurt. Not from anything tearing, like with Mr. Vuoso, but from the feeling that there wasn't enough room. But Thomas kept pushing anyway. "Oh my God," he whispered.

"What?" I whispered back.

"Nothing," he said. "It just feels so good."

"Oh."

"I'm sorry if it hurts," he said.

"It's okay."

"The first time is always painful for girls."

"Yes," I said.

He had an orgasm pretty quickly after that. I wasn't exactly sure what I was supposed to do to have one myself, so I just lay there. When he was finished, he rolled off of me and onto his side of the bed. We lay there for a long time, not talking. Finally he looked over at me and said, "Is there a lot of blood?"

I rolled to one side of the towel so he could see. There was no blood.

"Where is it?" he asked.

"I don't know," I said. "Maybe some girls don't have it."

He was quiet for a minute, then said, "It *was* painful, right?"

"Yes," I said.

"You just didn't look like it was bothering you that much."

"It was."

"I mean, it's not like I have a small dick or anything."

"No," I said, "you don't."

"Huh."

"Maybe you were just really careful," I said.

"I guess."

"Anyway," I said, "I'm glad it wasn't that bad."

"Yeah," Thomas said, "that's good."

"So you don't think I'm a racist now?" I asked him.

"Stop saying that," he said. "I already told you to forget about that."

"Sorry."

"It definitely should've hurt more," he said.

I didn't say anything.

"Why didn't it?" he asked. He rolled onto his side and looked at me. "Who'd you do it with before me?"

"No one."

"You never did it with anyone?"

"No."

"But what about the blood?"

"I don't know, Thomas." I got up off the bed and started to get dressed.

"I'm not going to be mad if you had sex with someone else," he said. "I'm just curious."

"I didn't," I said, pulling on my underwear.

"Was it back in Syracuse?"

"It was nowhere."

"Nothing popped," he said. "It's supposed to pop."

"Can you please call me a taxi?"

He sighed and went in the bathroom, the rubber hanging loosely off the end of his penis. When he came back, it was gone. After putting his clothes on, he walked out of the bedroom and thumped down the stairs. I followed him shortly afterward. He was standing at the kitchen counter, opening a jar of peanut butter. "The cab'll be here in fifteen minutes," he told me.

"Thanks," I said.

"Do you feel like a woman?"

"Uh-huh."

"I feel like a man," he said, spooning peanut butter into his mouth.

When the cab beeped, Thomas walked me outside and opened the car door. He gave the driver ten dollars and told him my address.

After he shut the door, the driver kept looking back at me through his rearview mirror. He did this all the way home. He had dark brown eyes and hair the same color. I thought he was probably Mexican.

At first I tried to stare back at him, but then I started to feel bad and looked away. It seemed like he was mad at me even though he didn't know me. When we got to my house and I opened the door to get out, he said something in Spanish. I didn't know what it meant, except for one word: *negro*.

That night while Daddy and I ate dinner on our TV tables, I thought about how I was a woman and he didn't know it. He just sat there watching the war. He thought I didn't have any privacy, but I did. I had a lot of privacy. The more privacy I had, the stupider he seemed to me.

After dinner, the phone rang. It was Grandma calling from Lebanon. Since the war started, she'd been calling a lot. Daddy hated it. I could hear him yelling at her in Arabic. Occasionally, mixed in with some of the Arabic, I would hear the word *Scud*. This was because Grandma thought Saddam was going to bomb her. She called every time there was an attack on Israel. After hanging up with her, Daddy would say how stupid she was. He said he told her fifty times that Saddam had no reason to bomb Beirut, and that no Scud would ever accidentally hit her. But she wouldn't listen. She would start crying and say he didn't love her.

The next day in school, Denise wanted to know if it had hurt. "Not too much," I said. She had come over to my locker before homeroom.

"Really?" she said. "It wasn't that bad?"

"No."

"What about blood?" she said. "Was there a lot?"

I shook my head.

"Wow," she said. "You're lucky."

"I guess so." It made me kind of mad that suddenly she wanted to know all about it, when just the day before she had said she was sorry she knew anything.

"Did you use protection?" she asked.

I nodded.

"What kind?"

"A rubber."

"Did it break?"

"No."

"The man is supposed to hold on to it when he pulls out so it doesn't fall off and spill inside you. Did he do that?"

"I don't remember," I said. "I think so."

"You could get pregnant if he didn't do it."

"I think he did," I said, mostly because I wanted her to be quiet.

After a moment, she said, "So that's it? He doesn't think you're a racist anymore?"

"No."

"Well, I guess that's what you wanted."

"Yes," I said. "It is."

At lunch, the first thing Thomas said when I sat down was, "Are you sore?"

"Not really," I told him.

"Oh." He seemed disappointed.

"You were very careful," I reminded him.

"I wasn't that careful."

"The cabdriver kept giving me dirty looks on the way home," I said. "I think he was a racist."

"Asshole," Thomas said, then we started talking about how we could find a way to report him.

When I got home that day, I called my mother. Somehow, being a woman made me miss her. "Hi," I said when she picked up the phone. I wondered if she could tell I was different from the sound of my voice. All day long, I had imagined myself to be calmer and more patient with people.

"Hello," she said. "How are you?"

"Good," I said.

"How did the interview go?"

"It was okay."

"Good," she said again. She paused, then said, "Aren't you going to ask me how I am?"

"How are you?"

"I'm great," she said. "I have a new boyfriend."

"Richard?" I said.

"I already told you?"

"Yes," I said. "Last time we talked."

"Well," she said, "he's very nice. Much nicer than Barry, that's for sure."

I was quiet. I never knew what to say when Barry came up.

"I really think you'd like him," my mother said.

"I'm sure I would."

"Richard and I went to a pickle festival last weekend."

"Oh."

"Guess who loves pickles?" she asked.

"Who?" I said.

"The Japanese," she said. "Who knew?"

We both laughed a little.

"Everything okay down there?" she asked.

"Uh-huh."

"Your father behaving himself?"

"Yes."

"What about Thomas?" she said. "Do you ever see your friend Thomas?"

"No," I lied.

She sighed. "That's too bad."

"You and Daddy said I couldn't see him."

"I know," she said. She sounded a little tense.

"Sometimes I see him in school," I said, "but I can't help that."

"The thing is, Jasira, I might've been wrong about him."

I put my hand on the kitchen counter. I felt a little dizzy to hear her say she was wrong about something. "What do you mean?" I asked.

"I'm just saying that maybe it wasn't fair to tell you you couldn't see him just because I had a hard time when I went out with your father."

"Oh," I said.

"I feel bad about it," she said.

"Does that mean I can see him?"

"Well," she said. "I don't know. Let me talk to your father about it."

"All right."

"You can't date him, though, because you can't date anyone. You're too young. But I think I might've been wrong about you visiting with him."

"Okay," I said.

After we hung up, I felt better than I had in a long time, like I had been smart to do the things I thought were right. I went in my room and lay down on my bed. I put my hands in my pants and started touching myself. I couldn't stop thinking about Thomas's face when he'd looked between my legs. I didn't care about the sex part. I just liked being stared at. I wanted to go back over to his house so he could do it again.

When my mother called back that night, Daddy yelled, "What do you mean you changed your mind?" After she answered him, he said, "Well, she's living with me, so I make the rules!" He hung up on her, then came back in the living room. "I don't care what your mother says," he told me. "You're not seeing that black kid. Do you understand?"

"Yes," I said, even though I didn't, not at all.

"If I ever find out that you've been seeing him, I will punish you severely. I mean it."

"But you're from the African continent," I said.

"Listen to me: When we fill out forms that ask our race, we check white. North African is considered white, and that's what we are. Then there's the black category for your friend. You see the difference? You should be glad we don't have to check this box."

He went back to his chair where he had been watching the war on TV. CNN was showing footage of Iraqi soldiers running away from a bunker just before an American plane bombed them. "Look at that," Daddy said, cracking a nut. "It's disgusting. There's only one man they need to kill, and they're not going to do it. It doesn't matter to kill the Republican Guard. These people will do whatever Saddam tells them. So if Saddam isn't there, they won't do anything. Just forget about these people."

I thought maybe he was trying to be nice to me by talking about the war, but I didn't feel like talking. I was mad that Daddy was a racist, and that he was trying to force me to be one, too. I wished I could just tell him the truth. That I had gotten as close as you could to a black person, and that nothing terrible had happened at all.

At lunch the next day, it was still bothering Thomas that there hadn't been any blood when we'd had sex. After I set my tray down and punctured my milk carton with my straw, he said, "Did you get raped?"

I looked at him. "What?"

"Is that why you won't tell me what happened?"

I didn't know what to say. I didn't know if I had gotten raped. I knew what rape was, of course, but I was pretty sure it was only when someone had sex with you, not when they used their fingers.

"Jasira?" he said.

"No," I said, "I didn't."

"What were you just thinking about now?"

"Nothing."

"Were you thinking about when you got raped?"

"No," I said. "I already told you. I didn't get raped."

"Then how come there was no blood when we had sex?"

"I don't know," I said.

"There was supposed to be blood," he said. "Since there wasn't, you either had sex with someone before you had sex with me, or you got raped. Which is it?"

"It's not any of those things."

He looked at me. "It was something, that's for sure."

"Maybe it's from using all those tampons. I got stretched out."

"I doubt it."

All the way home, I thought about what Thomas had said about getting raped. I knew that rape was bad, of course. I knew that when someone did that to you, it was scary and it hurt, just like with Mr. Vuoso. But then I didn't think it could be rape because I liked Mr. Vuoso again. On TV, people who got raped went to court and felt happy when the rapist was convicted and went to jail. They wanted bad things to happen to the rapist. But I didn't feel that way about Mr. Vuoso. Not at all. I didn't want him to get gassed or killed or called up or anything. I was in love with him, just like I had told Denise. Whatever he had done to me, it couldn't possibly have been rape.

When I got home, I did my homework, then went over to Melina's. She answered the door wearing an apron over her T-shirt and stretchy black pants. "Hey," she said. "Why are you knocking?"

"What?"

"Why didn't you use your key?"

"Oh," I said. "I don't know. I don't have it with me."

"Why not?"

"It's in my backpack."

"Well, next time I want you to use it."

"Even if you're home?"

"It doesn't matter if I'm home or not."

"Okay," I said.

"I gave it to you for a reason," she said.

I nodded. "Can I read my book?"

"Yes."

I followed her into the house. I noticed that her apron strings were tied in a tiny knot at the back since there wasn't enough of them to make a bow. "Help yourself," she said, gesturing toward the coffee table where the book sat.

"Are you making something?" I asked. I couldn't really smell anything cooking.

"Sort of," she said. "It's a salt substitute. You mix up all these different herbs and stuff in the coffee grinder, then when you put it on your food, it's supposed to trick you into thinking it's salted."

"You can't have regular salt?"

"Not with my blood pressure, no."

"Oh."

"Why don't you grab the book and bring it in the kitchen?" she said. "You can read while I grind."

"Okay," I said, heading for the coffee table.

I liked Melina's kitchen because it didn't look like ours or the Vuosos'. I could tell that she and Gil hadn't picked any of the kitchen designs that the housing development people had offered, but had done things their own way. I especially loved the big silver stove and refrigerator. They seemed like things you would find in a restaurant.

I sat down at the kitchen table, which also reminded me of a restaurant, a diner my mother and I used to go to. The seat cushions were covered in glittery red vinyl.

Melina went back to her work at the counter, and I opened my book to the rape section. It said that rape was any time someone

forced you to do a sex act you didn't want to do. It said that whatever
had happened wasn't my fault, no matter what kind of outfits I wore.
It said that Mr. Vuoso was an angry man with mixed-up values. If I
wanted, the book said, I could take up to three years to report him.

As I read, Melina turned the grinder on and off. She shook it a
couple of times, too, while it was grinding, like a maraca. When she
was done, she took the top off, licked her finger, and stuck it in the
mixture. "Is it salty?" I asked her.

"Come and taste it," she said.

I got up and went over to the counter. Melina licked her finger
again, stuck it in the powder, then said, "Open your mouth." I did,
and she put her finger in, and I closed my lips around it so that when
she pulled it back out, it was clean. I did this as if it was something I
had done with my own mother many times, only it wasn't. My
mother and I never did anything like this.

"What do you think?" Melina asked.

"It tastes like garlic," I said. "And parsley."

"But not salt," she said.

"Not really."

"Ah well." She unscrewed a small glass jar and began spooning
the powder into it. "Maybe Gil will like it."

"What would happen if you ate regular salt?"

"I could have the baby too soon."

"Oh."

"To save me, they would make me have the baby, even if she
wasn't ready to come out."

I nodded.

"They always save the mother first."

I was glad to hear this, since I didn't really care about Dorrie.

"But the mother always wants to save the baby," Melina said.

"Is that what you would want?" I asked her.

"Of course."

It depressed me that she said this, even though I knew that it shouldn't.

"I have to pee," Melina said, handing me the spoon. "Would you finish this for me?"

"Sure," I said.

She untied the little knot at the back of her apron and took it off. I started scooping the powder into the jar. A second later, I heard her say, "Rape?"

I looked up from what I was doing. Melina had stopped at the table on the way to the bathroom and was now looking down at my open book.

"Do you have a question about rape, Jasira?" she said. She was talking a little more quickly than usual.

"What?" I said.

"Why were you reading about rape?"

"I wasn't."

"Yes, you were," she said. "I want to know why."

"I'm reading the whole book," I said. "That's just the part I was on when you wanted me to taste the spices."

"There's no way you could've gotten this far in the book with the amount of time you've been over here. There's just no way."

"I know," I said. "I'm skipping around."

Melina looked at me. She didn't say anything for a long time. Then she took a deep breath and said, "Okay. It's your book. You can read whatever parts you want."

"Thank you," I said.

"But if you have any questions about anything you're reading, you should come and ask me."

"Okay," I said.

"I know about everything that's in this book."

I nodded.

"Do you have any questions you'd like to ask me now?"

I shook my head. "No."

"Are you sure?"

I nodded.

She sighed. "All right then."

After she'd walked out of the kitchen, I went and closed the book and put it back in the living room. Then I finished putting the fake salt in the jar and screwed the top on. Melina came back and said, "Where's the book?"

"I'm finished reading it," I said. "I put it away."

"Oh!" Melina said, and she put a hand on her stomach.

"What is it?" I asked, even though I could guess.

"Dorrie just kicked."

"Are you okay?"

She nodded. "She might do it again. Want to feel?"

"I should probably go home," I said.

Melina seemed disappointed. "Oh."

"Your spices are all in the jar," I said, picking it up to show her.

"Okay," she said. "Thanks."

I went home then and cried on my bed. First I cried because I hated the baby, then I cried because I felt terrible for hating the baby. Then I cried the hardest when I realized that hating the baby made me like my mother, whom I never wanted to be like, not in a million years. If I was mad at my mother for always being so jealous of me, then it seemed like Melina could get mad at me for always being so jealous of her baby. I didn't want that to happen, so I made myself stop crying. I told myself it was better to feel terrible and lonely than to hate a baby, and I tried to do that instead.

When Daddy got home that night, he was in a bad mood. He had heard on NPR that President Bush had announced a cease-fire with the Iraqis, even though Saddam wasn't dead yet—or even captured. He said Colin Powell should be fired for not doing his job, and President Bush should be impeached for ever listening to him.

He was also mad that Mr. Vuoso hadn't gotten called up in time to get gassed. Now that the Iraqis had surrendered, Daddy was pretty sure they wouldn't try anything funny against the Americans. "So this guy gets off easy," he said, "once again."

I wasn't sure what the other times were exactly, but I didn't want to ask, since Daddy was already upset. Instead I said, "Will Mr. Vuoso get called up at all?"

"Probably not," Daddy said, and he went and got himself a beer.

I tried to act depressed about this like Daddy was, but inside I was glad. Now, it didn't matter if I lost Thomas because he was black, or if Dorrie stole Melina from me. Because Mr. Vuoso was safe. He was going to stay living next door. And as long as he was next door, I would never be alone.

NINE

A week after the war ended, the shuttle launch in Cape Canaveral got canceled. Daddy said it was because there were some lug nuts with cracks in them, and because NASA had hired morons. He was mad that he was going to have to wait for his getaway weekend with Thena until April, which was when the launch had been rescheduled. He said he needed to recover from Colin Powell wrecking the war.

I was disappointed that Daddy's trip had been canceled, too. I had been looking forward to doing whatever I wanted for a couple of days, especially with Mr. Vuoso. I imagined his taking me out for dinner at Ninfa's again so we could celebrate that he wasn't going to get called up. Then I imagined that we would come back to Daddy's and use one of Mr. Vuoso's condoms to make love. I thought that by doing it nicely, it would prove once and for all that Mr. Vuoso hadn't raped me. That he had only been angry with me on that day he'd used his fingers.

My mother sent my father a letter saying she had read that his launch had been canceled, and that he and Thena must be so disappointed. She enclosed a picture of herself with her new boyfriend, Richard, at the pickle festival, and Richard was black. I guessed this was why she had changed her mind about my seeing Thomas. "This woman is the biggest hypocrite in the world," Daddy said, showing me the picture. Then he crumpled it up and threw it in the trash. After he walked out of the kitchen, I went and got it. It was true, what my mother had said about the Japanese liking pickles. There were a whole bunch of them walking around in the background.

I took the picture to school the next day to show Thomas, and he laughed and said, "Don't that just beat all?" I agreed that it did, and every time I saw him for the rest of that day, he would shake his head and smile. Even though Richard was black like Thomas, it was as if Thomas thought something bad had happened to my family by my mother dating Richard, and Thomas was glad about it.

Pretty soon, Daddy started calling my mother's new boyfriend Colin Powell. He said things like "Maybe your mother will marry Colin Powell," or "I guess your mother and Colin Powell must really like pickles." I waited for him to call Thomas Colin Powell, too, but we didn't really talk about Thomas that much.

Thomas and I hadn't had sex since that first time at his house. He said he wasn't going to do it with me again until I told him the truth about why I wasn't a virgin. When I told him I was telling the truth, he said he didn't believe me.

"What an asshole," Denise said when I told her.

"Yeah," I said, even though he was right that I was lying.

"Who needs him, anyway?" she asked.

I shrugged. I kind of did want to have sex with Thomas again. I liked how he seemed to know this enough to think he could black-mail me with it. At first I could've taken it or left it, but now that he was acting like he was depriving me of something, I played along. It made me feel like one of the girls in *Playboy* who always seemed to like sex so much. Sometimes I even said "Please?" to Thomas, but he would just say no, not until I was straight with him. Then I went home and had an orgasm thinking about how I loved sex but couldn't get any.

The school newspaper with my article about Mr. Vuoso came out after the war had ended, which made some of the questions seem a little out of date. Still, it was exciting to see my name in print.

"Who the hell is that?" Thomas asked, opening up the paper at lunch.

"My neighbor," I said.

"You mean that kid's father? You interviewed that kid's father?"

"He's a reservist," I said. "That's what the article was about."

"You could've written about something else," Thomas said.

"But I'm the war correspondent for the paper."

"No you're not. War correspondents are at the war. You're in Texas."

"I was interviewing someone who was probably going to be at the war soon."

Thomas stared at the picture of Mr. Vuoso in his army uniform. "He looks just like his stupid kid."

"I know."

"I hate that kid."

Denise thought my article looked good. She said if Mr. Vuoso really did get called up, I would have the interview as a souvenir of our time together. She was disappointed, though, by Mr. Joffrey's response to her horoscopes. She'd shown him the paper and told him to read it, but he said he didn't believe in astrology.

I didn't give Mr. Vuoso a newspaper, but Zack had a friend with a brother in junior high who gave Zack a copy. He showed it to his dad, and Mr. Vuoso came over one night to talk to me about it. "I never said this," he said, standing in our foyer and pointing to the last line of the article that my editor, Charles, had liked so much. "I would never have said anything like this."

I didn't know what to tell him. I was hoping he would like that I had made him sound tough and strong.

"None of this stuff sounds right," he said, hitting the paper with the back of his hand. "Go get that tape. I want to listen to it."

"I can't," I said.

"What do you mean you can't?"

"Daddy took it from me."

"What?"

"He was mad that I interviewed you, and he took the tape. That's why I had to make the whole thing up."

I thought he would feel sorry for me that Daddy was so mean, but he didn't. "This really fucking pisses me off," he said. "I'm a representative of the United States Army. These are not things that someone in the army would say."

"I'm sorry."

"Sorry?" he said. "What good is that?"

"I don't know."

"It's no good, that's what good it is."

"I'm sure no one in the army will see it."

"You can't say that. Plenty of kids in that school could have parents in the service. Jesus. I look like a fucking idiot."

"I tried to remember as best as I could."

He looked at me. "Your memory is for shit, you got that? Don't talk to me anymore. Don't come over; don't do anything. Just leave me alone."

"Why?" I said, and I felt myself starting to cry a little.

"Because you're a very stupid little girl," he said, and he walked out.

I didn't know what to do after he left. I stood in the same place for a long time, then I moved to the couch. Mr. Vuoso wasn't going to be nice to me anymore. He wasn't going to be sorry for what he had done. Instead, he wanted me to be sorry for what I had done.

Except what he had done was much worse. It didn't seem fair. I guessed I could still tell on him, since Melina's book said I had three years, but that didn't make sense, either. It would only make him madder.

There was still time before Daddy got home. I knew Mr. Vuoso had told me to leave him alone, but I couldn't help it, I went and knocked on his door. Zack answered. "Is your dad around?" I asked.

"That article sucked!" he said.

"Go get your dad."

"My dad never said those things. You made it all up."

"I know he's home," I said. "He just came over to my house."

"He doesn't want to talk to you."

"Just for a second," I said.

"Go home, towelhead."

"Don't call me that."

"Camel jockey." He looked over his shoulder to make sure his dad wasn't there, then added, "Raghead."

Suddenly, the little cat escaped. She raced out the open door and across the Vuosos' front lawn toward Melina's house. "Snowball!" Zack yelled. It was nearly dark, and he only had his socks on. "Move it!" he said, and he pushed past me out into the front yard. "Snowball!" he called again, hovering close to the ground and holding out his right hand like there was food in it. He made kissing noises, then said, "Snowball, Snowball," in a voice even higher than his regular one.

I stayed on the front porch, watching. When Zack had traveled across Melina's front yard and almost into the next one, I went inside his house and shut the door. Then I locked it. It was almost time for Mrs. Vuoso to come home, but I knew I had a few minutes. I walked quietly through the living room and into the kitchen, but Mr. Vuoso wasn't there. I went upstairs. He was in his bedroom, lying down with an arm across his forehead. A very dim light sat on his bedside table. It reminded me of the old-fashioned oil-burning lamps they used on

Little House on the Prairie, with the metal key on the side to turn it on and off. "Mr. Vuoso?" I said.

He took his arm off his forehead and lifted his head a little to look at me. "What are you doing here?"

"I just wanted to say I was sorry."

"Get out of here," he said, sitting up. "I told you never to come over again."

"But I said I was sorry."

Mr. Vuoso sat at the edge of his bed, staring at me.

"Can't you forgive me?" I asked.

"You crossed the line," he said. "This was too much, putting words in my mouth."

"I won't do it again."

He laughed in a mean way. "Well, of course you won't! I'll never give you another interview, that's for sure."

That made me cry a little, even though I didn't want another interview. It just seemed like everything he was saying was *never.* It all sounded so permanent.

"You can stop crying," he said. "It isn't going to work."

"I can't help it."

"Right," he said, like he didn't believe me.

"I can't."

Mr. Vuoso looked at me for a long time. Then he said, "Do you know what you do?"

I shook my head. I was afraid to hear what he was going to say, but I was also glad that he was at least talking to me.

"You act like you're so young and you don't know what you're doing, but you do know. You know exactly what you're doing."

"No, I don't," I said, because it sounded bad, what he was saying.

"Yes, you do. You know what you do to men."

I didn't answer him. Part of me still wanted to defend myself, but another part of me felt like he was giving me a compliment.

"Well," Mr. Vuoso said. "You're not going to rope me in anymore. I've had enough."

"I didn't rope you in," I said. "I just liked you."

"I don't want to be liked by you. There's something wrong with you."

"Stop saying those things," I said, trying not to cry again.

"I'll say whatever I want."

Just then the doorbell rang.

"Who the hell is that?" Mr. Vuoso asked.

"It might be Zack," I said.

"Zack?"

"I might've accidentally locked him out."

"For chrissakes," Mr. Vuoso said, and he got up and walked past me out of the room. I followed him downstairs and into the living room. When he opened the front door, Zack was standing there without the cat. "Snowball escaped!" he yelled. "That towelhead made her escape, and then she locked me out!"

I waited for Mr. Vuoso to tell Zack not to call me that, but he didn't. He turned to me and said, "Time for you to go home."

"You didn't find her?" I asked Zack.

"Did you hear what I said?" Mr. Vuoso said, and he grabbed my arm hard and pushed me outside. I didn't move after he shut the door behind me, just stood there on the steps, feeling dizzy.

A moment later, the door opened back up and Zack and his father came out. "Go home!" Mr. Vuoso barked when he saw I was still there. "Get out of my yard!"

I moved off the steps, and the two of them rushed past me and out onto the grass. Zack had his shoes on now and was carrying a plastic container of dry food, which he shook as he called, "Snowball, Snowball!" Mr. Vuoso called the cat's name, too. I walked home slowly, wishing I would see the cat somewhere, but I didn't. It was just the empty street.

In my room, I lay on my bed while my heart raced. I wasn't sure what I would do without Mr. Vuoso. He was the person I was closest to—even more than Thomas. He was the one who did things with me that he wasn't supposed to, since he was a grown-up. When someone did things with you that they weren't supposed to—things that felt good—that was when you knew you were special. That was why you couldn't lose them. If you lost them, you weren't special anymore. You were just blah. You would have to wait for someone else to do things with, but since the things you were doing weren't right, you probably wouldn't find anyone. You probably had to realize that you were going to be alone.

When Daddy got home that night, he said, "I just ran over a cat."

I looked at him. I had gotten out of bed and was sitting in the breakfast nook doing my homework. "What?"

"It ran out in front of the car," he said. "It was dark out. I couldn't see."

"Where is it?" I asked.

"What do you mean where is it? It's on the side of the road. It's dead."

"You didn't pick it up?"

"And do what with it?"

"I don't know," I said.

"I'm calling Animal Control," he said. "They'll come and get it."

"What did it look like?" I asked.

He took out the phone book and started flipping through the blue pages. "It was little and white."

I took a deep breath. "That's the Vuosos' cat."

"What?" Daddy said, looking up from the phone book.

"You hit the Vuosos' cat."

"How do you know?"

"Because," I said. "I went over there to see Zack this afternoon, and she escaped while we were talking."

"You must be kidding me," Daddy said. He put the phone book down on the kitchen counter.

I shook my head.

"What the hell were you doing over there? You don't even like that idiot kid."

"I don't know," I said.

"No!" Daddy yelled. "That's not true! We don't go knocking on people's doors because we don't know. You tell me right now why you went over there."

"I had to ask Mr. Vuoso something."

"Vuoso?" Daddy said. "What the hell are you talking about?"

"I had to tell him I was sorry about my article."

"What article?"

"About reservists. For the school paper."

"You didn't write that," he said. "I have the tape."

"I wrote it by trying to remember what was on the tape."

"You wrote a fake article about Vuoso?"

"No," I said. "I remembered a lot of the things right. It was just some of them that were wrong, and that made Mr. Vuoso mad."

Daddy paused for a second, then said, "Do you have this news-paper?"

I nodded.

"Go get it."

I went and got the paper out of my backpack and brought it to him. "Look at that idiot," Daddy said, poking his finger at the picture of Mr. Vuoso. Then he started reading. Almost immediately, he laughed. "This is what you remembered?" he said. "You have a terri-ble memory!" He read his favorite answers aloud, such as, "*No, I am not afraid to go to war. It's not that scary since I will just have to pass out food,*" and, "*We all need oil for our cars.*" When he was finished, he said that it was the best article he had ever read, and that he had clearly done the right thing to take the cassette away from me. Then he said, "Now go and get your coat."

When I came back from the closet, he was rummaging under the sink, pulling out the old white T-shirts with yellow sweat stains under the arms that he used to polish his shoes. "Here," he said, handing one to me. Then he grabbed the yellow dishwashing gloves hanging over the spigot and gave me those, too. "Let's go," he said, pulling his own coat from the chair where he'd left it.

We got in his car and drove to the end of our street, then took a left. I saw the cat as soon as she appeared in Daddy's headlights. She looked the same way some bugs did when they were dead, all curled up in a tight circle, as if being alive was the only thing that kept their backs straight.

"Go get it," Daddy said, pulling over, and I opened the car door. I was nervous to see her up close since I had never seen anything dead before. I wanted to hold her as soon as possible. I knew she would get stiff soon and I was terrified of feeling her that way.

The cat's eyes were open, which made me think she was alive for a second, but then when I saw how still she was, how the eyes weren't moving to look at me, I understood that she really was dead. I knew that on TV, when people died with their eyes open, other people brushed a hand over their lids to make them close. It was bad to have your eyes open if you weren't alive. I didn't think that would work now, though, since cats don't really have eyelids. Instead I just said, "Sorry, Snowball."

Daddy had made me think she would be covered in blood by giving me the rubber gloves, but she only had a small trail of it coming out of her left ear. Still, I put them on before lifting her onto the center of Daddy's T-shirt, which I had already laid out on the road. She wasn't stiff yet, but she didn't feel regular, either. Mostly she was just tight, like a flexed muscle. As I moved her, I realized I was closing my eyes a little, like when you watch a scary movie through your hand.

After she was on the T-shirt, I lifted all the edges around her, then carried her like a sack to the car. Daddy opened my door from the inside and said, "Just hold it on your lap."

We were quiet as we drove the couple of minutes back to our house. In our driveway, Daddy turned the car off and said, "Bring it inside."

"Don't you want me to take her back to the Vuosos'?" I asked.

"Are you kidding?" Daddy said. "So that asshole can call me a murderer? Forget it."

Inside, he stood over me at the kitchen counter, instructing me on how to wrap the cat first in Saran Wrap, then in several layers of plastic bags. He told me to put her in the freezer, and that we would put her out with the trash in a couple of days.

"Then they'll never know what happened to her," I said.

"Well," Daddy said, "you should've thought of that before you got her killed."

That night in bed, I couldn't stop thinking about what Daddy had said. That I had gotten Snowball killed. I thought he was probably right, but at the same time, I wondered how come it was me. I got her killed by trying to apologize to Mr. Vuoso, but I would never have had to apologize if Daddy hadn't taken my tape and I hadn't had to write a fake article. How did Daddy know where the problems all began? How could he be so sure? I guessed he was sure because he never thought he did anything wrong. But he did do things wrong. He was a racist, and he was mean, and it seemed to me that one day, somebody besides me was going to find out.

The next day at lunch, when I told Thomas about Snowball, he said, "I want to see her."

"You can't," I said. "She's all wrapped up."

"So we'll unwrap her."

"I don't know," I said.

"I'll do it. You won't have to touch her."

I didn't say anything. Mostly I was worried about the Vuosos telling on me if they saw Thomas visiting, since they might be outside looking for Snowball.

"C'mon," he said. Then he lowered his voice and said, "I'll have sex with you."

"You will?" I said.

He nodded. "I know you miss it."

When Thomas started talking like that, acting like I liked having sex with him so much, I got a good feeling. Daddy got mad when people made assumptions about him, but I liked it. It made me feel like someone wanted to know me. Even if they were wrong, it didn't matter. It mattered only that they were trying. "I don't have a rubber," I said.

"So?" he said. "I'll pull out."

"Will that work?"

"Duh."

"Okay," I said.

"Okay," he said, and he bumped my leg with his under the table.

When Thomas and I got off the bus that afternoon, Zack was outside, calling for Snowball. "Hey, Zack!" Thomas said, like they were old friends.

Zack ignored him.

"I heard you lost your cat," Thomas said.

"Screw off," Zack muttered.

"What's that?" Thomas asked.

Zack wouldn't repeat himself. Instead he yelled, "Snowball!" a little louder than usual.

"Snowball!" Thomas yelled, too.

"Don't!" Zack wailed. "She's scared of you. She'll never come if she thinks you're here."

"What if she never comes at all?" Thomas said.

"C'mon," I said to him. "Let's go."

"What if she's dead?" Thomas asked.

"Screw you," Zack said. "What do you know?" and he turned and walked in a different direction.

Inside my house, Thomas went straight for the freezer. "Is that her?" he asked, pointing to the oddly shaped package wrapped in a white plastic grocery bag, and I nodded.

He pulled her out and set her on the counter. She made the same scraping sound as a block of ice would. I guessed she actually was a block of ice. "I can't believe he made you wrap her," Thomas said, untying one of the many knots I had made with the bag handles.

"It was my punishment," I said. "I killed her."

"Bullshit," Thomas said. "You can't even drive."

I moved closer to him then, leaning my head against his shoulder.

"You sure put her in enough bags," he said, since every time he took one off, there seemed to be another.

"Daddy wanted to be sanitary."

"Three is sanitary. Five is crazy."

Finally he got down to the Saran Wrap. You could see her pretty clearly through it. "Oh, man," Thomas said. "That's just sad."

"She was a good cat," I said.

He nodded. "Are her eyes open?"

"Uh-huh."

"Why didn't you close them?"

I shrugged.

"We should close them now."

"We can't," I said. "She's frozen."

"Well," Thomas said, "I bet if we thawed her out a little, it would work."

"There's not enough time," I said.

"Sure, there is." He put his arms around me and kissed me lightly a few times on the cheek. He said, "We can go in your room and by the time we come out, she'll be soft."

"What if she smells?"

"She won't."

"Are you sure?" I asked, and he whispered in my ear that he was.

We went in my room then and Thomas told me to take off all my clothes. When he just stood there watching me, I said, "Aren't you going to take off yours, too?"

He shook his head. "I want to do it where you're naked and I'm not. I'll just unzip my jeans."

"Why?"

"Because it's sexy. It shows how much you want it."

I thought this made sense, so I said, "Okay." When all my clothes were off, he told me to get on all fours on the bed. "Why?" I asked again.

"Because that's how I want to do it."

"But I can't see you," I said.

"You'll feel me."

I did what he told me, even though it made me feel kind of embarrassed. I worried that by being that way, he could see inside my butt. I tried to turn around a little to look at him, but he told me not to. He said to just keep looking forward and not worry about it. I heard his zipper, then I felt him poking me with his penis. He tried to push it into a place where there wasn't a hole. "It's not there," I said.

"Hang on," he said.

After another try, he found the right spot. I was already excited from his kissing me in the kitchen, so it went in pretty easily. "Oh, man," I heard him say. Then he asked, "Does that feel good?"

"Yes," I said, even though I wasn't sure if it did. It didn't feel bad.

It just felt like exactly what it was: Thomas holding my hips and sliding in and out of me.

"Are you going to come?" he asked a minute later.

"I don't think so."

"The girl has to come first," he said.

"I don't think I'm going to."

"Why not?"

"I don't know," I said. "I don't know how to if I'm not by myself."

Just then, Thomas reached around the front of me and put his hand between my legs. I made a noise then that I didn't mean to make, like a long *ooh*.

"Can you come like this?" Thomas asked me.

"Yes," I said, and then very quickly after he started rubbing me, I did. I made another noise, like my voice was shuddering. It seemed so much better like this, to have an orgasm with someone else. It was incredible to think that I wasn't the only person who knew how to make myself feel good.

"Okay, now I'm going to come," Thomas said.

"Okay."

I felt him pull out of me. "Roll over," he said.

I rolled over. Instead of putting himself back inside me, though, he knelt in front of me, staring between my legs and touching himself. When it was time for him to come, he pointed his penis at my stomach and that was where the stuff came out. Some of it went in my belly button.

When he was finished, he lay down next to me on the bed. "Can I have a tissue?" I said.

"Hold on a second."

"I need a tissue," I said, feeling the tickle of liquid on my skin. "It's going to spill on the bed."

"Okay," he said, and he stood and went in the bathroom. When he came back with the tissue, he cleaned me up himself. "Did you like that?" he asked.

"Yes," I said. I wasn't actually sure if I'd liked it or not, but when Thomas's voice made it sound like he thought that I had, it made me want to agree.

"Next time I'm going to come on your tits," he said.

"Okay," I said. I tried not to show how excited I was that he seemed to be talking about doing it again without my having to tell him why I wasn't a virgin.

He balled up the tissues then and said, "Let's go see if she thawed."

She hadn't. Plus she was starting to stink a little. Thomas said he didn't smell anything, but I figured he was probably just doing that so he wouldn't have to admit that he'd been wrong. "We have to wrap her back up," I said.

"Or," Thomas said, "we could put her in the microwave. Just for, like, thirty seconds."

"No," I said. He was beginning to remind me of the boys at school who told gross jokes about animals in ovens and dryers and dishwashers.

"It's disrespectful not to close her eyes," Thomas said.

"It's more disrespectful to put her in the microwave."

"Not if you're only doing it to close her eyes."

I thought about this. I couldn't really tell what was right. "What if she starts to stink some more?" I said.

"She won't," Thomas said. "Not for thirty seconds."

She did, though. It wasn't too bad, but it wasn't very good, either. Even Thomas admitted he could smell her now. Plus, when the thirty seconds was up, he still couldn't shut her eyes. "We have to put her back in the freezer," I said, and this time he listened to me.

I watched Thomas wrap Snowball just as Daddy had watched me the night before. When he didn't do something right, I told him, but not in an unfriendly way, like Daddy. Thomas didn't like that he had to put her back inside so many plastic bags, but I said that if he didn't, I could get in trouble. "How are you going to get in trouble?" he asked. "I mean, is your dad seriously going to check how many bags she's in before he throws her in the trash?"

"I don't know," I said. "He might."

"I just find that very hard to believe," Thomas said, which kind of hurt my feelings, even though it was probably true that Daddy wouldn't check the bags. I just didn't know how to explain to Thomas that that wasn't the point. The point was that at all times, I needed to keep as many things as possible the way Daddy liked them.

We kissed good-bye in the living room; then I opened the front door. When we stepped outside, Mr. Vuoso was in his yard, taking down his flag. "There's the guy from your article," Thomas said, and he laughed a little.

"Shh," I said.

"Why?" Thomas asked.

"He doesn't really like the way the article came out."

Thomas shrugged. "It seemed all right to me. I mean, for being about an asshole."

Just then, Mr. Vuoso started walking toward us. "Oh no," I said.

"I'll handle this," Thomas said.

"Jasira," Mr. Vuoso said, stepping onto our lawn. He had his triangle-folded flag tucked under his arm.

"Yes?"

"What's going on here?"

"Nothing," I said.

"What do you mean what's going on here?" Thomas asked.

"Am I talking to you, son?" Mr. Vuoso said.

"I'm not your son," Thomas said.

"Does your father know he's over here?" Mr. Vuoso asked me.

I didn't say anything.

"Leave her alone," Thomas said, and he changed the way he was standing so that he suddenly seemed a little taller.

Mr. Vuoso ignored him. "You come and talk to me when he's gone," he said, then he turned and walked back to his house.

"Who the fuck does he think he is?" Thomas asked, so that Mr. Vuoso could probably still hear.

I shrugged.

"Don't you dare go and talk to him," Thomas said.

"I won't," I said, and I meant it. Something about the way Mr. Vuoso was acting was reminding me of the day he had hurt me.

"Go in the house and lock the door right now," Thomas said.

I nodded and went inside. After locking the door, I pulled back the living room curtain and waved to Thomas as he walked down the street. When he was out of sight, I let the curtain drop and went in the kitchen to look things over. Everything seemed fine except it still kind of smelled. I got a can of air freshener from the cupboard in the laundry room and sprayed it around, only that just made a grosser smell of the dead cat plus gardenias. I went around the house opening windows then, and while I was doing the ones in the living room, the doorbell rang. I froze. "Jasira," I heard Mr. Vuoso say. I didn't move. "I know you're in there," he said a second later.

"Yes?" I said, trying to sound as friendly as possible.

"Open the door!" he said.

I didn't open it.

"Now!" he yelled.

Finally, I pulled the living room curtain aside and looked out at him. "What is it?" I asked.

"Open this door," he said, craning his neck a little from where he stood on the steps.

"Just tell me what you want to say like this."

"Goddammit!" he said. "I told you to come and see me when that kid left."

"I don't want to come and see you," I said.

"Oh no?" he said.

I shook my head.

He just stood there on the steps for a second. Then he came down and walked over to the window screen. He didn't watch out for the little marigolds Daddy had planted under the sill, just stepped right on them. "What were you doing with that nigger?" he demanded.

"Nothing."

"You tell me what you did with him, or I'm going to come over and tell your father he was here, and I don't care how hard he beats you."

It made me catch my breath a little, to hear someone talk about Daddy beating me. "Please don't tell Daddy that Thomas was here," I said.

"Just tell me what you did with him."

I didn't say anything.

"Did you let him fuck you?"

I still didn't say anything.

"Jesus Christ."

"You said you wouldn't tell on me."

"Jesus Christ," he said again.

When Daddy came home, he said, "What smells?"

"Huh?" I said. I breathed deeply to show him that I had no idea what he was talking about.

"There's a bad smell in here," he said, pointing his nose in different directions.

"I can't smell it," I said.

"Is it the garbage?" He opened the door under the kitchen sink. The bag was full, and he said, "Take out this garbage, Jasira."

I nodded and went to tie up the white plastic bag.

"We're going to get bugs if you don't keep up with your chores," he said. "And if we get bugs, you're going to pay for the exterminator out of your savings."

"Okay," I said.

"They're very expensive," he warned.

I waited for Daddy to tell me to take Snowball out, too, but he didn't. I wasn't sure if he'd forgotten, but I didn't remind him. I knew she was dead, but still, I couldn't stand to think of her getting smushed in the garbage truck.

The next day at school, Thomas wanted to know what had happened with Mr. Vuoso. "Nothing," I said. "He came over and tried to talk to me but I wouldn't open the door."

"What did he want to talk about?"

"I don't know," I lied.

Thomas was quiet for a second. Then he said, "Is he in love with you?"

"What?"

"Does he love you?"

"No," I said, although the idea that Thomas thought Mr. Vuoso loved me made me want to hear more.

"He talks to you like he does," Thomas said. "That's what you do when you love someone. You boss them around, but they don't notice. Only other people can notice."

"I don't think he loves me," I said.

"He might."

"I don't think so."

Still, for the rest of the day, I couldn't stop thinking about it.

Mostly, I thought Mr. Vuoso didn't like me, but that he wanted to fool around. It had never occurred to me that there might be something else.

In study hall, Denise and I passed notes back and forth. Hers said: *Mr. Joffrey has a girlfriend. I can't believe it.* Then she made a frowning face with a small tear on the cheek.

I wrote back: *How do you know?*

She said: *Because he finally read my horoscopes, and he said the one about his girlfriend was really accurate.*

What did it say? I asked her.

That if you're a Gemini, this month will find you successful in your career and radiating beauty.

Oh.

It's like he was shoving it in my face, she wrote.

Maybe he just wanted to let you down easy.

No, she wrote, *he wanted to shove it in my face!*

I'm sorry, I wrote.

She asked me how it was going with Mr. Vuoso, and I said fine. I didn't tell her that he had gotten mad about my article, that he had frightened me the day before, that he might be in love with me.

She wrote back that she was jealous, that I was lucky, that if I found out his birthday, she would write him a good horoscope for next month.

That afternoon when I got home from school, I did my homework. Then I turned on the TV and set up the ironing board. Since I had lost my job with the Vuosos, Daddy had offered to pay me to press his shirts instead of taking them to be laundered. He gave me a dollar fifty each, and said that as soon as I started doing a crappy job, he would head straight back to the cleaners.

Each shirt took about fifteen minutes, and I had finished nearly five of them when the doorbell rang at around six. I went to the front door, but instead of opening it, I checked out the window first to see who it was. When I saw Mr. Vuoso, I opened the window and said, "Hi."

"Hi," he said. He seemed a lot calmer than he had the day before. "Can I come in?"

"I don't know," I said. "Daddy might be home soon."

Mr. Vuoso looked at his watch. "Are you sure? It's a little early yet."

"Can't we just talk like this?"

"Sure," Mr. Vuoso said, even though I could tell he seemed a little disappointed.

"Is everything okay?" I asked.

"Well," he said, "mostly I just wanted to apologize for yesterday. How I acted. I'm sorry."

"It's okay."

"No," he said. "It's not. That was no way to talk to you."

I didn't say anything. I didn't think anything would ever feel so good to me as when Mr. Vuoso felt sorry.

He took a deep breath then. "Also, I wanted to say good-bye."

"Good-bye?" I said.

He nodded. "I got called up."

I looked at him through the screen. He had stayed on the steps today and was just kind of leaning over toward me as we spoke. "But the war is over," I said.

He laughed a little. "The fighting part is over. They still need plenty of help."

I didn't understand. Not when Daddy had said that Mr. Vuoso probably wouldn't get called up. But I guessed that Daddy didn't know what he was talking about. He didn't know what he was talking about a lot of the time. "Could you get killed?" I asked.

"I don't think so," Mr. Vuoso said. "I mean, I hope not."

"I didn't think you would have to go since the war ended."

"Well, that makes two of us."

"I don't want you to go."

"I'll be back," he said.

I didn't know what to say then.

"Anyway," he said, "good-bye."

I watched him turn and go down the front steps. When he had gotten about halfway down the front walk, I said, "Wait," and I went and opened the front door.

He stopped walking and turned around.

"You can come in," I said.

He paused for a moment, then nodded and walked back toward me. On his way into the house, there was a breeze of his cologne. After looking around the living room for a moment, he went and sat in Daddy's chair. "C'mere," he said. "Come and sit with me."

I stood still. It was taking me a minute to get used to his being so friendly. "Thank you for not telling on me about Thomas," I said.

"Thomas?"

"My friend from yesterday."

"Oh," he said. "I don't really want to talk about that."

"Sorry."

"Can't you come over here?"

I walked toward him slowly.

"Sit with me," he said, patting his lap. As soon as I sat down I felt his penis against my bottom. I knew he wanted to do things with me, and that I should do them since he had gotten called up. Mostly, though, I felt like I should do them because I had done them with Thomas and Mr. Vuoso knew that. I felt like if I said no, he would ask me why I would do things with Thomas and not with him, and I wouldn't have an answer.

After I had sat in his lap for a while, he started rubbing his hand on my breasts. He pushed my shirt up and then my bra, then he leaned down and bit one of my nipples. "Ow," I said, and I put a hand over the breast he had bitten. "Don't do that." He didn't do it anymore, but he made a strange face at me. A face like he thought what I had said was funny. "Okay," he said, "we'll do something else."

He told me to kneel on the floor then, and I did, and he unzipped his pants and put his penis in my mouth. At first he moved my head for me in the way he wanted it to go, then he took his hands away so I could do it on my own. When I stopped doing it right, he put his hands back over my ears and started showing me again.

After a while, he told me to stop and to stand up. I did, and he unbuttoned my jeans and had me step out of them, along with my underwear. Then he had me lie down beside the coffee table on my stomach and he put his penis inside. It was just like the day before with Thomas, when he had clothes on but I didn't, and he was behind me. But he didn't reach around to rub me like Thomas had. He just pushed my head into the carpet.

After he had moved in and out for a while, he pulled out and told me to get up. He sat back in Daddy's chair and put his penis in my mouth again. I tried to act brave about how I would have to swallow the stuff, but at the last minute, he pulled his penis out of my mouth and pointed it at my face. Some went across my lips, and some went on my cheek. "Good," he told me, putting his penis away. "That was good." Then he zipped up his pants and said he would think about me in Iraq.

After he left, I put my hands to my face to keep it from dripping onto the carpet. I could feel it starting to fall from my skin. I walked to the bathroom naked, holding the drips, then got in the tub without looking in the mirror. I didn't want to see myself like that.

In the shower, I wanted Thomas. I wanted to tell him that he definitely wasn't right about Mr. Vuoso being in love with me. I wanted to tell him that I wished I had still been listening to him about not opening the front door.

I got out and toweled off. I put on new clothes and put my old ones in the washer with some of Daddy's, since he didn't like me wasting water with a half-full load. Then I went back to my ironing. I finished two more shirts before Daddy came home. When he saw them, he said they were better than the cleaners. He took out his wallet to pay me, and I tried not to cry from his being so nice.

TEN

Mr. Vuoso didn't get called up. I kept waiting for him to leave, but he didn't. He stayed. Every day I saw him taking out the trash, getting his mail, taking down his flag, pulling in and out of his driveway. It was a hard thing to think about. That he had lied to me, that I had believed him, that now he seemed to feel fine while I was ashamed. I was ashamed for being stupid. For doing something I hadn't wanted to do, and then, every day, having to look at the person I'd done it with.

The worst part was that when he saw me, he didn't ignore me. He smiled, or waved, or called out, "Hi, Jasira! How are you?" The second worst part was that I would smile back, or call back, "Fine, thank you." At first when he acted like that, so sincere, I thought maybe he was still getting called up, just that he hadn't left yet. Then when I asked Zack about it one afternoon, he said, "My dad's not getting called up! Didn't you hear, retard? The war's over. We kicked Saddam's ass."

I especially felt ashamed in front of Melina. When I saw her outside, I wouldn't go out. If she came outside while I was outside, I would make up a reason why I had to go in. I didn't go to her house anymore to read my book, and I didn't answer my door when I thought she was on my front steps. I ran out of tampons, and instead of asking her to get me more, I just used pads. Wearing pads was one of the few things that made me feel better anymore. They were like a punishment I could give to myself.

I thought I deserved to be punished because that time with Mr. Vuoso, my body had been excited. In my mind I hadn't been, but then when Mr. Vuoso had pushed himself into me, it had gone in easily. He had said things like, "You really want it, don't you?" and "This is what you like, huh?" I felt betrayed by my body. I felt like I had been thinking one thing in my head, but then in this other part of me, it was something very different. Whatever part of me was in control of between my legs wanted bad things to happen because it did the thing that made it easier for bad things to happen.

I got dizzy, thinking about all of this. Sometimes, when I thought too hard, my fingers tingled, and I could feel the inner lining of myself shrink up and curl into a ball. Like Snowball had been on the road.

In French class, Madame Madigan had to ask me three times how I was doing before I looked up and said, "*Je vais très bien.*" Thomas had to repeat himself so often he started calling me deaf. Only Denise seemed to understand why I couldn't pay attention to anything. *That guy doesn't love you anymore?* she wrote in a study hall note. *Yes,* I wrote back, and I drew the frowning face with the little tear like she had drawn for Mr. Joffrey.

Denise invited me to stay over at her house that Saturday, and I said I would ask Daddy. "Sure," he said, "as long as you do all your chores first." So I spent Saturday morning scrubbing my bathroom and vacuuming. Daddy also wanted me to help him weed the flower beds we had planted in front of the house, since we had stopped taking care of them after my mother went back to Syracuse. While we were outside, kneeling in the dirt with our work gloves, Melina's husband, Gil, came over. He said something to Daddy in Arabic, and Daddy answered him back. I knew they had small conversations like this sometimes when they met out in the street. Daddy would always come inside and say that Gil had a good accent but predictable politics.

"Nice day for gardening," Gil said now in English. He wore jeans and house slippers and carried his mail tucked under his arm. One thing I noticed about him was that he wore glasses only on the weekends, the same way other people wore sweatpants or old sneakers.

"Yes," Daddy said, looking up into the sun. "Jasira and I thought we should take advantage."

I hated it when he made it seem like something was our idea together, when really it was just his. Even if it was only gardening.

"Well," Gil said, "I don't want to interrupt you guys. I just came over to invite you for dinner. Melina thought we should all celebrate the end of the war."

"Celebrate?" Daddy said. "What do you mean celebrate?"

I thought the way Daddy was talking would scare Gil, but he didn't seem to notice anything. He just smiled a little and said, "You're not happy?"

"No," Daddy said. "I'm not."

Gil shrugged. "We don't have to celebrate. We can just eat."

I hoped Daddy would say no, we couldn't come. I hoped he would be his usual self and keep us away from other people. But he didn't. He said, "This is a very nice invitation. We would be happy to come."

"Great," Gil said, and he told us to come on Friday at seven-thirty.

After he left, Daddy said, "This guy is as bad as that idiot Vuoso, making assumptions about me."

"Then why do we have to go for dinner?" I asked.

He looked at me. "I thought Melinda was your best friend."

"Melina," I said.

"We don't call adults by their first names," he said.

"Sorry."

After lunch, he drove me over to Denise's. He waited in the car until she opened the front door, then drove away. Denise waved to him, but I don't think he saw. "C'mon in," she said. "We're just having lunch." I told her I'd already eaten, but she said I'd have to eat again, since her mom had made us a quiche.

Mrs. Stasney was taller than Denise and had short reddish hair. She shook my hand when I walked into the kitchen, then told Denise and me to take a seat. "Jasira is depressed," Denise announced.

"Really?" Mrs. Stasney said. She brought the quiche from the oven and set it on the table. "Why is that?"

"Because her boyfriend doesn't love her anymore. Just like what happened to me."

"You girls are too young to be getting depressed about boys."

"No we're not," Denise said. "We're in puberty."

After we had rinsed our dishes and put them in the dishwasher, Mrs. Stasney dropped us off at the mall. Denise wanted to get a pair of pants, but none of them fit. They were either too small for her butt and just right for her waist, or just right for her butt and too big for her waist. "This sucks," she said, and she sighed out of the corner of her mouth so that her wispy blonde bangs flew up in the air.

Since Denise couldn't find any clothes that fit her, we went to a store called Glamour Shots and had our pictures taken. It was a place where they put a lot of makeup on you, gave you a fancy dress to wear, then had you pose like models. I was embarrassed to do it, but Denise said it was the only thing that would cheer her up. Afterward, the photographer showed us proofs of all the pictures he had taken, and we picked the ones we liked best. I had enough money to order only one copy, but Denise bought me two more. "One for your mom and dad," she said. "Duh." I thanked her, even though I was pretty sure that the last thing my parents would want was a sexy picture of me.

Denise's dad picked us up at six o'clock. He was tall but chubby, and as I sat behind him in the backseat, I noticed the flesh-colored hearing aid Denise had once mentioned that he wore. Mr. Stasney had been at the gym when I'd arrived at Denise's house, and now he told us all about his workout: how many miles he had racewalked, how many crunches he had done, how much weight he had bench-pressed. He said he had lost three pounds in the last week, and Denise told him that was good but that she wanted to talk about something else. "Ask Jasira about herself," she said. "Try to learn something about my friends."

"Tell me about yourself, Jasira," Mr. Stasney said, looking at me through the rearview mirror.

"Not like that!" Denise said. "Ask her specific questions."

Mr. Stasney asked me a bunch of specific questions then about school and Daddy and my mother. It reminded me of when I had eaten dinner with Thomas's parents, except Mr. Stasney didn't seem quite as interested in my answers. He wasn't mean or impolite or anything. He just seemed like maybe he wasn't finished talking about his visit to the gym.

We went to the Olive Garden for dinner, where Mr. Stasney embarrassed Denise by talking loudly and introducing himself and us to the waitress. Then we went back to Denise's and watched a video she had rented called *A Patch of Blue*. It was an old movie from the sixties about a blind girl who loved a black man. "I thought it would remind you of you and Thomas," Denise said.

"I'm not blind," I said.

She hit me in the arm. "Not that part!"

In the middle of the movie, Denise lay her head on my legs, which I had pulled up onto the couch. Sometimes, when I would try to bite off a piece of my cuticle, she would reach up and grab my hand and say, "Don't bite." Then she would hold on to it a little while longer before letting go.

Mr. and Mrs. Stasney had gone out to visit friends, and when they came home, I worried about their seeing Denise lying on me. But Mrs. Stasney just stood in the doorway and said, "How romantic." Denise told her to shut up, and she just laughed and said good night. I couldn't imagine ever telling my mother to shut up. I couldn't imagine her ever thinking it was okay for me to be romantic.

I wished Denise would lie close to me in her double bed like she had on the couch, but she just kept to her side. I wondered a little if I was gay, then decided I probably wasn't. Mostly I just liked to have someone touch me in any way they wanted, but without it hurting or feeling bad.

The next morning, when Daddy came to pick me up, the *Playboy* Mr. Vuoso had given me a few months earlier was sitting on the front seat. I saw it through the passenger's-side window before I even opened the door, and for a second I thought of running back inside Denise's house and asking her family to protect me. But I didn't. I just stood there, staring through the window. "Get in!" came Daddy's muffled yell, and finally I pulled on the door handle.

I had to pick up the magazine before sitting down on the seat, and for some reason, this felt more embarrassing than anything I could've imagined: touching it in front of Daddy.

At first he didn't say anything. He just sat there, watching me put my seat belt on. I hadn't known what to do with the *Playboy* so I just set it in my lap after picking it up to sit down. I would've preferred to put it on the floor with my backpack, but I knew it was there for me to get in trouble about, and that Daddy would want us both looking at it while he yelled.

As soon as we were out of sight of Denise's house, Daddy punched me in the thigh really hard. Then he did it again and again in the exact same spot. I wanted to lay a hand over the spot to try to cover it, but then I thought he would just punch my hand. "What the hell is that?" he said finally, pointing to the *Playboy*.

I didn't want to say it was a magazine, because I knew that wasn't what he was asking. He was asking where I got it, why I had it, what I did with it. I knew I wouldn't be able to answer any of those questions. Ever. I knew he would keep punching my leg until I could, but that since I couldn't, he would have to just tire himself out.

Instead of answering him, I asked him where he had found the magazine. "What do you mean where did I find it? You know exactly where I found it."

"You were looking in my room?"

"No, I wasn't looking in your room. I didn't have enough laundry to fill the washer, so as a favor to you I was going to wash your sheets."

"Oh."

"When people do us a favor, we say thank you."

"Thank you."

We drove past a gas station, where a bunch of high school kids were holding a fund-raising car wash. They were carrying signs and jumping up and down and yelling things at people who drove by, like that their cars were dirty and support the United Way. I knew Daddy hated them. I knew if he ever saw me acting like that, even though that was probably how you were supposed to act at car washes, he would get mad.

"Where did you get that magazine?" he demanded.

I couldn't answer him. I just couldn't. It wasn't that I wanted to protect Mr. Vuoso, because I didn't. I wanted Mr. Vuoso to get in trouble. I just didn't want to get in trouble along with him.

"Answer me!" Daddy yelled.

When I still didn't talk, he hit me on the leg again and told me there would be more when we got home. He said, "You are not living in the moral universe. The things you do are very different from what normal people do. You are not normal. This is a magazine for men, not women. You are looking at pictures of whores, and you like them so much that you save the magazine. You do not obey me; you do not obey your mother. One day, Jasira, you will run out of places to live."

We pulled into our development and, a minute or so later, passed the spot where Daddy had hit Snowball. *Sorry, Snowball,* I said in my head. I said it every time we passed this place. I tried to imagine her dashing out in front of Daddy and Daddy not being able to stop. But it always ended up in my mind that he didn't want to stop. That maybe he could've, but instead he decided to hit her.

We turned onto our street, then pulled into our driveway. I still had the magazine in my lap, and now I reached down to get my backpack. It was the same pack I took to school, except with the books taken out and some pajamas and a toothbrush put in. "You are going to be sorry when we get in that house," Daddy said, opening his car door.

I opened mine, too. I felt slow and stiff. Part of it was my leg hurting and not wanting to move it around more than I had to, but another part was my feeling confused about going into the house with Daddy when I already knew what would happen. I didn't understand why I would do that, not really. "Hurry up," Daddy said. He was already at the back door, turning the house key. Then he pushed on the door and left it open for me to follow him. It didn't make sense. I was supposed to go in there and get hit.

I shut my car door and walked down the driveway until I reached the edge of the Vuosos' front lawn, then I cut across it. I walked faster, holding the magazine and with my backpack jiggling. Every time my left foot hit the ground, my thigh hurt.

I crossed Melina's driveway next, then began cutting across her front lawn. I reached her front walk and ran up the steps. Her car wasn't in the driveway, so I unzipped the tiny pocket in the front of my backpack and took out her house key.

As I opened Melina's screen door and pushed the key into the lock, I heard Daddy calling my name. I looked quickly over at our house and saw him standing in our driveway. I went back to turning the key and didn't look at him anymore, even though I heard the *whoosh* of grass under his feet and the sound of his calling was getting closer. It didn't matter, because the door was opening now and I was stepping inside and shutting it quickly behind me while Gil watched me from the couch.

He seemed a little surprised at first, but then he acted like it was no big deal. "Oh, hey," he said. "C'mon in."

I didn't move. I knew Daddy would be coming soon, and I wasn't sure what to do. "Is Melina here?" I asked.

Gil shook his head. "She's at prenatal yoga. She'll be back soon, though. You're welcome to wait." He wore a dark knitted cap that made him look like a friendly burglar. In front of him, on the coffee table, were several different piles of papers. I figured he was paying his bills.

Just then there was a loud, quick knock on the door. "Hello!" Daddy called. "Open the door, please!"

I looked at Gil. I was too ashamed to ask him to help me. I was holding the *Playboy* magazine, and after having glanced at it once, I could see he was trying not to look at it again. If Melina had been there, I would've asked her to do something, but she wasn't there. If I had been alone, I would've locked the door and listened to Daddy yell. But there was just Gil, so I moved to open the door.

"Hang on there," Gil said, getting up suddenly from the couch. "I'll get that." Then, coming toward me, he said, "You look like you need a tissue. Why don't you go and use the bathroom upstairs."

I touched my face. I guessed I had been crying. I wasn't sure if it was from my leg or running away.

"It's the second door on the right," Gil said.

I nodded and turned and started up the staircase. There was no carpet on it like at the Vuosos', so each wooden step made a sound. I thought I could feel Gil watching me as I climbed. I hoped he would wait to open the door until I stopped making so much noise, and he did. Daddy's knocking didn't stop until I had rounded the corner of the upstairs hall.

With every step, I could feel how bad it was for me not to go home with Daddy. It would've been pretty bad if I had turned back when he'd first called my name outside. And definitely a lot worse if I had answered his knock at Melina's door and gone back with him then. But now, with Gil talking to him instead of me, with my shutting myself into a room deep at the center of Melina's house, I couldn't imagine going back without Daddy killing me.

I didn't use a tissue like Gil had told me to. I just locked the bathroom door and held my body against it in case Daddy or Gil tried to come in. Because I was pretty sure Daddy would convince Gil to give me back. Daddy knew how to act with other people to make himself not seem crazy.

I could hear them talking for a long time, even though I couldn't understand what they were saying. My shoulder started to ache from pressing it into the door, but I held it there anyway. I didn't care about any pain I got from myself.

After a while—half an hour? forty-five minutes?—the talking stopped and I thought I heard the door close. I pressed my shoulder even harder now, hearing someone coming up the stairs, then down the hall. "Jasira?" Gil said, knocking on the door.

"Yes?"

"Did you get a tissue?"

"Yes." I was thinking that Daddy was secretly with him, and that Gil was trying to trick me into coming out so he could give me back.

"Well," he said, "I just wanted to let you know that your father went home. Okay?"

"Okay," I said, even though I didn't believe him.

"Okay," he said.

I didn't know what to do then. The door made a slight creak as I pushed my shoulder into it a little bit more.

"Jasira?" Gil said.

"Yes?"

"Melina will be home soon."

"Okay."

"Can I get you anything?"

"No, thank you."

"All right then," he said, and after a second I heard him head back down the hall.

I waited for it to be a trick and for him to turn around and come and get me, but he didn't. He just thumped down the stairs. I decided then that it was possible that we were the only two people in the house.

Finally, I moved away from the door. I sat on the toilet and rubbed my shoulder. A few minutes later, I stood up and washed my face. I went in my backpack and got my toothbrush and brushed my teeth, too.

Soon I heard the front door open downstairs, followed by Melina calling out that she was home. Then I didn't hear anything for a few minutes. Then someone was climbing the stairs and coming down the hall. "Jasira?" Melina said, knocking on the door.

"Yes?"

"Can you please open up?"

I unlocked the door and opened it.

"Hey," she said. She was wearing sweats and a man's blue oxford shirt. The buttons in the middle wouldn't reach, so she had just left them open.

"Do I have to go home?" I asked her.

"Do you want to go home?"

"No." I started to cry again because I had never told the truth like that before. Melina told me to come here, and I did, and I didn't even mind so much that we were hugging Dorrie between us.

We didn't really talk about anything after I came out of the bathroom. Melina just told me to put my stuff in Gil's study—except for the *Playboy,* which she didn't ask me about, but which she took away from me and put in her room. When she mentioned that the couch in Gil's study folded out to be a bed, I tried not to get too excited that I might be staying over.

We went downstairs then and sat in the living room. Melina knitted, I read my book, and Gil went back to his papers. It turned out that they weren't bills, but stocks that he was trying to change around to see if he could make more money. Now that he wasn't in the Peace Corps, Gil worked for Merrill Lynch.

I wasn't sure what to read in my book anymore. I wasn't sure what there was left to know about. Then I found a part about kids who had done sexual things that they hadn't wanted to do, but their bodies had gotten excited anyway, just like mine with Mr. Vuoso. The book said it wasn't my fault, and that I was human and not a plant, and that that was why it made sense that my body might've acted that way.

Melina said she was too tired to cook dinner that night, so Gil made food from Yemen. I was a little bit disappointed since it was kind of like the food Daddy cooked, but then when I tasted it, it was a lot better. "This meat is nice," I said. "Daddy's is always dry."

Gil nodded. "The Arabs overcook everything."

We were sitting around the Formica table, with Gil closest to the kitchen in case he needed to get up to get something. Melina had to sit with her chair pushed way far out from the table because of her stomach. Her fork had to travel a long way from her plate to her mouth, and sometimes food fell off of it and onto her blue shirt. It was funny to me because for some time, I had noticed that all of her clothes were stained in that exact same spot, and now I understood why.

It was beginning to feel weird that we hadn't really talked about what had happened earlier, so finally I asked Gil what Daddy had said to him.

"Well," Gil said, "that he wanted to take you home with him. That sort of thing."

"What did you say?" I asked.

"That you were in the bathroom."

Melina laughed. Gil laughed a little, too.

"Then what did he say?" I asked.

"He just kept kind of saying the same thing over and over again: that you were his daughter and he was there to pick you up."

"And you kept telling him no?" I said.

"Pretty much."

"Isn't he going to come back?"

Gil shrugged. "Maybe."

"Will I have to go back then?"

"I thought you said you didn't want to go back," Melina said.

"I don't."

"So don't worry about it."

"Don't tell her not to worry about it," Gil said. "She's worried."

"I just meant that no one's going to make her do anything she doesn't want to do," Melina said to Gil. Then she turned to me and said, "No one's going to make you do anything you don't want to do, okay?"

"Okay," I said.

Later, while we were all watching TV in the living room, there was a knock at the door. "That's Daddy," I said.

"How do you know?" Melina asked.

"I just do."

"Well," she said, "do you want to go upstairs?"

I nodded.

"All right. We'll wait to open the door."

I got up from the couch and went upstairs. Instead of locking myself in the bathroom, though, I stood just around the corner in the hallway so I could hear everything. Melina must've opened the door this time, because I heard her say, "Oh, hello."

Daddy said something I couldn't hear then, and Melina said, "Sure, c'mon in."

"What can we do for you?" Gil said.

Daddy laughed. "What do you think you can do for me? I'm here to take my daughter home."

"Well," Melina said, "she doesn't want to go home with you."

"So?" Daddy said. "This is enough shenanigans." Then he yelled, "Jasira! Let's go! C'mon!"

I didn't move. Part of me felt sorry for him that he didn't know where I was in the house, but part of me liked it, too.

"Excuse me," Melina said, "but I just told you: She doesn't want to go home with you."

"This is none of your business," Daddy said. "If you don't give her back, that constitutes kidnapping!"

"I doubt it," Melina said.

Then I heard Daddy say something to Gil in Arabic—something loud and long—and Gil said something back to him.

"Speak in English, please," Melina said, which I could've told her not to do since now Daddy would never speak in English around her. I was right, too. Even though Gil started speaking in English, Daddy kept going in Arabic. "What's he saying?" Melina asked Gil.

"He wants to call the police," Gil said. "I'm trying to talk him out of it."

"And tell them what?" Melina asked Daddy.

He ignored her and said something in Arabic to Gil. "Well," Gil told Daddy, "I guess I just don't see the harm in her staying with us for a couple of days. She'll come back when she's ready."

Even though he was still speaking in Arabic, I was beginning to think I could understand what Daddy was saying. Like when Gil said I would come back when I was ready, he probably said, "Who cares about when she's ready? I'm her father and she'll come back when I say." And when Gil said that Daddy might be sorry if the police came since information could come out that might not help Daddy, he probably said, "What information? There is no information." And when Gil said, "Well, there's got to be some information because she's limping a little on her left leg," Daddy probably said, "She's making it up."

Finally, I heard the front door open and close. "You can come down now," Melina called, and I came out from around the corner and walked down the stairs. "We got rid of him," she said.

"Thank you," I said.

"He'll probably be back," Gil warned.

"So?" Melina said. "We'll get rid of him again."

We went back to watching TV again. During one of the commercials, Melina said, "Go to the upstairs bathroom and get me the brush in the left-hand drawer of the sink cabinet."

I nodded, then went upstairs and got the brush. When I came back, Melina took it from me, then patted the spot beside her on the couch. She started brushing the back of my hair first, followed by the sides. "Good Lord, you have a lot of hair," she said.

"Thank you," I said, since I could tell she meant it as a compliment.

"Doesn't she have a lot of hair, Gil?"

It embarrassed me that she was forcing him to say something about how I looked, but he didn't seem to mind. He just agreed that I did without really looking up from his stock papers.

After that, I started to enjoy having my hair brushed a lot more. It made my scalp tingle and get so goose-pimply that I was sure Melina could probably feel the bumps under her brush and was just being polite not to tease me about them. It reminded me of how nice it had felt when Barry used to shave me, except it was even better since we didn't have to keep it a secret.

At around ten, Melina said it was her bedtime and that I should probably get some sleep, too. We said good night to Gil, then went upstairs. I took my backpack in the bathroom to change and wash up, and when I looked down, I saw that the big orange Syracuse T-shirt my mother had given me for Christmas didn't totally cover the purple bruise on my leg. I wasn't sure if I should try to stretch the T-shirt down or just let Melina see it.

"You okay in there?" she asked, knocking lightly on the door.

"Yes."

"Well, come on out and try this bed. See if you can stand it."

"All right," I said, pulling down on my shirt a little. I opened the door and stepped out.

"Jesus Christ," Melina said, her eyes going to where my hands were tugging the shirt. She reached out and took my wrist so I would let go. The shirt sprang back up.

"Daddy was mad about the magazine," I said.

"Uh-huh," she said. I liked how she seemed angry, but not at me. "Can I get a picture of that?" she asked.

"My leg?"

"I just think it's a good idea."

"Okay," I said, even though it made me nervous.

"I'll be right back," she said, and I watched her waddle down the hall.

I went in Gil's study then and got in my bed. I could see what Melina meant when she worried that it might not be comfortable. There was a bar that ran across the middle, just under my back. It wasn't too bad, though, especially since I didn't sleep on my back.

Melina came back with a Polaroid camera. "How's the bed?" she asked.

"Good."

"You don't mind that bar?"

I shook my head.

"Well," she said, "we'll see how you feel in the morning."

I nodded, even though no matter how I felt in the morning, I planned to tell her that the bed had been comfortable.

"Hop out for a second so I can take a couple pictures."

I pulled back the covers, got up, and stood beside the bed. The first picture Melina took was a picture of all of me. Then she came in closer and took one of just the bruise. After each picture shot out of the camera, she caught it in between her fingers. Now she started waving them lightly through the air. "Is there anything else I should take a picture of?" she asked.

"No," I said.

"Good."

I got back in bed and covered myself up again. I noticed the pictures starting to come clear as Melina waved them. "Can I see them?" I asked.

"Why would you want to see them? You've got the real thing right in front of you."

"I just want to see."

She gave them to me, and as I held them, they seemed to come into focus even more. "It looks like a jellyfish," I said.

"Well," Melina said, taking the pictures back, "it's not a jellyfish."

"Thank you for helping me," I said.

"You're welcome." She leaned down and kissed me, then turned the light off and shut the door behind her. After she left, I thought about the pictures. I thought about her showing them to Daddy, and his knowing that she knew about our life together. It was a nice thing to think about in a way, but then, in another way, I understood that the more things I didn't keep secret, the angrier Daddy was going to be when I finally had to go home.

Melina took me to school on Monday morning, since I was worried that Daddy would try to get me at the bus stop. She said she'd pick me up and take me home, too. Then she handed me a bag with a lunch she'd packed. No one had ever really done that for me before. With my mother I had packed my own, and with Daddy I bought.

In study hall, Denise passed me a note asking why I was wearing the same outfit from last Saturday. I wrote back saying that I liked this outfit. At lunch Thomas asked where I had gotten the freaky lunch. "It's not freaky," I said.

"Who eats a lamb sandwich?" he wanted to know. Since I had said I liked Gil's dinner so much, Melina had given me the leftovers. I lied, though, and told Thomas that Daddy had made me eat the lamb so it wouldn't go to waste.

After school, Melina arrived in her little Toyota with the seat pushed back all the way to fit her stomach. "How was school?" she asked when I got in the car.

"Good."

She waited for me to get my seat belt on before she started driving, which I thought was nice. Daddy always started driving as soon as he had his own belt on, even if mine wasn't on yet. It always made me feel like he hoped we would get in an accident before I could buckle up.

Melina sang along with the radio as she drove. She had a really nice voice, like a professional singer, and I liked how she wasn't shy to let me hear it. When the song ended, I asked her what she had done while I was at school. "Well," she said, "I ended up sleeping a lot. I was kind of tired."

"Oh."

"Yesterday was maybe more excitement than I'm used to."

"I'm sorry," I said.

"For what?" She downshifted as we approached a red light. "What are you sorry for?"

"For giving you too much excitement."

She shook her head. "It had nothing to do with you. You didn't do anything."

"Okay," I said, even though I couldn't see how it didn't have anything to do with me.

When we got to our development, Melina asked if I had my house key. I said yes, and she suggested that maybe we should go to Daddy's to get some of my things—clothes and stuff. "Okay," I said.

We parked in her driveway, then walked over to my house. Melina had never been all the way inside, so I gave her a quick tour. In the kitchen, I was surprised to find Daddy's dirty dinner dishes from the night before still in the sink. In his room, the bed was unmade.

In my bedroom, Melina said, "He couldn't be bothered to decorate this place for you?" She had really worked on Dorrie's room, painting it yellow, hanging pictures, sewing little pillows with felt appliqués of a giraffe, an elephant, and a lion.

I shrugged.

"Anyway," she said, "let's pack your stuff."

We had gotten a plastic garbage bag from the kitchen, and now I started putting clothes from my dresser drawers inside it. At first I only put in a few things, but then Melina said, "What's the matter? Don't you like staying with Gil and me?" and she reached in and grabbed more clothes. Next I went to my closet and got some things from there—sweaters, pants, blouses, and shoes. There wasn't really much more to take except for a couple of schoolbooks on my dresser. "All set?" Melina asked, and I nodded.

As we passed back through the kitchen, I stopped in front of the refrigerator. Snowball was still in our freezer. Daddy hadn't mentioned her since the night we'd wrapped her up and I was beginning to think that maybe he couldn't stand to put her in the trash, either. Even so, I didn't feel right, leaving her behind. Part of me worried that he would get mad when he noticed all my clothes were gone and put her in the trash just to be mean. "What's the matter?" Melina asked.

"There's something I need to take from the freezer."

"Sure," she said. "Some food you like?"

I shook my head. "No. It's kind of gross."

"What is it?"

"Snowball."

"Snowball?"

"Zack's cat that he lost."

"You mean it's dead?"

I nodded.

Melina looked at me. "Did you kill Zack's cat?"

"Sort of," I told her, and I explained what had happened.

"I see," she said.

"We were supposed to put her in the trash, but then Daddy kept forgetting. I don't want him to put her in the trash."

Melina thought for a second. She said, "I have a lot of food in my freezer for when the baby comes, you know? I'm not sure I have room for a cat."

"It's okay," I said.

She sighed. "Let me see how big she is."

I opened the freezer and pulled Snowball out.

"Well," she said, "I guess she's not that big."

"She's only a kitten," I said.

"All right then," Melina said, and she took Snowball and put her in the garbage bag on top of my clothes.

When we got back to Melina's, she made room for Snowball in the freezer, then we went upstairs to find a place for my clothes. Melina ended up clearing a couple of shelves for me in the linen closet, and we piled my things onto those. After we'd finished, she said she needed to lie down for a few minutes, but that I was free to go and watch TV or help myself to a snack or whatever. "Okay," I said.

"I'll be out in a while," she said, and I tried not to feel sad when she shut her bedroom door all the way.

I went downstairs in the living room and didn't do anything. Mostly I just concentrated on all the things that could happen once Daddy found out I'd taken my clothes and Snowball. None of them were good.

The phone rang at one point, and since it wasn't my house, I waited for the machine to get it. When the person came on, it was my mother. "Jasira? Are you there?" She paused for a second, then said, "This is a message for Jasira. I understand she's staying with you. I'm her mother, and I would like her to please call me so I can find out what's going on. Her father is very upset. Thank you."

Suddenly this all felt like such a bad idea to me. The longer I stayed away from my real life, the worse it was going to be when I went back. And I just knew I would have to go back. No matter how nice and strong Gil and Melina were, they would get tired of all of this soon. Especially when Dorrie came. When Dorrie came, I wouldn't stand a chance.

I went in the kitchen and erased the phone message from my mother. I got the garbage bag Melina had folded up and put away, took it upstairs and loaded my clothes back into it, then went back down to the freezer to get Snowball. I let myself quietly out of the house and walked down the front steps. Just then, Gil pulled into the driveway. "Hey," he said, getting out of his car. "Where you going?"

"Home."

"Home?" he said. "Already? You sure you're up for it?"

I nodded.

"Does Melina know?"

"She's taking a nap," I said. "I didn't want to bother her."

Gil jingled his car keys lightly in his hand. He was wearing contact lenses and a suit today, with no burglar cap covering his sandy hair. "Did Melina tell you about her blood pressure?" he asked me.

"Yes," I said. "I think so."

"Well," he said, "the thing is, if she doesn't know you're going back home, and she wakes up and finds you gone, that could be very bad for her. She's not supposed to get too upset."

"Oh."

"Do you think as a favor to me you could go back in and at least wait until she wakes up?"

"Okay," I said. "I'm sorry."

"Nothing to be sorry about," he said, and he took the garbage bag out of my hand and carried it back inside for me.

When Melina woke up and came downstairs, she said, "What stinks?"

"I don't smell anything," Gil said. He had loosened his tie and was sitting in the living room with me, reading the paper.

"It's like rot," Melina said, making a face. The hair at the back of her head was sticking up so that you could see it from the front.

I realized then that I had forgotten to put Snowball back in the freezer. "It might be the cat," I said.

"What cat?" Gil asked.

"Jasira has a dead cat that she froze," Melina said. I could tell Gil wanted to ask more about it, but Melina cut him off and said, "I can't believe it's stinking all the way from the freezer."

"No," I said. "It's not."

She noticed the garbage bag on the floor beside my legs. "What's that?" she said. "Is that the bag from your house?"

I nodded.

She put her hands on her back for support. "What are you doing with that?"

Before I could answer, Gil said, "When I came home, I ran into Jasira coming out of the house. She was thinking she was ready to go back to her father's."

"No," Melina said, looking at me. "What are you talking about? Absolutely not."

"If she wants to go back, she can go back, Mel," Gil said.

"You're serious?" Melina said. "You really want to go back?"

"I don't want to be any trouble," I said.

"Give me the cat," she said.

I opened the bag and took Snowball out and brought her over to Melina. As she headed for the kitchen, she said, "I want you to take those clothes up to the linen closet and put them away."

"Okay," I said.

"You have to let her go home if that's what she wants," Gil called after Melina.

"That's not what she wants!" Melina called back.

Gil watched as I picked up the garbage bag and headed upstairs. I thought it was nice of him to try to stick up for me, which was why I didn't want to hurt his feelings by telling him that Melina had been right: I really didn't want to go home.

The dinner Melina made that night was called chicken tetrazzini. It was chicken in a sauce that you poured over rice. It was really good. We all said so. After dinner, Gil did the dishes, and Melina asked me to come upstairs with her. She sounded serious, which made me think she wanted to look at my bruise again, but that wasn't it. Instead, she took me in her room and told me to sit down on her bed. Then she pulled my *Playboy* from her bedside drawer and sat down next to me. "Where'd you get this thing?" she asked.

I didn't answer. I knew she wouldn't hit me like Daddy had. I was just too ashamed.

After a moment, she opened up the magazine and flipped through a couple of pages. "I wouldn't mind this stuff so much if it wasn't for the airbrushing. If it was just plain old women without air-brushing, I could probably handle that."

"What's airbrushing?" I asked.

She flipped a couple more pages, then turned the magazine around to show me a picture of a lady in a horse stable leaning forward with her hands on a saddle so that her butt stuck out. "See how smooth her skin is right here?" Melina said, pointing to the backs of her thighs.

I nodded.

"She probably has cellulite. But they painted over it so that her skin looks perfect, and now men look at these pictures and think that's how women should look. And women look at these pictures and think that's how they should look."

"Women look at these pictures?" I asked, remembering how Daddy had said that they didn't.

"Sure they do," Melina said. "Why shouldn't they?"

I shrugged.

"They look at these pictures and feel bad about themselves."

"Oh." I thought for a second, then said, "Do some women look at the pictures and feel good?"

"Maybe," Melina said. "Is that how you feel?"

I didn't answer.

"I mean, they're sexy pictures."

"I guess so," I said.

"The thing is," she said, closing the magazine, "how anyone feels when they look at the pictures—it doesn't matter. It's private."

I nodded.

"But how a kid your age has a magazine like this isn't private. You see what I'm saying?"

I nodded again.

"This is a magazine for adults only."

Now she sounded like Daddy.

"If you found this magazine, that's one thing. But if an adult gave it to you, that's different." She paused. "Did an adult give it to you?"

"Yes."

"Was the adult your father?"

"No."

She sighed.

"I'm sorry," I said.

"For what?"

"For reading an adult magazine."

"Don't worry about it," she said, and she reached over and put it back in the drawer.

Later, when we were all watching TV in the living room, there was a knock at the front door. Gil got up out of his chair to answer it. He usually got up and did everything after dinner, since that was when Melina was tired. "Oh, hi," he said. "C'mon in." I braced myself to see Daddy, but that wasn't who it was. It was Mr. Vuoso. He was dressed in a lightweight jacket and a baseball cap, and he carried some envelopes in his hand. When he stepped into the foyer, he took his cap off. As soon as Melina saw him, she hit the Mute button on the remote control. Mr. Vuoso heard the silence and turned to look at us.

"Hi," Melina said.

Mr. Vuoso opened his mouth to say hi back, but then he saw me and didn't say anything.

"What's up?" Melina asked him.

"Oh," Mr. Vuoso said. He held up the envelopes in his hand. "I just—we got some of your mail today. Mrs. Vuoso asked me to bring it over."

"Thanks," Gil said, taking the envelopes from him.

"That mailman sucks," Melina said. "I mean, there's hardly any of us on the damn street, right?"

Mr. Vuoso seemed confused, like he wasn't sure if Melina was trying to be friendly or not. "Yeah," he said. "He's pretty careless."

Melina nodded.

"Hello, Jasira," Mr. Vuoso said finally. He didn't say it in a mean way, but like he wanted Melina and Gil to think we were friends.

I didn't answer. I didn't want to talk to him. If Daddy had been there, he would've forced me to say hello since Mr. Vuoso was an adult before he was someone Daddy hated. But Melina and Gil didn't seem to care. They didn't tell me to do anything.

Mr. Vuoso wouldn't leave. He just stood there, holding his hat. Maybe he was waiting for Melina to explain what I was doing there. She didn't, though. She said, "Actually, I think we have something of yours, too."

"Oh really?"

"What is it?" Gil asked.

"It's in my bedside drawer," Melina told him. "Would you mind going up and getting it?"

He didn't move right away, but then Melina gave him a look that I'd seen a few times since I'd started staying with them. It was a look that said he should do what she wanted without talking about it anymore.

"Sure," Gil said now. "Hang on."

We all watched him climb the stairs. While he was gone, I stared at Melina, Melina stared at Mr. Vuoso, and I was pretty sure I felt Mr. Vuoso staring at me. "So, Jasira," he said. "I didn't know you spent time over here."

I didn't say anything, just kept looking at Melina. "Here's Gil," she said a few seconds later. We all turned to look at him. He was holding the *Playboy*. He came downstairs and handed it to Mr. Vuoso, who waited a moment before taking it. He looked so shocked that I had to work hard not to feel sorry for him.

"That's yours, right?" Melina asked.

It seemed like he nodded, but I wasn't sure.

"Good," she said.

Mr. Vuoso looked at me, and I quickly looked down at my lap. I wished he would go. I wished it weren't so hard not to feel guilty.

"Well," Gil said, and I heard the front door opening. "Good night."

Soon the door closed. I looked up. Gil turned the deadbolt. He sighed and said he was going up to bed. Melina told him she'd be there in a little while. After he'd climbed the stairs and rounded the corner, she turned to me and said, "Did he do anything else to you?"

I thought about what Gil had told me earlier, that Melina wasn't supposed to get upset. That I wasn't supposed to tell her things that would upset her, since it could hurt the baby. Part of me still wanted to hurt the baby a little, like I always had. But then part of me didn't. I didn't really like the baby, but I knew Melina did, and I knew that if I wanted her to keep liking me, I would have to like the baby, too. Or at least pretend that I did. "No," I said. "He didn't."

"Are you sure?" she asked.

"Yes."

"I don't want you ever speaking to him again, do you understand?"

"Yes."

"And don't you dare feel sorry for him."

I didn't ask her how she knew I felt that way. I just nodded. She picked up the brush then, which we now kept downstairs on the coffee table, and started brushing my hair. After a moment, I said, "Let me do yours," and she said okay. The brush slipped through her straight hair easily. There were no catches or tangles to work through, no strands of ripped-out hair to shake off my hand. She never once said ouch. Dorrie would have this kind of hair, too, I thought. If the three of us ever walked down the street together, everyone would know who the real daughter was.

ELEVEN

I waited all week for Daddy to come to get me, but he didn't. And since Melina was always driving me to school, I never saw him out on the street in the mornings. When he got home at night, I was eating dinner with Melina and Gil. It wasn't that I wanted to see him, really. But I did wonder about him sometimes: what he was doing or eating; what shows he was watching on TV; whether Grandma still thought Saddam was going to bomb her. My mother called once more, but it was at the same time of day when Gil wasn't home and Melina was taking a nap. This time I went and stood by the machine and almost picked up. But then I didn't. I was too afraid she would tell me I had to go back to Daddy's. When she hung up, I erased the message.

All that week, waiting for Daddy to come, I had strange dreams. I couldn't remember what they were about, but they always woke me up because of something I was doing in real life, like holding my breath or yelling. Melina came in my room and turned on the light whenever I yelled, but when I woke up holding my breath, I was by myself. Sometimes I thought about making a fake yell so she would come, but that didn't seem very nice.

When I yelled and she came in my room, she told me it was just a bad dream, then she lay down beside me in bed and went to sleep. In the morning, when she woke up, she said she had no idea how I could stand that bar underneath me. She asked me to rub the spots on her back where the bar had hurt her, and when I did, she said I had the magic fingers.

I began to think that with each day that passed, the end of my life was coming. Not the end of my real life, but the end of my good life. I knew that once Dorrie got here, Melina would go to her room in the middle of the night, and not mine. Probably I wouldn't even have a room. I would be back living with Daddy, or in Syracuse with my mother. On those nights when Melina came to stay in my bed, I didn't sleep. I stayed awake and watched her sleep. I tried to be awake as much as possible while the thing I liked best was happening to me.

"You look tired," Thomas said to me in school on Friday.

"I do?" I had just sat down at the cafeteria table and was opening up the lunch Melina had packed for me.

"You have circles under your eyes."

"Oh." I unwrapped the aluminum foil around my sandwich. Melina never asked me what I liked to eat. She just packed the food and I was surprised by it. I preferred that to actually liking the food. Today it looked like egg salad.

"Aren't you getting enough sleep?"

"Yes."

"Then why do you have dark circles?"

I shrugged and bit into my sandwich.

"I'm coming home with you after school today," Thomas said. "We can take a nap."

"You can't," I told him.

"Why not?" He watched egg salad squeeze out the sides of my sandwich, then, when it landed on the foil, he reached over with his plastic fork and scooped it up.

"Because," I said. "I don't live there anymore."

"What?"

"I live with Melina."

"That pregnant lady?"

I nodded.

"Why?"

"Daddy was hitting me too much."

Thomas didn't say anything. Some more of my egg salad squeezed out, but he didn't pick it up. "Why did he hit you?"

"He found my *Playboy*."

"Just for that?"

"He said it was a magazine for men and I shouldn't be reading it."

Thomas thought for a second, then said, "Let's take a nap."

"I can't," I said. "Not at Melina's."

"Then come to my house."

I shook my head. "Melina likes me to stay with her."

Thomas walked outside with me after school and waited for Melina to come. When she pulled up, he opened the passenger door of the Toyota and stuck his head in. "Hi," he said.

"Hi," Melina said. "Thomas, right?"

He nodded.

"You need a ride somewhere?"

"Can I come over to your house and hang out with Jasira for a while?" he asked.

"Sure," she said. Then she leaned forward and looked at me on the sidewalk. "Is that what you want to do?"

I nodded.

"Okay," she said. "Get in."

Thomas pulled the front seat forward and climbed in back. When

I got in front, I could feel his knee against my spine. "Want me to pull the seat forward?" I asked, but he said no, he was good.

Melina pulled away from the curb and followed the circular drive that led off from school property. She asked us if we wanted to rent a video or something, and Thomas said no. He said, "Hey, Melina, does Jasira look tired to you?"

She took a quick glance at me as she drove. "I don't know. Maybe. Are you tired?"

"Not really," I said.

"She has dark circles," Thomas said.

"Well," Melina said, "she's sleeping on this crappy hideaway bed we have. That's probably the problem. She's just too polite to say it sucks."

"It doesn't suck," I said.

"Jasira is the most polite person I know," Thomas said, which embarrassed me since he didn't laugh afterward like he was making a joke.

We stopped at the supermarket and Melina gave us twenty dollars to go in and buy milk, bread, and some snacks for ourselves. When we got in the store, Thomas went straight to the pharmacy section and got a small package of condoms. "I can't do that at Melina's," I said.

"Why not?" he asked. "What's the difference between taking a nap and having sex? We'll close the door either way."

"I already told you," I said. "I can't take a nap."

"She won't care," Thomas said. "She's cool."

Thomas had his own money and paid for the rubbers separately. I worried that the checkout lady would say we were too young to have them, but she didn't. She just looked at us like she was thinking that—especially when Thomas took the rubbers out of the bag with the food and stuck them in his backpack.

Melina had fallen asleep by the time we returned to the parking lot. Her head was leaning against the window, and her mouth was a little bit open. "Home, James," Thomas said, climbing into the back-seat, and that woke her up.

We passed Mr. Vuoso's copy shop on the way, and I didn't say anything. Neither did Melina. Ever since she had given him back his *Playboy,* it was like he didn't exist anymore. Only I knew it wasn't true. He did exist. So did Daddy. Just because I didn't see them didn't mean they weren't there. They would stay afraid of Melina and Gil for only so long. I had an idea that they were both just waiting for Melina to go to the hospital to have her baby so that they could come over and get me.

When we walked into Melina's house, Thomas said, "Man, this place is nice. Really modern."

"Thanks," Melina said, dropping her purse onto a chair.

"Hey, Lawrence of Arabia," Thomas said. He set the bag of groceries on the coffee table and walked over to the wall with all of Gil's desert pictures.

"My husband was in the Peace Corps," Melina said.

"He dug toilets in Yemen," I added.

"He's a white guy?" Thomas asked.

"Yup," Melina said.

Thomas nodded. "That's cool."

"Listen, you guys," Melina said, "I need to take a nap for a while. Feel free to watch TV or whatever. Just give me an hour or so."

"Sure," Thomas said.

"Just hang around the house if you go outside, okay Jasira?"

I nodded.

"Thanks for the food," Thomas said.

"You're welcome," Melina said, and she turned and went upstairs.

After she left, we went in the kitchen to unpack the groceries. "We can eat later," Thomas said, laying a couple of bags of chips on the counter. "We should take a nap now, while she's taking a nap."

"But I'm hungry," I said.

"You can wait."

"I always have a snack after school."

"Don't you want to have sex with me?" he asked, lowering his voice.

"Yes."

"Well," he said, "this is a really good chance. Right now."

"If Melina finds out, she'll send me back to Daddy's."

"No way," Thomas said. "She's not going to send you back to someone who hits you."

"Then she'll send me to my mother's."

Thomas didn't say anything, just folded the paper grocery bag.

"I don't want to live with my mother," I said.

"Where do you want to live?" he asked.

I thought for a second, then said, "Here."

He laughed. "You can't live here. You can't just move in with the neighbors."

"Why not?" I asked.

He shrugged. "You just can't. It doesn't happen."

It made me feel really bad to hear this. Especially since Thomas sounded so sure of himself.

"C'mon," he said. "Let's go upstairs."

I didn't get up from my chair.

"C'mon," he said again, walking over to me. He took my hand and laid it on the front of his pants. "See how excited you make me?"

I nodded.

"Nobody makes me that excited. You're the only one."

I let him move my hand across his pants a little.

"Don't you want to be the only one?" he asked.

"Yes," I said, because I did. It was the main thing I ever wanted, with anyone.

Thomas got a rubber from his backpack, then we took our shoes off and walked upstairs. This time I was glad that Melina had shut her bedroom door all the way. "There's the bathroom," I whispered as we passed it.

When we got to Gil's office, I motioned for Thomas to come in, then shut the door. "Let's still whisper," I said, and he nodded. He sat down on the bed to test it out. "Damn," he said. "This really does suck."

"It's not so bad," I said.

He took his jacket off, draping it over an arm of the couch. Then he lay back on the foldout bed, slipping his hands between his head and my pillow. "Suck my dick," he whispered.

I sat down on the edge of the bed and unbuckled his pants. I liked how they always got tight across the front when he had an erection. When I finally unzipped him and pulled his shorts down a little, his penis sprang out. Mostly, I liked how he was lying there with his hands behind his head. He was telling me what to do, but he wasn't forcing me. It was only the way he was acting, but it made me feel more excited than anything.

"That's good," Thomas whispered when I was crouched over him. He did put his hand on my head then, not to move me up and down, but to touch my hair. "That's good," he kept saying. After a while, he said, "I want to eat your pussy."

I stopped sucking on his penis and waited for him to move over so I could lie down beside him. Once I had, Thomas knelt in front of me and pulled off my jeans and my underwear, then pushed my legs apart and held them like that, in the stretched-out way he liked. He stared for a while, then put his mouth there, and I touched his hair.

It felt really good, what he was doing. I didn't say anything, but I tried to touch his hair very softly, so he would know. I thought maybe I was going to have an orgasm this way, but then Thomas decided to stop to put his rubber on. He told me to get on top, and I did, and that was very different from when he was on top. I could feel everything a lot more, even too much. Thomas reached up and held on to my breasts, and it was like every part of me that knew how to feel good was being touched at the same time. I had an orgasm very quickly, but it wasn't the same kind I was used to. It felt like it came not from the outside of me, but from the inside, where Thomas's penis was. It felt like it started very deep, then traveled to the surface. Like it began earlier than ever and ended way past when it was supposed to. I couldn't help it. I yelled.

Immediately Thomas and I both stopped moving against each other and listened. "I don't think she heard anything," he said.

"No," I said. "She did."

"How do you know?" he said. "C'mon, keep going."

He started to move again, but I got off him. "She hears everything," I said, reaching for my clothes.

"What about me?" Thomas said. He looked down at his penis, which was still hard inside the rubber.

"I'm sorry," I said. "You have to get dressed."

Just then I heard Melina's door open. "Jasira?" she called from down the hall.

"Hurry up!" I whispered to Thomas.

"Oh shit," he said, and he hopped up and started pulling his shorts on over the condom.

"Jasira?" Melina said again. Her voice was closer and more nervous-sounding. A couple of seconds later there was a knock at the door. "Hello?" she said.

"Yes?" I said. I was already dressed, just buttoning up the top of my shirt. Thomas was still pulling his jeans on.

"What are you doing?" Melina asked.

"Nothing," I said.

"Why is this door closed?"

I waited for her to open it, but she didn't.

"I was just taking a nap," I said.

"Did Thomas go home?"

I was quiet for a second. "No."

She opened the door right away then. Thomas had just pulled his sweater over his head. "Hi," he said.

"What's going on in here?" Melina asked.

"We were taking a nap," I said.

Melina looked at the bed, which was still made, but rumpled, then down at the floor. I worried that maybe Thomas's condom wrapper was there, but if it was, she didn't notice. "You're too young to be alone in your room with a boy," she said. "If you're tired, Thomas should go home so you can rest." She looked at Thomas then. "Should I take you home?"

"Do I have to?" he said.

"Are you still tired, Jasira?" Melina asked me.

I shook my head.

"All right," she said to Thomas. "You can stay. But you guys need to go downstairs. C'mon. We'll all go downstairs."

"Did you finish your nap?" I asked her.

"Not really."

"You could finish it now," I said. "I promise we'll go downstairs."

"It's okay," she said. "I'm not that tired anymore."

"I just need to go to the bathroom," Thomas said.

Melina stepped out of the way so he could pass by. After he left, she looked at me. I was still standing at the foot of the bed. "I'm sorry I shut the door," I said.

"Why did you yell?"

"What?"

"I heard you yell."

"Oh." I tried to think of something to tell her that wouldn't be embarrassing but that also wouldn't be a lie. I couldn't.

"Were you having a bad dream?" she asked.

"No," I said.

Just then the toilet flushed, and the bathroom door opened.

"Okay," she said. "We'll talk about this later."

"Sorry," I said again.

We all went downstairs and had snacks. Thomas told Melina about how he had to eat a big plate of spaghetti the night before he had a swim meet so he could carbo-load. He laughed and said all the blond kids' hair turned green from the chlorine. Gil came home at around six and Thomas asked him about the pictures in the living room. They went to look at them while Melina and I stayed in the kitchen, eating. "He's a nice kid," she said.

I nodded.

"A little bossy, but nice."

"He's a really good guitar player," I said. "He likes Jimi Hendrix."

"Well," Melina said, "he has good taste."

We started to cook dinner, which was two homemade pizzas. Melina had made the dough while I was at school, and now she took the mounds out of the refrigerator and we each stretched one out on a cookie sheet. We spread sauce on top, then cheese, then pepperoni on one and low-salt ham on the other. They both had peppers, mushrooms, and onions. After putting them in the oven, we went to sit in the living room. "*Marhaba,*" Thomas said when we walked in.

"What?" I said.

"That's how you say hi in Arabic. Gil taught me."

"Oh," I said.

"You didn't know that?" Thomas asked.

"I don't speak Arabic."

"It's a hard language to master," Gil said.

"Dinner will be ready in fifteen minutes," Melina said.

"Great," Gil said.

"Do you need to call your mother?" Melina asked Thomas.

"Oh yeah," he said. "I guess I better. Where's the phone?"

She pointed toward the kitchen. "On the wall by the pantry."

Thomas nodded. As soon as he left, the doorbell rang. Melina had already sat down, so Gil got up to get it. "Oh," he said, "hello there."

"Good evening," I heard Daddy say. It was the first time I'd heard his voice in days. He sounded like he was trying to act pleasant.

"Um, come in," Gil said.

Daddy, who was wearing a navy blue suit, stepped inside, followed by his girlfriend Thena, I hadn't seen her since the morning she'd put makeup on me, though sometimes we spoke briefly on the phone when she called to talk to Daddy. Now that she was here, I'd forgotten how pretty she was, how shocked it made me feel that she would want to be with Daddy. Tonight she was dressed in a silky dark green dress and a pearl bracelet. Her eye makeup was swirly greens and coppers, and she had pale peach nail polish on her fingertips. Her hair looked like it had just been brushed. I was certain that she must smell good, though we were standing far apart. She was carrying a bottle of wine with curled shiny ribbons around the neck, and Daddy held a rectangular glass baking dish. I knew he'd made baklava, since that was his specialty. He'd tried to show me how to make it once, saying maybe I could surprise him with a batch when he came home from work, but I never did.

"This is my friend Thena," Daddy said to Gil.

"Hello," Gil said, shaking Thena's hand.

"Pleased to meet you," Thena said.

"We're here for the dinner," Daddy said. "To celebrate the end of the war." When nobody said anything, Daddy handed Gil the baklava and said, "This is for you."

"And this," Thena said, handing Gil her bottle. "Sparkling cider," she added, looking over at Melina.

Gil looked at Melina, too, like he didn't know what to do. In the silence, I could hear Thomas's low talking in the kitchen.

"Good evening, Melina," Daddy called across the room. "This is Thena."

Melina nodded. "Hello."

After a moment, Daddy said, "Hello, Jasira."

"Hi," I said.

"Say hello to Thena," he said.

"Hello," I said to Thena.

"It's good to see you again, Jasira," she said.

I nodded.

"Okay," Thomas said, walking into the living room. "My mother says I can stay."

Daddy turned to look at Thomas. Everyone did.

"Hi," Thomas said. He was standing in the wide doorway leading from the living room to the kitchen. He had reached his arms out so that a hand touched each side of the door frame. He wore a T-shirt, and when he did this, you could see his biceps. Swimmers, he had once told me, were not buff, just cut.

Daddy was still staring at Thomas. I tried not to feel sorry for him that I was going against his rules and there was nothing he could do about it. It was hard, especially now that he was here in his suit, trying to make a good impression. "This is Thomas," I said finally, figuring that since he was my friend, Daddy would at least want me to be the one to introduce him to Thena.

"Hello, Thomas," Thena said, and she stepped forward to shake his hand. "I'm Thena."

Thomas let go of the door frame and stepped forward, too. "Nice to meet you," he said. Then he looked at Daddy and said, "Hello."

Daddy didn't say anything.

"It's Thomas," Thomas said, prompting him.

Daddy nodded. "I remember."

There was quiet for a moment, then Thomas turned to Melina and said, "My mom says I can stay."

"Good," Melina said.

"Well," Daddy said, "I guess you forgot about our dinner tonight."

"It's not just that," Melina said. "I mean, yes, we forgot, okay. But circumstances have changed, don't you think?"

Daddy shrugged. "The war is still over."

"You know what I mean," Melina said.

"May I say something?" Thena asked.

"Of course," Gil said.

"Thank you," she said. She smiled a little and took a breath. "We don't want to intrude, do we, Rifat?" She looked at Daddy. When he didn't answer, she continued, "It's just that I think Rifat would like the chance to visit with Jasira and let her know that he misses her." She looked at Daddy again.

"Yes," Daddy said. He looked at me and added, "This is what I'm interested in doing."

"So even if we don't stay tonight," Thena said, "perhaps we could make plans for another night?"

"Sure," Melina said.

"There're only two pizzas," I blurted out.

"It's okay," Thomas said. "I'm not that hungry. I had a lot of snacks."

Nobody said anything then. It was hard to know what the decision was, or who was going to make it. I was nervous for a second that Melina would say I had to, but she didn't.

"Well," Gil said, "why don't you both at least come in and sit down for a few minutes?"

"Thank you," Thena said. "That would be very nice."

"Let me take your coat," Gil said, and he helped Thena off with hers. As he headed for the closet, Melina motioned Thena and Daddy into the living room. Daddy took Gil's chair, and Thena sat at one end of the couch. I was still standing in front of the middle seat, while Melina had long ago settled into the other end. When Gil came back, he took the chair nearest to Melina's end of the couch. It hardly ever got sat in since it was too close to the TV.

"Come and join us, Thomas," Gil said.

Thomas nodded and took a seat on the floor in front of the coffee table.

"That pizza smells good," Thena said.

"Thank you," Melina said.

"It's homemade," I said. "Even the crust."

Thena nodded, like she was impressed. "May I ask when your due date is?" she said to Melina.

"Officially, April twenty-third. But it feels like it could be any day now. She's already dropped."

"Dropped?" Daddy said.

"They reposition themselves in the uterus as the birth gets closer," Melina told him.

Daddy looked embarrassed then, like he wished he hadn't asked. "Oh."

"So you know it's a girl?" Thena asked.

Melina nodded.

"How exciting," she said. "Congratulations."

"Thank you," Melina said.

"Girls are so much more fun than boys," Thena said.

"Why?" Daddy said. "How do you know?"

"Everyone knows that," she said. "Girls have more personality."

Daddy raised an eyebrow. He probably wanted to say something like I didn't have much of a personality, but he didn't.

"I agree," Thomas said. "About girls."

Daddy glared at him. "Excuse me," he said, "but may I ask what you're doing here?"

"I'm a friend of Jasira's," Thomas said.

"Uh-huh," Daddy said. "Except Jasira isn't supposed to be seeing you."

Thomas shrugged.

"Why not?" Melina asked.

"Because I'm black," Thomas said.

Daddy didn't say anything.

"Is that the reason?" Thena asked Daddy.

He didn't answer.

"My God," Thena said. "That's ridiculous."

"First of all," Daddy said, "she's too young to go with boys—that's the first thing."

"I agree," Melina said.

Daddy looked at her. He was quiet for a second, then said, "And second of all, it can be very hard for white women in interracial relationships. It was hard for Jasira's mother, for example."

"Jasira's not white," Thomas said.

"Oh, yes she is," Daddy said. "On the forms, North African is considered white. Caucasian."

"What forms?" Thomas asked.

"Any forms!" Daddy said. I could tell he didn't think Thomas should be speaking to him in that way, and that was the real reason he was getting mad.

Just then, the oven timer rang. "Time to get the pizza," Melina said, getting up from the couch. "Come and help me, Jasira."

"Sure," I said, following her into the kitchen.

When we got there, Melina said, "Take down six plates, would you?" I nodded. I felt the heat of the oven on my legs as she opened the door and took out the two trays. While they sat and cooled on the stovetop, she went to the silverware drawer and got out a bunch of knives and forks. She didn't think there would be enough sparkling cider for all of us, so she filled six glasses with lemonade and put them on a tray, along with the silverware and some napkins. I kept waiting for her to say something about what she was thinking, but she didn't. She just worked, cutting the pizza with a round roller and putting a slice of each flavor on everyone's plate. Finally, she sighed and said, "I guess they're staying for dinner."

"I guess so," I said.

"Sorry about that, kiddo."

"It's okay," I said, and that was the truth. It was always okay when Melina knew what I was thinking without my even having to tell her.

We took everything out to the living room then—the plates with pizza and the tray with everything else. As soon he saw the food, Daddy said, "Oh, we're eating in here?" Thena immediately began clearing magazines off the coffee table. Daddy started to help her until he came across my *Changing Bodies, Changing Lives* book, then stopped. "What's this?" he asked.

Melina and Gil looked at each other.

"Whose is this?" Daddy wanted to know.

"It's mine," I said.

"Yours?"

I nodded.

"Where did you get such a book?"

"It's for teenagers," I said. "Teenage boys and girls."

"Look at this," he said, and he handed the book to Thena.

She wouldn't take it. She said, "It's time to eat now, Rifat."

"But look at this book," Daddy said, showing her some of the pages. "With these pictures."

Thena took the book from him and looked at it. "This is just a basic book," she said. "With basic information."

"No, it's not," Daddy said. "This is not basic information. This is very graphic material. I can't even repeat most of this."

Melina sighed. "Look," she said, "I gave Jasira that book as a gift. She had a lot of questions, and I thought the book might help."

"Who are you?" Daddy asked. "Why should you help? Who told you to help?"

Gil said something to Daddy in Arabic, and Daddy stopped talking to Melina that way. Gil said something else and held out his hand,

and Daddy handed him my book. We all sat and ate pizza then. "This is really good," Thomas said.

"Thank you," Melina said.

"It really is," Thena agreed.

"There's a little left for anyone who wants it," Melina said.

"Count me in," Thomas said, even though he'd already said earlier that he was full from snacking.

"Save room for baklava," Daddy mumbled.

"Daddy makes a very good baklava," I said.

Daddy looked at me then. He didn't smile, but some of the lines in his forehead relaxed a little.

After we finished eating, Thena helped Melina and me carry the dishes into the kitchen. She started to put on one of the rubber gloves Melina always left at the edge of the sink, and Melina said, "Oh no, don't worry about the dishes. Gil will do them later."

"I insist," Thena said, putting on the other glove.

"Okay, well, I'm too tired to stop you," Melina said.

"Jasira will help me dry," Thena said, which made me kind of mad since I wanted to go back in the living room with Melina. I always wanted to be with Melina. Instead, though, I picked up a dish towel.

Melina put her hands on her back and watched Thena and me at the sink. I pretended that maybe she didn't like the idea of my not going with her either, but then finally she just said, "All right. Don't be long."

"She's very nice, isn't she?" Thena said after Melina had walked out.

I nodded.

"I can see why you like her so much."

I worried that Thena might ruin her nice dress with soapsuds, so I said, "Would you like an apron?"

"Sure," she said. "That's probably a good idea."

I went to the deep drawer next to the refrigerator that held clean aprons and dish towels. I knew where everything was in Melina's house: Scotch tape, pens, extension cords, writing tablets, phone books, shoe polish, lightbulbs, the broom, umbrellas, toilet paper. I was allowed to go and get whatever I needed, whenever I needed it, without asking. I could eat any food I wanted at any time of day. I could turn on the TV and watch my favorite shows from when I used to live with my mother. Whenever I did anything new without asking permission, I could feel Gil and Melina trying to ignore me, so I wouldn't feel self-conscious about it. I knew I wasn't supposed to notice this, but I did. I noticed everything, all the time. I couldn't help it.

"Here," I said, handing Thena the apron that barely reached around Melina's stomach. "You can use this."

"Thank you." Since her hands were all soapy and wet, she smiled and said, "Would you mind?"

I said no, slipped the loop over her head, then made a full bow with the apron strings in the back. Thena returned to her washing and I picked up a plate from the drainer and dried it. "So," she said, "when do you think you might move back in with your father?"

I went to the cupboard on the other side of her and put the plate away. "I don't know," I said. I didn't tell her that I hoped never. That I wanted Gil and Melina to be my new parents.

"He really does miss you, Jasira," Thena said.

I didn't answer, just went and got another plate to dry.

"Do you miss him?"

"No."

"Oh."

"Sorry," I said.

"No," she said, "I understand. It's just—I mean, the thing is, all parents lose control and hit their kids at one time or another. My parents were wonderful and they did it, too. Gil and Melina will probably do it."

"No, they won't," I said. I glanced in the sink then, trying to gauge how many more dishes I would need to dry before everything that was left would fit in the drain board and I could go out the living room.

"Maybe that was the wrong thing to say," Thena said. "I can't really speak for Gil and Melina, and I shouldn't try to."

"It's okay," I said. I went and put the second plate in the cupboard. I wished she would wash the pizza trays next since they were so big. I knew it was either wash them now so I could go, or save them for the end and I'd be stuck here.

Thena sighed. "How's your mother?" she asked.

"Good," I said, even though all I'd heard from her recently were her insistent phone messages.

"That's good," Thena said.

I started to feel guilty then that Thena was just trying to be nice to me, so I said, "She has a black boyfriend."

"Really?" Thena asked.

I nodded.

"What does he do?"

I couldn't remember for a second, since the main thing about him always seemed to be that he was black. Finally, I said, "I think he's a guidance counselor at my mother's school."

"Ah," Thena said, like that explained something, except I wasn't sure what. She put a glass on the drain board that still had a few soapsuds on it, and I wasn't sure what to do. I couldn't remember if soapsuds were bad for Dorrie. Part of me didn't feel like caring, but another part of me thought I should.

"Can you rinse this a little more?" I asked, picking up the glass.

"Sure," Thena said.

"Thanks," I said, taking it back when she was done.

"Well," Thena said, "I can tell you this: I disagree with your father about having Thomas as a friend. That's simply wrong. I'm sure he knows it, too. He's just worried about your well-being."

I went and put the glass in its cupboard. I wished she wouldn't always come back to defending Daddy. Melina never did that. She never believed that Daddy had any good parts inside him. Even if that was wrong, I didn't care. I didn't want to think about Daddy's insides anymore. I was too tired.

Just then, Thomas came into the kitchen. "Hey," he said, "I'll finish drying. Your father wants you to show him your room."

"Why?" I said.

Thomas shrugged. "He says he has a right to see where his daughter is sleeping."

"He cares about you, Jasira," Thena said. "He wants to make sure you're comfortable."

I decided then that I would rather show Daddy my room than listen to Thena talk like that anymore, so I handed Thomas the dish towel.

Out in the living room, Daddy stood and said, "I would like a tour, please."

I looked at Melina, who was wedged into her usual corner of the couch, then at Gil in his chair. "C'mon," he said, immediately standing up. "I'll come, too."

I could tell Daddy was disgusted that I thought I needed protection from him, but I didn't care. I knew he wouldn't hit me; it wasn't that. But he might've said terrible things to me when we were alone, like what the hell did I think I was doing over here, and if I didn't come home this instant he was going to penalize me heavily. I wasn't even sure if I would really have believed it, but I didn't want to find out. I didn't want to be with him and have him say those things and learn that I was still afraid.

Gil went up the stairs first, then me, then Daddy. When we reached the upstairs hall, Daddy said, "It's loud with the wooden steps."

"Not too bad," Gil said. Then he motioned to the door on his right. "This is the master bedroom."

Daddy peered in and nodded.

A little farther down the hall, Gil said, "And here's Jasira's bathroom." Neither he nor Melina had ever called it that before, and I wondered if it meant anything that I now had two rooms in the house.

We stopped so Daddy could flip the light on and take a look. "Very nice," he said, though he didn't really sound like he meant it. He turned the light off and said, "I thought about getting a two-story for Jasira and me, but then it seemed too big for just the both of us."

"Sure," Gil said.

"And now just one," Daddy said.

"Here's Jasira's room," Gil said, turning the light on and stepping inside. I followed him, and Daddy followed me. He put his hands on his hips while he looked around. My bed was still rumpled from Thomas and me using it earlier, but he didn't seem to notice. Instead, he said, "Whose jacket is that?"

I looked at Thomas's coat, draped over the back of the couch. It was a blue windbreaker.

"That's not your jacket," Daddy said.

"No," I said. "It's Thomas's."

"What?"

"I came up here to show him my room. He must've left it."

"Did he sit down?" Daddy asked. "I don't understand why he would leave his coat if he hadn't sat down."

Gil went and got the coat. "Well," he said, "I'll give it back to him."

"What does that solve?" Daddy demanded. "I want to know why it's here in the first place."

"Jasira just said that she was showing Thomas her room."

"But why would he leave his jacket here if he hadn't stayed?"

"He didn't stay," I said.

"Uh-huh," Daddy said.

"I'm ready for baklava," Gil said.

Daddy didn't move. "Don't you and your wife perform any type of supervision?"

"Of course we do," Gil said. "Melina already agreed with you that Jasira was too young to go with boys."

Daddy didn't say anything.

"C'mon," Gil said. "I'll make us some coffee."

Daddy looked like he didn't really want coffee. He looked like he wanted to keep searching for evidence. Finally, though, he turned and walked out of the room. He said he would have a few questions for Melina when he got downstairs.

"No," Gil said. "No questions, please."

"I have a right to ask questions about my daughter's well-being," Daddy said.

"Jasira already answered your questions."

"She's a liar," Daddy said.

"Excuse me?" Gil said.

"She lies about everything," Daddy said.

"I have never known Jasira to be a liar," Gil said. "She's always been very truthful with Melina and me."

"Well," Daddy said, "you wait and see."

"That's enough," Gil said. "Enough nasty talk. We'll go have some baklava, then you and Thena should probably go."

"Fine," Daddy snapped. "Whatever you say." Then he went in my bathroom and shut the door.

"C'mon, Jasira," Gil said to me, and he put a hand on my shoulder and guided me toward the stairs. I felt terrible as we walked. Like I should tell him to take his hand away since it was true, I was a liar.

"Where's your father?"Thena asked when we reached the living room. She and Thomas must've finished up the dishes because he was back on the floor and she was sitting on the opposite end of the couch from Melina.

"Using the bathroom," I said.

"Here," Gil said to Thomas, dropping the jacket in his lap.

"Oh, thanks,"Thomas said.

"No more going upstairs, okay?"

Thomas nodded. "Sure."

"Now," Gil said, clapping his hands together. "Who would like coffee?"

"I'd love some decaf,"Thena said.

"One decaf," Gil said.

"Me, too,"Thomas said.

"How about you, Jasira?" Gil asked.

"Okay," I said. No one had ever asked me if I wanted coffee before. I'd always thought I was too young.

"I'll have some milk," Melina said.

Gil nodded and went in the kitchen.

I sat down on the couch between Melina and Thena. Melina reached out and touched my hair a little. "Everything okay?" she asked.

"Yes," I said.

"Good."

I looked over the coffee table at Thomas, who was now lying on the floor. He had folded up his jacket and tucked it under his head like a pillow. His eyes were closed.

"You ready to go home, Thomas?" Melina asked him.

"Sure,"Thomas said, opening his eyes and looking over at us. "I want to try some of that baklava first, though."

Thena nodded. "Rifat is a good cook."

A few moments later, Daddy came down the stairs. He had a

strange look on his face, and he was holding a piece of toilet paper in his hand.

"Rifat," Melina said, "we're ready for your baklava." It was the first time I had heard her say his name.

Daddy didn't answer. He just kept coming down the stairs. When he reached the bottom, he walked over to where Thomas was lying on the floor and said, "Get up."

"What?" Thomas said.

"Get up," Daddy said again.

"What's the matter?" Thomas asked, sitting up. "What are you talking about?"

Daddy turned the toilet paper upside down then and something dropped into Thomas's lap.

"What the hell!" Thomas said. "That's disgusting."

"This is yours," Daddy said.

At first I couldn't tell what it was, but then Thomas picked it up, and I saw that it was his rubber from earlier.

Daddy turned to Melina and said, "What did you let them do?"

"I didn't let them do anything," she said. "What are you talking about? What is that?"

"It's a rubber!" Daddy said.

"Oh my God," Melina said, trying to stand up. I held out an arm to help her, but she didn't see it.

Gil must've heard Daddy yell because he came in and said, "What's the problem?"

"I found a rubber in your toilet," Daddy said. "In *Jasira's* toilet!"

"What rubber?" Gil said.

"His rubber!" Daddy said, pointing to Thomas. "He's the only one here who needs a rubber."

Thomas grabbed a napkin off the coffee table and put the rubber inside it. He stood up.

"Where do you think you're going?" Daddy barked.

"To throw this in the trash," Thomas said. "It's disgusting that you took it out of the toilet."

"Give it to me," Daddy said.

"No," Thomas said.

Daddy lunged at him and grabbed the napkin out of his hands.

"Jesus!" Thomas said.

"You're not going anywhere!" Daddy said. "You stay right here!" Then he looked at Melina and said, "I want to know why you're letting my daughter use rubbers."

"I'm not," Melina said. "I didn't." For the first time, it seemed like she was stuck. Like she didn't know what to say.

"Then why did I find this?" Daddy demanded.

"Honestly," Melina said, "I don't know."

"You think I'm so terrible!" Daddy said, looking from Melina to Gil. "You both think I'm so terrible. But then you let my daughter take boys in her room and use rubbers!"

His skin was red and he was spitting, and I couldn't tell if his face was sweaty or if he was crying. I worried that he would try to hit someone, except there was no one for him to hit, not really. If he had tried to hit Thomas, Thomas might've hit him back.

"Rifat," Thena said. She got up from the couch and went to stand by his side. "Let's try to calm down for a moment. Please."

"No!" Daddy yelled, and he shook her hand from his arm. He turned to me and said, "Go and get your things. You're coming home." When I didn't move from behind the coffee table, he yelled, "Now!"

"Hold on a second there," Gil said.

"You have a picture of her leg, and I have this rubber!" Daddy said. "If you show the police her picture, I will show them this. You are terrible, too. You let terrible things happen, too!"

"Look," Thomas said, "I'm really sorry, okay? It's all my fault. Blame me."

"Of course I blame you!" Daddy said. "I blame you, and I blame her!" He pointed at Melina.

"That's enough," Gil said sharply. "Just calm down. You don't even know what happened."

"I know exactly what happened," Daddy said. "I know that my daughter lost her virginity in this house!"

"That's not true," Thomas said.

"Shut up!" Daddy yelled. Then he turned to me and said, "Go and get your things. I already told you!"

Nobody said anything. Not Melina, not Gil, not Thena. It was like they all thought Daddy was right for once. Like they had no way to fight him. And I guessed they didn't. Not really. But I did. And I didn't want to go back with him. I just couldn't imagine it. I couldn't imagine living with him or my mother ever again. I could imagine visiting them, but then, in the end, I would need to come back to Gil and Melina's. To my foldout bed with the bar in the middle. To my bathroom. To my clothes in the linen closet. I said, "I didn't lose my virginity in this house."

"She lost it at my house," Thomas said to my father.

"No, I didn't," I said.

Thomas looked at me.

"I lost it at your house," I said to Daddy. "Mr. Vuoso did it. With his fingers. I didn't want him to, but he did."

As soon as I'd said it, I didn't want to see anything. Especially, I didn't want to see anyone seeing me. I didn't want to know anyone who knew this thing about me, and I wished I hadn't said it. It was disgusting, like pulling a rubber out of the toilet. I turned then to the only person who was a stranger to me anymore. I turned to Dorrie, and I pressed my face against where she was, and I cried harder than I knew I could, and when I felt her kicking me lightly in the face, I was glad to know that one of us was so alive.

TWELVE

Melina cried. She said it was all her fault. Gil told her it wasn't and tried to put his arms around her, even though she already had her arms around me. "Don't hug me," she said. "Nothing happened to me."

Thomas picked up his coat from the floor, put it on, and said he was going next door to kill Mr. Vuoso. Gil said no he wasn't and went and stood in front of the door. Daddy sat down in Gil's chair and put his face in his hands. I guessed he felt the same way as I had, like he didn't want anyone to see him. Thena went and stood next to his chair and put a hand on his shoulder. Instead of watching Daddy, I just watched her hand shake from his body.

I was glad that everyone was worried about how sad they were and whose fault it was. I was glad not to have anyone talk to me. It was embarrassing, the things I had said, the things they all knew. Even in front of Thomas, who I did intimate things with, I felt embarrassed.

Nobody could really calm down for a while. I said I wanted a glass of water and went in the kitchen and sat by myself at the table. Thomas came in and said where was my water, then filled us both glasses from the faucet. He came and sat down next to me and said, "You should've told me." When I didn't answer, he picked up my hand and held it. He was the calmest of everyone, maybe because he was too young to think it was his fault. I didn't really think it was any of the adults' fault, but I liked how they thought it was. I liked how terrible they looked and how they shook and cried. It felt like I didn't have to worry about things anymore, now that they were doing it for me.

Thomas played with my hand. He scratched each one of my fingernails with the tip of his own. "Did it hurt?" he asked.

I nodded.

"Was there a lot of blood?"

I nodded again.

"That was my blood," Thomas said. "Not his."

Normally I would've liked when Thomas said something like that. Acting like he owned me. But now it didn't make me feel like anything. Mostly I just thought that it was my blood, and that Thomas shouldn't bring it up anymore.

There began to be the low sound of adults talking in the living room, and Thomas and I stayed quiet so we could listen. It was hard to hear them. They didn't want us to hear. I got worried that they were talking about sending me back to Daddy's, so I went and stood in the doorway between the kitchen and the living room. "What are you saying?" I asked. They all looked at me. No one answered. I could feel Thomas at my back, breathing.

"I live here now," I said to everyone in the room, and no one said that I didn't.

After a few moments, Thena said, "Thomas, I should at least take you home."

"Why?" he asked.

"Your mother will be worried."

"I don't want to go," he said, and no one talked about it anymore.

They all looked tired and scared. Daddy didn't have his face in his hands anymore. He'd turned his head from me and was staring straight ahead at the TV, which wasn't on. Melina had slumped back onto the couch. Gil wasn't directly in front of the door anymore, but he was nearby, like a goalie who felt safe coming out a little ways.

"What's going to happen?" Thomas asked.

I thought Daddy would yell at him and tell him to butt out, but he didn't. He said, "We have to call the authorities."

"Why?" I said. I worried that I would have to tell my story again to people I didn't even know.

"Because," Daddy said, turning around to look at me. "What that son of a bitch did is illegal."

"But I don't want to talk about it anymore," I said.

"Too bad," he said.

Gil said something in Arabic then, even louder and more sharply than the thing he had said to Daddy when Daddy had snapped at Melina. Daddy made a hard face at him but didn't say anything back. I knew Gil was defending me, and it made me feel terrible that I couldn't understand any of the words.

Melina sighed. "You're right, Rifat. We have to call the police."

"No," I said.

"I'll sit with you," she said. "The whole time."

I almost said no again, but then Daddy said, "Melina will sit next to you," and I stopped. I didn't want to ruin Daddy and Melina's getting along.

"Should we call them now?" Gil asked.

Nobody answered.

"Or wait until tomorrow?" he said.

"I don't know," Daddy said. "I can't think."

"Maybe we should wait until tomorrow," Thena said.

All along, there had been the smell of Gil's coffee drifting out from the kitchen. It was strange to have something bad happening when something was smelling so good. "Coffee's ready," Thomas said.

Everyone ignored him.

He shrugged and went back in the kitchen. I heard him open cupboard doors and get down cups and saucers. I heard him open drawers and pull out silverware. "Help me, Jasira," he called a couple of minutes later, and together we carried in the coffee for the adults. We put the cups on the coffee table with milk and sugar, but no one would drink from them. Thomas went back in the kitchen and brought out the baklava. He had removed the foil from the top of the dish, and now it sat at the middle of the table, the filo pastry cut in Daddy's neat, perfect diamonds. Thomas tried to scoop out the pieces with a spatula, but it just made the flaky leaves crumble and fall apart. I waited for Daddy to yell at him to stop, but he didn't. I waited for Daddy to tell him you had to recut the diamonds after it was baked to be able to lift out the pieces, but he didn't. I waited for Daddy to get mad at me for knowing all of this and not telling Thomas myself. But he just sat there, watching the whole thing fall apart, all of his hard work.

Gil took everyone home that night, even Daddy and Thena. He walked them past the Vuosos' house so Daddy wouldn't get mad and bang on the door. I knew Daddy wouldn't have done that, though. He wasn't like Thomas.

That night, Melina slept with me in my bed from the beginning. I guessed she thought I would definitely have a bad dream, so she might as well just tuck me in and stay. "I'm sorry," she said while we lay there in the dark.

"Why?" I said.

"Because I should've figured all of this out."

"I didn't want you to," I told her.

"Yes, you did."

I was quiet for a moment. I had to think if this was true.

"Jasira?" she said.

"Yes?"

"Were there any other times?"

I didn't answer.

"Tell me if there were any other times, please."

"It's not good for the baby," I said.

"The baby is fine."

"Yes," I said.

"How many?"

"One."

"You're going to have to tell the police that, too."

"What if I wanted to do it that time?" I asked, then I started to cry from being ashamed. Not because I really had wanted to, but because I had acted like I did with Mr. Vuoso, and he would tell the police that, and that would make it true.

Melina pulled me next to her and whispered, "It doesn't matter. If a grown man has sex with someone who's under sixteen, it's rape. Even if she wants to do it."

"I didn't really want to," I said. "I just acted like I did."

"Why?" Melina asked.

"I don't know."

She touched my hair while I tried to stop crying. It was hard when she was being so nice to me. Before we fell asleep, I said, "I used to hate Dorrie."

Melina laughed a little. "I got that."

"I don't anymore," I said, even though I kind of did.

"You can hate her," Melina said. "Older kids always hate their little brothers and sisters."

I hoped Melina wouldn't say anything else then. I just wanted to hear the words play over and over again in my head. They were so bright and shiny, like when you looked into the Texas sun, then shut your eyes tight, and there was still the outline of the circle.

The next morning, Saturday, I talked to the police. Daddy brought them over while Melina and I were eating breakfast. There was a man and a woman officer, but I didn't have to talk to the man, just the woman. The man stayed in the living room with Daddy and Gil. The policewoman had asked Daddy if he wanted to be present for the interview, but he said no, that Melina would sit with me. The policewoman wanted to know if Melina was a relation, and Daddy explained that she was a friend of the family. I thought this was kind of funny since no one in my family except me actually liked Melina. Still, it was nice that Daddy said that. Mostly, though, I was just glad that he wouldn't be listening to me talk.

We were sitting in the kitchen. The policewoman was recording me on a tape recorder, but sometimes she would write something in a notebook as well. Melina had her knitting, probably because she didn't want me to feel like she was paying too much attention to me while I was feeling ashamed.

I told the policewoman what I had told everyone the night before, except she had a lot more questions. She wanted to know every little thing Mr. Vuoso had said to me, every way he had looked at me or touched me. Some of the things that had been nice between us now sounded kind of bad when I was telling them to the policewoman. Like Mr. Vuoso taking me out for dinner, or visiting me while Daddy was at Thena's to say that the floodlight wasn't on, or letting me interview him for the school newspaper. After I told these stories, the policewoman would ask a question, like, "And when he visited you, he could tell that your father wasn't home?" That was when I would know I had been seeing things in the wrong way.

When it seemed like the interview was over, the policewoman asked, "Is there anything else?"

I looked down at the table. I just didn't want to talk about the other time, when I had let Mr. Vuoso do it to me because I'd thought he was going to war. I didn't want anyone to know how stupid I had been to believe him.

"Jasira?" the policewoman said.

I looked at her. She was black and stout, and I liked the way her uniform fit, rising snugly over the mounds of her bottom and breasts. "Yes?"

"Did you have any other contact with Mr. Vuoso?"

When I didn't answer, Melina said, "Yes, she did."

"Can you tell me about it?" the policewoman asked.

I looked at Melina.

"Go ahead," she said.

I waited for a second, then told the policewoman about the other time. I was getting tired of having to say words like vagina and penis and breast and erection. Even saying fingers or mouth was embarrassing. I noticed that in the worst parts of the story, Melina knitted faster than usual. I watched her and pretended like I was her engine. Like my talking was pushing a kind of pedal that could make her hands speed up. I didn't cry until the end, when I described how Mr. Vuoso had called me a slut while we were doing it. Melina put her knitting down then and told the policewoman that we had probably talked enough for that day. The policewoman nodded and capped her pen. She turned off the tape recorder and stood up. Before she left, she touched my arm and said, "You're a good girl. You remembered lots of details."

A few minutes later, Daddy came in the kitchen. "How did it go?" he asked. "Did you answer all her questions?"

Melina nodded. "She did very well."

Daddy looked at her, then back at me. "Why are you crying?" he asked.

"Rifat," Melina said, "it was hard. These were hard things to talk about."

Daddy kept looking at me. "I can't understand why you never told me about this before."

"I thought you would be mad," I said.

"Why would I be mad if someone was hurting you?"

"I don't know."

"Well, I wouldn't," he said, looking at Melina. "I'm not that kind of person."

Melina didn't say anything. Just then Gil came in. "Everything okay?" he asked.

I nodded.

"I'm pooped," Melina said.

"Well," Gil said, "maybe we should all take a little time to ourselves."

"What does that mean?" Daddy said.

"I'm just saying maybe we could take a break for now, then get together a little bit later."

"You mean you want me to go home?" Daddy said.

"Just for a little while," Gil said.

"What if I want to stay with my daughter?"

"You can see her later," Gil said. "After she has a rest."

"She can rest at my house," Daddy said. "She has her own room there."

"C'mon, Rifat," Gil said.

Daddy didn't answer. He'd been holding a business card from the policewoman, and now he flicked the edge of it back and forth with his fingernail.

"You can come over tonight, okay?" Gil said.

Daddy shrugged. Then he turned to me and said, "You can't come home? Even for just one afternoon?"

I didn't know what to say. I looked at Gil.

"No," Daddy said. "I'm talking to you, not him."

I took a deep breath and said, "I can't."

Daddy was quiet for a second, then he said fine and went home.

Melina and I went and sat in the living room then. She asked me how I was doing, and I said okay. She told me again that I had done a good job with the policewoman, but that I should probably prepare myself for the fact that I would have to tell my story a few more times to different people. Plus, she said, I would have to go to the doctor. "What kind of doctor?" I asked, even though I already knew.

"My doctor," she said. "The doctor who takes care of me when I'm pregnant. She's very nice. We'll go together."

"Will Daddy come, too?" I asked.

"God, no," she said. "I mean, I guess we can't stop him from sitting in the waiting room, but he can't come in the examining room. It's not allowed."

"Okay," I said. I got my book about teenagers from the coffee table and read about how, when you have an exam, they put a kind of tool in you to spread your insides so they can see. It said you were supposed to relax while they're doing it, so it wouldn't feel uncomfortable. It said that the doctor might try to show me my insides with a mirror, since they were fascinating.

While I was reading, the phone rang. Gil, who was still in the kitchen, answered it, then called me to come in. "It's your mother," he said, handing me the receiver. I wished I could tell him that I didn't want to talk to her, but I figured I shouldn't, since he'd already had to defend me against Daddy. I was worried that someday soon he might get tired of having to tell people to leave me alone.

"Thank you," I said, taking the phone.

He nodded, then grabbed the magazine he'd been looking at and headed into the living room.

"Hello?" I said, wishing Gil had stayed.

"Jasira?" my mother said.

"Yes?"

"Is that you?"

"Yes."

She was quiet for a moment, then said, "Daddy just called me. He told me what happened."

"Oh," I said.

"I'm going to come down there next weekend, okay?"

"I live with Melina now," I said.

"Yes," she said. "Daddy told me."

"You can stay with Daddy, but I live with Melina."

"Okay," she said.

I didn't know what to say then. I couldn't think of anything. Finally I asked, "What will you do when you come?"

"Well," she said, "just see you, I guess. Talk to you."

"Oh."

"Maybe I shouldn't have sent you down there to live."

"I like it," I said, which was the truth. I did like it.

My mother started to cry. "How can you like it?"

"It's not so bad."

She was quiet for a moment, then said, "You were very brave to talk to the police."

"Thank you."

"Now that man will go to jail, and he won't hurt any other little girls. You prevented him from hurting other girls."

"Uh-huh," I said. I didn't really like to think of Mr. Vuoso going to jail. It bothered me. I knew he had done bad things, but he had done good things, too. He had been my friend sometimes. He had been jealous of Thomas. He had yelled at his son to be nice to me. He had protected me from Daddy.

"Anyway," my mother said, "I'll be front and center in that courtroom, giving him the look of his life."

"What if it's on a school day?" I said.

"What?"

"What if court is on a school day and you can't come?"

"They'll have to get a substitute," she said.

After we hung up, I went in the living room and told Melina and Gil that my mother was coming in a week. "I've never met your mother," Gil said.

"I met her," Melina said, but she didn't say anything else.

"I don't want to live with her," I said.

"Okay," Melina said.

"Will I have to?" I asked.

"Not if you don't want to."

"Will I ever have to live with anyone I don't want to?"

"Of course not," Melina said.

"Thomas says I can't live with the neighbors."

She sighed. "Well, Thomas doesn't know everything."

Daddy didn't come back that night, even though Gil had told him that he could. Part of me was glad, but part of me missed him a little. If we had been together, we could've made fun of my mother and how terrible it was going to be when she visited. Or we could've talked about how the police car had stayed outside the Vuosos' house late into the afternoon. Or how when they had left, Mr. Vuoso had been with them, carrying a small duffel bag.

Denise gave me the pictures we'd had taken of ourselves at Glamour Shots. She said that I looked like a model and that I could be in a magazine someday. She said she looked like a model, too, but if it had been a shot of her whole body, then forget it. She gave Mr. Joffrey a copy of one of her pictures, and a couple of days later he gave it back to her, saying that he couldn't accept it but that she looked very nice. She asked me if I was going to give a copy of my picture to Mr.

Vuoso, and I said probably not. "You're not in love with him any-more?" she asked, and I shook my head.

I gave Thomas one of the pictures, and he said he would cherish it always. He'd started walking me everywhere in school, like he thought someone was going to get me. He met me at the curb when Melina dropped me off in the morning, and he waited with me in the afternoon until she came to pick me up. He told me he'd decided that he didn't want to have sex with me anymore, not until I was older. In-stead he held my hand and kissed my cheek. He didn't say anything selfish about what I should do for him. He came back to Melina's one day after school, but all we did was sit and watch TV.

Daddy must've seen Thomas's parents come to get him, because he came over that night and knocked on the door. He said I wasn't allowed to see Thomas anymore, not because he was black, but because we'd had sex. Melina said I was allowed to see him, except with supervision. Daddy said I was his daughter, and he would make the rules; and Melina said it was her house, and she would make the rules. Daddy said he couldn't believe he didn't have a say in how his own daughter was raised anymore, and Melina said he was over-stating.

My mother arrived on Friday night with her new boyfriend, Richard. Daddy let them stay at his place while he went to stay with Thena. It seemed strange to me that he was letting a black person stay in his house. Part of me thought he was doing it to try to impress Melina, who he felt had unfairly judged him as a racist. "How could I be a racist?" he'd asked me one night on the phone. Sometimes he called to tell me good night or to ask if I'd done my homework. "I mean, just take one look at me!" When I didn't answer, he answered for me, saying, "Well, I couldn't be a racist. Hardly. It's a joke."

My mother called from Daddy's house and asked if I'd like to come over and meet Richard. Melina was standing nearby in the kitchen, her fingers spread out across the front of her T-shirt. It was like she was trying to massage Dorrie through her stomach. "I don't usually go over there," I told my mother.

"You can't come over for just a night?" she asked. "I mean, we've come all this way."

I looked at Melina. She shook her head slightly, like she was agreeing with me that I didn't have to go over there. "You could come over here," I offered.

Melina nodded approvingly.

"Come over there?" my mother said.

"Melina says it's okay."

"Uh-huh," my mother said.

"You could meet Melina and Gil."

"I think I already met her," my mother said. "Didn't I?"

"Oh yeah," I said.

"I guess I just thought you might break your rule and come and stay the weekend. I mean, your father's not even here."

Melina made a face. I could tell she was getting bothered by how long this was all taking, by how my mother wouldn't do things our way.

Finally I said, "I don't like to go to the place where Mr. Vuoso hurt me." It wasn't actually true, but I was learning that whenever I talked about Mr. Vuoso to my mother, she didn't bother me so much.

"Oh," she said. "I see. Well, okay. Why don't we all just go out for dinner then? Richard and I rented a car."

"With Melina?" I asked.

"Well," my mother said, "I guess I was thinking it could be just us for tonight. What do you think?"

I looked at Melina. She shrugged. "Okay," I said to my mother. Mostly I just wanted to get off the phone. "I'll meet you in the driveway."

"Great," she said. "You're going to love Richard."

"Okay," I said.

"Maybe you could invite your friend Thomas to come."

I didn't understand why Thomas could come but not Melina, so I said no. After we hung up, Melina said, "What's her problem?"

"She doesn't want to meet you," I said.

"She already met me."

I shrugged. "She doesn't want to meet you again."

"How can you not want to meet the people your kid is living with?"

"I don't know," I said.

"Weird," Melina said.

"Can I go to dinner with them?"

"Sure," she said. "I mean, I guess I'd prefer to meet this Richard guy first, but whatever."

I nodded and went to get my shoes. I wondered if it would always feel good, asking Melina for permission. It wasn't so much the yes or no part I cared about, but the extra parts. The parts that said she was worried that someone was going to hurt me.

It was strange, walking back to Daddy's house. I wasn't usually outside at this time of night anymore, since this was when Gil and Melina made dinner. And when I was outside, I wasn't alone. Melina had relaxed a little about my going out since Mr. Vuoso had gone with the police, but then he paid bail a couple of days later and came back and she got nervous again. Even though she said there was no way he would dare to do anything now, I noticed that whenever I said I wanted to go out lately, she made up a reason that she wanted to go out, too. Or else she looked at Gil, if he was there, and he made up a reason.

Daddy hated that Mr. Vuoso was out on bail. He said fifty thousand dollars wasn't enough for what Mr. Vuoso had done, and that he couldn't wait for the real punishment to start. I didn't really like seeing him, either, but not for the same reason as Daddy. I didn't like seeing him because it was too hard not to feel sorry for him, and I knew

I wasn't supposed to do that. Every time I felt sorry for him, I felt like I was disappointing Melina, even though she might not have known what I was thinking.

Today when I walked past the Vuosos', I noticed a new white cat in the front window. I couldn't believe it. She looked so much like Snowball that I thought maybe it was her, maybe she'd come back to life. But of course she hadn't. She was still in the freezer, wedged in with all Melina's frozen dinners.

My mother ran out of Daddy's house and hugged me. She was wearing jeans and a blue oxford shirt and sneakers. Her hair was in a ponytail. I thought she was trying to look like Melina, even though I wasn't sure she remembered what Melina looked like. I hugged her back until it seemed like maybe she was going to start crying, then I pulled away. She sniffled a little, then introduced me to Richard, who was bald and had a beard. He leaned forward to shake my hand. I got the sense that he didn't want to come too close to me, and I liked that.

We went to a place that served a lot of grilled meat. I liked how instead of saying you wanted a certain dish with a name, you just said, "I'll have the chicken," or, "I'll have the steak." We got a curved booth, and my mother sat between Richard and me—closer to Richard, though. Sometimes, when he said something she thought was funny or smart or nice, she reached over and scrubbed his beard with her fingers. When she started to get upset that her steak had been cooked wrong and that Richard's was more what she had wanted, he passed his dish to her and she felt better. The two times he got up to go to the bathroom, she asked my opinion of him. I said I thought he was different than Daddy and that he had a soft, low voice. She nodded. "I know. It's very romantic." I was glad when Richard came back so I didn't have to think of more things to say about him. When my mother went to the bathroom, he asked me about school and how I liked living with Melina and Gil. I said I liked it a lot, and he said that people could find family in all kinds of different places.

The next day, my mother still wouldn't come to Melina's. This time she said she wanted to go to meet Thomas and his family. I was embarrassed because I was pretty sure she just wanted Mr. and Mrs. Bradley to see that she had a black boyfriend. I wondered if Richard was embarrassed, too, but if he was, he didn't say anything. He just shook Mr. and Mrs. Bradley's hands, then we all sat down in the living room and talked about different planets Mr. Bradley had seen through his telescope.

At one point Thomas asked if we could go upstairs so he could play me a song. None of the adults seemed to know which one of them was supposed to answer. Finally my mother said, "Um, sure. Just don't be too long." I said we wouldn't, and Thomas and I got up from the couch. When we reached his room, he said, "Your mother is weird."

"I know."

"She didn't want you to come up here."

"She doesn't like when boys like me," I said.

"Why?" he said. "She's got her own boyfriend."

I shrugged.

Thomas picked up his guitar and played a few chords, then put it back on its stand and asked if he could eat my pussy. I said no, since our parents were downstairs, but he said he would hurry. He said he wouldn't have asked if I'd been wearing pants, but that since I was wearing a skirt, it would be really easy for him to get down there.

"I thought you didn't want to do stuff anymore," I said.

He thought for a second, then said, "It's more that I don't want you to do stuff for me. But this is something for you. That's different."

I said okay and lay back on his bed. He pushed my skirt up, pulled my underwear off, and put his face between my legs. I pushed myself against his mouth when it started to feel like I was going to have an orgasm, and it seemed like that made him lick me even better.

When it was finished, he came up to my face and asked me if there was anything else I'd like him to do, and I said that I'd like him to let me suck his dick. I could tell by the way he was leaning his hips back that he wanted me to see his erection and say something like that.

"Okay," he said in a serious way. "I mean, if that's what you want."

I said it was and unbuckled his belt. While I was sucking on him, I felt relieved. Ever since I had told everyone what had happened to me, and they had all tried to do the right things, I had felt lonely. It wasn't that I didn't want people to do the right things, or that I didn't want to be helped. I did. But I still wanted my old life, too. I wanted to make love to people. I wanted them to tell me what to do. I couldn't imagine those feelings ever going away.

When we went back downstairs, my mother asked what song Thomas had played for me. She said she hadn't heard any music.

"That's because my amp wasn't plugged in," Thomas said. "I was playing without my amp."

"Oh," my mother said.

When we got back to Daddy's, my mother asked me to come in just for a second, so she could give me a present. I asked her if she could give it to me in the driveway, and she said no, I had to come in. When I didn't move, she sighed and said no one was going to make me stay at Daddy's if I didn't want to. "We'll leave the back door wide open," Richard said, "in case you need to make a quick getaway." I smiled at him, but my mother gave him a look that made me think she might get mad at him later.

Finally I said okay and went inside. We walked back to Daddy's study, where my mother's suitcase was open on the floor. It held clothes I'd never seen before, including a silky pink nightgown. From there, I glanced briefly at the unmade bed, trying to imagine some-

thing about my mother and Richard from the way the sheets and pillows were positioned.

"Here," my mother said, handing me a small wrapped box. I
opened it and found a razor inside. Not the disposable kind, but a
heavy metal kind that came with replacement blades. "Do you like
it?" she asked me.

"Yes," I said. "It's very nice."

She nodded. "Let's go in the bathroom. I'll show you how to
use it."

"I already know how," I said, sticking out one of my bare, shaven
legs. I knew from Barry, from Thomas, and just from doing it myself.

"Oh," she said, looking hurt.

"I really like this present," I said. "It's my favorite present you ever
gave me."

"I'm glad," she said, even though she didn't look glad. She looked
like she was going to cry again. I put the razor down and gave her a
hug. "I'm a terrible mother," she said.

"No, you're not," I said, since it seemed like that was the right
thing to do.

"Yes," she said. "I am." She pulled away from me and dried her
eyes.

I didn't say anything. All of a sudden, I felt tired. I wanted to go
home.

"I'm very jealous of that Melina," my mother said.

"I'm sorry," I said.

"I just don't want to meet her."

"Okay."

"You can live with her if you want, but I can't go over there. I just
can't."

I nodded. We made plans to have breakfast at Denny's the next
morning, before she and Richard left. I picked up my razor, along

with the wrapping paper and ribbon. I thanked my mother again and kissed her. I told her I loved her and that I'd had a nice time with her that day. I didn't tell her that I'd already changed my mind about what the best gift she'd ever given me was.

Mr. Vuoso pled no contest. It was like saying you were guilty without actually having to say it. The judge would still punish him, though, as if he had said he was guilty. The good part was that I wouldn't have to tell my story to any more people, or go to see the doctor. I didn't know if Mr. Vuoso had done this to try to be nice to me, but it felt like he had. When I suggested this to Melina one day, she said absolutely not, that I shouldn't be fooled. "He's doing this to be nice to himself," she said. "So that if your father brings a civil suit against him later, he can still plead not guilty."

Melina and Daddy started to talk a lot about Mr. Vuoso's sentencing, and how much jail time they hoped he got. They still fought about different things—what time I should go to bed, how short I should be allowed to cut my hair—but more and more they were becoming friends over how mad they were. At first I was glad that they liked each other better, but then the things they said about Mr. Vuoso made me nervous. Especially when they talked about how other people in jail didn't like men who hurt children, and how they did mean things to those men.

In the end, I didn't really want anything bad to happen to Mr. Vuoso. I just wanted him to be sorry, like he'd been back when he'd first hurt me. I wanted him to always be sorry, to always worry that I was still feeling hurt, to always want to try to make something up to me. Then, sometimes, I wanted him to try to get something for himself from me. But to do it in a nice, soft way that scared me only a little.

One morning, when I hadn't had bad dreams the night before and Melina hadn't come to sleep with me, I woke up early and got out of bed. Gil had already showered and left for work, since it took at least an hour for him to get to the center of Houston with all the traffic. Melina was still asleep. I dressed in my clothes from the day before and went downstairs. It was just getting light outside, and I waited for Mr. Vuoso to come out with his flag. When I saw him, I went to the freezer and got Snowball.

I took her outside with me and stood on the front steps. I watched Mr. Vuoso in his front yard, attaching the hooks on his flag post to his flag. When he saw me, he stopped what he was doing. It felt like we looked at each other for a long time. I came down off the steps and walked to the edge of Melina's lawn. There was her driveway in front of me, then the Vuosos' lawn started. After a moment, I crossed Melina's driveway. It was as far as I would go. "Hi," I said.

"Get away from me," he said.

I didn't know what to do then, since that was so different from what I had hoped he would say.

"I'm sorry I told on you," I said.

"Get the fuck away from me!" he hissed.

I stood and watched him pull the rope so his flag would run up the pole. When he was done, he headed for his front door. "Daddy killed Snowball," I said.

He stopped and turned around. "What?"

"It was an accident. He ran over her, and then we froze her. We didn't know what to do."

"Jesus Christ."

"This is her," I said, holding out the package.

He paused for a moment, then walked to the edge of his lawn, stopping at the place where his grass met Melina's concrete.

"Here," I said.

He took Snowball from me and looked at her frozen body. He felt it a couple of times, like he was trying to figure out how she was positioned.

"This is her head," I said, showing him, and he nodded. After a moment, I said, "I'm sorry."

He sighed. "It's not your fault."

"She escaped when I was talking to Zack."

"It's not your fault," he said again.

"Okay," I said.

He looked at me then in a very sad way, and I knew that I loved him. I would never tell Melina or anyone else, but it was true. I couldn't help it. He was sorry. He really was. He hadn't meant to hurt me. He loved me, too.

He reached out then and put his hand on my face. It was still very early in the morning, and the sky was pink and hazy. The heat of summer was coming, and it was hard to believe that this was as cool as it was going to get all day. His palm on my cheek felt damp and warm. As he pulled it away, I heard a scream behind me. I turned around to see Melina on her front steps. She was wearing the clothes she had gone to sleep in the night before. "Stop!" she yelled. "Stop it right now! Don't you dare touch her!" And then she fell. Down the front steps, and into a strange, bulging heap on the walkway.

I turned and ran across the lawn toward her. Her eyes were closed, and she had a cut on her wrist that was starting to bleed a little. "Melina?" I said. She didn't answer. She was lying on her side across the walkway. "Melina?" I said again, touching her shoulder. When she still didn't wake up, I ran to get Daddy. Mr. Vuoso had already gone back inside his house.

Daddy was awake and finishing packing for his Cape Canaveral trip. He and Thena were leaving that night, right after work. Now, as I yelled at him that Melina had fallen down the front steps, he wanted to know what I was talking about. "Where's her husband?" he asked, even though he was already moving toward the back door to get his shoes.

We went outside together, skipping the sidewalk and cutting across Mr. Vuoso's front lawn instead. "Melina!" Daddy yelled as he ran. "Hello! Melina!"

She still hadn't opened her eyes by the time we reached her, and Daddy made little slaps on each side of her face. "Melina!" he said. "Time to wake up!" When she didn't respond, he told me to go and call 911. "Tell them we need an ambulance for a pregnant woman who has fainted," he said, and I nodded and went inside. As soon as I picked up the phone in the kitchen, though, I heard a siren. It was coming closer and closer, and I waited a moment to dial. When I understood that it was actually driving down our street, I hung up the phone and went back outside. "They're here already?" Daddy asked, turning around to look at the flashing lights, and I shrugged.

Not even the loud siren woke Melina up. Only when one of the two men paramedics waved smelling salts under her nose did she open her eyes. "You fainted!" Daddy yelled at her, in the same loud voice he'd been using to try and wake her.

She nodded, even though she also looked confused.

"How long has she been out?" the paramedic with the salts asked. He was still holding the broken packet in his hand, and I was both afraid and fascinated to smell it.

Daddy looked at me. "How long?"

I thought for a moment, then said, "About five minutes."

"Do you remember why you fainted, ma'am?" the other paramedic asked. This one had a stethoscope around his neck and was pushing up the sleeve of Melina's shirt so he could wrap a blood pressure cuff around her arm.

"My hand hurts," she said.

"You have a cut," I told her, pointing to the bloody spot.

"We'll clean that up in just a second," the paramedic with the salts said.

"They want to know why you fainted," Daddy said.

"I don't know," Melina said, looking at me, and I knew then that she did. Then she made a strange face and grabbed her stomach. "Oh my God."

"Contraction?" the paramedic with the stethoscope asked.

"I don't know," she said. "This is my first baby."

We all watched her. "Breathe," the paramedic said, and she did, huffing and puffing lightly.

When it was over, she moved a little to try to sit up, and that was when I noticed the bloodstain between her legs. It stood out on the light blue surgery pants she wore as pajamas. "Uh-oh," I said.

"What?" Melina said.

"Your pants."

She looked down. "Oh my God."

Daddy turned away quickly.

"Okay," the paramedic with the salts said, standing up from his kneeling position. "Time to go to the hospital."

"Okay," Melina said, sounding nervous.

Both paramedics went to the back of the ambulance to get the stretcher. "Want me to call Gil?" I asked Melina.

"There's no time," she said. "We'll call him from the hospital."

"I can call him," Daddy said. "Before I go to work."

"You're going to work?" Melina said.

"It's almost seven o'clock," Daddy said. That was when he left every day.

Melina looked at him. "You're not coming with us?"

"Me?" Daddy said.

She nodded. "Gil might not make it to the hospital in time."

"You'll have Jasira," Daddy said. "Jasira will go with you."

Melina seemed like she was going to cry. "I can't believe you're not coming!"

Daddy looked at her. He looked at me. I didn't know what to tell him. It was hard to say no to Melina. It was hard because when she really wanted you to do things her way, that was when you most felt like she liked you. So when Daddy changed his mind and said okay, he would go and get his car, that was when I knew it for sure, that he cared what she thought.

In the ambulance, the paramedic with the stethoscope stayed in back with us, monitoring Melina's heartbeat. As we drove, her contractions started to come faster, and she squeezed my hand until they passed. It actually kind of hurt, but I didn't want to make her feel bad by saying so. She kept telling the paramedic that she wanted to push, and he told her she had to wait until we got to the hospital.

"Why?" she said. "Don't you know how to deliver a baby? I'm sure they train y'all to deliver babies!"

"I do know how, ma'am," the paramedic said. "You're just not ready yet. Try to hold on."

"How do you know?" she said. "You haven't even examined me."

"Ma'am?" he said. "We really are very close to the hospital."

Melina didn't say anything, just grabbed my hand and huffed her way through another set of contractions. Out the back window, I could see Daddy following us in his Honda. I waved to him at a stoplight, and he waved back. When Melina finished her contraction, she turned to me and said, "You know you're not supposed to talk to that man. Why did you talk to him?"

For a second, I thought she meant Daddy. Then I realized she was talking about Mr. Vuoso. "I wanted to give him Snowball," I said, "before he went to jail."

"I don't care what you wanted to give him," she said. "You live with me now, and you'll do what I say. When I tell you not to talk to someone, I expect you to listen."

I noticed that ever since I'd said the word *jail,* the paramedic had turned his back on us as much as he could in the cramped space and had started filling out some paperwork on a clipboard. I wished I could tell Melina that Mr. Vuoso had called the ambulance for her, but I was pretty sure she would just say that any idiot could pick up the phone. So instead I said, "Sorry."

"I'm punishing you," Melina said. "After I have this baby, you're getting punished."

"Do I have to go back to Daddy's?" I asked.

"No!" she said. "Not that kind of punishment. You're going to have to wash extra dishes or something."

"Okay," I said.

She had another contraction then, and I liked how hard she squeezed my hand this time, like she was trying to hang on to me.

At the hospital, Daddy had to find a parking place, while Melina and I got out at the emergency room entrance. A Mexican nurse named Rosario met us just inside the automatic doors. She told the paramedics to follow her, and we wheeled past all the people sitting in the waiting room, then through a set of double doors. It wasn't actually a room they put Melina in, but a space sectioned off with curtains. The paramedics took down one side of the stretcher, then lifted Melina onto her new bed, which was shorter than the stretcher. They made jokes about how much she weighed, and she laughed until another contraction started to come.

Rosario worked very quickly, rolling Melina one way, then another, as she took all her clothes off. She did the same procedure to dress Melina in a gown, then gave her a sheet to stretch across her stomach. I wasn't sure why she did that until she went to the foot of the short table and pulled out two foot holders. When she took each of Melina's feet and stuck them in the holders, her legs were wide open. Without the sheet to cover her, everyone could've seen everything.

I'd grabbed Melina's purse before we left in the ambulance, and now she told me to take out her wallet and get some change to call Gil. There was a pad and paper on the table at her bedside, and she wrote his number down for me. "Tell him to hurry up," she said. "And find your father." I nodded and took the paper. As I left the room, I noticed the nurse putting on a rubber glove and rolling a stool between Melina's open legs.

The pay phones were out by the waiting room. Gil was in a meeting, but when I told his secretary what was happening, she said she would go and get him. After a moment, he came to the phone and said, "Jasira? Is Melina okay?"

"Uh-huh," I said. "But you better hurry. She wants to push."

"Already?" he said. "She's that close?"

I was too ashamed to tell him it was my fault that everything was happening so fast, without any time for him to get here. "Yes," I said.

"Okay," he said. "Tell her I'm on my way."

I told him I would and hung up. Just then Daddy walked in. He looked around the waiting room like he didn't know what to do. "Daddy," I called.

He saw me and walked over to the phones.

"Melina is in a room," I said. "C'mon, I'll show you."

"I'll just wait here," he said.

"But she wants you to come."

"Why?"

"Because Gil isn't here yet."

"I have to call work," Daddy said. "They'll wonder where I am."

"But Melina is almost ready to push."

"Well," he said, "come out and tell me when she's finished."

"I don't think she'll like that," I said.

"I'm not watching her have a baby," Daddy said. "It's none of my business."

"But you told her you'd come."

"I told her I'd come to the hospital. Not her room."

"I think she really wants to have a grown-up there."

Daddy sighed. "I'll go and say hello. That's all. Then she'll have to wait for her husband. He's coming, isn't he?"

I nodded.

"Good," he said. "Hopefully there won't be too much traffic."

"She's behind those doors," I said, pointing, and since he wasn't moving, I took his hand and led the way.

When we got to the room, Melina was telling an older nurse I hadn't seen before that she really wanted to push. "Not quite yet," the nurse said. "Just hang on."

The nurse walked out and I said, "Gil is on his way."

"Good," Melina said.

"I'll just stay for a moment," Daddy said. He glanced at Melina's feet in the holders, then looked away.

"Didn't you see Jasira's birth?" she asked.

Daddy shook his head.

"Why not?"

"Those were different times."

Melina laughed. "They were not! It was only thirteen years ago!"

"So?" Daddy said. "Thirteen years is a long time."

Melina sighed. The hospital was air-conditioned, but her face was sweaty from the pain of the contractions. "You really can't stay?" she said.

"I'd rather not," Daddy said.

Melina didn't say anything, just looked disappointed.

"Jasira will stay," Daddy said. "That will be much better for you." He looked at me then and said, "She's a good girl."

"Yes," Melina said, "she is."

I didn't know what to do with the two of them talking about me like that, so I looked at the clock on the wall behind Melina's head. A moment later, she started having a contraction, and I went and stood by her so she could hold my hand. By the time it was over, Daddy had left. "What a chicken," she said.

"He doesn't like bodies," I told her.

"I guess not."

Gil didn't make it in time to see Dorrie get born. But I saw her get born. I saw Melina push her out, along with all the other stuff that came with her. They cleaned her up and weighed her, and since Gil wasn't there, they let me cut the umbilical cord. Afterward, they put a gauze pad over the stump. When it healed, it would become her belly button. I hadn't known that. Not until that very moment. I also hadn't known that when I first saw Dorrie, I wouldn't feel jealous. Not at all. Not even when Melina started crying. Dorrie made me cry, too. She was very small and tired, and I knew it was only right to love her.

ACKNOWLEDGMENTS

This book took three years to write. During that time, I leaned heavily on Holly Christiana, Nina de Gramont, Ben Greenman, and Bill Kravitz. I thank each of them for their love and friendship.

For their invaluable support, I thank Deborah Ballard, Niezka Ebid, Stephen Elliott, Faulkner Fox, Don Georgianna, David Gessner, Carol and Georges de Gramont, Hania Jakubowska, Alison Lester, Toby Lester, Laura Maffei, Giovanna Marchant, Michael Martin, Gunther Peck, Linda Peckman, Melissa Pritchard, Martin Rapalski, Cory Reynolds, Samantha Schnee, Barbara Schock, Alissa Shipp, Jeremy Sigler, Lisa Stahl, Terry Thaxton, and John and Ann Vernon. Thanks also to Gail Ghezzi, Daniel, and Jake, my surrogate Brooklyn family.

My editor at Simon & Schuster, Marysue Rucci, bought this book both unfinished and in an entirely different form. She offered a few incredibly pertinent suggestions, then turned me loose to finish the job. I ended up tossing the hundred pages she bought and starting over. I thank her immensely for bearing with me on this, and most of all, for her great trust.

I am very grateful to Mary-Anne Harrington, my editor at Hodder/Headline in the UK, who bought this book before it was even an idea. Never once has she mentioned the fact that I delivered it to her two years late.

Thank you to my publicists at Simon & Schuster: Victoria Meyer, Tracey Guest, and Kristan Fletcher. They have each, without reserve, thrown their weight behind this book, and I feel lucky to be working with them.

I very much appreciate the constant support I receive from Tara Parsons at Simon & Schuster, and Leah Woodburn at Hodder/Headline. As well, I would like to thank Loretta Denner at Simon & Schuster for her expert production editing, and Nora Reichard, my equally wonderful copy editor.

A huge thanks to Jesse Holborn at Hodder/Headline, who did such an incredible job designing the book. Thanks also to Jackie Seow and Davina Mock at Simon & Schuster for their patience and sharp modifications.

Thank you to Tony Peake at Peake Associates, who continues to provide help and encouragement from across the pond.

Chapter 4 of this book was written in Seaside, Florida, where I was given a residency through the Seaside Institute's Escape to Create Program. I would like to thank everyone at the Institute, most especially Peter Horn, Marsha Dowler, Nancy Holmes, Richard Storm, and Don and Libby Cooper, who loaned me their gorgeous house for a month. Thanks also to Susan Horn, Peter Jr., and Tennyson, who welcomed me like family.

I thank my in-laws—Margery Franklin, Mark Franklin, and Diane Garner—for helping to underwrite this book. It would've taken so much longer to finish had I not gotten to work on it full-time.

Thank you to Joy for always seeing me through.

Thank you to Aunt Suzie and Uncle Conrad, who really mean it when they say that their home is also mine.

Shortly after I finished this book, Howie Sanders and Andrew

Cannava at United Talent Agency showed it to Alan Ball, who then optioned it. Whether or not the film gets made, I thank each of them for their intense commitment. I also want to thank Joe Regal, Bess Reed, and Lauren Schott at Regal Literary for welcoming me so warmly into their agency.

My agent, Peter Steinberg, has made good thing after good thing happen for me since I met him in 1999. He has cared about me not only as his writer, but as his friend. There is little that feels better than falling under his protective wing.

Finally, I want to thank David Franklin. We separated during the writing of this book, but never once did that stop him from doing what he has so generously done for years: paying the bills, and editing every word I write.

ABOUT THE AUTHOR

Alicia Erian received her BA in English from SUNY Binghamton and her MFA in writing from Vermont College. Her fiction has appeared most recently in *Playboy, Open City, Zoetrope, The Sun,* and *The Iowa Review.* Her first book of short stories, *The Brutal Language of Love,* was published by Villard in 2001.